HER SECRET WAR

Pam Lecky is an Irish historical fiction author. Having been an avid reader of historical and crime fiction from a young age, it was inevitable that her books would be a combination of the two. Pam lives in north County Dublin with her husband and three children. She can be contacted through social media or by visiting her website www.pamlecky.com.

HER SECRET WAR

PAM LECKY

avon.

Published by AVON
A division of HarperCollins*Publishers* Ltd
1 London Bridge Street
London SE1 9GF

www.harpercollins.co.uk

HarperCollins*Publishers*
1st Floor, Watermarque Building, Ringsend Road
Dublin 4, Ireland

A Paperback Original 2021

1

First published in Great Britain by HarperCollins*Publishers* 2021

Typeset in Bembo by Palimpsest Book Production Limited, Falkirk, Stirlingshire
Printed and bound using 100% Renewable Electricity at
CPI Black Print, Barcelona

MIX
Paper from
responsible sources
FSC C007454

*Dedicated to Lorna and Terry
with thanks for your steadfast support*

1

It was almost Whitsuntide Eve. Sarah Gillespie ran down the last few yards of the laneway to the rear of the terrace of houses. Blinded by tears, she careered into a stack of boxes in the poor light, cursed and almost stumbled. Sarah glanced down at her footwear in disgust; dancing shoes weren't ideal for a girl in a hurry. Why hadn't she thought to bring a spare pair in her bag? To catch her breath, she leaned against the wall. Dismayed by her own feebleness, she concentrated hard on her breathing. She hated to lose control. With trembling fingers, she roughly wiped away the offending tears.

Damn you, Paul O'Reilly! Sarah Gillespie does not cry over any man.

Though falling out with Paul and inappropriate footwear weren't her biggest problems right now. What if Da returned home before her? What if he went into the girls' bedroom and discovered the pillows stuffed under Sarah's blankets on her bed? If he were drunk, and there was a fair chance he would be, he wouldn't twig; but if he wasn't . . . A shiver ran through her; there would be hell to pay. Sneaking out to meet Paul wasn't the cleverest thing, but with Da so vehemently opposed, what was a girl to do?

'No daughter of mine will be mixed up with a good-for-nothing bicycle repair man!' Da had almost choked on the words.

The irony wasn't lost on Sarah. With petrol rationed, Paul was inundated with work, keeping those lucky enough to be employed with a reliable means of transport. As their father had bellowed and cursed, Sarah had clenched her fists, but had remained silent. Beside her, her younger sister, Maura, wore that bleak and helpless expression which always came over her when Da's temper blew up. Neither Sarah nor Maura would ever have the courage to gainsay him because there was no reasoning with Da.

Sarah continued down the laneway at a slower pace until she reached a streetlight. Peeking at her watch, she was relieved to see it was ten minutes to midnight. Her abandoned date meant she was home earlier than usual. Da wouldn't be in for ages yet. Having told Paul in no uncertain terms that she didn't need his help to get home, she had hopped on the first bus to arrive at the stop. In her pique, she hadn't noticed it was the wrong bus and she had had to get off at a stop some distance from North Strand, leaving her with a long walk. To avoid the possibility of meeting Da or any of his mates, she had slipped through the side streets. She knew Da and his cronies would be up on Newcomen Bridge, overlooking the canal, smoking their filthy Woodbines and putting the world to rights. Herr Hitler and Mr Churchill, look out!

Still, something of the weekend could be salvaged, for she

2

had persuaded Da to accompany them to Howth the next after-noon. And, God willing, he'd be sober. Even he didn't start drinking till late afternoon. Most days. She loved the journey along the coast road, then up the hill to the summit. It was one of her favourite places, with its stunning views of Dublin and beyond down to Wicklow with the distinctive shape of the Sugar Loaf Mountain standing proud in the distance. Nothing could be easier, with the tram for Howth passing right outside the door of No. 18. Maura had suggested a picnic. Not that there was much to take in the way of food; rationing was biting hard lately. But a flask of tea, a bottle of porter for Da and some sandwiches would keep them going. Maura was such a sweet girl, but very innocent for a seventeen-year-old. Sarah worried about her, mostly because Da didn't bother. There were times Sarah resented the responsibility, but someone had to shield Maura from Da's bad temper . . . and his fists.

As Sarah approached the back gate of No. 18, she heard the sound she dreaded most; the deep throbbing of those blasted Jerry bombers flying over the city. For months now, they had been making their way up the Irish Sea at night, en route to bomb the poor unfortunates up in Belfast or Liverpool. Belfast had taken a real battering six weeks before. It had been so bad that the Irish government had sent fire crews up to help put out the fires and dig out the bodies. The newspapers had been full of the Blitz with shocking pictures of the devas-tation. For days after, a line of miserable refugees from Belfast had streamed out of Amiens Street railway station, just up the road. Her heart had gone out to them, especially the children, bewildered and scared.

Recently, there had been rumours that the Luftwaffe had been spotted over land in the south of Ireland, ratcheting up the country's anxiety. What if they mistook Dublin for Belfast and dropped their deadly cargo? Thank God for the Taoiseach, Éamon de Valera. He had declared that Ireland was neutral and the Brits and the Jerries just had to accept that. Of course, Da had something to say about it. As a true republican, he and his daft mates thought Ireland should join the German cause and help crush the British. Pub talk, most of it, but Sarah knew Da had history. He'd led a flying column during the War of Independence, and he boasted about it whenever the opportunity arose. Some locals avoided him because of his pro-republican rhetoric.

Suddenly the clear night sky was illuminated by the sweeping searchlights trying to pinpoint the planes. Sarah stood rooted to the spot. The hum of the engines was louder tonight.

A warning flare went up, bursting like a star. The flares usually worked, warning the Germans off, though at times it took a few shells to remind them it was Dublin – move on! More flares shot up, and still the planes circled, like vultures. Sarah shivered. Maura was on her own and would be terrified. She needed to hurry.

The rattle of gunfire ripped through the air just as Sarah put her hand to the gate. She stalled, unsure what to do. It was some time since the anti-aircraft gun at Clontarf had fired. Suddenly, the sky was alight with a fireworks display. Between the searchlights, the flares, and the streaks of light from the shells, it was spectacular. Sarah wondered what make of plane they were. Paul would know; he was mad keen on aircraft. So keen, in fact, that he wanted to join the RAF. Just typical, that. You find a nice lad who treats you well, and he decides to dash off to England and enlist. Hurt and disappointed when he'd told her tonight, she had lashed out and told him they were finished. God! The look on his face; she knew she had wounded him. Irrevocably. The thought of what she had done made her cheeks burn. Her temper was always getting her into scrapes. Now that she had cooled down a little, the regrets were creeping in. She had been too hasty, as usual.

Soon, Paul will be fighting the likes of those bombers flying so low overhead. Then it struck her. She had never seen them fly so low. They were skimming the rooftops. Horrified, Sarah could see the pilot of one plane as it swooped past. Scared, she drew back into the shadows. That was close! There was a bang as another flare went up, and a minute later another barrage of shelling. Surely the Germans would move on now?

But then the strangest thing; some planes were coming back the other way towards the south of the city. They never did that. Were they lost?

Disconcerted, Sarah pushed open the gate and scuttled up the path through their small back yard. The ancient sycamore, conveniently located close to the house, was her ladder. As she contemplated the climb, Maura's head popped out from their bedroom window, but her gaze was directed at the light show above.

'Hey, kiddo!' Sarah yelled and waved, but Maura couldn't hear her above the din. Sarah called out again, louder this time.

Maura leaned out. 'Is that you, Sarah?'

'Of course it's me! Who else would be daft enough to stand out here shouting up at you?'

'Well, I can't see you behind the blasted tree, now can I?' Maura replied. 'You're all right. Da isn't home yet. Hang on; you can save yourself the climb and your stockings into the bargain. I'll let you in the back door instead.'

'Good woman,' Sarah shouted back. A few minutes later, Sarah heard the key turn and the door swung open. Maura's head popped out, her expression fearful as she glanced skywards.

There was a whoosh overhead as a Jerry plane swept past. 'Janey Mac, I've never seen the like,' Sarah gasped, watching as the bomber disappeared northward. 'There's so many of them. God help Belfast.'

'Come in, Sarah,' Maura urged. 'I don't like it. Look, they've broken formation. See that one,' she pointed upwards, 'he's circling back. They *never* do that.'

Maura looked terrified and despite the fear settling in her own stomach, Sarah knew she had to appear calm. 'Relax! They know it's Dublin. They're not stupid.'

'All the same, don't linger out there.' Maura tugged her sleeve and pulled her inside. 'It could be dangerous.'

Once inside, Sarah pulled off her jacket, stretched her arms and yawned. 'Calm down, Maura. They're just acting the maggot.'

Maura didn't look convinced. 'I wish they'd take their antics elsewhere. Preferably Berlin.'

'They'll move on soon, you'll see.' Sarah gave her a smile, hoping to dispel her fears.

'So, how was the date?' Maura asked.

'Grand. Mostly. We went to that new place on the quays.'

'The Flamingo?'

'Yes. Daft name isn't it, for a Dublin club? And the crush!'

'Was the band any good?' Maura asked wistfully. Sarah knew it was weeks since her little sister had been out dancing. It was always a battle to get Da to agree to her going out.

'I've heard worse.'

Suddenly, Maura leaned closer and frowned. 'Have you been cryin', Sarah? Your mascara is all smudged.'

Sarah pushed her away. 'No! Don't be daft. Just something in me eye. Any tea in that pot?'

'I'll check,' Maura answered, picking up the chipped teapot from the centre of the table. She grimaced and shook her head. 'No joy.'

Sarah sat down with a sigh on one of the rickety chairs. 'I'm parched; be a love and make some fresh. There should be enough of a glimmer to heat the water.' She kicked off her shoes and rubbed the soles of her feet. 'I swear I have a blister on both feet. Dratted shoes.'

Maura still stood by the stove, frowning. 'What if the glimmer man comes? We'd be in awful trouble.'

'Maura, it's a bank holiday weekend. I'm sure the man is suppin' pints in the pub along with the rest of the male population of North Strand.'

'All right,' Maura replied, taking up the kettle and half filling it. Then she leaned against the counter and stared off into space, waiting for the kettle to boil. Maura's soft, rounded cheeks and petite frame only added to her childlike appearance. And in many ways, Maura was still a child. Sarah had done her best the last five years, but she was no substitute for Ma. That void could never be filled. Da's neglect made her so angry. And tonight, with all the bizarre stuff going on, why wasn't he home to check on them? Maura was scared of her own shadow; he knew that. Surely, it was his job to protect his daughters? But it appeared they could not compete with the lads in the pub. There was no chance of Da abandoning his pint. Not a chance in hell.

The drone of a bomber broke the silence. Maura flinched and crossed herself, before peeking out the window. 'What is going on tonight?'

'I've no idea, kiddo. Come on, the kettle is boiling now. Get a move on,' Sarah cajoled. But her palms were sweating. She wiped them on her skirt while Maura's back was turned. Heart thumping, Sarah took a furtive glance out the window. Something didn't feel right. Why was Jerry still over Dublin? Were they deliberately trying to scare them for a joke?

Maura finished making the tea and handed her a cup. 'Sorry, no milk. Best drink up. We don't want Da finding us up when he gets home.' The boom of the anti-aircraft gun could be heard in the distance. Maura threw up her hands, a fierce frown marring her delicate features. 'How are we going to get to sleep with that racket going on out there?' With that, she stomped out of the kitchen and up the stairs.

'They'll be gone soon, I'm sure,' Sarah called after her. No response. Great! Maura was now in one of her moods. Sarah gulped down her tea then brought her cup to the sink under the window to rinse it out. Suddenly weary, her throat tightened, and tears threatened to flow once more. *Blast Paul and blast the Germans!* Blinking the tears away, she stared up into the night sky, only to spot another bomber caught in a searchlight as the anti-aircraft gun rattled once more. Could this night get any worse?

2

Sarah disliked the idea of a blackout. If pushed, she would admit to a fear of the dark, her childhood fear of those multi-armed creatures that inhabited the space under her bed never having been truly conquered. Not that blackout regulations were strictly enforced in Dublin. There had been no clear ruling from Dublin Corporation, or 'the Corpo' as it was fondly known as by the majority of Dubs. Some advocated Dublin being fully lit, so the Germans knew the city was neutral; others favoured the safety of darkness. What they had was a ridiculous mix of the two. So far, Ireland had been relatively untouched, bar a few stray Jerry bombs which the German embassy insisted were dropped in error due to faulty navigation.

Tonight, like most nights, Sarah left the curtains open, hoping to glimpse the stars. Even with all the strange activity this evening, it was preferable to see what was happening out in the world. The window was open, but the bedroom beneath the eaves was stuffy and claustrophobic. Sarah lay on her side, tense and uncomfortable, scanning her view of the night sky framed by the sash window. Perhaps, for once, it would be better not to focus on the world outside. With a sigh, she turned over onto her back and stared up at the ceiling, subconsciously tracing the line of the crack that stretched from the door to the far corner. Like much of the rest of their rented house, the bedroom was showing signs of age and decay. Da said it was the trams passing that had caused the subsidence in their stretch of Victorian terraces, but his complaints to the landlord fell on deaf ears. The upside was that their rent was low and with three wages coming in, they could afford to be the sole occupants. Most of the other houses in their terrace were sublet. One family Sarah knew lived in one room, all five of them.

The house creaked and settled. Sarah strained to hear. Was that Da coming in? Silence. She breathed out her relief. If only . . . What if he never returned? Would it be so very bad? Life would be simple; they could be happy, just the two of them. No tension, no watching what you said. He was so difficult to live with. Everything was black and white to Da. Reality and Jim Gillespie were strangers since Ma had died, Sarah suspected, but he was not the kind of man who would take kindly to that opinion being voiced. As a result, there wasn't much joy at No. 18.

Sometimes, Sarah struggled to remember Ma clearly, but then she would hear one of her mother's favourite songs on the wireless, and she would cease what she was doing as the memories flooded back. Her mother used to sing along to those melodies, her voice low but sweet as she toiled over the washing or the preparation of the dinner. Ma would turn and smile and encourage them to sing with her. It was a comforting reminiscence, which, along with the scent of rosewater, were guaranteed to spin a comforting web to cushion Sarah's grief. The tiny glass bottle, its contents almost dried out, still stood on the dressing table in her parents' room. Whenever she went in, Sarah would uncap it and breathe in the memories. Everyone said Sarah was her mother's image, but when she picked up her mother's photograph that brought little consolation. It was five years now since they had stood at Ma's graveside in Glasnevin Cemetery. No other family members had been present at the funeral. Da had alienated them all, as only he could.

If Da had been cantankerous before, he was a tyrant now without Ma's softer influence. The rumour he might be going on reduced hours at the factory didn't help matters. Where would that leave us, Sarah often wondered. The war was crippling the country, and there was so little work. She was employed in a small architect's practice in town, but it paid a pittance, and Maura's typing job didn't bring in much more.

'You still awake?' Maura asked in a whisper from the other side of the room. 'I can't get to sleep.'

'Me neither. Best try though. You won't enjoy the outing this afternoon if you're tired.'

'I can't wait, Sarah. I love going to Howth.'

Sarah turned over and gazed across at her sister. Despite the heat of the room, Maura was clutching the sheet under her chin. Sarah suspected she was shivering, even though it appeared Jerry had scarpered. They hadn't heard a plane for at least fifty minutes.

'Hey, you know, you might meet someone nice out in Howth tomorrow,' Sarah said, hoping to take Maura's mind off the Luftwaffe's earlier antics. 'It's bound to be packed with day-trippers. A holiday weekend always brings them out in their droves.'

Maura's face lit up. 'Oh yeah; wouldn't that be lovely. Let's walk down the harbour to the lighthouse. Of course, I'll have free rein with you joined at the hip to Paul O'Reilly,' Maura said with a giggle. 'How is the gorgeous Paul, by the way?'

'I neither know nor care,' Sarah snapped. 'I despair of him; he's plane mad. All he talks about is joining the RAF and doing his bit. Some fella he knows went up to Belfast to enlist, so he's thinking of doing the same.'

'No! Ah, God, I'm sorry.'

Sarah huffed. 'Don't be.'

'But won't Paul's da kill him if he enlists?' Maura asked.

'Course he will. Pat O'Reilly is a fierce IRA man, same as our Da. Sure, he'll skin Paul alive if he finds out.'

'So, is Paul just going to sneak off and say nothing?'

'What else can he do?'

Maura's glance brimmed with sympathy, setting Sarah's irritation level to high. 'Will you be all right? You'll miss him if he goes.'

Sarah snorted. 'Plenty more fish and all that.'

'Get away with ye! Sure, you're crazy about him,' her sister answered.

Sarah took a swipe at her with her pillow but the gap between the beds was too wide. 'For your information, I've finished with him.'

'No! Get away! I don't believe it for a second. You'll be back together in no time. Paul's the nicest lad you've ever dated.' Maura sighed. 'Those blue eyes and that blond hair. He's only gorgeous.'

'He has brown hair!' Sarah scowled at her.

'No, no, it's definitely blond. All right, keep *your* hair on! Maybe dark blond. Anyway, perhaps he won't go? It could just be talk. Probably trying to impress you; you know what fellas are like.'

'I tell you; he's made up his mind, and so have I!'

Maura turned over, pulling the sheet up over her head, but Sarah heard her mutter: 'You're mad in the head.'

For a moment, Sarah was rigid with anger, but Paul's face flashed into her mind. He was a handsome fellow with a ready smile and a wicked sense of humour, but he was abandoning her. It wasn't even their war. What was he thinking? But their row replayed in her mind. God! Maybe her silly sister was right. Had she made a stupid mistake? It wouldn't be the first time she'd messed up. She had said some harsh things. But he had just stood there taking it, which made her even angrier. When she had run out of steam, he had given her a look that would have curdled milk. In that moment, she realised she had hurt him deeply. But it was ridiculous, this plan of his. She couldn't understand why he wanted to enlist when he had a well-paid job. It was only those who couldn't find work that went to England – there were plenty of jobs over there in the factories. Probably the only good thing to come out of the war. But what if Paul joined up and then got himself killed? The thought made her ill.

Thumping her pillow, she moved around until she found a more comfortable position on the lumpy mattress, then turned her head to look out the window. The sky was beautifully clear. It was peaceful at last.

An awful thought struck her, and she broke out in a cold sweat. What if Jerry did the same thing coming back from Belfast? They often dropped their surplus bombs out over the Irish Sea to save fuel on their way home from bombing runs.

The silence of anticipation was almost worse than the earlier pandemonium.

Sarah was just dozing off when she heard a strange whistling sound, accompanied by a tremendous bang. The entire house vibrated. In horror, she watched as the crack in the ceiling snaked across to the window, the plaster dust floating down on top of her, making her cough.

'Mother of God! What was that?' she cried, scrambling to sit up in her bed. Then it happened again, followed by rumbling. 'Is it an earthquake?'

Maura crossed herself, then frantically kicked off the sheet and bedcover. 'No, Sarah. That sounded like bombs to me, and they're close by.'

Sarah flung back her bedclothes and flicked on the light. She glanced at the clock. It was twenty minutes to two. 'Come on, get dressed, Maura. We need to find out what's going on.'

'Turn off the light!' Maura cried.

'I think it's a bit late to be concerned about blackout.' Sarah buttoned up her blouse with shaking fingers. 'Did you hear Da come in yet?'

'No. I'm certain he's still out.'

They finished dressing in a rush, then headed downstairs. Sarah pulled open the hall door and they stepped down onto the pavement. It was mayhem outside. All the neighbours were out, looking about wildly, most in their night attire. The men were running down towards Portland Row, their terrified wives standing in the doorways, screaming at them to stay put. Sarah spotted a plume of smoke to the west.

She grabbed the arm of a passing man, forcing him to stop. 'What's happened?'

He shook her off. 'What do you think? Bloody Jerries, that's what!' He raced away.

'What should we do, Sarah? Should we go look for Da?' Maura's face was deadly white.

Sarah gnawed at her lip. 'I don't know.' She nodded towards the chaos. 'Looks like Summerhill was hit. Da wouldn't have been up there. He should be all right.' *Blast him*, she thought. *Why hasn't he come home to check on us?*

Maura shuddered, her eyes wide with terror. Sarah put an arm around her shoulder and tried to smile, but panic was almost choking her. She couldn't think straight. Should they stay in the house or leave? Where would be safer if Jerry came back? Seconds later, they heard a distant rumble. Maura clutched at her neck. 'Oh my God, that must be another one.'

Sarah pulled her back into the house. 'Maura, it's a Blitz! We need to find shelter. Quick, under the stairs.' Sarah tussled with Da's bike and flung it across the hall. They squeezed into the gap left by the bicycle and clung to each other, shivering.

'I don't understand,' Maura said after a few moments of silence. 'There was no warning, no siren. Why would they bomb us? We're neutral!'

'I tell you what, why don't I go out and flag the bastard down and ask him in my best German?'

Maura scowled back at her. 'That's not helpful!'

'Then don't ask stupid questions, Maura.'

A few minutes passed as they sat in silence.

'Do you think Da's all right?' Maura asked.

Sarah didn't give a fig, but she didn't want to frighten Maura any further. 'Sure he is. It would take more than the Jerries to do him in. He was either in the bar at Egan's or on the bridge having a smoke. He'll have got a fright, that's all. No doubt he'll return home to check we're not hurt . . . soon.' More likely, he'd head back to the pub if at all possible, Sarah knew. The men would like nothing better than to dissect tonight's activities over a few malt whiskies.

Time dragged, but they were too afraid to move. Sarah heard the noises out on the street; people milling about, talking loudly, someone shouting instructions. A fire engine sped past, siren blaring. Maura crossed herself and muttered a prayer under her breath.

Then, the drone of a bomber could be heard again. 'Jaysus! He's back,' Maura cried. 'I can't stand it, Sarah, I can't stand being cooped up! We'll be trapped if we stay under here.' Maura pushed her way out and headed for the front parlour. Ma's best room: the room they only used for special occasions. Ma's wake was the last time they had used it.

Sarah followed, reluctant to be left alone under the stairs.

'What should we do? What if there are more bombs? Would we be safer outside?' Maura asked, tilting her head, listening out for the plane. 'It sounds fainter. Has he moved away, do you think?'

With growing alarm, Sarah stood in the centre of the room, running her fingers through her hair. Her hands were shaking. 'I don't know, Maura, ok? I'm trying to think.' Her voice shook.

'Sorry, Sarah. I'm dead scared. Why won't it stop? I want them to go away. Why can't they leave us alone?' Maura asked, sitting down on the edge of the armchair. She wrapped her arms around herself, her lower lip trembling. 'Oh, no! Look!' Maura pointed to the window.

Sarah moved closer to the large sash window – Ma's photograph had pride of place on the deep sill – and saw that the upper pane of glass had cracked, probably when the bombs fell. Da would be livid about the damage. The picture was the only decent one they had of Ma, and Sarah couldn't bear the thought of it getting damaged; best it went into a drawer. As she reached for the silver frame, there was an ear-splitting whistle, followed by a huge boom.

The window exploded inwards, and Sarah fell into darkness.

3

31st May 1941, North Strand, Dublin

'By all that's holy; she's alive!' The voice sounded far away, as if she were dreaming. Sarah tried to focus on it. The light from a torch played on her face, hurting her eyes. She struggled to cry out but choked on dust and grit. Any attempt to move brought wave after wave of pain in her limbs. With growing horror, Sarah realised she was pinned up to her neck in rubble, the pressure around her body almost unbearable. Everything stung; her eyes, her face, her nose. She could hear the pathetic moans of someone in pain. *Oh God, that's me!*

The light swung to the left and Sarah could make out the shape of a person behind, crawling towards her, inch by inch, through the gloom. To her dismay, he halted. 'Jaysus, it's very unstable here, lads. Stay back!'

No, no! Sarah wanted to cry out. *Please don't leave me here in the darkness. Get me out!*

'Mick! I can smell gas,' a distant voice shouted. 'We'd best hurry. Have you far to go?'

'A couple of yards, that's all,' the man replied, sweeping the torch around. ''Tis just the one.'

Sarah prayed. '*Hail Mary . . .*'

With painstaking slowness, the man picked his way forward. 'Hello, love. I'm Mick Ward. Don't you fret, now. We're going to get you out. What's your name? Are you one of the Gillespie girls?' Sarah nodded and tried to speak, but no words would come. She started to cry. Where was Maura?

Mick reached out and removed a large section of brickwork which had been pressing down on Sarah's shoulder. Passing it behind to another man, he flashed Sarah a grin. 'Won't be too long, love. You just hold tight.' She didn't have much choice.

Sarah had no idea how long it took Mick to dislodge her. As each piece of rubble was removed, he did his best to reassure her. But if she moved, searing pain shot through her body.

'Maura?' she croaked. It came out as a whisper.

'What's that love?' Mick asked, tilting his face closer.

The dust caught in her throat as she tried to speak. A fit of coughing was all she could manage.

'Just a few more minutes, now.' He patted her free shoulder and turned away as a second man crawled forward.

'Let's try to pull her free,' he said to Mick. 'We're running out of time. The smell of gas is getting stronger.'

Frantic, Sarah tried again. 'Sister.'

'What's she saying?' the second man asked.

'No idea. Best get her out. Ok, missy, this is going to hurt a bit,' Mick said. With a nod to the other man, they both grasped a shoulder and heaved. Sarah screamed in pain and passed out.

★　★　★

20

That's odd, Sarah thought, looking up at the ceiling through a sleepy haze. *The crack has disappeared. Did Da get it mended?* Mystified, she drifted back into a deep sleep.

The next time she woke, sunlight was streaming in through a window directly onto her face. A large, clean sash window. And her precious bookcase was missing. Blinking to full consciousness, she took in her surroundings. It wasn't No. 18. In fact, it looked very much like . . .

'Poor lamb, you awake, love?' A young woman in a nurse's uniform came into focus. She was leaning over her, her brow marred by a deep frown. 'You've certainly been through it. They had to sedate you for the pain. How do you feel?'

Sarah's throat was raspy dry. 'Where?' was all she managed.

'You're in the Mater Hospital. I'm Nurse Agnew. Do you remember what happened?'

Sarah shook her head, and immediately regretted it as pain sliced through her skull, taking her breath away. As she moved, Sarah sensed the heaviness of her leg and arm. Glancing down, she realised both were in casts. All of a sudden, she recalled the droning of the bombers, the explosion, and Maura sitting in the front parlour, shaking in fear.

'Oh my God! Maura!' Sarah exclaimed, struggling to sit up. 'Where is she?'

'Take it easy; you're safe now. Don't be fretting about anyone else for the moment,' Nurse Agnew said, gently rubbing Sarah's upper arm. 'Would you like some water? Let's get you sitting up.' With surprising deftness, the nurse pulled Sarah up, plumping up the pillows behind her. Now Sarah could survey the entire ward.

As Nurse Agnew held a glass to her parched lips, Sarah took several sips before pushing the glass away.

'How long have I been here?' Sarah asked.

'It's Monday afternoon. They dug you out on Saturday. Can you tell me your name and your age, love?' the nurse asked.

'Sarah . . . Gillespie,' Sarah croaked, as a pulse of terrifying blackness encroached on her peripheral vision. 'Nineteen.'

Through a haze, Sarah saw Nurse Agnew grab a file at the end of the bed. 'Ah, that's grand. You see, we weren't too sure who you were, and no one on the ward recognised you.' The nurse gave her a sympathetic glance. 'Probably because of the swelling to your face. Anyway, there are loads of people looking for family and friends. I'll get your name posted up so your loved ones can find you. Hopefully, it won't be too long.' Nurse Agnew sighed. 'It's been chaos these last few days. We've never seen the like.'

'Maura?' Sarah asked, fighting off dizziness and losing the battle.

'Who's that, love?' The nurse leaned down towards her.

'My sister,' she whispered.

Nurse Agnew straightened up. 'I'll see what I can find out.'

Sarah grabbed the nurse's arm as she moved away. 'And my Da?'

'What's his name?' the nurse asked, her eyes full of sympathy. 'Jim Gillespie.'

'Right. They might both be here; you never know. But don't fret if they aren't. They also took casualties to Jervis Street Hospital. You must rest, now. The doctor will be along to see you soon.'

Sarah watched the nurse move to the next bed, then looked about only to come up short. The ward was full of injured women; faces she recognised from all around North Strand.

★　★　★

22

On Tuesday morning, Sarah awoke to the gentle squeezing of her arm. She looked up into Nurse Agnew's face.

'Sorry to disturb your sleep, Miss Gillespie, but there's a Garda here who wants to speak to you,' the nurse said. 'Here; let me help you sit up.'

A young policeman was standing at the end of her bed, pale-faced and cap in hand. Nurse Agnew pulled the curtains around Sarah's bed. 'Quick as you can, Guard, please. Miss Gillespie needs her rest,' was the nurse's parting shot to him.

'Morning, Miss,' he said, coming around the bed to stand beside her. 'I'm Garda Burke, from Store Street Station. We understand that your sister and father are still missing.' She nodded. The colour rose in his face and he cleared his throat. Sarah felt sorry for him; he didn't look much older than Maura.

'Have they been found?' Sarah asked, clutching the sheet. The fog lifted from her brain. He could only be here to deliver bad news. Her stomach heaved.

'Well, Miss, I . . . we can't say for sure. There's a lot of confusion and they are still digging people out.' His voice wavered. 'The thing is, a number of bodies have been brought to the morgue and we have no way of identifying them, other than through personal belongings.' He opened a small bag. His hands shook. 'Perhaps I could show you some of these and you could tell me if you recognise them?'

Sarah cringed. *Please, God, no!*

Garda Burke pulled out several pieces of jewellery, a purse and a leather wallet. Sarah scanned them and shook her head.

'Ok,' he said, 'Just a few more.'

Da's signet ring; his wedding band. She recognised it immediately. With a shaking hand, she picked it up from the policeman's palm. 'JG' was engraved on the top. Her fingers curled around it.

'Miss?'

'This belongs to my father,' she said at last, gulping down her tears.

'I'm very sorry, Miss. Thank you for your help,' the young man said, biting his lower lip. He pulled out a notebook. 'Would you mind giving me his details; address, date of birth?'

Somehow, she managed to tell him all, even as a creeping numbness began to take hold.

Despair hovered; hope vanished. All she could do was cling to the tiny chance that somehow Maura was still alive.

It was late on Wednesday afternoon when Sarah spotted him as he entered the ward and her heart leaped. Paul O'Reilly scanned the beds, a frown cutting across his brow. Relief swept through her only to be instantly replaced by regret and shame for the awful words she had thrown at him the night they broke up. For a moment, she squeezed her eyes shut, consumed by guilt. He had not deserved her scorn. It spoke so much for his character that he would even consider visiting her now. Would she be as magnanimous if their roles were reversed?

Sarah waved her good hand to catch his attention. For a moment he hesitated before slowly walking up to her bed. His grim expression added to her already fractious state. The fact he was here at all set off some alarm bells. Was he the bearer of news about Maura, or had he come to commiserate about Da? As he stood at the bottom of her bed, gripping the end rail, Sarah noticed his eyes were red-rimmed; in truth, he looked wretched. Her heart galloped.

At last, Paul cleared his throat. 'Thank God they got you out, Sarah,' he said, his voice low.

'Oh Paul! I'm so glad to see you. Have you heard about my Da?' Her voice broke.

He hurried towards her, concern flooding his face as he grabbed her good hand. 'Yes, I'm sorry, of course, but right now, I'm more concerned about you,' he answered. He gently caressed her cheek. She almost burst into tears.

'It could have been worse,' she whispered. From the one peek in the mirror that morning, she knew she still looked a sight; she had bruising and swelling to her face and a bandage covered the deep cut just above her shoulder to the side of her neck.

'God, yes, I know!'

'Please sit down, Paul. You're the first visitor I've had. It's very kind of you to come . . . especially after, well, you know.'

Paul nodded, a flicker of embarrassment crossing his features.

As soon as he sat down, she leaned towards him. 'Paul, tell me; is there any news of Maura? I haven't heard a thing and they won't let me out of here. I'm desperate for news. She must be in Jervis Street Hospital, but I've no way of finding out for sure. Could you check for me?'

Paul wouldn't meet her eye, but stared down at his clasped hands. Eventually, he looked up. 'It's not good news, Sarah.' Then he gulped and his expression scared her. 'I was down at your house all day yesterday, looking for you. No one down there knew what had happened to you or Maura. With the state of the house, everyone assumed both of ye had been buried. But they're still digging people out, all along North Strand; so there was hope.' He shook his head. 'I've never seen anything like it. There is total devastation.' Sarah frowned at him, barely able to take in what he was saying. 'Well, eventually, they burnt off the gas. The bomb ruptured the main, you see, and they couldn't risk digging in that area in case a spark set it off. Anyway, they found her . . . Maura . . . yesterday, late afternoon.'

Sarah gasped and clutched his arm. 'Will she be all right? Is she here? When can I visit her?'

Paul's eyes welled up. 'I'm sorry; there was nothing they could do. Your entire terrace crumbled like a stack of cards when the last bomb exploded. All that's left is the charred remains of that tree in your back yard. The house completely buried her.' He halted, swallowing hard, a solitary tear rolling down his cheek. 'They said she died instantly. We must take comfort in that.'

'No! I don't believe she's dead; she can't be. She was only feet away from me, Paul, sitting in the armchair by the fireplace. It must be someone else they found. Maybe it was someone from next door, blown into our house by the force of the explosion? It has to be a mistake.' Sarah started to cry and shake uncontrollably.

Paul squeezed her hand, his own torment plain to see in his face. 'No, listen to me, Sarah.' His voice was low and urgent. 'It was her. I'm sorry, but you must accept it. She simply wasn't as lucky as you.' Paul released her hand to wipe his tears. 'I had to identify Maura at the morgue. That's where I found out where you were. I was asking about you, in case you had been brought there too, and Mr Nugent heard me talking to the clerk. He told me he'd seen you here when he was visiting his wife. You have no idea how relieved I was. I nearly hugged the man when he told me.'

Sarah did her best to stem the flow of tears, but there was a terrible ache in her chest. As she looked up, she was aware of the curious glances of the other patients. Paul gave her a watery smile and handed her a handkerchief.

'Thank you.' She blew her nose and took some shaky breaths. As they sat in silence, Sarah tried to compose herself. She closed her eyes, but it only took her back to the darkness, choking on dust, the building pressing down on her body. Maura was very close, she knew it; she could sense her presence. Her eyes flew open to the crushing reality of a hospital ward and her worst fears confirmed.

'Where is Maura now, Paul?' she asked at last, gulping down fresh tears.

'Still at the morgue. She will be moved, along with the others, to the church later this evening. The funerals will be tomorrow.' Paul's voice broke. 'The first batch. They're taking them all to Glasnevin Cemetery afterwards. I told them to bury her with your Ma. Did I do right?'

'Yes, thank you. That's perfect.'

'I'm so sorry, Sarah,' he said, his voice shaking.

But Paul's words barely registered through her sorrow.

Maura was gone forever.

On Thursday morning, the ward was cloaked in melancholy silence. Everyone knew what was happening today. As if in keeping with their sorrow, the skies threatened rain from the early morning. Right on cue, as Sarah envisaged the procession of coffins being brought out of the church, the clouds released their fury. Sarah leaned back into the pillows and let the tears fall unchecked. Still, no one on the ward spoke; each was mourning a family member, a friend, or a neighbour.

St Laurence O'Toole Church was only a short walk away, yet Sarah was not allowed to attend, despite her pleas to the doctor. Paul had promised to attend the funeral in her place and to bring flowers. White roses if he could find them, as they were Maura's favourite. Gradually, news filtered in from the visitors, some of whom brought in newspapers which were devoured by the patients. Sarah now knew Da had met a similar fate to many others that night. He and his mates had been seen on the bridge not long before the last bomb had fallen.

There was universal praise for those working to rescue survivors and find those who had been lost. What they had to deal with and the things they had to witness were unprecedented in Dublin's history.

That fourth bomb, the one that had destroyed her home, had been a 500 lb landmine; the destruction it had caused was all too visible in the newspaper photographs. One picture showed the tram tracks outside where their house used to stand, mangled and twisted like great metal fingers reaching up into the sky, as if in supplication to the angry god of war. The only consolation was that it would have been instant death for those, like Da, caught out in the open. But, try as she might, she could not grieve for him.

Then Sarah heard it. The faint sound of a marching band. Mrs McCluskey, in the bed beside her, pulled back her blankets and hobbled over to the window beside Sarah's bed. 'Do you hear the music, love?' she asked.

'Yes.' Sarah eased around in her bed, swinging her legs out.

'Let me help,' Mrs McCluskey said, throwing back the blanket for her. Then she offered Sarah her arm to lean on. They stood together in their grief, arm in arm. 'Aren't we lucky to be at the back of the hospital? They're due to travel past us towards Glasnevin.' Mrs McCluskey pointed to the rear gate which stood open. A huddle of hospital staff stood near it; umbrellas raised in a hopeless battle with the high wind. Gradually, those patients who were well enough to get out of bed crowded around the other windows, eager to see what was happening. The music grew louder, and Sarah saw the first of the cortege pass by.

"Tis grand,' Mrs McCluskey murmured. 'The Garda Band, bless them, leading the way; only fittin''.

Then it was the turn of the hearses drawn by magnificent black horses, their black plumes almost bent over with the force of the wind and rain. Which coffin held Maura? Which held Da's remains? Sarah clenched her fists as a wave of anger and worst of all, guilt, hit her. Mrs McCluskey must have sensed her distress, for she squeezed her arm. 'Are you going to be all right, love? Your father and sister, isn't it?'

Sarah managed a nod.

'God, I've been lucky. No one close to me was lost. You and those other poor families!' Mrs McCluskey wiped her eyes. 'Ah, Jaysus, look! Tiny coffins for those unfortunate, innocent children. How could those Jerries do such a terrible thing? If I live to be a hundred, I'll never understand.'

Immediately behind the hearses were horse-drawn carriages, full of mourners; flashes of white faces pressed up against the glass. Even at a distance, their hopelessness was palpable. Sarah closed her eyes for an instant in silent comradeship.

A procession of emergency services marched by and Sarah thought fleetingly of her rescuers. They had risked their lives to free her, and so many others. Those men who had patiently dug Maura out of the ruins of their home, or brought her father's remains to the morgue; were they marching too?

Sleek black cars went past. 'Pah!' Sarah's companion almost spat out the word. 'There's de Valera and his cronies in their fancy cars. So much for his neutrality; look where it has brought us today. I don't think Hitler is paying much attention to it. We can't even defend our citizens.'

'Will you stop!' a lady at the other window called out. 'We don't want war here again. It will only mean more of the same. We'll end up a smoking ruin like London or Liverpool.'

'Better to fight an honest war than take this lying down,' barked Mrs McCluskey. 'The whole world thinks us Irish are cowards.' She beat her fist against the window shutter. 'Well, just let Jerry set foot in Dublin and I'll show him what for!'

'I don't doubt you would and all, Martha McCluskey. Sure, your own husband is terrified of ye,' was the reply from the other window.

Mrs McCluskey stiffened in anger. Sarah threw her a pleading look. Now was not the time to argue about politics. Sarah turned back to keep watch, doing her best to hold on to her self-control. Still the mourners came. Sarah watched as hundreds of ordinary Dubliners snaked out behind the cortege, despite the foul weather, paying their respects and united in mourning the city's dead. Sarah could not speak or think clearly as raw emotion constricted her throat. At that moment, she would have given anything to walk with them.

Unable to bear it a second longer, she pulled away from Mrs McCluskey and crawled back into bed. Sarah turned her back on the window, her mind paralysed by sorrow and a growing desire for revenge.

4

19th July 1941, Glasnevin Cemetery, Dublin

The sun broke through the clouds as Sarah stood at the front gate of the graveyard, clutching a bunch of white roses. A check of her watch confirmed Paul was late, but she would wait; she was reluctant to visit the family grave alone. Paul had been so kind since the bombing, despite their awful breakup. Most days he had visited the hospital after work, and he had even brought his mother in to see her. When Sarah was discharged, Paul had accompanied her to the temporary refuge in the local convent near her old home. When he had suggested escorting her to the cemetery, Sarah had agreed without hesitation.

Paul's unstinting kindness only emphasised how awful her behaviour had been. What had gotten into her the night the bombs fell? Surely, the fact that he was so willing to help her now meant he had at least forgiven her. Could she dare to hope for a reconciliation? She needed him more than ever. During her weeks of recovery, she had little else to think about except her grief and an overwhelming loneliness. A future without Maura was bad enough; one without Paul was both bleak and dark. She would have to swallow her pride and admit she had been in the wrong.

But how would he receive that admission? What if he was acting now out of pity, not affection? He was attentive, but the easy relationship they had enjoyed before was gone. There was no intimacy now, when all she longed for was the comfort of his arms around her. Friendly affection was not enough for her; but perhaps it was all she deserved. Either way, it was too late if he was determined to enlist. The last thing he would want would be ties back in Dublin.

Now she understood why he wanted to contribute to the war effort. Jerry had unwittingly given her that insight. That night would always be a watershed in her life: the world before, when all Sarah Gillespie thought about was books, going to the pictures and nights on the town, and then the painful reality of life after, without a family and without Paul. Perhaps it was better to remember the good times. Sarah could still recall the first time she met him at the local drama group. It had taken her weeks to work up the courage to attend, not least because Da had belittled any ambitions in that direction as pure foolishness. As Sarah had walked into the dingy backroom of the church hall, Paul's had been the first friendly face she had seen. When he had asked to walk her home afterwards, she was delighted. Within a week, they were walking out together.

A hearse pulled up and swung in through the gates, followed by a car of mourners. Sarah's heart went out to the funeral-goers as the cortege wound its way down the narrow track through the jumble of headstones. Sarah's thoughts drifted to the last time she had visited. It had been with Maura to refresh the flowers on their mother's grave, just a week before the bombing.

Hearing the revving of an engine at the bus stop, Sarah turned, and was relieved to see Paul jumping down from the rear of the bus. Paul sprinted up to the gate, holding on to his hat. With an effort, she pushed any sad thoughts away and greeted him with a smile. He looked smart today, and for the hundredth time, she regretted her impetuosity. If only time could be reversed. As he greeted her, he didn't quite meet her eye. Sarah sighed; he felt just as awkward as she did. After a moment's hesitation, he gave her a peck on the cheek, when all she longed for was an embrace.

'So sorry, Sarah; I had to finish a rush job before I could leave. Saturday morning is always mad busy. Then I missed my bus; had to wait for the next one.'

'Not at all, Paul, I understand. I'm just glad you could come. Shall we go in?'

Paul offered her his arm, glancing downwards. 'How's the leg? Any better now the cast is gone?'

'Yes, thanks. It came off on Monday. My leg is stiff, and I don't think I will be wearing heels for a while.'

'You must be patient and let your body heal.'

Sarah gave him a sad smile. 'I know, and I'm unlikely to be going dancing any time soon anyway.'

Paul squeezed her arm in sympathy. 'Ah, you will, someday, Sarah. Maura wouldn't want you to stop living your life and having some fun.' Sarah nodded and gulped, too emotional to respond. His glance was full of concern. 'We don't have to do this today. Are you sure you are ready?'

'Absolutely,' she replied.

'Good. Now, let's take our time; we have all afternoon,' he said.

They turned down the gravel path to the left, following the

old stone wall that sheltered plots dominated by elaborate Victorian gravestones, some crumbling with age and covered in lichen and moss. It was peaceful under the trees as they walked along, an oasis of calm away from the city noise. From visiting her mother's grave, Sarah was familiar with the path, and a little further on, she turned in amongst the headstones until she found the small Gillespie plot.

The headstone was small and plain compared to some of its neighbours, and slightly lost amongst the towering Celtic crosses and weeping angels. Jim Gillespie had gone to a moneylender to help pay for it: the one decent thing he ever did for Ma. Mind you, he never visited the grave after the funeral; never bothered to see what his money had secured. It bore only Sarah's mother's name and the date of her death. The minimum of acceptable detail; the maximum of acceptable cost to Da. Beneath the stone, the disturbed soil was heaped up in a mound, and two bouquets of roses lay on top. The petals on both were turning brown at the tips and curling back.

'Did you leave these? Is there no end to your kindness?' Sarah asked, turning to Paul in amazement.

Paul cleared his throat as two patches of colour sprung up in his cheeks. He stooped down to pick up the decaying flowers. 'Don't mention it. I've been coming out every week as you couldn't come, and I couldn't bear to think of her . . . alone.' Paul took a deep breath and looked away. 'I'll put these in the bin.'

Sarah watched him disappear down the path, grateful for his thoughtfulness not only in visiting her family's grave, but for giving her a moment to grieve alone. She let out a long, slow breath before placing the roses down. Then she stood back and tried to pray. But as she stared down at the earth, the words would not come. It was hard to imagine her young sister now resting, forever silent, in this grave. Beautiful, funny Maura; a mere child. It was harder still to think of Maura's final moments. Had it truly been instant, or had she suffered for hours? Most nights, Sarah woke from nightmares in which she was being buried alive, watching helplessly as Maura disappeared beneath the tumbling rubble. The dreams were awful; she dreaded sleep.

Every day, her anger grew; and the focus of that anger was Nazi Germany. But how could she, a mere nobody, strike back? She could only hope that someday an opportunity would arise.

As the horrors of the bombing faded in the minds of Dubliners, Sarah tried to cope with the uncertain future she now faced. All the constants in her life had been pulled away. Her family was gone, and she was homeless. Then, to cap it all, she had received notice from her job. In her absence, they had taken on someone else. Sarah had never liked her boss and knew he was only too relieved to have an excuse to get rid of her. The worst possible timing, of course, but it would force her to make decisions.

Like many others displaced by the bombs, she had taken refuge with the nuns, but that could only be temporary until she found her feet. The city was slowly returning to normal and although the nuns had been kind, Sarah could sense a growing impatience for her and the others to move on with their lives. If one were cynical, one might even believe it was because the generous flow of donations from the public to support the refugees had now dried up.

Glancing at the inscription on the headstone, Sarah wondered what she should do. Maura's name would have to be added. Da's as well. The cost would empty her Post Office savings account, but it had to be done.

Paul stepped up beside her and put an arm around her shoulder. 'Are you all right? This must be hard for you; but for her sake, you must get on with your life, Sarah. Maura adored you. I know how close you two were, and that you will miss her dreadfully, but she would not have wanted you to give way under this.'

'I will try, but it will not be easy. I will miss her very much!' Sarah wiped her eyes. 'Maura was wonderful, the best of sisters. It is such a waste, Paul. Her life was only beginning.' Sarah placed a hand over her heart. 'I'll never forget her. I will carry her with me in here, forever.'

Paul nodded. 'Come; there's a bench over there. Let's sit down for a few minutes. You can rest your leg but still see the grave from there.'

They sat down and Paul took her hand, lacing his fingers through hers like he used to when they were courting. Sarah found it comforting, finding solace in the memory of happier times. She leaned her head against his shoulder. A blackbird, perched up in a tree above them, burst into song every so often. And suddenly, Sarah was at peace. She glanced over to the grave, finally able to say a prayer.

After several minutes, Paul harrumphed. 'Sarah, I have some news.'

She lifted her head and smiled. 'Yes?'

'I've . . . Well, after all that has happened . . . and I've been thinking for some time that—'

'You're going to enlist; you're going up north.'

His face relaxed into an apologetic smile. 'Yes. I'm sorry. It's terrible timing, particularly now when you need all your friends around you, but the bombing and your situation have made me even more determined. I don't want to wait any longer.'

A spark of hope ignited for an instant; had he delayed departing for her sake? No, it could not be that. He saw himself merely as her friend.

Hiding her disappointment, Sarah nodded. 'Trust me, I now understand completely. I'm only sorry . . . the things I said . . . I was hurting. As for your leaving to enlist, I am glad,' she said in a rush. 'In fact, I admire you for it.' She squeezed his arm. 'I wish you well, I really do. Hitler must be stopped.'

Paul turned to her, swallowing hard. 'I agree. We have to fight this goddamn evil. But you don't need to apologise about that night. I sprung it on you too suddenly, I realise that now.'

'Still; I should have tried to understand your point of view. It was a selfish reaction on my part, and I regret it.'

'Thank you,' he said. 'But perhaps it was for the best, you know, with me leaving. I don't know what lies ahead for me, Sarah. And you've had enough loss to deal with for one lifetime.'

His words turned her insides to stone. Couched in soft words, it was still a rejection. And one she deserved. Fighting back the impulse to cry, she said: 'You mustn't worry. I'm tough as old boots, me. When do you leave?' she asked, staring ahead. Sarah knew if she looked into his eyes the pain would leak out and she would howl.

'The end of the week. I'll report to a recruiting station up in Belfast, but then I'll be moved to an airfield somewhere in England once they complete all the paperwork.'

'Will you tell your family?'

'No. You know why that is impossible,' he answered with a sigh. 'Da would be livid. He might even try to stop me. And as for my Ma, she would try to talk me out of it. I'll leave a letter explaining why I have to go. Maybe, in time, they will accept it.'

'I understand. You will have quite the adventure. I admit to being quite envious.' Sarah looked out across the graveyard, a hollow feeling in her stomach. 'I'll miss you, but I wish you luck.'

Paul squeezed her hand. 'I'll take revenge for both of us, I promise you that.'

Sarah sucked in a breath. 'Don't go with hatred in your heart, Paul. Go because it is the honourable thing to do. There is too much evil in the world as it is.'

'And decent men must act,' he said, his voice catching.

Sarah nodded and they sat in silence for several minutes.

'Have you heard anything from your Da's family?' Paul asked.

'No. And I won't. There was no love lost there.'

'Jim Gillespie was a hard man,' Paul said with a frown. 'At least now you are free of him.'

'I cannot speak ill of him; he was my father, no matter what he did.' Sarah shifted on the seat and withdrew her hand from his grasp.

'Sorry, Sarah, but I must speak plainly. It was hard not to notice your bruises, and your excuses were always so flimsy. He was a brute of a man. Jim's reputation for violence was well known. Half the men in North Strand feared him, my own father included, and you don't find many men harder than my Da.'

Sarah shivered and drew herself in. 'I know you mean well, but I don't want to talk about him. And please don't tell anyone about . . . what he did. Best forgotten now, anyway.'

'I understand,' he said, though his frown said otherwise.

'I wonder where you will be posted,' Sarah said, hoping to change the subject. 'Will you write to me? I'd love to stay in touch. But only if you wish it.'

'Of course I do!' He turned to her. 'Sarah, I'm worried about you. What are you going to do?'

'I have a few ideas bubbling away.'

'Good for you. But I was thinking. There is nothing to keep you here after what has happened to your family. Why don't you leave and go to England too? There's plenty of work in the English factories, and that helps the war effort and hurts Germany.'

'As a matter of fact, I have been thinking along those lines,' she said. 'I've had plenty of time on my hands these last few weeks, courtesy of Herr Hitler.' Paul frowned at her, but she smiled back. 'A few days ago, I received a letter from my Uncle Tom, my mother's younger brother who lives in Hampshire. He and his wife have offered me a home. My uncle works for Vickers Supermarine and says he might get me a job there. I'd be contributing to the war effort, something I cannot do here. Best of all, it's an opportunity to get revenge on Jerry too. The chance to stay with family and start over is a compelling reason to take them up on their kind offer.'

Paul grinned back at her. 'Indeed, it is. That's fantastic if he can get you a job in Vickers. They make Spitfires, you know. The best planes in the world. That's why I want to join the RAF; I hope to fly a Spit someday.'

'I'll ask them to make one especially for you,' she said. 'It will have "Ace O'Reilly" emblazoned on the fuselage.'

'I wish you could! But tell me, are you seriously considering leaving Ireland?'

How she longed to tell him what was really in her heart; that she loved him and wanted him to stay, that she wanted them to build a life together here. But it would be unfair on him to do so. Her gaze lingered on the grave of her mother and sister, and a father she could not grieve. She had never felt so alone in her entire life.

'There is nothing to keep me here, Paul, and I think I owe it to them, don't you?'

5

20th August 1941, North Strand, Dublin

It was a humid afternoon as Sarah left the convent. It was one of those rare days when the distinctive smell of hops and malted barley from the Guinness brewery on the quays wafted that far east. But she was heedless of the weather and the pungent odour. She had to remain single-minded, for this journey could not be put off any longer. No matter how awful, she could not contemplate leaving Ireland without visiting her old home one last time. As Sarah walked along, the tightness in her stomach turned into a cold, hard knot of dread. Would the very sight of No. 18 in ruins trigger even more grief? The nightly terrors were bad enough as it was.

Rounding the corner into North Strand, she came to a dead stop. The black and white images in the newspapers hadn't prepared her for the scale of the devastation. North Strand lay in ruins; the familiar was no more. The houses, Nugent's shop, the post office: all gone. For a moment, Sarah was overcome, and she had to stretch out her hand to support herself against the post-box, which had miraculously survived. Some passers-by cast her curious glances, but she stared straight ahead, determined not to make eye contact. It was several minutes before she had the strength to move forward again.

Further down the pavement, the long-familiar sight and sound of a tram caused her to stop and stare in surprise. It trundled past, packed with passengers. She hadn't expected the trams to be back working so soon. Surely the damage to the road had been too great? Frowning, Sarah scanned the surface of the roadway. An area of clean cobblestones and shiny tram track revealed where the landmine had exploded. That certainly made the priorities of the city's bureaucrats more than clear. *Pity the lives lost could not be replaced so easily*, she thought with a sting of sadness.

She looked across the road to where No. 18 once stood and caught her breath. Her body became rigid as a wave of pure anger hit. Her fists clenched at her sides. For weeks she had wallowed in grief, but what did that achieve? It couldn't bring Maura back . . . or even Da. She needed to act. This was her new reality and Germany was to blame. Grief was replaced by a burning desire for revenge for Maura's pointless murder. Whatever it would take, no matter how small her contribution to the war effort would be, it had to be better than this paralysing neutrality. She knew in that instant her decision to leave for England was the right one.

The twisted metal of the lamp-post which had stood outside their house and the gaunt outline of their old sycamore showed the ferocity of the explosion. Their terrace, once home to over ten families, was now a pile of debris. Further along, the next terrace still stood, but the roofs and windows were missing, and the front walls of some were bulging out at odd angles. It would soon face the wrecking ball.

For several minutes, she could only stare as memories came flooding back. Ma standing at the door waving them off to school; escaping down the steps to play with the other children as soon as Ma's back was turned; watching Da head off to the pub of an evening from the window in the front parlour. Everyone in the house would relax for those few hours they were free of him. But those memories tumbling through her mind only made the loss of Maura more acute. What she would give to have one last conversation with her: one last laugh; one last hug.

Sarah waited for a break in the traffic and crossed the road. Either side, at the ends of their terrace, parts of the gable walls still stood with stranded fireplaces hanging out into the abyss below. It was uncomfortable to look at remnants of the houses. It was, as if the inhabitants' lives were exposed for the world to gape at and mock. The bricks, beams and rubble from the houses were pushed back from the pavement into great dusty piles. Her main reason for visiting had been the faint hope of finding personal belongings. But that was doomed, and the ignominy of scrambling through the rubble to find trinkets struck her as ridiculous now that she could see the result of the blast. Even if anything had survived, it would be damaged beyond repair. She had escaped with her life; that would have to suffice.

Looking around, Sarah wondered how they had found her that day and rescued her. The risk those men had taken almost overwhelmed her. She could remember them now, their anxious expressions belying their comforting words. They must have been scared too. Would it be possible at this stage to find out who they were, and thank them in person before she left?

Sarah wiped away her tears with the back of her hand. One thing was certain: she could never come back here again. The past had been wiped in one horrific twist of fate. She recalled seeing that German pilot swooping low over the roofs on the night of the bombing. What had he or his fellow pilots been thinking as they had released those bombs? Did they know it was Dublin or had it been a genuine mistake? Not that it mattered: the outcome had been the murder of innocents and the annihilation of a close-knit community. That she could never forgive.

'Is that you, Sarah Gillespie?' a familiar voice called out, breaking into her thoughts. 'I saw you pass my window, and I thinks to meself, that's young Sarah, that is.'

Sarah turned to see one of her old neighbours coming towards her, leaning on a walking stick. Sarah had always been fond of Mrs Twohig, affectionately known as Mrs T by the locals. The elderly lady had treated her and Maura with kindness when they were kids. With no children of her own, she had loved to spoil them with sweets and cake; luxuries they never got at home. It was said she had buried two husbands and some local wags had christened her 'the Black Widow', but a more generous soul it would be hard to find in North Strand.

'Yes, Mrs Twohig, it is. It is good to see you.' Sarah walked up to her and gave her a hug. 'How have you been?'

'As good as can be expected after all of this dreadful business. You are a welcome sight, my dear. I'd heard they dug you out, but I didn't know what happened to you after that.'

'I was lucky, Mrs T. I've been staying up at the convent since I was discharged from the Mater. Were you hurt in the explosion?' Sarah asked.

Mrs Twohig crossed herself. 'No. The good Lord was looking out for me, he was. A few broken windows was the size of it, and those nice boys from the Corpo came and fixed them.' Her tiny cottage was back down the street, further away from the blast zone.

'I'm glad you were unharmed. Too many others weren't so lucky,' Sarah said.

The old lady leaned on Sarah's arm, breathing hard, her face full of sorrow. 'I'm so sorry about your sister Maura. Lovely child, she was. And . . . of course, your Da.' The lady's hesitation wasn't lost on Sarah.

'Thank you, Mrs Twohig.' Sarah glanced back at the pile of rubble. 'This is my first time back. I've been avoiding the street ever since . . .'

'I can understand that, you poor love. And all those innocents lost. You heard about the Butler family?' Mrs Twohig shook her head. 'Even the tiny babe lost. They found her in her mother's arms.' She took a deep breath. 'North Strand will never recover from this.'

'You may be right.' Sarah glanced around. 'I've heard people are being offered new homes on the outskirts of the city in Cabra.'

'Aye, that's so. They say it's a soulless place, and sure it's miles from everywhere and not a shop to be had, but folks need a roof over their heads and at least the city is doing something for the poor craturs.' Mrs Twohig sighed. 'Maybe someday if they rebuild, they'll come back here again.'

Sarah doubted anyone would return, not least because of the awful memories the place would hold. The community was scattered forever now. 'This must be hard for you,' she replied.

'True. Many of my oldest friends have upped and gone or been made homeless,' the lady said with a sad smile. 'And a couple are now six feet under up in Glasnevin.'

'Would you not consider going out to Cabra to be near your old neighbours?'

'No, I'll stay put. I have lived here all my life, Sarah, and I'm too decrepit to be gallivanting all over the city. Just me and my cat Montgomery left now. I suppose you're moving out to Cabra, then?'

'No, Mrs T. It's likely I'll go to England, to my uncle. I came today to see if I could find a few things before I leave . . . but this doesn't look promising.' Sarah gave a mirthless laugh. 'I feel foolish now that I can see the level of destruction. What was I thinking?'

All of a sudden, Mrs Twohig's grip on Sarah's arm tightened. 'But didn't you know? Those Corpo lads who were working here left a box of recovered items with me. Why don't you come back to mine and see if there is anything belonging to your family? I'm afraid I hadn't the heart to look through the box.' The lady sniffed and blew her nose before smiling at Sarah. 'Do come. I can put the kettle on. I'm sure I have a few biscuits. If I recall, you have a sweet tooth.'

'Thank you, I would like that,' Sarah replied warmly. How could she resist the pleading in the old lady's eyes? She must be lonely, with only memories and piles of rubble for company. With a bit of luck, there might even be something to salvage from Mrs Twohig's box of recovered items. They linked arms and strolled back towards the Twohig cottage.

'You know, your dear mother was incredibly good to me when I lost my Joe. She used to call in nearly every day to see how I was. A very kind-hearted woman, and God knows she had enough troubles of her own to be worrying about the likes of me.'

Sarah stiffened, but at least she could detect sympathy in the woman's tone. Many others had reacted differently to her mother's plight, as if it were her mother's fault that Jim Gillespie had been a violent man.

'Now, where did I put that box?' Mrs Twohig muttered as soon as they entered her disorderly sitting room. Tiny patches of ancient, faded wallpaper were visible where there was a gap in the jumble of household items and keepsakes. Sarah's elderly hostess stood frowning at the mess. 'I'm sure it's in here somewhere. I throw nothing away, you know.'

Sarah smiled. That was more than evident. Even the sofa was piled with bric-à-brac of all kinds. Only a solitary armchair, stationed at the front window, was free of clutter. Mrs Twohig turned her attention to the alcoves either side of the fireplace that brimmed with an assortment of bits and bobs, tut-tutting under her breath. 'Must be here somewhere, eh, Montgomery?' This Mrs Twohig addressed to the cat, a large Persian laying atop a stack of magazines, who flicked his ears and yawned.

'May I help you? Can you recall what the box was like?' Sarah asked, beginning to think this would be an impossible task.

Suddenly, Mrs Twohig turned around. 'Ah! Of course, now I remember. There it is, Sarah. Can you reach it? It's that large red box on top of the books.' The lady pointed to the top of her bookcase with her walking stick. 'You have a look, dear, while I stick the kettle on the gas.'

Once Mrs Twohig had quit the room, Sarah gave the cat a wary glance. Retrieving the box would entail disturbing him, and Montgomery was never slow to use his claws. 'Come on, kitty, you need to move,' Sarah coaxed, giving his head a tentative rub. With a wide yawn, the cat gave a languid stretch before bestowing a haughty stare upon her. He jumped down, and with his tail in the air wandered out the door after his mistress.

It took a few minutes, but Sarah retrieved the box without spilling its contents or injuring herself as she balanced on the arm of the sofa to reach up. She sat down on Mrs Twohig's armchair and placed her hands reverently on top of the box. It contained the remnants of so many lives. Heart pounding, she opened the flaps. A cloud of dust rose, making her cough. Each item was covered in a fine powder and tiny bits of grit. Using her handkerchief, she removed as much dirt as she could and sorted through the items, examining each one, hoping to find something familiar. By the time Mrs Twohig returned, Sarah had reached the bottom of the box, her hands shaking. Nothing. Not one item in the box had been recognisable: they were all other people's memories.

'Any luck, dear?' her hostess asked.

'No, nothing.'

'That's a shame. Never mind, Sarah. Come down to the kitchen for your tea.'

'I'll just put the box back,' Sarah replied, jumping up to hide the tears that threatened to fall.

There wasn't a puff of air in the tiny kitchen despite the back door standing open. Mrs Twohig had to hooch the cat off the only other chair. 'That cat has no manners!' she exclaimed, but with affection. 'Now, drink up, Sarah, and tell me about your plans.' She pushed a cuppa towards Sarah as she sat down.

'I'm leaving for England in a couple of weeks. I'm just waiting for the approval to travel to come through.'

'I'm sorry to hear it, Sarah; I'll miss you. Are you sure it's the right thing to do? I hope you won't regret it.'

'It hasn't been an easy decision. All I've ever known is No. 18 and North Strand. But everything has changed. There is this huge void in my life, now. It was hard when Ma died, but at least I had Maura. She was only twelve years old and the responsibility of her care fell to me. That made the grief easier to bear. It gave me purpose.'

'That's understandable. I always said your Ma would have been proud of the way you took the poor chick under your wing. You had to grow up before your time.' Mrs Twohig's eyes narrowed slightly. 'Your Da wasn't there much, was he?'

'No.'

'Perhaps it was his way of coping? Men are never any use when it comes to domestic matters.'

Sarah almost laughed. 'Da didn't like his routine to be disturbed and if he didn't like something, he just ignored it. That included us. God forgive me, but I will not miss his harsh ways. However, Maura has left a hole in my life. I miss her so much. And I can't help it; I want revenge for her needless death.' Sarah took a deep breath. 'Seeing the ruins of our home today has only reinforced it. It was murder, plain and simple.'

'It was! You're right, my dear. Those nasty Germans have a lot to answer for.'

'As long as I live, I won't understand why they did it,' Sarah said.

'Pure evil, my dear. My late father always said it. He fought them in the Great War.' She paused to pour them both a fresh cup of tea. 'Did you know Peter Roche died up on the bridge?

Just like your poor Da.' She shook her head. 'His poor widow could only identify him from a mole on his back.' She shuddered. 'An awful business. At least you were spared that.'

'Yes. The only way to confirm it was Da was his wedding ring. At least I haven't been left wondering what happened to him. Some of the bodies were never identified. They just buried them together in a plot up in Glasnevin.'

'Terrible for the poor families,' the old lady said with a shake of her head. 'You must miss him a little, all the same?'

'He wasn't the most loving of fathers, but he was my Da,' she replied with a sad smile.

The old lady nodded, her eyes full of understanding. 'And what about your young man? Is he not going to help you out?'

Sarah caught her breath. She had done her best to reconcile herself to losing Paul and since he had left, she had struggled with remorse. But she knew he had to enlist. It was too important to him, and above all, she wanted him to be happy. That day in Glasnevin, she could have appealed to him to stay, but she had realised it would only have destroyed whatever friendship was left. It would have been an incredibly selfish act on her part. However, it was still painful to think she might never see him again.

'Paul has left Dublin already. He's enlisting in the RAF up north and then he will be stationed somewhere in England.'

'Ah, now, good for him. Do you hope to join him there?'

'No, we broke up a few months ago. We are still friends, but our lives are taking us in different directions. My uncle has invited me to come and live with his family in the south of England and there is hope of a job, too.'

Mrs Twohig reached across the table, squeezed her hand, and spoke in her soft way. 'I'm delighted for you. A fresh start. It does no good to dwell on the might-have-beens, *a stór*. Life has taught me that over and over again. You have your life ahead of you. It seems to me, war or no war, that your future lies across the water.'

Mrs T stood up and took a small black metal box down from a shelf. 'Take this with you. It has always brought my family luck.' She reached inside the box and pulled out an object. She blew on it, then rubbed it with the sleeve of her cardigan before handing it over.

Sarah stared down at the metal cross on a black-and-white ribbon, lying in her palm. 'No, no, I couldn't accept this!'

'Please take it. It was my father's, and he swore it got him through the Great War. Survived the Somme, he did. Told us he took that medal from a Hun he shot who tried to kill 'im and his pal. I've no need for it now, and it might prove lucky for you.' Mrs Twohig held up her hand as Sarah protested. 'No, I'm determined. I want you to have it, especially as there was nothing of yours in that box from the Corpo. No arguments, please.'

Sarah gulped down her tears, still staring at the medal. 'Do you know what it is, Mrs Twohig?'

'My father called it an Iron Cross. German medal for bravery. Now there's a piece of irony for you. Bravery! Cowardly Huns dropping bombs on the innocent!'

The cross was black with a raised silver border. There was a crown at the top and 1914 at the bottom. In the middle was the letter 'W'. 'I wonder what the "W" stands for,' she said, looking across at her hostess.

'Sorry, my dear, I've no idea, but my father was convinced that war trophy was a lucky charm.'

Sarah glanced up. 'I will treasure it and keep it always. Thank you.' It was the most bizarre gift she had ever received, but if it were as lucky as Mrs Twohig claimed, it would be foolish to refuse it. Besides, she did not wish to offend the old lady.

'May God go with you, and keep you safe, *a stór,*' Mrs Twohig said, her eyes bright with tears. 'I'll keep you in my prayers.'

6

Sarah awoke as the train from Bristol crawled to a stop. Her fellow passengers were putting on their coats and retrieving their bags from the racks above their seats but Sarah waited, her excitement building. For a moment, all she could do was count her blessings, relieved to have made it to Southampton. Her journey from Dublin had been long and uncomfortable, the sea voyage nerve-racking due to the threat posed by the Luftwaffe. She had boarded the train with relief only to find there wasn't a seat to be had. The train was full of soldiers on the move and she spent most of the journey in the corridor, nose to nose with the troops. Luckily, the men were a happy-go-lucky bunch and they had entertained her royally as the miles flew past. When they had disembarked several stops ago, she had been lucky enough to get a seat in a compartment for the rest of the journey.

Now, a new adventure beckoned. Another surge of excitement ran through her as she pulled out Uncle Tom's letter for the umpteenth time. Sarah scanned it once more before putting it back in her handbag. What would he be like? Ma had always spoken fondly of Uncle Tom and his wife Alice. They must be tender-hearted to have offered her, a virtual stranger, a chance to start over. Pulling a small mirror compact from her bag, she tidied her hair, applied some lipstick and adjusted her hat. Now she was ready.

Stepping down onto the platform, Sarah took in the surroundings and the people milling about. She had a vague idea of what her uncle looked like from old photographs Ma had treasured. As no one appeared to be waiting for her on the platform, Sarah followed the other passengers towards the exit at the far end. Outside, the first thing she noticed were the barrage balloons being buffeted about in the wind, the implication of their existence above the city plain. Sarah looked away with a grimace. Nearby, a group of men were working close to the station entrance, shovelling rubble and debris into wheelbarrows. Part of the wall had a gaping hole; the station must have been hit in recent days.

Spotting a gentleman standing near the entrance, Sarah thought it might be her uncle. He looked about the right age.

'Excuse me, would you be Tom Lambe, by any chance?' she asked on approach.

The man swung around and weighed her up with a sweeping glance, his expression one of aversion. 'I am not,' he barked. 'Bloody Irish! Why don't you crawl back to your own country? We don't need the likes of you here.' With a snort of derision, he moved away, leaving Sarah stunned, her heart thumping. She had never encountered such animosity before. It left her feeling ill.

'Sarah? Is that you?' a tentative voice enquired.

Sarah turned with relief. A middle-aged man stood a few feet away; he might have grown older, but she recognised her uncle immediately. Relieved, she closed the gap at speed, and held out her hand. 'Yes! Uncle Tom. I'm very pleased to meet you at last.'

Seconds later, she was hugged. 'Ah,' her uncle said, 'I'd know you anywhere. Sure, you're the image of your dear mother; same chestnut hair and green eyes. You are most welcome. I'm only sorry it's just yourself; very sorry indeed.'

Sarah gulped at the reference to Maura but returned the hug, choking back her tears. Uncle Tom cleared his throat and held her at arm's length. 'It's incredible . . . the resemblance. Well, now, we still have a way to go, my dear. Let me take your case. We can catch the Supermarine bus home to Hursley.'

'The Supermarine bus? Isn't Supermarine the company you work for?'

'Yes, it is. Since they had to disperse operations throughout the county, they have provided a bus service from all our different locations. Luckily, there is one that will take us straight home. It was that or cycle, and I assumed you'd have some luggage and would find that difficult. I'm afraid I don't own a car.'

'The bus is perfect. I'd much prefer it to a bicycle with this old case to lug about. How far is Hursley from here, Uncle Tom?'

'About nine miles,' he replied.

Taking his offered arm, Sarah studied him as they walked along. Tom was a tall man, with a lean face. Flecks of silver at his temples, in otherwise dark brown hair, peeped out from under his hat, and when he smiled encouragingly at her, his blue eyes crinkled at the corners. There was little physical resemblance to her mother, but she warmed to him straight away.

'Here we are. Shouldn't have to wait too long,' he said, coming to a stop and lowering her case to the ground. 'How was the journey? Crossing the Irish Sea these days must be nerve-racking.'

'I was anxious about it. There are so many stories about ships being attacked by U-boats or planes, even when flying the Irish flag. Everyone on board was nervous, even the crew – you could see it in their faces. I was never so glad to reach dry land when we docked at Liverpool.'

'I had hoped to meet you there, but work is hectic, and I just couldn't get away.'

'Oh no; I didn't expect it,' Sarah replied. 'The instructions in your letter were perfect, and I made all of my connections without too much trouble. Most folk are helpful, I find, if you need directions.'

'I'm relieved to hear it; I was worried about you travelling alone. So many people on the move these days.' He nodded towards an approaching bus. 'Excellent! Here's our transport.'

They hopped on and uncle Tom ushered Sarah to seats up near the top. 'I must warn you, my dear. The journey can be a bit hair-raising. You'd think the hounds of hell were after these drivers. They seem to believe they are a target for the Luftwaffe because they transport the workers. However, I doubt the Jerries know they even exist.'

As the bus travelled through the streets of the city, Sarah was shocked by the damage. Many buildings were mere shells with blackened walls and yawning holes. Each one represented a family torn apart, or a business destroyed. It reminded her of North Strand. From the Irish newspapers, she knew the Germans had bombed Southampton, along with most of the south English coast, but she hadn't realised the full extent of the destruction. When she remarked upon it to Uncle Tom, he grimaced.

'Damned Jerries! Did their best to blow us to kingdom come, but it will take more than that to beat us. We knew we would be targeted because of the naval base and Supermarine. We lost some good people when the factory was hit, you know. It was heartbreaking.' He regarded her gravely. 'Poor lass, sure you have experienced it first-hand. A dreadful business. What were they thinking, bombing Dublin?'

'No one knows. There are plenty of theories, but only the pilots can answer the question. The German Ambassador said it was an error, if you can believe him.'

'Well, it shows the level of depravity of Hitler and his maniacs, and no mistake. Now tell me truthfully, are you fully recovered from your injuries? There's no need for you to start work straight away if you need to convalesce.'

Suddenly self-conscious, Sarah touched the scar at the base of her neck before pulling her hair across it. 'Oh, no, there is no need for that. I'm fine. My leg is a little stiff sometimes, but I was lucky not to sustain more serious injuries. So many others were not so fortunate.'

Uncle Tom patted her arm. 'Indeed, you were blessed, my dear. Your dear mother must have been looking out for you. But oh my! We were so sorry to hear about your father and Maura. A tragic waste.'

'Thank you. There are days I still cannot believe it, but I have to focus on the future now,' Sarah said, anxious to change the subject. She still found it difficult to talk about Maura's passing, and any reminder of her father was unwelcome.

'That is the best attitude, my dear,' Uncle Tom replied. They sat in companionable silence for some minutes.

'How long have you lived in Hursley?' she asked.

'Only since January this year. The factory at Woolston was bombed last September, as I said, and then in the Blitz in November the house we rented, here in Southampton, was irreparably damaged. Supermarine dispersed all the different operations throughout Hampshire in December. Makes it more difficult for the Germans, you see. My section, the Drawing Office, was sent to Hursley Park. It's an old house and estate next to Hursley village. Anyway, I didn't fancy the commute, and as my son Martin also works in the Drawing Office and our Judith was a secretary in Supermarine at the time, we moved to the village. We were one of the first families to arrive and were lucky enough to find a cottage to rent. It's tiny, but sure it's grand. Your Aunt Alice is so glad to be away from Southampton. The bombing destroyed her nerves, poor love. Shortly after, our Judith took off for London. She found Hursley slow after Southampton, I think.'

'Do they build the Spitfires at Hursley?'

'No, only the prototypes. The main factory is now at Castle Bromwich, up north. Have you ever seen a Spitfire?'

'Only once. Maura and I witnessed a dogfight over Sandymount Strand one afternoon, but they moved out over the sea so I don't know how it ended.'

'My bet is our plane won. Damn fine machine, my dear; can out fly a Messerschmitt any day. Saved our bacon last autumn and no mistake. They'll win us the war yet.'

As the bus left the city behind, it picked up speed and Sarah turned her attention to the countryside as they raced along the leafy laneways. She could see rolling hills and a chequerboard of farm fields through the gaps in the trees. Would country life suit her, she wondered? It was bound to be very different to life in Dublin city. Would she be able to settle?

'Your aunt is looking forward to meeting you. And Martin, of course. We do miss our Judith since she went up to London. It'll be grand to have a young woman about the place again,' Uncle Tom remarked.

Sarah smiled up at him. 'That's a shame. I'd love to meet Judith – she's about my age, isn't she?'

'About a year older. Don't worry, she will be home in a few weeks for the weekend. Got herself a nice job, so she did. An important one, too, from what she says in her letters. We are extremely proud of her.'

'I'm looking forward to meeting all the family. It is so generous of you to offer me a home and the possibility of work. While I was recovering in hospital, my job was given to someone else.'

'Good gracious; that was mean-spirited after what you had gone through.'

Sarah shrugged. 'Yes, but I was relieved, to be honest. The boss was a terrible snob and we never got on. I would have changed jobs at the first opportunity, anyway.'

'Still, that must have been a blow.'

'I had more pressing problems. When I was discharged, I had to go to a refuge set up in the local convent.'

'Why was that? Was the house that badly damaged?'

'Yes. There is nothing left but a pile of rubble, Uncle Tom. I have no idea when or if they will rebuild. There is a plan for some residents to move to council houses on the outskirts. As I'm on my own, they probably wouldn't offer one to me. Families are considered more urgent, as is only right. But the problem was I found it strange in the refuge. There was no privacy, and although I was thankful to have a roof over my head, I couldn't settle. The nuns meant well, of course, and were kind. But when your letter was redirected to the refuge, it was more than welcome.'

'Not at all! Family always comes first, I say. And, as it happens, Supermarine is constantly on the lookout for suitable employees. Our workload has increased dramatically in the last six months.'

'Did the RAF lose many planes during the Battle of Britain?'

'Aye, and the demand is rising all the time. Production has ramped up to meet it, with the factories working twenty-four hours a day.'

'A good friend of mine has enlisted in the RAF.'

'Where is he based?' Uncle Tom asked.

'I don't know as I haven't heard from him since he enlisted. I gave him your address so that he could write to me. I hope that was ok?'

Tom chuckled. 'Of course. Was he someone special?'

Sarah felt the colour rush into her cheeks. 'Yes, at one point.'

There! She had mentioned him without falling into the abyss. All these weeks she had repressed any memories of him. It was the only way she could cope, move forward, and make a new life. Leaving Ireland had been difficult enough without lingering on recollections of their time together and their favourite haunts: walks down the Bull Wall wooden bridge to Dollymount Strand or strolling down Howth harbour; nights out on the town; these were filed under 'the past' now. But it did make her a tiny bit sad that she was almost reconciled to his loss. Was she becoming heartless?

Uncle Tom hesitated for a moment and gave her a sheepish look. 'I know so little about your lives. How remiss I have been. I should have made more of an effort to stay in touch after your mother died. I had meant to visit ye in Dublin, too. But the timing was never right.'

'When were you last home to Ireland, Uncle Tom?'

'Ah, my dear, I'm so long living in England I don't think of Ireland as home any more.' He paused a moment. 'Isn't that sad? But I came here as a lad of fifteen. There was no work in Galway then; it was emigrate or starve.' He sighed. 'But to answer your question, it would have been your grandmother's funeral in Roundstone in '24. You were only a young 'un in your mother's arms then, so I doubt you remember.'

'No, I don't. But Ma always spoke of you and Galway with great affection. We never visited, though. Da didn't like . . . well, he objected to the cost of going. It was Ma's dearest wish to return to see Aunt Peggy, but then Ma fell ill with TB . . .'

Uncle Tom grunted and pursed his lips. 'Aye, well, your Da and I never got on, I'm afraid. We would have been there for your mother's funeral but we didn't find out about it until it was too late to travel.' With a sigh, he continued. 'Jim could be a difficult man.'

Sarah looked away. 'Difficult' was not the word which most readily came to mind.

7

Half an hour later, Sarah clambered off the bus after her uncle. They were in the centre of a village with a beautiful old church sheltered by ancient trees on one side of the road. Opposite was a two-storey Georgian building, a sign proclaiming 'The King's Head' swinging gently in the breeze in the front garden. From the little Sarah had seen so far, the village consisted of rows of red-bricked cottages hugging the main road. It was a charming place.

'Welcome to Hursley, Sarah,' Uncle Tom said, taking her suitcase. 'Come along. If we are in luck, Alice will have the kettle on.'

'Some of these cottages must be ancient,' she said, admiring a fine example with latticed windows and a white front door which contrasted beautifully with the old brick.

'Yes; ours is at least two or three hundred years old. Not a straight wall in the place! We were lucky; some people ended up in huts which were specially built at the farthest end of the village. Not half as nice as our cottage, nor as cosy.'

As they passed a forge, the blacksmith shouted out a greeting to her uncle. 'Fine afternoon, Tom!'

Uncle Tom responded in kind but kept walking. 'Time enough for you to meet the locals,' he said quietly with a wink. 'And . . . here we are.' He stopped in front of a dormer cottage with a green door and pots of white geraniums on either side.

Without further ado, he pushed open the door. 'Alice, we're here!' he called out. Taking a steadying breath, Sarah followed. They walked straight into a small parlour which served as a sitting and dining room with an enormous brick fireplace at one end and ancient rafters hugging the ceiling. There was clutter everywhere, but it had a welcoming feel. Sarah liked it on sight. As she moved into the room, a woman and a young man rose from the table. Her aunt came forward and clasped Sarah's hand warmly. Aunt Alice was bird-like, a tiny woman with greying hair and a rosy complexion.

'You are very welcome, Sarah,' her aunt said, her grey eyes twinkling. There was still a strong Galway lilt to her voice. 'We're delighted you have come to us.' Then she turned to the young man. 'This is Martin, your cousin.' Martin nodded and grinned. He was the image of his father, Sarah thought, as she shook hands with him.

'Come and sit down, *a stór*; you must be exhausted, coming all that way. Take the seat here beside the fire,' her aunt urged. 'Martin, take Sarah's coat and pop her suitcase up to the bedroom, there's a good lad.'

'Alice, I could murder a cuppa,' Uncle Tom said, sitting down at the table. Sarah grinned at him as she handed her coat to her cousin.

Martin headed towards the stairs, passing a dresser on which there were several framed photographs.

'May I?' she asked her aunt, indicating the collection.

'Of course, my dear.'

Sarah walked over and recognised a photograph of her mother, and one of Maura and herself as children. Uncle Tom came to stand beside her. With a lump in her throat, Sarah picked up her mother's picture. 'All of ours were destroyed in the bombing.' She looked up at her uncle. 'It's wonderful that you have these.'

Tom pointed to the photo of her and Maura. 'She sent me that one shortly before she died. If you like, we can try to get them copied for you. Come along, your tea will go cold,' he said. 'And I suspect, if we are very well behaved, there may even be cake.'

Whether it was because Tom was a link to her mother, or because of the peace and homeliness of the Lambe house, Sarah's weeks of anxiety regarding her decision to emigrate began to evaporate.

The following day was Sunday, and after returning from Mass in Winchester, Martin suggested he show Sarah the sights. They walked up a meandering laneway from the centre of the village until they reached higher ground. With a majestic sweep of his arm, Martin invited her to sit on the wall. Once she was settled, he pointed down to the cluster of cottages. 'Behold, the great metropolis of Hursley!' Martin grinned at her. 'Actually, it's not half as quiet as it seems today. Between all of us working at Supermarine and the evacuees from Southampton, it can get quite lively. As you saw this morning, Winchester isn't far either for a night out.' Martin hopped up onto the wall beside her. 'I suppose it's all very different to Dublin?'

'Yes, it is, but I'm sure I'll get used to living out in the sticks, as we say at home.'

'Ah! Do you think we are nothing but bumpkins? Huh, you city slickers are all the same.' Sarah giggled as he elbowed her gently. 'Poor old Judith couldn't stand it here and high-tailed it to London some months ago. Now she has a fancy job in the civil service. It's given her airs which it is my great pleasure to deflate every time she comes home. The parents miss her, so having you to stay is a wonderful distraction.' Martin studied her for a moment. 'Yes, I think you will do just fine.'

'Why, thank you!'

'Don't mention it! Seriously though, you'll settle in quickly once you start working. In the meantime, make the most of it. It will be long hours at Supermarine, as like as not.'

'You work in the Drawing Office, same as Uncle Tom, don't you?' Sarah asked.

'Yes. I've been in the company since I left school. Just as well, because with my poor eyesight I couldn't enlist.' Martin tapped the side of his glasses, his expression suddenly glum. 'Thank heaven I had a talent for drawing. I couldn't bear not to be doing something for the war effort.'

'That's part of the reason I wanted to leave Ireland and come here. Nothing I could do at home was going to help matters. Even after what happened, there is no hope of the Irish government changing their minds about neutrality. It was difficult for me to accept that, so your father's invitation couldn't have arrived at a better time. Leaving Ireland, in the end, was an easy decision.'

Martin nodded. 'I can understand why you must want revenge on Jerry. Must have been a beastly experience.'

'Yes, it was dreadful, and as I recovered from my injuries

the full consequences of that night hit me. At first, I didn't know what to do. Our house was gone, and with Maura and Da . . .' Martin patted her shoulder, '. . . I was in a kind of limbo. My Da's family are all down in Cork and Ma's in Galway; I barely know them, and the situation is worse in both cities from what I hear: no jobs and rationing hitting hard. Then a friend encouraged me to consider leaving, like he planned to do. Paul has joined the RAF.'

Sarah picked a blackberry from a branch which straddled the wall and popped it into her mouth. She plucked another one and offered it to Martin.

'Lucky sod! What I wouldn't give to join up. All I can do is help to design the planes,' Martin said with a sad smile, before tossing the blackberry in the air and catching it in his mouth. 'I'll never fly one.'

'But what you're doing is vital work.'

'Yes, yes, it is, but a man can have a dream, can't he?' Martin's expression was wistful.

'And I'd love to be a film star, but that's not going to happen either,' Sarah said, and Martin burst out laughing.

'Oh, I don't know. You seem to me to be quite a determined young lady. I'm a huge film fan myself, as it happens. Try to go once a week. You wouldn't be interested in joining the amateur dramatic society, would you? It's a lark and a great way to meet people. Quite a few from Supermarine have joined.'

Sarah was delighted. 'Gosh, I'd love to. I was in one at home, but only briefly.'

'Perfect, I'll drag you along to the next meet-up. We're always looking for people to help out. They hope to put the play on at Christmas.'

'What are you doing?' she asked.

'*Hay Fever*. Do you know it?'

'That's a Noël Coward play, isn't it?'

'Yes, that's the one. It's hilarious. I was lucky enough to be cast as Richard Greatham. A diplomat, would you believe?'

'No typecasting then,' Sarah quipped, which earned her a dirty look. 'Where does the group meet? Is it far?' Sarah asked.

'No, not at all. We use the Hut on Port Lane. The building is fairly rudimentary, mind, and a bit damp. It's two old army huts joined together, but it does for rehearsals. I think the plan is to get permission to stage it in one of the large reception rooms at Hursley Park.'

'Are the huts from the last war?' she asked.

'Gosh, yes, but I don't know any of the history. There is talk that the army may want to use the grounds again at some stage, but so far they have left us in peace.'

They sat in silence for a while, looking at the rooftops down below. Sarah was lost in thought. Eventually she spoke up: 'Will I be accepted here? Could my nationality be an issue?' she asked.

'I shouldn't think so, no more than my family's,' he replied with a frown. 'You let me know if anyone says anything. I'll sort them out.'

'Thank you! I've always wanted a knight in shining armour.'

'Happy to oblige.'

Sarah acknowledged this with a nod. 'I'm dying to get started at Supermarine. How long will it take for my ID card to come through? I don't want to be a burden to your parents.'

'Don't you worry about that; they are only too glad to have you here. It shouldn't take too long to sort out the paperwork. Father said you will need to go into Winchester with him during the week to sort all that official stuff out, but I can't see any difficulty. With your work experience, you will be snapped up. Supermarine are crying out for workers. Father has already spoken to Mr Hargreaves — he's the Employment Manager — and there's a spot for you on the tracing team. The tracing girls are good fun; you'll like working with them. They're always organising outings to the cinema and picnics. We even had a sports day last month. That was hilarious. Don't worry — you'll be part of the gang in no time. Miss Whitaker will be your boss. She might look like a dragon, but she's really rather sweet. Oh, and we even have a social club where they hold the odd dance. One word of warning, though — the canteen food at Hursley Park is vile.'

'Thanks for the warning.' Sarah jumped down from the wall. 'Now, shall we explore some more?'

'Certainly, my lady. Your wish is my command.'

8

15th September 1941, Hursley Park

It was Monday morning and Sarah's first day at Supermarine. She surveyed the wood-panelled office with admiration. Much like the rest of the house she'd seen so far, it was beautifully decorated, contrasting sharply with the utilitarian office furniture. She would have loved to have caught a glimpse of the original antiques that must have been here before, but she assumed those items were stored somewhere safe until the war was over.

The window afforded a view of the parkland, lush and green with a stand of oak trees in the distance. The grounds were extensive, Uncle Tom had told her, housing many different departments both in the outbuildings and in the huts hidden beneath the vast woodland canopy. Her aunt had mentioned that Lady Cooper, the widowed owner, was still in residence, occupying the upper floor of the mansion, and was often to be seen about the place.

'This all seems in order, Miss Gillespie,' her manager, Miss Whitaker, said, pulling Sarah's attention back into the room. The lady looked up from Sarah's paperwork, which lay in front of her on the desk. Her steel-grey hair was pulled back in a severe style. Silver-framed spectacles only emphasised her stern gaze.

'Your previous experience in an architect's office will be invaluable, of course. Most of the girls sent to us lately are fresh from school and don't know one end of a sheet of tracing cloth from another.' Miss Whitaker glanced down again and frowned. 'Your uncle has vouched for you and I hold Mr Lambe in high esteem. We have been colleagues and friends for many years.' The dour gaze was once more directed at Sarah. 'I would be very disappointed if you were to prove unworthy of his trust.'

Unsure how to respond, Sarah gave her a half-hearted smile and shifted on her feet. 'I'll do my best, Miss Whitaker. I'm grateful for the opportunity to work here.'

'One final thing, Miss Gillespie. Security on these premises is, of necessity, tight. The work you will do is vital to the war effort. Please don't forget that. It is only fair to warn you that we carry out periodic checks to ensure staff are not removing secrets from the buildings. We also discourage discussing your work with anyone except your immediate colleagues. As the posters say, Miss Gillespie, careless talk costs lives. Is that clear?'

'Yes, of course,' Sarah answered.

'Hmm,' was the reply. Miss Whitaker rose from her chair. 'Come, I'll introduce you to the girls and show you to your desk.' Sarah grabbed her bag and coat and followed the lady down a long corridor. Stopping halfway down, Miss Whitaker pointed to a door. 'You may leave your coat and bag in there.

We allow nothing of that nature in the Tracing Room for security reasons. Quickly now, pop your things inside.'

Sarah soon returned to the corridor to find Miss Whitaker standing outside a room further down. A plaque on the door said 'Tracing Office'. Sarah joined her by the door, and as they were about to go in, Miss Whitaker paused with her hand on the handle. 'One further thing, Miss Gillespie. If you meet Lady Cooper, remember to be polite. She still lives in the house but keeps to herself. This was her morning room,' she continued, before opening the door.

They stepped into a sizeable room with long sash windows overlooking the grounds. It was a fabulous space, Sarah could see, despite the rows of drawing boards. She could imagine the Cooper family sitting around their breakfast table in years gone by. It was a far cry from her humble origins in Dublin. The walls were pale blue with white floor-length panels containing delicate oblong and oval motifs of dancing figures against raised blue backgrounds. Sarah had seen nothing like them.

'They are rather splendid, are they not, Miss Gillespie?' Miss Whitaker said, waving towards the nearest panel. 'Those are priceless Wedgwood panels.' Sarah had never heard of Wedgwood, but she thought the figures were delightful.

The desks were occupied by young women and the eyes of each now swivelled to look at the newcomer with curiosity. A middle-aged lady with a round face and bright blue eyes sat at a desk at the top of the room. Miss Whitaker made straight for her.

'This is Miss Sugden, your supervisor,' Miss Whitaker said to Sarah. 'My right-hand woman.'

Sarah shook Miss Sugden's hand. 'How do you do?'

'Very well, thank you, Miss Gillespie. You are very welcome

to the tracing team.' The supervisor smiled up at her and turned to the manager. 'Don't worry, Miss Whitaker, we'll take good care of her.'

'I have no doubt, Miss Sugden.' Miss Whitaker turned and addressed the sea of faces. 'Ladies, let me introduce Miss Sarah Gillespie, who is joining us today.' Miss Whitaker beckoned Sarah forward before walking away towards an empty desk in the corner at the far end of the room. She turned to Sarah. 'This will be your desk, Sarah. If you have any questions, Gladys and Ruth will help you.' The manager nodded to the women who occupied the desks closest to Sarah's. Each smiled and shook Sarah's hand.

'Work hard, Miss Gillespie, and we will get along famously,' Miss Whitaker said before departing.

Gladys winked at Sarah and returned to her work.

'Come along, Sarah, I'll talk you through it all and show you where everything is kept,' Ruth said.

The girls were sitting on a rug under the ancient oak trees, having their lunch. Sarah was delighted they had invited her to join them.

'Well, Sarah, welcome to the Dragon's lair. You have survived your first morning,' Gladys said. 'What do you think of us all? Be honest, now.'

'I couldn't be happier. This is a much nicer place than my last job. Any hints or tips? Anyone I should avoid?' Sarah asked.

'No, Miss Sugden is an absolute pet. A very motherly sort,' Ruth said.

'And Miss Whitaker?' Sarah asked.

'Perhaps not quite as *motherly*,' replied Gladys. An amused glance passed between the two friends. 'But don't be concerned.

She's a stickler all right, but once your tracing is up to scratch, she leaves you alone.' Gladys pushed her blonde hair back from her face.

'My cousin Martin told me about her. I'm relieved the work is similar to what I was doing in Dublin. More detailed but I think I'll manage.'

'Good for you! Some new girls struggle at the start. Just remember if you have questions ask me or Gladys. We're old hands at this stage,' Ruth chimed in.

'Thanks, I appreciate that,' Sarah replied. 'Is this a regular spot for your break?'

'We have our lunch here most days if the weather is fine. You're welcome to join us. Some of the other girls prefer the canteen, but it's a squeeze. It used to be the servants' dining room. We prefer it out here. It's bad enough being cooped up all day without spending your free time in the house as well.'

Sarah looked around the park. 'And what about in the winter? Or do you sit out here in hats and scarves, freezing to death?'

Gladys grinned. 'Funny! No. We suffer the canteen when needs must. Best to bring your own food though.'

'I'll bear that in mind. Could we not eat at our desks?' Sarah asked.

'It's forbidden to bring food or drink into the Tracing Room in case of accidents. The slightest smudge or mark and the tracings must be washed out and you have to start over, which is a complete pain, trust me.'

'Now that will have you up before the Dragon,' Gladys said, 'and no mistake.'

Ruth laughed. 'Gladys has some experience of that, don't you know.'

Gladys made a face at her friend and turned back to Sarah.

75

'The Spanish Inquisition had nothing on her! The usual punishment is the delightful task of cutting fresh sheets of tracing cloth off the roll.' Gladys held up her right hand. 'A tiresome job. I still have welts on my palms from the last time. The scissors are *always* blunt.'

'In my last job, the sheets came pre-cut,' Sarah said.

Ruth snorted. 'And cost a hell of a lot more, I'm sure.'

'Most likely,' Sarah said. 'Forgive me, but I'm curious. I didn't see either of you in Hursley during the week. Do you rent close by?'

'No, I wish! Not enough room in the village, I'm afraid. We share a room in a boarding house in Winchester and use the Supermarine bus in and out. You're living with the Lambe family, aren't you?' Ruth asked.

'Yes. Tom Lambe is my uncle.'

Ruth sighed. 'And Martin is your cousin. He's lovely.' Gladys snorted but Ruth ignored her and continued: 'Lucky you to live so near to work. But, hey, come into Winchester some Friday night. We usually go to the cinema.'

Gladys nodded. 'Definitely. Much livelier than Hursley, unless sitting in the pub with the locals is your idea of fun. Drag your cousin along. Ruth will be ever so grateful.'

'Swine!' Ruth cried, swiping her friend with her empty sandwich bag. Gladys dodged and laughed at her.

'I'd love to,' replied Sarah with a grin.

9

'Come on, slowcoach, nearly there!' Martin called over his shoulder to Sarah. 'The Ritz is just around the next corner.'

'Hold up, Martin. I'm not used to such a long cycle. I've run out of puff,' Sarah gasped. Her injured leg was objecting to the strenuous exercise, but she hated to be beaten.

'Ha, ha, such a weakling!' he replied as he rounded the bend ahead of her.

With a spurt of effort, Sarah caught up with him. She had enjoyed the journey and chatting with Martin, but now the evening was drawing in and she worried about the cycle home in the blackout. It would be a challenge, but at least there were few cars about because of the petrol rationing.

Ahead of her, Martin braked. 'That's a relief; there're the girls. Good of them to wait for us, but I hope we aren't late. They won't let us in if the picture has started,' he said. 'I've wanted to see *Cottage to Let* ever since I read about it in *Picturegoer Weekly*. Nothing like a good spy film.'

Martin locked the bikes together and they crossed over the road to where Ruth and Gladys were waiting at the cinema entrance. Ruth smiled shyly at Martin as they approached.

'Evening, ladies. Shall we?' Martin asked, holding out his arm to Ruth, who blushed furiously.

Gladys tucked her arm through Sarah's, and they followed the others inside. The foyer was crowded, and they had to squeeze through to get near the ticket booth.

'Hold on here, ladies; I'll get the tickets,' Martin said before joining the queue.

Sarah looked about the jammed hallway. 'I recognise quite a few faces,' she remarked to Gladys.

'Yes, most of the younger staff come here on a Friday night. It's a tradition; cinema Friday, dance Saturday, if there's one on locally.'

A few minutes later, Martin pushed his way towards them and handed them their tickets. 'Best seats in the house,' he quipped.

'Circle tickets; how posh, Martin. Who are you trying to impress?' Gladys asked with a cheeky grin. Martin glowered at her before turning his attention back to Ruth.

'I didn't realise my cousin was such a charmer,' Sarah said to Gladys.

'I heard that!' Martin grunted.

'You were meant to,' she replied.

Gladys squeezed Sarah's arm and wiggled her brows. 'Just ask Ruth; she'll tell you how charming Martin Lambe can be.'

Sarah loved going to the cinema; always had. Scraping money together whenever she could, she used to take Maura to the Savoy on O'Connell Street. Da didn't hold with 'that muck', as he used to call it. His attitude only made Sarah more determined to see as many films as she could. The Savoy was the grandest cinema in Dublin with its Venetian-inspired interior, and Sarah loved to soak up the atmosphere, imagining herself the leading lady at an opening night. But she had to be content with being an observer and avid fan, her only regret not being able to afford to visit more than twice a month. It wasn't just escape from the humdrum routine of her life; it fed her dreams. And when she couldn't afford to go to the cinema, she used to lose herself in film magazines or books. The local library had a good range of fiction, but her favourites were Dorothy L Sayers and Agatha Christie. The librarian used to joke he was running out of books for her to borrow. Unfortunately, the few books she had bought over the years were lost when No. 18 fell around her ears, but within a couple of weeks she intended to start her collection anew.

Though not as splendid as the Savoy, the Ritz was a large cinema, and Sarah sighed contentedly as she settled into her seat. The first week at Supermarine had been exhausting as she had learned about their tracing process and got to grips with the specialist equipment and the more rigorous routine. Each day her confidence had grown, and that very afternoon the Dragon had complimented her on her work.

Home life, too, was proving pleasant. Her rapport with Martin was a source of quiet joy and went a little way towards helping her deal with her grief. He had brought her along to the drama group the previous Wednesday, which had been great fun. All the acting parts were already cast but Sarah didn't mind. She was happy enough to help backstage with scenery and costumes. Martin had one of the main roles and surprised her with his performance. He was a natural on the stage and clearly enjoyed himself in the role. It was a friendly group and she had enjoyed talking to them over tea and biscuits at the end of the night. She was looking forward to the following Wednesday already.

Tom and Alice were generous in spirit and had made her feel part of the family. They spoke lovingly of their daughter Judith, who Sarah was increasingly curious about. Judith's job in London was spoken of in reverent tones but when Sarah asked what her cousin did, they couldn't tell her. Afterwards, Martin had hinted that her work was top secret, but Sarah wasn't sure if he was serious or not. She doubted someone as young as her cousin would have such an important role.

Tonight, Sarah didn't want to dwell on anything but the future. For the first time in months, it looked promising. Now, as she relaxed, she was ready for escape to another world. As she waited for the curtain to go back, three young men climbed the steps, stopped at their row, and called out cheerfully to Ruth and Gladys. One of them was rather handsome, Sarah noted; tall and dark with a mischievous glint in his eye. Martin, who was seated next to the aisle, chatted to the men before they continued on their way. Sarah guessed they worked at Hursley too. They didn't go far, taking seats in the row behind. Ruth glanced at them but then looked away quickly, her face flushed and her breathing laboured. Sarah wondered if there was history there. She'd have to ask Gladys about it later.

Gladys caught her eye and whispered: 'Lads from Wages.'

'I haven't seen them before.'

'You wouldn't have. Their office is in Southend House, the old house near the other entrance.'

'Won't you introduce us, Gladys?' one man said, leaning over

Gladys's shoulder. Sarah looked up. It was Mr Handsome, and his charming smile was directed at her.

'Sarah Gillespie, this is Rob McArthur,' Gladys provided with a roll of her eyes and a knowing smile.

Sarah shook hands. 'Nice to meet you, Rob.'

'You're new, aren't you?' he asked. 'I'd have to be blind to miss a pretty girl like you.'

'Yes, just started this week,' Sarah replied, as Gladys smothered a giggle.

Rob nodded and looked as though he was all set for a chat, but before he could say anything more, the lights went down, and he had to sit back. Gladys winked at Sarah.

Sarah turned towards the screen, a little flattered to be singled out. Mind you, she wouldn't be taken in by a bit of patter. She was well used to that back home and knew just how to deal with forward young men. Fleetingly, she thought of Paul and wondered where he was. Was he in England yet? There was still no sign of a letter from him, even though he had promised to write. Could he have forgotten about her already in the excitement of his new adventure? It was a lowering thought. But it could be that he was busy training or moving about the country to different bases. That had to be it. Once things were more settled, they would meet up again.

Martin had already filled her in on what the picture was about on the cycle to Winchester. A touch of espionage was just the ticket and two of her favourite actors were in *Cottage to Let*; Alastair Sim and John Mills, who played an RAF pilot. Sarah bit her lip. She might try to envisage Paul in the role. It would be something they could laugh about if they met up. Of course they *would*, she thought: there would be no 'if'. But as friends, nothing more. And that was her own fault. How she still regretted those angry words and her fumbled attempt at a reconciliation that day at the graveyard. She should have tried harder.

The curtain rose, and Sarah dismissed her gloomy thoughts. Around her, the hubbub died down as the projector kicked into life.

About forty minutes into the film, an air-raid siren went off. Everyone groaned as the projector juddered to a halt and the lights went up. Sarah's heart raced.

'Here we go again!' Gladys said with a sigh, pulling on her coat, before moving along the row, following Ruth and Martin down the steps.

But Sarah could not move; she was overcome with terror. She squeezed her eyes shut and shook; she was back in No. 18, North Strand. The wall was falling towards her as if in slow motion and the dust was choking, blinding. The pressure was pushing the breath from her body. That was Maura crying out behind her! Sarah was stuck fast; she couldn't reach her, couldn't move a muscle.

With a jerk, she opened her eyes as she felt the weight of a hand on her shoulder. 'You can't stay here, Miss Gillespie.' Sarah looked up into Rob McArthur's anxious face. 'Come on, the shelter isn't far.'

Sarah stared at him, too afraid to move. 'I can't!'

All around, people were filing out towards the exits. There was no trace of Martin or Gladys. Panic rose in Sarah's throat.

Rob clambered over Gladys's vacated seat and into Sarah's row. He stood regarding her with concern. 'What's the matter? Seriously, we must move now. Far too dangerous to stay here – and you'll get into trouble.' Rob grabbed her hand and gave it a tug. 'Come on, your friends will wonder where you are.'

Sarah nodded and took a deep breath.

'Good girl,' he said, pulling her to her feet. 'That's the ticket. Don't forget your gas mask.'

Sarah scooped up her things and let him lead her to the end of the row and down the steps. Rob kept a firm grip on her arm, leading her out through the foyer to the street. For a moment all she could do was breathe deeply, the cold air helping to ease her fear. However, she was still shaking.

'There's a shelter in the grounds of Holy Trinity Church; it's the closest one. It's not far,' Rob said.

'Is it underground? I could not bear that.'

He flashed her a puzzled glance. 'You'll be fine; don't worry,' he answered, taking off at pace. Around them, people were scurrying off in different directions. Sarah was disorientated; the darkness of the blackout made it almost impossible to see anything but vague outlines. She had to trust that Rob knew where he was going. Clinging to Rob's arm, she could make out a terrace of houses to their left, the roofline dark against the slightly lighter sky. Not a chink of light was to be seen at a window or door.

In the distance, a searchlight suddenly swept the sky. Sarah's heart beat even faster, her ears straining for the engine drone that haunted her nightmares.

'How much further?' she squeaked.

'Nearly there, don't fret.'

People ahead of them slowed down, before turning left. Rob followed, pulling her through a gateway. Now it was almost pitch dark under the trees, and they had to slow down even more. Head bent, Rob said: 'This is the cemetery. Have to follow the path through to the side of the church. Don't want to end up in an open grave, now do we?'

How he could joke at such a moment, Sarah could not fathom, but she remained silent, concentrating on keeping her footing on the uneven path.

'Here we are,' he said, as they emerged into an open space. He pushed her ahead of him. Sarah squinted into the darkness and could make out the outline of the shelter. An ARP warden stood at the entrance and waved them in with his torch. There were about fifteen others inside, huddled together and speaking in hushed voices. A few candles had been lit, but the place smelled damp and it was surprisingly chilly. There was no sign of Martin or the girls. Sarah hoped they had found a safe place to shelter.

'Are there other shelters nearby? I don't see my cousin here,' Sarah said.

'Yes, quite a few. Don't worry, they'll be safe.'

Sarah wrapped her arms around her body, but she continued to shiver. 'Did you hear any planes?' she whispered frantically to Rob. 'Do you think they are near?'

'Can't imagine it's too serious. Might be a stray Jerry looking for Southampton. They're just being careful sounding the alarm. It happens a couple of times a week.' Rob tilted his head. 'You sure you're all right? Is this your first air raid by any chance?'

She almost laughed. 'No, not exactly. I'm the only one of my family to survive one. Back in Dublin, a few months ago.'

'Oh! Of course,' Rob exclaimed. 'I should have realised you're Tom Lambe's niece, the Irish girl. So sorry, yes, I'd heard about that. Damn Germans!' He looked embarrassed; it was sweet, really.

Sarah smiled weakly back at him. 'I'm sorry I reacted like

that in the cinema, but I have this fear of being buried again . . .'

Rob touched her arm. 'Gosh, how awful! Is that what happened to you?' He shuddered and grimaced. 'It's perfectly understandable to be afraid if that's what you experienced. Forgive me, but didn't you lose your sister? I heard your cousin Martin talk about it.'

'Yes, my younger sister, Maura. My father died too.'

'What rotten luck. I have a brother in Africa. Did you know Jerry has bombed Cairo? I don't know how I'd feel if anything . . .' He dug the toe of his shoe into the dirt floor and frowned. 'Sorry, that sounds silly considering what you've been through. Bloody war,' he said at last, casting her a bleak look.

'But you're helping to end it.'

Rob wouldn't meet her eye. 'Calculating weekly wages isn't all that heroic. I'd much rather be fighting somewhere like my older brother.'

Sarah longed to ask him why he couldn't enlist, but it was hardly polite on such a brief acquaintance. 'How much longer will we have to stay here do you think?' Sarah asked instead.

As if on cue, the all-clear sounded. 'You see, false alarm,' Rob said. 'I'll take you back to the Ritz. I'm sure your cousin will be worried and wondering what happened to you.' He frowned down at her. 'He should take better care of you.'

'Oh no, he does. He mustn't have realised I didn't follow them out.'

Rob nodded. 'It can be chaotic when the sirens go off. People panic. I'm afraid our entertainment is over. It's unlikely they will restart the film at this stage. Tickets should be good for another showing though.'

'I hope so. I was enjoying the picture. Thanks, Rob, and

'sorry to have been such a coward.' Sarah took his proffered arm as they clambered out of the shelter and up onto the grass.

'Not at all, and I don't think you are a coward. Most people would react the same if they had gone through what you have. Besides, I'm always happy to help a damsel in distress.' Rob paused, smiling down at her. 'Would the damsel care to go out for a drink with me next Saturday?'

Sarah didn't hesitate. 'The damsel would.'

10

27th September 1941, Hursley Park

It was Saturday lunchtime. Sarah strolled down to the main entrance of Hursley Park with Gladys and Ruth, both girls teasing her about her upcoming date with Rob McArthur. Despite her protestations that the date was only a drink and a chat, they would not let up – to the point that she wanted to scream. Gladys hinted that he had something of a reputation and seemed to be inordinately fond of the Tracing Room girls, which Ruth vigorously denied, leaving Sarah confused. With a promise to give them all the details on Monday morning, she parted company with them at the military hut at the entrance to the grounds. The girls dashed off to catch the bus back to Winchester.

Spotting her Uncle Tom on the path just ahead, Sarah called out: 'Uncle Tom, wait for me!'

Her uncle turned and smiled as he waited for her. 'Did you have a good morning, Sarah?'

'Yes, thank you. Busy as usual. And you?'

Tom nodded as they fell into step. 'The work has ratcheted up in the last few weeks. There are new marks of Spitfire being planned all the time.'

'Why are there so many versions? The way my friend Paul talked about it, the Spitfire is already the epitome of perfection.'

Uncle Tom chuckled. 'Is this the lad who has enlisted?' Sarah nodded. 'He'll soon find out the RAF is always tinkering with the design. But with good reason: they need different modifications for specific uses. Sometimes it is only minute changes, or it might be a substantial redesign if the RAF request, say, bigger engines, or want to use the plane for an alternative purpose, such as surveillance. Then cameras are fitted to the wings and that has a knock-on effect on wing design. You'll see new drawings coming through all the time to the tracing team. At the moment, I'm working on the Mark VII. Miss Whitaker will get those drawings soon for you ladies to work on.'

'What happens after the tracings go to the printers?' Sarah asked.

'Once the instruction manual is printed, the lads in the Experimental Hangar down at the south entrance build the prototype, which then has to be tested by an RAF pilot over at Worthy Down.'

'Oh yes, I've heard the engines being revved up, but I wasn't sure what was happening down there.'

'They are busy lads, let me tell you. Anyway, if the prototype passes, it goes into production. But that entails the manufacture of new jigs and tools. The process is never quick enough for the RAF, I'm afraid.'

Sarah was impressed. 'Do the constant changes not put pressure on resources? Are they always necessary?'

'That's debatable! But what the RAF wants, it gets.'

'There is so much involved in the process, and so many people! I wish I knew more about the planes. The drawings I have been working on so far are complicated, but I believe the Dra— Miss Whitaker is happy with my work.'

Uncle Tom guffawed. 'Do they still call her that? How naughty!'

'Sorry,' Sarah replied meekly.

'Not at all; in fact, she knows that's her nickname. She's rather proud of it, I think.'

'Really?'

'Yes. Nearly all the long-term staff have monikers of one sort or another.'

'What's yours?' Sarah asked.

'Can't you guess?' Tom asked with a grin. She shook her head. 'Chops!'

'Why on earth . . . Oh, I see . . . *lamb* chops.'

'I think it's rather good, don't you? Better than Paddy or Mick any day. But we are insulated from that nonsense here in Hursley. It was different down in Southampton. Tiresome stuff on the whole – hopefully you never encounter it.'

Sarah recalled the incident at the station in Southampton and smiled sadly. 'Indeed.'

'The problem is they have short memories. They seem to forget it was the Irish navvies who built the London under-ground and half the buildings in every city in the country. Ah, sure, there has always been animosity to some extent, but now with Ireland staying neutral, there's resentment too. Not sure I agree with the stance, myself.'

'I definitely don't, Uncle,' she said.

'That I can understand; but you see, most English don't

appreciate the history, or can't be bothered to learn about it. In fairness to them, it is irrelevant to their lives. The ordinary English working man had little to do with Ireland's woes.'

'My father would not have agreed with you on that, Uncle Tom. He was always going on about the Black and Tans and how vicious they were.'

'They were a small minority, Sarah, and them half-crazed after the Great War. Shell-shocked, most of them.' He sighed heavily. 'Not that I'm excusing what they did, for those boyos perpetrated some terrible things in the name of the Crown, but the likes of your father returned the compliment whenever possible, and in his case, with great relish.'

'You knew Da was involved in all that?'

'On the few occasions I met him, he wasn't shy about discussing it or showing his anti-British prejudices. There's still many like him, as I'm sure you know,' he said.

'Is that why I was vetted so thoroughly before I could be taken on? Because I'm Irish? Could they have known about Da's past?'

Tom shrugged. 'I'd say it was likely. But it's understandable considering where we are working. We are dealing with secrets which will win us the war, my dear. It isn't personal.'

'No, I understand. Miss Whitaker was very vocal on that point; that I wasn't to discuss my work with anyone, even in other departments.'

'Not even with your favourite uncle?' he asked, eyes wide in mock horror.

Sarah laughed. 'Not even with *him*.' Tom smiled and they walked on. Sarah continued: 'I have noticed how each department keeps pretty much to themselves during the day.'

'Yes, that is encouraged. Careless talk, and all that.' Tom halted and gave her a knowing look. 'Except I've heard of late that a certain lad in Wages is keen to get to know a tracing girl, eh?'

Sarah stifled a giggle. 'Did Martin tell you?'

Uncle Tom took her arm and they walked on. 'Aye, and it's hardly surprising that my pretty niece has attracted attention.'

'I'm meeting Rob McArthur later in the King's Head. It's only a drink, nothing serious.'

'Are you indeed? Good for you.'

'Do you know him?' she asked, a few yards further on.

'Well, as far as I am aware, he only joined Supermarine just before we left Southampton. I have little interaction with that section, but he seems a nice enough lad. Though I do recall one morning finding him in the Drawing Office. He'd lost his way in the grounds, he said, and I had to direct him back to Southend House. All apologies he was. Seemed a nice enough young man.' Tom frowned at her. 'But remember; should there be any trouble you come straight to me or Martin, do you hear?'

Sarah squeezed her uncle's arm in gratitude. 'Thank you.' How different Uncle Tom was to Da. *He* had never shown the least interest in her safety. And didn't he prove that tenfold the night the bombs fell. Already she felt at home in the Lambe household. *If only poor Maura could have experienced it,* she thought, sadly. *She would have fitted in here so perfectly.*

Tom glanced up at the sky. ''Tis a fine day! I think I shall do some work in the garden after lunch. Did you have a victory garden in Dublin?'

'No. Some of our neighbours grew potatoes and onions. Mr Nugent a few doors up used to take pity on us and share some of his veg. Da had no interest in growing things. Maura tried to persuade Da to let her . . . but he wasn't keen. He had some strange notions about us getting our hands dirty. So silly.'

'That's a shame. It's a great way to relax after a day bent over a drawing board, I can tell you.'

'Have you always been an avid gardener?'

Uncle Tom chuckled. 'Not at all! I only started out of necessity when rationing began. But I soon found I enjoyed it immensely; particularly being out in the fresh air. Alice was finding it difficult to get decent vegetables in the shops, so she's delighted I've developed green fingers. I had to leave a lovely patch of garden in Southampton but sure I have a much bigger one here. It all worked out very well, you see, because we had to dig out a big patch for the Anderson Shelter and I was able to use some of the soil to make raised beds for my veg.'

'Have you used the shelter yet?' she asked, suddenly anxious.

'No, not even once. I check it once a week to make sure all's right and tight.' Tom winked at her. 'It's the perfect temperature. I have a couple of cases of porter stored in there, in case of emergencies, of course. However, it's unlikely we will ever use the shelter. Jerry tends not to bomb villages in the middle of nowhere.'

'Unless they find out about Supermarine,' Sarah said.

'Don't you worry; that's highly unlikely. The huts in the grounds are well camouflaged or hidden under the trees. They'd be difficult to spot from the air. Now, would you care to join me in the garden for a while before the big date this evening? I could do with some help with the weeding and the spuds won't harvest themselves.'

'I'd love to,' Sarah replied.

'Do they fit?' Uncle Tom asked, looking down at Sarah's feet clad in Martin's boots.

'They are far too big, but I have three pairs of socks on.

And Aunty Alice gave me this old jumper of yours,' she said. The Aran sweater was huge on her, swamping her small frame. Sarah stamped her feet and grinned. 'Will I do?'

Tom broke into a chuckle: 'A regular land girl! Come on, you need to earn the title.' He headed down the path.

The garden was long and narrow, edged by stone walls and ancient trees. Every available inch of ground had something growing in it. Mystified as to what any of it was, Sarah followed her uncle down to the end of the garden where the Anderson Shelter was located. He turned around, swept out his arms and breathed in deeply. 'Isn't it grand? I'm rather proud of how much we have grown. Alice rarely buys vegetables now. I even have room to grow a few flowers to brighten the place up.'

Sarah followed his gaze, taking in the rows of plants and the raised beds bordered by planks of timber. It was all neat and tidy, testament to the hours her uncle put into the garden's upkeep. 'You will have to teach me, I'm afraid. I don't have a clue what anything is or what I should do.'

'I'll make a gardener out of you yet, missy, wait and see. Right, you can start by weeding between the rows of parsnips over there. Here's a wee trowel and a trug; you can put the weeds into that. The parsnips are the bright green broad-leaved plants, the other blighters in between are the weeds.'

Sarah hunkered down, pushing back the leaves of what she hoped was a parsnip. 'Shall I take this out?' she asked, pointing to a yellow-flowered plant lurking beneath.

'Aye, now be careful you don't disturb the roots of the parsnip. I'm looking forward to tasting 'em with a few roast spuds some Sunday.'

'When do you harvest them?' she asked, as Tom started on the next row.

'Well, you see, the trick with those boyos is to leave them in the ground to be frosted – they have a much sweeter taste then.'

They worked along their rows for several minutes in silence. Sarah found her rhythm and enjoyed the work. As she looked up from a parsnip, she caught a wistful glance from Tom. 'What is it?'

'Oh, I was just thinking of your mother. You are so like her, Sarah, it's uncanny.' He looked about the garden. 'I'm surprised she didn't grow veg at home. As children, we helped your grandfather with harvesting. Mind you, the soil was poor in Galway. Full of stones. The only fertiliser we had was seaweed, and we dreaded those days we had to go down to the shore and pick it. Back-breaking work, that was.'

'I can imagine,' Sarah said, trying to visualise her mother lugging baskets of seaweed.

'Thankfully, I have an arrangement with a local farmer who supplies me with manure in exchange for some of my veg. Isn't it funny how we have fallen back on the old ways of bartering? Makes sense though, in times like this.'

'Uncle Tom?'

'Yes, love?'

'How did my mother and father meet?' she asked. 'Ma never told us.'

A shadow flitted across Tom's features. He placed his trowel on the soil and sat back on his hunkers. 'It was just before I left Galway. You know about your father's involvement in the War of Independence?'

'Yes, he spoke of it.'

'Hmm, well he and some of his mates were active in the local area.'

'But he was a Dub. What was he doing in the west?' she asked.

94

'Michael Collins sent him to head up a brigade in Galway.'

'But why Da?'

'Didn't you know he was a Dublin Fusilier? Survived France and came back with valuable knowledge of how the British Army operated.'

'I never knew that!' Sarah exclaimed.

'Well, it wasn't something he wanted people to know in later years: not good for his republican image.'

'Of course not. But I find it hard to believe; he hated the British so much,' she replied.

'Ah, but like many of those who volunteered in 1914, your father had been blacklisted for striking during the Lockout the previous year. He had no hope of work and army pay was decent. Don't forget, at the time everyone said the war would be short-lived. But Jim wasn't home long from the front when he realised the public mood had swung in his absence, especially after all that happened in 1916. Now, he found he was a pariah in the eyes of many. However, Michael Collins needed men with the inside knowledge your father had gained. It wasn't long before they had recruited him to the IRA ranks.'

'So, when he came back to Ireland, he switched sides.'

'Precisely, though I doubt he was ever loyal to anyone except Jim Gillespie. Anyway, he arrived in Galway out to prove himself. One day he and his flying column turned up at our farm. We'd had a visit from the Black and Tans the previous week, looking for information and generally being a nuisance. Your father wanted to know why they had picked on us. He coerced my father into giving his brigade refuge for a few nights in our hay shed. It was a guerrilla war, you see. They were lying low, waiting to ambush British soldiers who they believed were due to pass through our valley that week.'

'And that's when he met my mother.'

Uncle Tom nodded as he picked up his trowel again. 'Oh, we were all very impressed by him. Fine-looking man, full of talk and a man of the world.' Tom's expression hardened. 'She fell for him, of course. Soon after, me and Alice left for England. It was only when we came back to Galway for your grandmother's funeral that I met him again. And, I'll be honest with you, love, I didn't like him one bit. I was older and less likely to be impressed by talk at that stage. I remember remarking to Alice that he had changed, or more likely, he was showing his true colours at last. But what could I do? Your mother defended his behaviour and would not discuss him. Alice tried talking to her, but she was having none of it. My suspicion was that he wasn't treating her well. She had changed; gone awful quiet, not like the lively girl she'd always been growing up.'

Sarah blew out a slow breath, fighting back her tears. 'No, he didn't treat her well at all.'

With an angry exclamation, Tom shoved his trowel into the soil before coming around to her row. 'Ah, and it wasn't just your mother, was it?' She nodded. He knelt beside her and put an arm around her shoulder. 'He can't hurt you any longer.' Unable to speak, all she could do was smile sadly. 'You're safe here with us, Sarah. I'm only sorry I didn't do more to help ye, but I have every intention of making up for it by ensuring your life with us is as happy as possible. We have little, *a stór*, but we have each other, and we will always be here for you.' He squeezed her shoulder. 'Here, take this and blow your nose, you daft thing.' He handed her a clean handkerchief. 'Now, those weeds need seeing to. Let's get back to work!'

11

27th September 1941, Hursley

Later that evening, as the hands of the clock crept forward, Sarah grew jittery. Uncle Tom's teasing over dinner about Rob didn't help matters. Martin on the other hand was remarkably restrained, though she could tell he was bursting to make a comment. Was that kindness, or was he waiting for the right opportunity to maximise his teasing? You could never quite tell with Martin.

When the time came to get ready, she climbed the stairs slowly, chiding herself for being foolish. It was only a drink, so there was no reason for nerves. Rob was an attractive lad with a pleasant manner, so why wasn't she excited about the evening ahead? She thought fleetingly of her first date with Paul. That night she had been so excited and almost sick with nerves on the bus into the city. Tonight she would gladly stay at home. What was different now?

If she were honest, she didn't want to get seriously involved, particularly if Gladys was to be believed and Rob McArthur had a roving eye. Above all, it was too soon after the fiasco with Paul and her regrets were still raw. Much as she hated to admit it, Paul was often in her thoughts; teasing might-have-beens she really ought to suppress. However, it was too late to back out. Rob was probably already on the bus down from Winchester.

Sarah had only been in her room a few minutes when there was a tap on the door and her aunt appeared in the doorway.

'Is everything all right, Sarah? You mustn't mind your uncle. Sometimes he doesn't know when to stop his joking.'

Sarah laughed. 'Not at all. Don't worry, I can take it.'

Alice sat down on the bed and smiled. 'I'm glad to hear it, but I've scolded him all the same. Above all, I want you to be happy here.'

'Aunty Alice!' Sarah exclaimed, sitting down beside her, and taking her hand. 'I am exceedingly happy, and you must not worry about me: I'm a lot stronger than people think.'

'I've no doubt; I can tell you're a little powerhouse, but you seem nervous about this date tonight. Are you having second thoughts? I can always get Martin to let the lad down gently for you.'

Sarah chuckled at the image her aunt's words conjured up. Martin would love to have that kind of ammunition to throw at her. 'That is kind of you but it won't be necessary. You are right; I'm regretting my hasty acceptance of the invitation. But he had just rescued me from my own stupidity, and it would have been churlish to refuse.'

'Nonsense! Your reaction to that air raid was perfectly under-standable. But I suspect that Irish boy you told me about is still in your head. I reckon it has more to do with that.'

Sarah marvelled at how astute her aunt was and nodded. 'Paul was special.'

'Is there no hope?' her aunt asked, gazing at her with concern.

'He made it clear we would only ever be friends. I've had to accept that and move on. Besides, I haven't heard from him, even though he promised to keep in touch,' Sarah replied.

'He'll be busy, though. I'm sure the RAF will have him training hard.'

'That will be it.' Sarah glanced at her watch. 'Now, I must get ready. Would you help me pick out something to wear?'

Her aunt beamed back at her, delighted. 'Oh yes. I always used to help Judith choose, you know.' Alice went over to the small wardrobe. 'Oh dear, we will have to do something about these,' she said, pursing her lips as she inspected Sarah's few items of clothing.

'I'm lucky to have even those, Aunt. Everything in there was given to me by the nuns,' Sarah said.

'Well, I think this green dress might be the best option. I always like it on you.' Alice pulled the dress out and handed it over.

Sarah buttoned up the dress, smoothed down the skirt, and sighed. 'It doesn't fit well, but I do like the colour.'

Alice came up behind her and gazed into the mirror. 'I agree. It brings out the green in your eyes.' Her aunt then tilted her head and frowned before reaching out and pulling in the sides of the dress. 'Hmm, it swamps you, Sarah. If you slip it off again, it wouldn't take me long to take in the side seams on the sewing machine. It would fit much better and show off your lovely figure.'

'Really?' Sarah turned and gave her a hug. 'You are the best!'

'Quick, hand it over, there's a good girl.'

Sarah slipped out of the dress, then stood regarding her reflection. Pulling back her hair, she groaned, thinking her aunt had left the room. The scar on her neck stood out livid and ugly; it was difficult to hide. She felt along the ridge of the scar and grimaced.

'Does it bother you?' Alice asked from the doorway.

Flustered, Sarah turned to her. 'Oh! Not normally, but it seems to bother other people. Some of the girls at work are the worst culprits. I have been wearing a scarf around my neck to hide it, but that feels like giving in. That doesn't sit easy with me.' It amazed Sarah that in a country where most of its citizens had experienced bombing and its devastating effects on lives and bodies, they still recoiled to see the physical markers of it. No one ever alluded to the scar or asked how she got it, but she had caught the fleeting looks of distaste.

'Hold on, I may have just the thing,' Alice said, putting the dress down on the bed and slipping out of the room. Moments later she returned, holding a small round box. 'Try some of this.' Her aunt pulled off the lid. It was a powder puff. 'Dab it along the line of the scar. It won't hide it completely, but it won't be as obvious.'

As Sarah patted the powder along the raised ridge of skin, the delicate scent of it was heavenly, but the translucent powder didn't hide much. Pulling her hair down to obscure it as best she could, Sarah forced herself to smile back at her aunt through the mirror. Perhaps in a few months it would be less obvious, but there was no way she was going to let an injury dent her confidence. She was still Sarah Gillespie, survivor, and proud of it. 'Just the ticket, thank you.'

Alice beamed back at her before heading out the door with the dress. 'Won't be long.'

Sarah walked over to the window and stared out into the gathering dusk. Could she be any luckier? Her aunt was so kind-hearted and motherly. It still amazed Sarah how quickly she had settled into life with the Lambes. After work in the evenings, the family settled down before the fire and the wireless was turned on to hear the news. Uncle Tom would sit, head bent, listening intently, a glass of stout in his hand. Once the news was over, Tom was fond of regaling her with stories of his and Ma's childhood. Aunt Alice would chuckle and shake her head over her knitting, even though she must have heard his tales many times. With a groan and a roll of his eyes at Sarah, Martin would look up from a book or a magazine and wink. Sarah treasured the moments, adding them to her arsenal of happier memories to buffer the bad. Not since Ma had died had she experienced the novelty of being at ease at home. At No. 18, they used to sit in dread in the kitchen, waiting for the sound of the key in the lock and Da coming in. You never knew what kind of mood he'd be in.

In sharp contrast to her own parents, her aunt and uncle's love for each other could not be clearer. It was plain to see in looks and smiles exchanged, soft teasing and gentle caresses. Uncle Tom treated Alice with respect. That was the biggest difference. Sarah wondered how Ma could have been content with *her* choice; had death been a happy release? On several occasions, she had spied the bruises on Ma. Embarrassed, her mother would always turn away, covering up with shaking fingers, but not before Sarah saw the look of mortification on her face. Thank God Ma was free of Da's brutality and could rest in peace, no more than poor Maura. With a pang, Sarah realised the bomb which had destroyed her home and her family had set her free from fear and the threat of violence.

It felt a little strange to be going out on a date; something so normal after all the madness of the last few months. Sarah sat down at the small dressing table. As she applied the last of her lipstick, she suddenly remembered Mrs Twohig's strange talisman. Some luck wouldn't do any harm in the circumstances. It took her a few moments to find the medal, which she had wrapped in tissue paper and stowed in her suitcase before leaving Dublin.

Unfolding the paper, she gazed upon the metal cross and shivered as she recalled how Mrs Twohig's father had retrieved it from a dead soldier. How could such an object be lucky? Maybe it wasn't such a good idea, on balance. She placed it back in the case. A positive outlook was all she needed. She had spotted Rob several times during the week in the grounds of Hursley and he had finalised their arrangements the previous day, in the canteen. She hadn't experienced any doubts as she watched him walk away.

However, as soon as he was out of earshot, her lunch companions had ribbed her. Ruth was very keen for Sarah to go out with him. But then Ruth had been limpet-like all week, always trying to steer the conversation round to Martin. Initially, Sarah had indulged her, but Ruth was chasing Martin too hard, and unnecessarily too, for she was a good-looking girl and could have her pick. Was she one of those girls who loved the chase, then dropped a lad once she'd caught him? Sarah had grown fond of Martin in the short time she'd known him, and didn't want to see him get hurt. But without fail, Ruth manoeuvred herself to be in Sarah's company on the way out of Hursley Park in the evenings. As often as not, Martin would catch up

102

with them and offer to walk Ruth to the bus stop. Sarah teased him afterwards, but he would just grin and shrug, clearly enjoying the attention.

The clock struck eight fifteen as Sarah entered the King's Head. Despite her aunt's assurances, it felt strange to enter a public house; but Aunt Alice told her all the locals frequented it. Back in North Strand, the pubs were almost exclusively male; only a certain class of woman would enter them. Whenever Sarah had courted back in Dublin, it had involved going to dances, the cinema, or out to Dollymount Strand, if the weather was fine.

The pub was busy and it took her several minutes to find Rob, who was sitting over a pint close to the fireplace in the rear bar area. As soon as he saw her approach, Rob jumped up and greeted her with a friendly smile, taking her hand and squeezing it. 'What a relief! I was afraid you had changed your mind,' he said. 'I even thought of calling to the house. I suppose that's what I should have done anyway,' he said with a frown.

'Not at all. And sorry I'm late; I was helping my uncle in his garden earlier and we weren't watching the time. Then my aunt offered to adjust my dress just as I was about to leave.'

'It doesn't matter, Sarah,' he said as he helped her take off her coat. 'You're here now.' Rob stood back and looked her up and down. 'You look amazing.'

Sarah was taken aback. Why was he gushing? 'Thank you.'

Rob clasped his hands together and nodded towards the bar. 'What would you like to drink?'

'A gin and tonic, please,' she replied, sitting down. Rob headed off to the bar and she heard him give the order to the barman. Leaning on the counter, he smiled back at her as he waited. How attractive Rob was, with his dark hair and brown eyes. Smartly dressed, he had attempted to look his best. Physically though, he was the direct opposite to Paul. Lord! She'd have to stop comparing them. It wasn't fair to Rob.

On the far side of the counter, Sarah spotted Martin. He raised his glass and winked. Smothering a smile, Sarah looked away from him and turned her attention to her date.

Soon, Rob joined her, carefully carrying the drinks. 'Here you go,' Rob said, placing her gin down on the table. 'Is this spot all right or would you rather sit somewhere else? Sorry, I didn't realise the place would be so busy. I tried to find a more secluded spot so we could chat in peace.'

'No, this is fine, thanks,' she replied.

'To new friendships,' he said, raising his glass, his eyes bright.

'*Sláinte*,' Sarah replied. 'Your good health.'

'Is that Irish? Sounds wonderful.'

'Yes, it is a traditional toast.'

'How clever of you to know that,' he said with an earnest look.

'Not at all. Everyone learns Irish in school.' The lad was too eager to please, she thought; but perhaps he was nervous. Though why someone like him would be anxious about a date was strange. In her head she could almost hear Maura, in that quiet teasing way she had had, scolding her for being dippy, and urging her to give him a chance.

Rob's expression clouded momentarily as he glanced towards the bar. 'Isn't that your cousin over there?'

Sarah followed his gaze. 'Yes, he's a regular in here, same as my uncle. In fact, I think Uncle Tom was going to follow me over.'

Rob licked his lips and cast her a quizzical look. 'I'd forgotten how full of Supermariners this place would be. Let's move over to the other corner. It's more . . . private.'

'Sure,' she replied, wondering why Martin or her uncle's presence bothered him. Rob really *was* nervous.

When they settled down at the other table, Rob manoeuvred himself so they were sitting side-by-side, out of sight from the other part of the bar. 'Now, isn't this better?' he asked, sliding an arm along the back of the seat. 'You poor thing! I do hope you have recovered from last Friday. You were very shaken by that air raid. No long-term effects?'

All too aware of his closeness, Sarah moved forward on the seat, a tad uneasy. 'Gosh, no, thank you. I don't know what came over me. All of a sudden, I was reliving the bombing in Dublin. It was strange how the siren triggered it, for there was no warning the night of the bomb in Dublin. Just as well you were on hand.'

'My absolute pleasure. I could see you were distressed, and you would have been in trouble if you hadn't left the cinema. They're strict about evacuation.'

'Yes, I can see how that would be, as you'd be putting other people at risk. Hopefully, it won't happen again. It was embarrassing to lose control like that.'

'Well, it must have triggered terrible memories. Don't worry, I understand. We won't mention it again.' Sarah smarted at his patronising tone while he took a sip of his beer. 'Other than that, how are you settling in here?'

'Very well – my aunt and uncle have been exceedingly kind to me. I was so lucky they reached out to me.'

'The Lambes are good people; everyone says so.' Rob frowned. 'I'm sorry; it must be difficult, grieving for your family and having to adjust to everything new. Do you miss home?'

'I miss certain things, but after all that happened, I couldn't see a future there. The prospect of useful work and living with family was hard to resist.'

'Will you ever go back? Do you still have family there?'

'It's unlikely, there's nothing there for me any more and any family left are virtual strangers. At the moment, I'm taking things day by day. I'm just happy to be working and to have the support of my family. What about you? Are you from around here?' Sarah asked, hoping he'd stop dragging up unpleasant memories. Speaking of Ireland left a cold leaden sensation in the pit of her stomach. Surely he must realise there were things she would rather not remember, particularly on a night out.

'No, I hail from Kent.'

'Isn't that rather far away? What brought you to Hampshire?' she asked.

'My father plays golf with a director at Vickers. As it happened, I was looking for something better than the job I was in. I tried to enlist, but my asthma prevented me, even though I haven't had an attack since I was knee-high; but there was no persuading them.'

'Which service did you want to join?'

'The navy.'

'You mentioned you have a brother overseas? Is he in the navy?'

'No, Richard is in the army, over in Egypt.' He grimaced and stared down into his beer. 'Oh well; it wasn't my destiny to go into the fray. What bothers me is the way people look at me sometimes, as if I'm shirking my duty. You can tell they're thinking "Why are you at home when my son is off . . . wherever, putting his life on the line to save your sorry skin." If only they knew what I'm doing for this country.'

Rob's whining tone was jarring, but what could she say? 'That's awful, but you need not justify yourself to anyone. We can't all take up a gun and fight. What you are doing is helping the war effort, just differently. Besides, I'm sure your parents are relieved.' He shot her a frowning glance. 'I mean, that they don't have to worry about two of you being in the line of fire.'

Rob relaxed. 'Yes, well, it's not something I can change, and the job here pays well. I hope to save up enough to go to university when the war is over.'

'That's wonderful, Rob. What would you like to study?' Sarah asked.

'Languages, as I want to be a teacher. I found learning them easy at school. I seem to have a talent for it. So far, I've learned French and German, but I'd like to try Spanish and Italian too.'

Sarah smiled. 'I can't imagine there's much call for teaching German or Italian in England these days.'

Rob chuckled. 'Perhaps not, but the war can't last forever.'

'Didn't they say that about the last one? Look what happened!'

'Once the Yanks join in, it will be over quickly,' he said, inching closer to her. 'You shouldn't worry too much about it.'

'They don't appear to be in a hurry to join us.'

'It's only a matter of time.' Sarah felt his arm sliding around her shoulders and had to force herself not to tense up. 'Tell me,' he said, his voice low. 'I'm curious about the Irish situation. Aren't you afraid of being invaded by Jerry? I don't understand why you've declared neutrality instead of joining the Allies.'

Taken aback, Sarah chose her words with care. 'It's not long since Ireland gained independence, and then it was ravaged by civil war. We're a relatively new country with few defences.

The government felt it was best to stay out of it. Most Irish people agree.'

'Does it not have more to do with the history between our countries?' he asked.

Was he being sarcastic? She wasn't sure. 'There is an element of that, I suppose. After eight hundred years under British rule, we value our freedom; it was hard won.'

'I doubt Hitler values it much.' Rob rubbed his chin. 'I would have thought the Irish would be only too glad to give us Brits a kicking by joining the Nazi cause.'

Increasingly uncomfortable, Sarah shifted in her seat and took a sip of gin. 'There are some, a small minority of republicans, who do spout that nonsense. Most sensible people do not agree. We can see for ourselves how evil the Nazi regime is.'

'Yes, of course.' He didn't sound convinced. Caressing her shoulder, he leaned in close and twirled a lock of her hair. 'I'm ever so glad you threw in your lot with us Brits, otherwise we might never have met.'

'That would have been a shame, for sure,' she replied, glancing at the clock above the bar and wishing time would speed up.

'You're lovely, Sarah. I'm so glad you agreed to meet me tonight.' He was so close she could feel his breath. Then he kissed her on the cheek.

'Hey!' Sarah pulled away. 'Steady on, Rob.'

His eyes widened. 'Sorry, I couldn't help myself.' He glanced down at her empty glass. 'Are you ready for another?' he asked, his voice cracking and his cheeks flaring red.

'Yes, please.' Sarah sat back with relief as he wandered over to the bar. He stood glaring at the barman who was serving another customer.

'Can't you hurry up there, mate? I don't have all night,' Rob snapped.

Horrified, Sarah cringed. Why was he being rude to the poor man? Was it a reaction to her rebuffing him? At that moment, she knew it would not work between them. His overt attempts at intimacy left her cold, which made little sense since he was a handsome young man. Sarah thought back to the first time she saw him in Winchester. She had been instantly attracted to him. It went to show how wrong those first impressions could be; and if the spark wasn't there, you couldn't force it. Yet it was more than that; something wasn't right about the way he was behaving. She could not understand why someone like Rob, who surely never would have a problem finding a girl with his looks, was acting in such a forced manner. His behaviour smacked of desperation and it was off-putting. No wonder his history with the ladies was so poor.

To her relief, when he returned with the drinks, he sat a little further away. He had taken the hint. The conversation turned to work colleagues and Supermarine for a while before he asked again about the political situation in Ireland. Sarah was thankful, an hour later, when Rob suggested he walk her home. They parted at her door, with Rob giving her a peck on the cheek before heading off for his bus back to Winchester. Sarah watched him walk away, mystified by his behaviour, and unsettled by his comments about Irish politics. Every time she had attempted to turn the conversation and asked about his interests and family, he had prevaricated. He had kept probing her, obsessed by the notion that the Irish would side with Germany.

Well, no matter. Sarah was certain of one thing; she was determined not to repeat that experience any time soon.

12

29th September 1941, Hursley Park

As Sarah sat down for lunch the following Monday, she was immediately bombarded with questions by Gladys and Ruth, dying to know how her night out with Rob had gone. The increasingly bad weather had forced the girls to have their lunch indoors. Once she was sure Rob or any of his colleagues weren't in the vicinity, she broke the news that she wouldn't be seeing him again.

'Really?' Ruth asked. 'But he's so nice! And goodness me, he's a handsome lad. Everyone says so. What's wrong with him?'

Was that annoyance Sarah detected in Ruth's tone? Why would Ruth be annoyed with her for not liking Rob? Sarah found her attitude bizarre. 'Yes, he's good-looking, but I just didn't feel comfortable with him,' Sarah answered, exchanging a bemused glance with Gladys.

'Why ever not?' Ruth continued to glare at her.

Sarah sighed and put down her cup of tea. 'He was more interested in politics than me. I'm not saying there is anything wrong with being interested in such things, it's just that I do not wish to spend a date discussing political affairs, and the decisions of governments in far-off lands.'

'I agree. Very boring stuff, on the whole,' piped up Gladys. A dreamy expression came into her eyes. 'Though, if Cary Grant wanted to talk about international affairs, I'd probably put up with it. I'd just stare into those wonderful eyes and nod every so often.'

'Yes, thank you, Gladys,' Sarah ground out. 'The truth of the matter, Ruth, is that there wasn't any spark between us. I don't see any point in encouraging him if I don't see a future in it.'

'That's happened to me, too,' Gladys remarked, between mouthfuls. 'Not the politics thing: I mean lack of a connection. Looks can't make up for lack of personality, Ruth, you have to admit.'

'Rob has plenty of personality. He was just nervous,' Ruth replied. 'You should give him another chance.'

'For goodness' sake, Ruth, let the girl choose for herself. If she doesn't like him, she doesn't like him!' Gladys turned to Sarah. 'Ruth thinks a girl can only be happy if she has a fella in tow.'

'That's not true!' Ruth exclaimed.

Gladys ignored her. 'Don't mind her, Sarah; she's grumpy today. Martin hasn't asked her to the dance.'

'Yet!' Ruth pouted.

'Is that the dance advertised on the poster over there?' Sarah asked, looking towards the social club notice board.

'Yep, this Saturday in the old Entertainment Hall at the back of the stables. They're usually a good laugh. You're bound to find a replacement for Rob at it.'

Ruth rolled her eyes skywards. 'Nonsense!'

Gladys smothered a grin and elbowed Sarah. 'If only we were near an RAF base. Something very dreamy about those RAF uniforms, don't you think?' Sarah smiled back at her. She had recently told Gladys in confidence about Paul. It had felt so good to be able to talk about him to someone. Gladys had been sympathetic and understood her feelings of guilt. She hadn't insulted her with platitudes but had called her an idiot, which was well deserved, and had laughed that she would probably have behaved in the same impulsive way.

'They are feckless daredevils, if you ask me,' remarked Ruth with a huff. 'I'd stay well clear if I were you, Sarah.'

'One of my closest friends has just joined the RAF, and I can assure you he is one of the most honourable men you could meet,' Sarah snapped.

Ruth had the good grace to blush.

'Ha! I see you don't warn *me* off, Ruth,' Gladys said with a wink at Sarah. 'And I thought we were pals. Goes to show how wrong you can be about someone, Sarah, eh?'

Ruth quirked her mouth and hissed. 'I have been acquainted with you long enough to know you can look after yourself.'

Gladys burst out laughing.

Sarah hid her growing irritation with Ruth by looking at her watch. 'I think it's time to return to work, don't you?' Not waiting for a reply, she hopped up and made her way back to the Tracing Room, her mind already on the substantial pile of drawings awaiting her attention.

'Well! Would you look at those two lovebirds,' Gladys said to Sarah a few days later, throwing an amused glance over to the table where Martin and Ruth were having their lunch. 'All's well again in paradise!'

'He asked her to the dance on Saturday then?'

Gladys grinned. 'Yes, thank God. Didn't he tell you? I thought you two were as thick as thieves.'

'We don't tell each other *everything*. In fact, he never mentions her to me, but that's because he knows we are friends and workmates, I suppose. It could be awkward.'

'Perhaps. Anyway, she was all aflutter on the bus home yesterday and didn't shut up about him all evening. Sorry, I know he's your cousin and he's a pet but . . .'

Sarah grinned back at her. 'Enough said. And what about you? Do you have a date lined up for Saturday?'

Gladys winked at her. 'I'm working on it, never fear. And even if my plans don't bear fruit, I shall find someone on the night. There's usually a good mixture of lads. It's not just Supermariners who turn up. There will be lads from all the villages.'

Sarah finished her tea and sat back. 'I'm looking forward to it. The last time I was dancing was . . .' *the night of the bombing*, she thought, '. . . a while ago. Do you think Rob will be there? I was hoping to avoid him.'

Gladys's eyes lit up with mischief. 'Ooh, yes, that will be tricky for you. The scorned lover shadowing your every move, standing in the corner all alone, nursing a pint.'

Sarah spluttered. 'You should join the dramatic society.'

'Why aren't you taking me seriously? Poor lad must be heartbroken. You must be very cold-hearted if you think you can ignore his anguished sighs and forlorn glances. A quid says you'll feel sorry for him and give in.'

'Stop! Don't say things like that.' Sarah's heart sank at the thought she might not be in jest.

Gladys smirked. 'I'm afraid he usually does attend, but I

thought you intended to put him straight as soon as possible. Didn't I see you talking to him on the way out yesterday evening? It didn't look like a cosy chat. He was on our bus home, but he didn't say a word to anyone, which isn't like him.'

'Don't! I feel awful. You're right; he didn't take it very well. In fact, he was astonished. But what else could I do? I had to be honest with him.'

'Of course you did, but how conceited of him. You do know that Ruth went out with him a while back?'

'What? No, she never mentioned that to me.' Sarah stared across at her friend. 'Why didn't *you* warn me?'

Gladys looked surprised. 'It didn't seem important. Sorry, I thought you knew already.'

'How could I? Bother! Was I stepping on her toes do you think?' Sarah frowned across at her friend. 'But, why then was she so encouraging and so upset when I told you both I wouldn't see him again?'

'No idea. Ruth is a mystery to me most of the time,' Gladys replied, picking up her sandwich and finishing it in one bite. 'I've stopped trying to figure her out.'

'Why did they break up?'

'It was before we shared the flat in Winchester, so I don't know the ins and outs of it. Rob has walked out with a few of the girls but it never seems to last long. They must have parted on good terms though for Ruth to be ok with you going out with him.'

'Yes, I suppose so,' Sarah said. 'But it is odd.'

Gladys shrugged. 'Ruth is odd. Anyway, plenty more fish in the old pond for you to hook.'

Sarah gasped, trying not to laugh. 'You have a very blunt way of putting it.'

115

'I don't stand on ceremony, Sarah. You'll soon discover that about me. I speak as I find.'

'I much prefer that, Gladys.'

Gladys's expression became serious. 'Life hasn't always been easy for me. As a result, I don't put up with nonsense from the likes of Ruth. Getting the job here at Supermarine was a blessing. This bloody war has been a godsend, if I'm honest.'

'How so?'

'When I was fifteen, I had to leave home and find work as my dad was ill and couldn't support us. He was injured in the last war and came home a broken man. He was bedridden and struggling to breathe for most of my childhood.'

'That's awful,' Sarah said. 'Is he still alive?'

'Yes, if you can call it that. But it was hardest for my mother with four of us little ones. She had to take in washing just to put food on the table. Once we were old enough, we had to move on. I wasn't a great one for schooling, so I didn't have much choice when it came to finding jobs. I did shop work in Southampton, mostly. When the war broke out, I spotted a job going at the works in Woolston. I couldn't believe my luck when they took me on as I had no experience. Miss Sugden trained me up, you know. It's been a life-changing experience, Sarah, working here. I have decent money for the first time in my life and I can even send some home to my mother.'

'I'm sorry. It sounds like you had a rough time.' Sarah suspected Gladys wasn't telling her the half of it.

'It wasn't easy living hand to mouth. Much like you, I've seen the rotten cards life can deal you. But surviving makes you stronger, doesn't it?'

Sarah nodded and sighed. 'This war is shaping both of our lives.'

'And for the better. I've no intention of tasting poverty again. I intend to live life to the full!'

'Not a bad philosophy, Gladys,' Sarah said with a sad smile. 'If I have learned one thing, it is that life can be very short.'

'To making the most of it,' Gladys said, lifting her teacup in a toast. They clinked cups and Gladys laughed. 'And to fishing in that great big pond on Saturday night!'

13

Sarah heard the opening bars of 'In the Mood' as they walked up the path towards the stable block. It was Saturday evening and she was determined to enjoy the dance. With a grin, she turned to Martin. 'I love that song. The band sounds great.'

'Why so surprised? We have only the best here, madam; not bad for the middle of nowhere, eh? And, if we hurry, we might get to dance to some of it too,' he replied, increasing his pace, tugging her along by the hand.

The hall was jam-packed, and Sarah stalled at the entrance. Martin threw her a questioning glance. The sudden over-whelming fear was irrational, she knew, but she was determined to fight it. Once she was aware of where the exits were, she would be fine. A quick scan of the hall and she relaxed.

'Ok?' Martin asked.

She forced an answering smile and Martin pushed forward through the crowd, not stopping even when his mates tried to hold him up. Sarah let herself be pulled along. She had to smile: Martin's enthusiasm was infectious. Not that Sarah needed any encouragement, for she adored dancing; always had. He found a space among the dancers and launched into the dance with gusto, swinging her around until she was almost doubled up with laughter. Within minutes, all traces of fear had vanished. Faces flashed past in a blur. All too soon, the music ended with an appreciative roar from the crowd.

'I need a drink, Martin!' Sarah gasped.

'Right-ho!' he said with a wink, leading the way to the side of the room, where there was a makeshift refreshment table set up. Martin queried what was on offer from the young man behind the table. 'I'm afraid the only alcohol is rather warm beer or some kind of punch,' Martin informed Sarah with a grimace.

'What do you recommend?' she asked. But Martin was frowning over her shoulder and didn't respond. 'What is it?' Sarah followed his gaze. Ruth was in deep conversation with Rob McArthur near the doorway. *What could they have to talk about?* she wondered. There didn't appear to be any ex-lover awkwardness, but it looked odd. All of a sudden, both of them turned and looked in her direction. Sarah turned away, and her heart sank. She had hoped to avoid Rob – she still felt embarrassed about their date. Martin continued to scowl at the pair, and Sarah had to nudge him to get his attention. 'Punch, please, cousin, or I shall expire.'

'Sure,' he replied. 'Two punch, there's a good man,' Martin ordered. He then looked across the room and glowered. 'Your friend Rob is up to mischief over there.'

'You know they dated for a while?' she asked. Martin nodded. 'And by the way, he's not my *friend*, as well you know.'

'Then why was he asking me about you again in the pub last night?' Martin replied.

'You never said.' The knowledge only made her more determined to avoid Rob. There had been no spark between them; it would never work. These things could not be forced.

Martin shrugged, still looking put out. 'I only remembered now. If he turns his attention back to Ruth, I'll blame you.'

'Don't be silly. Go over and rescue Ruth: she'll be delighted. I've just spotted Gladys over there. I'm going to join her.' With a harrumph, Martin handed her the punch and left her side to push his way through the crowd.

Gladys waved across the room and Sarah made her way over to her, trying to protect her drink.

'What a crush!' Gladys said after giving her a quick hug. 'Have you been here long?'

'Not long at all.' The band started up again and Sarah had to raise her voice. 'Martin has just gone to find Ruth.' Gladys nodded and they made for a couple of empty chairs.

'I don't suppose we'll see much of those lovebirds for the rest of the evening,' Gladys remarked. 'Have you spotted anyone nice?'

'Not yet, but give me a chance.' Sarah made a face. 'Rob's here, though. I was half hoping he wouldn't turn up.'

Gladys laughed. 'Poor fellow; I almost feel sorry for him. He has no chance with you at all.'

'I'd rather not talk about him. What about you? Do you have your eye on anyone in particular yet?'

Gladys leaned closer. 'Well, there is that new lad in the Drawing Office. I was hoping your Martin might make the introduction. Here, what's that punch like?' Sarah handed her the glass and Gladys took a sip. 'Whoa! That's potent stuff, that is.' She sprang up. 'Do you want another one? You might as well as I'm going up.'

'No, thanks, I need to pace myself,' Sarah replied and watched Gladys disappear through the crowd.

Minutes later, there was a tap on her shoulder, and she looked up to see Ruth smiling down at her, Martin close behind.

'Gladys has just gone to get drinks,' Sarah shouted up to her.

'I'll help her. Anyone want one?' Ruth asked. Sarah and Martin shook their heads.

Martin sat down beside Sarah. 'Is it always this manic?' she asked.

He looked around. 'Actually, I've seen it worse, and it's early yet.'

The band finished another song just as the two girls returned. Martin hopped up to let Ruth sit down, and Sarah shifted to let Gladys share her seat.

The next song was announced. 'Oh, my favourite!' Gladys jumped straight back up again.

Sarah didn't recognise the tune. 'What is it?'

'It's so much fun. "The Blackout Stroll". Come on, dance with me, Sarah, you'll soon get the hang of it. When they switch off the lights, you have to grab another partner in the dark. You never know who you will end up with. It's a great laugh. Quick!'

Martin grinned at Sarah as he took her glass. 'Go on,' he said. 'And try to keep out of trouble.'

Sarah and Gladys lined up behind the other couples as the singer stepped up to the microphone. They moved off, arm-in-arm, swaying to the gentle beat, but after about a minute and a half, the lights went out. This was met by squeals and shrieks of laughter. Sarah felt Gladys move away from her and then her arm was grabbed. Seconds later, the lights came back up.

Rob was her new partner.

He beamed down at her and her heart sank. Would he ever give up? Ahead, Gladys twisted around and gave her a cheeky, wide-eyed grin. She appeared to be very happy with her new dance partner, whoever he was.

When the song finished, Rob kept a firm hold of her arm and steered her off the floor away from Martin and the girls.

'Gosh, I was hoping you'd come tonight. I've been looking out for you. Are you enjoying yourself?' he asked.

'Yes, I am,' Sarah answered, flustered. How to get away without causing a scene or hurting his feelings?

'Can I get you a drink?'

'No, thank you, really, I'm fine,' she said. 'My drink is over there.'

Rob ignored the hint and pulled a packet of cigarettes from his pocket, offering her one. Sarah declined. 'It's rather warm,' he said. 'Come on; let's go outside for a minute. It's difficult to talk with all this racket.'

Sarah followed him out of the door, hoping she could come up with the words to let him down gently. Why had he not believed her at lunchtime the other day? Was he one of those creepy fellows who wouldn't take no for an answer? She didn't want to hurt his feelings, but honesty was always better, and most of all, she wanted him to stop pestering her, once and for all.

'There, that's better.' Rob leaned against the wall of the hall and took a long drag on his cigarette. 'Don't suppose you'd rather go to the King's Head for a quiet drink?'

'No, thanks all the same.'

'The thing is, I really like you, Sarah. Won't you give me another chance?' he pleaded.

'Look Rob, you're a nice lad but I'm just not ready to get into another relationship right now. After all that has happened in the last few months, and, well, I only broke up with someone before I left Dublin. I still have feelings for him. Do you understand?'

Rob gazed at her, his expression blank; she could not fathom what he was thinking. Eventually, he smiled. 'That's Ok. You just need time. I won't give up, you know. Maybe in a week or so you'll feel differently. I believe we have a lot in common.'

Sarah gnawed her bottom lip. Was he being deliberately obtuse? 'I'm sorry, but I feel there is no future in this. Look, I'd better get back to the others. Enjoy your evening. See you around, Rob.'

Sarah sensed his gaze following her as she made her escape back inside. It wasn't a comfortable sensation.

14

The Hursley Amateur Dramatic Society had just wrapped up rehearsals for the evening and Sarah was waiting outside for Martin, acknowledging the salutes of the other members as they passed and headed for home. Through the open door she could hear Martin laughing and joking with the last few members of the cast. It was always the same: he took ages to say goodbye. Like Uncle Tom, he was a great talker and thrived in company. Content to wait, she breathed in the chilly evening air and gazed above the treetops to the south of the old huts. The heavens were so much clearer here in the country than they had ever been back in Dublin. Tonight, the sky was velvety black with tiny pinpricks of starlight. Much to her relief, for weeks there had been no sign of enemy planes in the sky. Her initial fear that Jerry might find Supermarine's new location and try to bomb the area had dissipated, and she was feeling much more comfortable in her surroundings. Now, as Sarah gazed upwards, she wished she knew more about the night sky.

At last, Martin appeared, pulling on his coat. He greeted her with a nod, then stood beside her. 'What has you so intrigued?'

Sarah pointed skyward. 'Any idea what they call those stars?'

'Haven't a clue. Anyway, I don't know why you're stargazing; all the stars you could ever wish to know are here tonight.' Martin waved his hand back towards the rehearsal space and grinned.

Sarah tut-tutted and gave him a mock scowl. 'You're getting a big head, cousin.'

His eyes widened in response and his chin went up. 'I shall ignore that unjust remark! Is it my fault you do not recognise greatness when you are in its midst?'

Sarah tried not to smile. 'It's sad how a little Noël Coward has turned your head completely. I suppose next stop for you is the West End.'

Martin quirked his lips. 'Jolly right!' Then he offered his arm, and although she hesitated long enough to glower at him, she linked arms and they set off down the laneway. 'I detect sour grapes,' Martin sniffed. 'I'm sorry you joined our merry band too late to audition for a part. Of course, the backstage folk are just as important.' He sniggered as a smug expression settled on his features.

'Huh! I could act you off the stage any day,' she replied, her nose in the air.

Martin came to a stop and faced her. 'That sounds like a challenge to me. Very well, next production we will see who lands the best part. Loser must stand the drinks for an entire evening in the King's Head.'

He held out his hand and Sarah shook it and said: 'Deal.'

They walked on towards the main road. 'Seriously, what did

you think of tonight's rehearsal? I didn't fluff my lines once, I'll have you know,' said Martin.

Sarah smiled into the darkness. 'True, but everyone else did. How long did you say you've been rehearsing?'

Martin's expression turned sheepish. 'Since June. I know, I know, and let me say it is cruel of you to laugh. Some of them aren't very good, but they make up for it in enthusiasm.' He sighed as she spluttered. 'Are we doomed, do you think?'

Sarah tried her best not to laugh. 'I think it's as well it's a comedy.'

With a grunt, Martin started walking again. 'Ha-ha, of errors you mean. Well, we have a few months yet. And don't you dare say "just as well" or mention miracles.'

'Actually, I was going to offer to say a novena. Who's the saint for lost causes again?'

Martin treated her to a frowning look and a dig of his elbow. 'You're hilarious!'

'Ah, don't despair. A lot can change in a few weeks. I'm surprised you haven't encouraged Ruth to join the society. I thought she'd be eager to be near the great actor and bathe in his glory.'

'I tried to persuade her, but she said she is too shy and can't act.' Martin cleared his throat and cast her a serious glance, his nose wrinkling. 'I've been meaning to ask. What do you really think of her, Sarah? Honestly now?'

'She's mighty keen on you.'

'That's not what I asked, and you know it,' he huffed.

'Truthfully? I don't know her very well, Martin. I get on better with Gladys. Ruth is inquisitive yet reveals nothing about herself . . . and she is overenthusiastic about some things, which can be trying at best.'

'Such as?'

'I don't want to—'

'No, please. I value your opinion. You see, I like her very much, but sometimes I can't make her out. Mind you, young women are an enigma most of the time, present company excepted, of course.' Martin squeezed her arm to his side. 'And I don't have Judith here to advise me any more on matters of the heart.'

'She was your confidante?'

'And vice versa. Though of late, I've heard little from her. London has made her forget us, I fear.'

'It's a big city. It's bound to be . . . exciting and distracting, if you know what I mean.'

'I know she's having a grand old time. In fact, that's why she hasn't been home in months. But it upsets the folks and I hate that.'

'Do you think there is a fella involved?' Sarah asked.

'I wouldn't be surprised. Judith is a stunner. She's never been short of admirers.'

Sarah thought of the photograph which had pride of place on her aunt's dresser. The girl was beautiful. 'I doubt she lacks for suitors, as they would have said in the old days.'

Martin nodded. 'Indeed. Anyway, stop changing the subject. I want your thoughts on Ruth.'

'All right. My peeve with Ruth at the moment is that she is driving me nuts about Rob McArthur. No matter what I say, she goes on and on about how nice he is, and that I should give him another chance. It's kind of unnerving as I've made it plain I have no intention of going out with him again.'

'Hmm, she said something similar to me the other night,' Martin said with a frown.

'Well, I don't think my love life is anybody else's business,' Sarah snapped, then regretted her words as she felt Martin stiffen. 'I don't include you in that, obviously.'

'Well, as it happens, I told her something along those lines and that I would never interfere. Well, unless there was a need, and you were in trouble, you know.' Martin frowned into the darkness.

'You're a dear!' Sarah reached up and kissed his cheek.

'Get away with ye! That's what families are for.'

'Well, it's a novelty for me and I'm grateful,' she said softly.

'Stop that now, Sarah. You're a proud young woman and I know that's because you had a hard time of it with your father. Mother told me about it.'

'She shouldn't have burdened you with any of that. Anyway, it's in the past now. Buried, just like him.'

'Still, you must let us . . . well, I suppose what I'm trying to say is that you should let us care for you and look out for you. You're not on your own any more; you're an honorary Lambe, and that's not something to be sniffed at.'

'Martin, stop! I will be blubbing in a minute. You need not say any more about it. I know how lucky I am to have found you all.' Sarah swallowed hard. 'Now, what were we talking about?' She was anxious to change the subject.

'Ruth. I think you are being too hard on her. She just wants everyone to be happy,' he said at last. 'She's very interested in you, always asking me about the family back in Ireland and how you are settling in.'

'Really? She never asks me about it.'

Martin shrugged. 'She said she was concerned about you after all that had happened. I think she's just being kind, Sarah.'

Sarah wasn't quite so sure; she found Ruth's questioning of Martin strange. But she didn't want to upset him. 'Yes, that could be it. More importantly though, does she make *you* happy?'

There was a slight hesitation. 'Yes, as I said, I like her a lot and she's terribly pretty, but I wish she weren't so reserved. I prefer a more open personality. Sometimes . . .'

'What?'

'Well, it's as if she thinks through everything she says before she says it. I find it disconcerting. Am I that intimidating, do you think?'

'Gracious, no! As it happens, I've noticed that about her too, but maybe she is as shy as she claims. Perhaps she hasn't walked out with many lads. Though I know she and Rob were an item, a few months ago. Any idea what happened there?'

'No. She's never mentioned it, but that's why I was put out on Saturday night, seeing them together. I can't help but wonder.'

'That's the trouble with old flames: it's hard to let them go.' The words were out of her mouth far too quickly. She could have kicked herself.

'Do you think she still likes him?' he asked, his tone anxious.

'Heavens, no! She'd hardly be urging me to date him if she did,' Sarah replied. 'Sorry, I didn't mean to imply anything. I was thinking of my own circumstances. Hearts are wayward things, aren't they?'

'If you say so. I guess you are referring to that RAF chap?' he asked.

'Yes. I think he is part of the reason I didn't want to take things further with Rob. In fact, the trouble is I compare every lad I meet to Paul.'

'And none of them measure up?' he asked with a glint in his eye. 'You must stop doing that. You'll never move on otherwise.'

'Yes, I suppose you are right,' she answered with a sigh. 'But Paul was special. I think it will take time.'

'Maybe Ruth is right: give poor old Rob another try.'

'Oh, don't you start!' she exclaimed in exasperation, just as they reached home. But her cousin only grinned at her as she swept past him and into the house.

15

14th October 1941, Hursley Park

It was a dull Tuesday afternoon. Sarah looked up from her drawing board and rolled her shoulders to ease out her muscles. She had been working for hours on this tracing and she was finding it hard going. The level of detail required, compared to the architectural drawings she had traced in her old job, still astonished her. She had a newfound respect for the engineers and draughtsmen designing the planes, not to mention the men who built the parts based on the new specifications she and the other girls worked on so diligently. There was a certain satisfaction in being a small part of the process. And if it helped defeat Germany, as it must, all the better. Sometimes she could not believe how lucky she had been to get the job here.

Gazing out into the park, Sarah fell to daydreaming. What would it be like to be wealthy and live in such a fabulous house as this, with grounds so extensive you could get lost in them? Sarah wondered if Lady Cooper wandered around the house and gardens alone at night, decrying the Ministry of Aircraft Production's appropriation of her home. Did she lose herself in her memories of better times? With such a beautiful house, the Coopers must have entertained lavishly in days gone by. Sarah had taken a peek at the grand reception rooms whenever the opportunity arose. Despite the ugly modern office furniture, the grandeur of the rooms, with their beautiful floors, ornate plasterwork and rich drapes, was still breathtaking. Sarah would fantasise by stepping back in time, conjuring up magnificent dinner parties with champagne and cocktails flowing, and the participants altogether splendid in their evening attire. Would those happy-go-lucky days and nights ever return for the landed gentry? Or, like the last war, would their houses be left bereft of fathers and sons, lost on some far-off battlefield, never to return?

Sarah doubted Hursley Park would ever be the same again. There would always be reminders of the war and its effect on the house. At least no walls had been knocked down or plasterwork removed, but there was bound to be some damage with so many people working in the building. The room she and her fellow tracers occupied had those priceless Wedgwood panels, and though they were mindful of them, it was inevitable they would be affected by the girls' day-to-day activities. Still, Sarah hoped Lady Cooper would get her estate back in one piece, someday. But it wouldn't be any time soon. It was common knowledge Supermarine was recruiting aggressively and needed more space at Hursley. Luckily, the grounds were expansive, and additional huts, camouflaged under the trees, were being erected to house more departments. Uncle Tom and Martin worked in one of the huts, and there was a rumour the tracing team might also move out to something similar in a few months' time.

A discreet cough and a raised brow from Miss Sugden at the top of the room brought Sarah back to reality. A glance at her watch told her it was still early afternoon. At this rate, she might get to start on another sheet today. Sarah took up her ink pen and traced a curve onto the sheet of tracing cloth. It was almost done; just one more loop . . . and now it was finished. Sitting up straight, she scanned the page before signing off at the bottom of the sheet. She smiled – the draughtsman who had signed off the drawing was Uncle Tom. Then she added the date. It was always satisfying to complete a tracing.

As Sarah added her tracing to the batch of sheets awaiting collection and despatch to the printers, the door opened. Miss Whitaker stood in the doorway staring at Sarah's vacant desk for several seconds before looking around the room, her gaze eventually landing on her target. 'Ah, Miss Gillespie; there you are. Come with me, please.'

The Dragon's tone gave nothing away, and Sarah shared an anxious glance with Gladys before following Miss Whitaker out into the corridor. Had she made a mistake on one of her tracings? Was she in some kind of trouble? It was a regular occurrence for one of the girls to be hauled before the Dragon for inaccuracy or tarnished tracings.

Miss Whitaker turned and walked back down the corridor towards her office. A few feet away, she stopped and beckoned Sarah forward. 'This is highly unusual and I'm not sure I approve, Miss Gillespie. There is a gentleman here to see you. He says it is urgent and cannot wait until after office hours. He's waiting for you in my office,' the Dragon said, staring hard at her over the rim of her glasses. Sarah was puzzled. Who on earth could it be?

'I wasn't expecting a visit from anyone, Miss Whitaker,' she replied.

The Dragon's lips compressed. 'He has pulled rank, so I could not refuse. Very well. Run along; don't keep him waiting.' Sarah's manager treated her to one more reproving glance before walking off in the opposite direction.

Sarah's spirits lifted. *Could it be Paul?* she wondered, her heart beginning to pound. But he wouldn't arrive unannounced, and he wouldn't even know for certain she was working here. If not Paul, then who else could it be? As she entered the room, she saw a man in naval uniform with his back to her over at the window, staring out into the grounds. The stranger turned and smiled. He was what her mother would have described as 'a fine figure of a man'. Sizing him up from beneath her lashes, she reckoned he was in his late forties. His hair was dark with silvery threads at his temples, and his bearing was military-like. With sharp features, and high cheekbones, he had an attractive face.

The officer moved towards her, limping badly. He held out his hand. 'Miss Gillespie?' he enquired.

'Yes, I'm Sarah Gillespie. I understand you wished to see me, sir?' she said after a firm handshake.

'Please.' He indicated she should sit down with a wave of his hand. Sarah sat on the edge of the seat and waited as he limped around the desk and took Miss Whitaker's seat.

The man sat forward and steepled his fingers, elbows resting on the desk. 'Well, I'm jolly glad to meet you at last, Miss Gillespie. My name is Captain Northcott, Royal Navy. At present, I work for the government on special assignment. Dashed sorry I had to interrupt your work. Your manager, Miss Whitaker, was kind enough to allow me the opportunity to speak to you. Please be reassured that there is no cause for alarm, young lady, and I have no wish to detain you from your vital work for longer than is necessary.'

'Not at all, sir. What can I do for you?' she asked. All the while, her mind raced with questions. Who was he and what was going on? Why would someone in the Royal Navy wish to speak to her?

'Miss Gillespie, how can I put this delicately? You have come to our attention.' Again, the dazzling smile. Puzzled, Sarah raised a brow but remained silent. 'Unfortunately, a red flag has been raised and it's my job to ascertain . . . How best to say it without giving offence . . . well, to ascertain if you are a bona fide friend to this country.' He wrinkled his nose as if saying it caused him physical hurt.

'I'm sorry. I do not understand what you mean, Captain.' Sarah straightened in her seat, her heart thumping. Unfortunately, she *did* have a sneaking suspicion what he meant.

'Oh dear, I'm not making myself clear, am I?' He sighed, and with exaggerated slowness, opened a folder which lay on the desk. Sarah noticed 'TOP SECRET' had been stamped on the front cover. Northcott tapped the open page and treated her to a quizzical glance. 'Your file was passed on to me, and makes for interesting reading.'

'Captain, I don't know what's going on, but I can assure you I was thoroughly checked before I started here. I can understand how my nationality might be an issue, but if that was a problem when I applied for this job, I'm sure it has been resolved. I doubt I would have been employed otherwise. Miss Whitaker could confirm that for you.' Northcott's brows shot up. Clearly, there was a problem. Fear sliced through her. Was she about to lose her job? She fought to stay calm. 'What exactly is the issue, sir?'

Captain Northcott sat back with a surprised expression. 'Please don't be alarmed. You have done nothing wrong; quite the opposite. My dear young lady, there is a difficulty, for want of a better word, but it is one we very much hope you can help *us* with. Think of it as a bargain in which we both get what we want. However, first, I'd like to ask you a question, if I may?' Sarah nodded. 'Why did you come to England?'

For a moment it was on the tip of her tongue to make a smart comment. The question was disingenuous if he was familiar with her file, but Northcott was leaning towards her, clearly interested in what her answer might be. She stared at her file on the desk. 'I think you must know. I'm sure it is all in that file.'

'Humour me, Miss Gillespie,' Northcott replied with a coaxing smile. 'I'd like to hear it from you.'

Sarah relaxed slightly and recounted the details of the night of the bombing. 'My family and home were wiped out that night and I could not see any way to make a meaningful difference to the outcome of this war by staying in Dublin. My relatives' invitation to come live and work here was just the opportunity I sought. Obviously, I cannot fight, but I can help the war effort by doing a good job here.'

'Very laudable, my dear Miss Gillespie. So, would it be fair to say revenge was your primary motivation for coming to England?' he asked.

'Partly, but also dissatisfaction with the stance my country has taken. And, if I am honest, I also wished to meet my mother's family.'

'That is understandable in the circumstances. It must have been a very distressing time for you. Life changing, in fact.'

'Not just me; countless others were left bereaved and homeless. And worst of all, there was no logic to it.'

'Indeed; but then the whole Nazi regime is rotten to the core. There's no accounting for anything they do.' Northcott grunted then rubbed his chin, his gaze fixed on the window. Sarah wished she knew what was going through his head. Eventually, his gaze focused back on her. 'It is your courage in the face of that tragedy that has sparked our interest, Miss Gillespie. Courage and resourcefulness.'

Sarah chuckled and Northcott's eyebrows shot up once more. 'I'm sorry, sir, but I'm no heroine in a Gothic romance. A survivor, perhaps, but no more.'

'On the contrary, I believe you have the . . . personality and aptitude we could harness for great good.'

Baffled, Sarah gazed at him, hoping he was going to clarify what he meant. 'I'm intrigued, sir, but I'm not sure—'

'Indeed, I'm being far too vague. My wife complains of it all the time.' Northcott gave a little laugh. 'Well, to be frank, Miss Gillespie, the British government needs you.'

Sarah stared back at him, perplexed. Northcott continued: 'You see, there is a Nazi spy – a fifth columnist – here at Supermarine. We'd like you to help us root him out. By so doing, you would get a measure of revenge and we would catch our impostor.'

Sarah straightened up in surprise. 'A spy? Here?'

The captain nodded. 'I know; quite shocking. It is difficult to believe he managed to get a job here.' Northcott lowered his voice. 'However, during the Blitz last winter things were chaotic. He got through the recruitment process rather quickly as they were short-staffed. Checks may not have been completed.'

'That is surprising. They were very thorough with me,' she replied.

'Yes, but things have been calmer since the move here to

Hursley.' Northcott tilted his head. 'What do you say? Are you game?'

'I don't know what to say, sir. I have no experience in such matters. There must be others more suitable for this job?'

'No, no. That's just it. Because you are Irish, our spy will think you are ripe for turning. He will assume you have republican leanings and that you are pro-German. He will home in on that. It wouldn't take much encouragement from you . . .'

'Yes, I can see how that might be; and it is important that this person is exposed. I'm not sure I'm the right person, though.'

'But think, Miss Gillespie – what better way to avenge your family's misfortunes at the hands of Nazi Germany than to help take down one of their spies?'

Sarah gave him a wan smile. 'It would be extremely satisfying, I have to admit. Let me think about it, please.'

The captain grimaced. 'Ah, unfortunately, there is very little time. This person is eager to gain access to plans, and so far, he has been unsuccessful in finding a co-conspirator. Our fear is he will move on, that we will lose track of him and that he will attempt his treachery elsewhere without our knowledge. These chaps are very clever, you know, and change identity frequently. It is sheer luck we know about him at all.'

'I see.'

'I do regret having to put pressure on you, but I would need your answer within twenty-four hours, Miss Gillespie.'

'So little time! This is all a bit of a shock, sir. I would like to get my uncle's advice.'

The captain went rigid. 'No! You cannot discuss this outside this room. I cannot stress that enough. Secrecy is of the utmost importance.' Northcott held her gaze for several seconds, during which time Sarah realised that for all his outward charm there was steely strength in the man too.

'And if I don't agree to help you?'

Northcott sat back in his chair. 'I would be very disappointed. And,' he looked down at her file, 'we would have to explore your past more *vigorously*. I hate to mention it, but there is the small matter of your father being a notorious republican.'

And there it was: Da's ghost. Sarah almost groaned aloud. 'My father is dead, and I never shared his misguided ideology, Captain. Ask anyone who knows me and they will tell you what my feelings are in relation to the republican movement,' Sarah replied, growing more agitated. How could she reassure him?

'You cannot have lived in the same house with the man for . . .' he glanced down at the file, '. . . nineteen years, and not have been influenced by his views.'

'Yes, I had to listen to his nonsense for years, I cannot deny that. He was not a man to gainsay. His nature was violent. But you cannot in all seriousness tar me with the same brush as my father. His involvement in the IRA was in the early 1920s, around the time I was born.'

'Be that as it may, if we were to find anything untoward in your family history, we would have little choice but to ask you and the Lambes to leave the country. We are at war, Miss Gillespie, and must be sure of our friends. You must see the logic in this.'

'I do. I also see that, in effect, I have no choice but to help you,' she ground out.

'Miss Gillespie, it is not as bleak as that. Besides, I would have thought you would jump at the chance to strike back,' he said with a quirk of his lips.

With a sigh, Sarah returned his gaze. 'I had hoped that by

141

doing war work, I had already achieved that. I hadn't envisaged such a role as you are hinting at, I have to admit.'

'Few do, but war has a way of bringing out the best in us all. I'm sure when you think this over you will be more than happy to help us.'

'Can you tell me more about what it is I would have to do?' Sarah asked, resigned to her fate.

'Help him steal the secrets he desires.'

'What? You cannot be serious.'

'I am deadly serious, my dear young lady. How else are we to unmask him?'

'Who is this spy?' she asked.

'Rob McArthur.'

Sarah blinked rapidly, grappling with the insanity of the idea. 'No! I don't believe it.'

'I can assure you our information is correct.' He treated her to a penetrating stare which set her nerves on edge. 'I understand you are acquainted with him.'

For a split second she was about to deny it, but based on Northcott's knowledge of her so far, it would be futile. 'Yes. Rob is a colleague. He helped me during an air raid in Winchester by showing me the way to an air-raid shelter.'

'And?'

Sarah sighed; her attempt to downplay their acquaintance clearly doomed. 'We met one evening for a drink, but I have little desire to further the acquaintance. He seems a nice enough fellow, though he is rather fond of talking politics. It was one of the things that put me off him. He reminded me of my father.'

'That, my dear lady, is hardly a coincidence. So, you *are* acquainted with him.'

142

Sarah sighed. 'Yes. He asked me out again, but I didn't wish to take things any further. Of course, you know all of this already.'

'Yes, rather.' He tapped the file and smiled.

'Is everyone in Supermarine under surveillance?' she asked.

'You can hardly expect me to answer that, Miss Gillespie.' The captain chuckled. 'Suffice to say, I am well informed.'

Then why bother to ask these questions? she thought with a great deal of annoyance. Sarah's stomach plummeted as it occurred to her that there was only one way Northcott's plan would work. 'Let me guess. You want me to befriend him and pretend to like him so he will reveal his scheme?'

'How very astute, Miss Gillespie. You're a quick thinker: I like that. However, your task will be a little more complicated than that.'

'I've a feeling I will regret asking this, Captain, but what do you wish me to do?'

'You must rekindle your romantic relationship with Mr McArthur; it cannot be just a friendship.'

She felt her stomach turn. 'Really? I'm not sure I could be convincing, sir. I left him in no doubt that I wasn't interested. Besides, I'm not sure I'm comfortable with the notion of using my femininity in such a way.'

'Miss Gillespie, this man and his vile objective must be exposed as quickly as possible. He has already shown interest in you. Gain his confidence. Our information, which is utterly reliable, is that he has been placed at Supermarine to steal Spitfire plans for his masters in Berlin.'

'Through someone like me,' Sarah said. Northcott nodded. 'But if your source is reliable, why not just arrest him now?' she asked, puzzled.

'We need evidence, or the case would be thrown out in a

court of law; hearsay is not enough to hang a man. He has no access to Spitfire plans working in Wages. My reports tell me he has been ingratiating himself with the girls in the Tracing Room in particular. He needs someone to provide the drawings. And who better than an Irish girl, fresh off the boat?'

Sarah recalled Gladys's comments about Rob and nodded slowly. 'Do you believe he was targeting me? I met him almost by accident at the cinema.'

'Are you sure it was chance? It is well known that the girls here frequent the cinema in Winchester most Friday nights.'

Sarah's heart sank. 'It was no coincidence then.'

Northcott sniffed. 'Highly unlikely. He hopes you are sympathetic to his cause. If we were to catch him receiving plans . . .'

Sarah's heart dropped. 'From someone like me,' she continued.

Northcott smiled. 'Exactly, Miss Gillespie, from you. That will give us all the proof we need; and it will prove your loyalty to our satisfaction such that there will be no need for any . . . unpleasantness.'

From a landing window, Sarah watched Captain Northcott limp across the front courtyard to a waiting car and wondered how he had received his injury. She had never met anyone like him. He was a strange mixture of jolly upper class one minute and tough resolve the next. On the surface he had seemed sympathetic to her situation, almost apologetic, but she had sensed how much he had enjoyed revealing his hold over her. Which was the true Northcott? she wondered. And what drove a man like that? Was it ambition, or a genuine desire to out a spy? If he succeeded, it would boost his career; even though Sarah Gillespie, prize idiot caught in the middle, would be the one taking all the risks.

A man in naval uniform was waiting for Northcott, leaning against the driver's door, smoking. He stamped out the cigarette and stood to attention as Northcott approached, then they both climbed in. There were no markings on the car. So, who did he work for? Was he Naval Intelligence or some other secret organisation? As the black car drove away, Sarah realised her heart was pounding.

She glanced at her watch. It was only four o'clock; still another hour and a half before she could leave. How she was going to get any work done with this to think about, she wasn't sure. Pondering it all, she made her way back to the Tracing Office. She was relieved she didn't bump into the Dragon, who would have undoubtedly taken the opportunity to interrogate her about her meeting. Both Gladys and Ruth threw her questioning glances as she entered the room, but Sarah went straight to her drawing board and kept her head down for the rest of the afternoon.

Working helped a little. There was no room for error; concentration was key, or you'd have to start from scratch with a new sheet of tracing cloth and a dressing-down from Miss Whitaker about careless work and the shortage of supplies. If her hands shook slightly as she relived the conversation with Northcott, no one knew but Sarah. It took a great deal of resolve to stay calm. But one thing was certain; she would give Northcott's proposal – or to be more accurate, his command – the time and consideration it deserved when she was alone.

16

14th October 1941, Hursley

Dinnertime was pure agony for Sarah that evening. She longed to be alone to sort out her conflicting thoughts and the arguments which had been circulating in her head since meeting Northcott. The conversation flowed around her as she picked at her food, but she found it difficult to concentrate and was only half listening.

But then Uncle Tom exclaimed, and everyone looked up. 'Well now, this is very interesting. An American warship has been attacked by a U-boat in the Atlantic.'

'When was that, Dad?' Martin asked.

'Last week. President Roosevelt has warned the Germans and Italians that the US will open fire if they enter waters America deems necessary for maintaining defence,' Tom read out. 'The US Navy will shoot on sight if any ship or convoy is threatened.'

'That's good, isn't it, Dad? Surely the Americans must come

in now and help us? They must see Jerry will not abide by any declaration of neutrality?' Martin said.

Uncle Tom placed the newspaper down on the table and sighed. 'It's not as simple as that, Martin. Roosevelt is determined to win another term; he won't upset his voters by reneging on his promise to keep the US out of the conflict in Europe. There is no appetite for war there. They still remember the last one and the loss of life.' Her uncle shook his head sadly.

'But they can't stand by and watch Hitler run amok here. They must see that he and his regime are pure evil.' Martin frowned at his father.

'I know, but they are removed from it across the water. Right now, it's politics before people. The world has gone mad, if you ask me,' Tom said, his expression glum.

'I believe it's only putting off the inevitable. When American lives are lost, the tide will turn in our favour. It has to. What do you think, Sarah?' Martin asked.

'I don't know,' Sarah replied. 'I can see why they want to stay out of it, but with things so bad for us right now, it would be a relief if they did join the fight.'

'If they keep attacking the convoys, the Yanks will do the right thing, I'm sure of it, Martin.' Tom gave Sarah a sly look. 'You're awful quiet, this evening, missy. Away with the fairies, in fact.' Uncle Tom laughed. 'Some lad caught your eye?'

'Don't mither her, Tom,' Aunt Alice said, casting her a concerned glance. 'Are you not hungry, Sarah? Are you unwell? I could make you some hot milk, if you like?'

'Heavens, no thank you, Aunt. I'm sorry; it's just that I'm tired this evening.' Sarah glanced out the window. 'Once we clear up after dinner, I'll go for a cycle. That should clear my head.'

'I'll come with you if you like?' Martin piped up, to her dismay.

'Thanks for the offer, but I don't think I'd be good company. I need to work off my mood and silence would be best.' She tapped the side of her head. 'Some demons to sort out.'

Martin shot her a puzzled glance but nodded. 'Ok.'

'The Dragon working you too hard?' Uncle Tom asked with a wiggle of his brows.

'Yes, yes, that's it exactly.' *If only!*

It was a mellow evening. The dying autumnal light painted the trees in glorious golds, yellows and ochre, and the hedgerows were bursting with shiny blackberries, waiting to be plucked. But Sarah kept moving. A chorus of birdsong and the whirr of the bicycle were the only sounds she heard. Heaven, or as close as. Sometimes, it was difficult to believe they were in the middle of a war when surrounded by such beautiful country-side. In the short time since she had arrived, Sarah had grown to love the place. The possibility of returning to Dublin had never entered her head until today's shock, but now she might have to consider it, albeit reluctantly.

Sarah breathed in deeply as she cycled up the Winchester Road and felt the tension in her body ease. If only she could confide in someone! But the captain had made it clear what would happen if word got out. Besides, who could she tell? Moreover, who could she trust? Sarah hoped it would be easier to think away from the house. And boy, did she have a lot to mull over.

Turning off to the left, Sarah pedalled along the narrow road, searching for the spot Martin had shown her the week before on one of their long walks. A few yards down she found it. Sarah dismounted, leaned the bike against the wall, and hopped over it where a fallen tree made access easy. Strictly speaking, the ruins of Merdon Castle were out of bounds. If

149

the military patrol caught her, she'd get into trouble, even though it was part of the Hursley Park estate. But Sarah reckoned it was unlikely they would bother to patrol this end of the grounds in the evening, and she skipped down the embankment into the old moat, now overgrown, the water long gone.

The ruins, at the top of a rise, provided a view of the rolling fields stretched out below. A more idyllic scene would be hard to find; just a pity she had such a knotty problem to mull over. Sarah plonked down on the grass and wrapped her arms around her knees. Staring off into the distance, she relived the conversation with Northcott. In effect, he'd given her an ultimatum, even though it had been couched in benign language. The consequences could be ghastly, no matter what she decided. Act for Northcott and a man's life could be forfeit; refuse, and her family would be snatched away from her.

From the pocket of her jacket, she pulled out the card Northcott had handed her and twirled it through her fingers. There was no crest or address, only Northcott's name and a Southampton phone number. An uninvited image of the man flashed into her mind. Was he who he claimed? He'd given little away, other than that he was in the Navy, but she assumed he worked for some other secret government organisation from the hints he had dropped, and the fact he had access to Supermarine's personnel files. That limp of his was bad. Had he been invalided out of the naval service and gone to work for the security services as a result? She knew next to nothing about how the security services worked or how they recruited. Was it normal to enlist the help of young girls just off the boat from Ireland? It didn't sound plausible, and yet that's exactly what Northcott had done.

A small part of her was flattered that someone like Northcott would consider her capable. And of course she wanted vengeance; a way to hit back. It burnt brightly in her mind all the time. And here was the British establishment handing her the perfect opportunity to bring down a Nazi sympathiser. A thrill went through her. Yes, it would be dangerous, but wouldn't it also be exciting? Wouldn't it ease the pain of Maura's – or even Da's – violent death? Perhaps not, but it was better than nothing. Above all else, it proved she had made the right decision to come to England. An opportunity like this would never have arisen back home.

But it was all very strange. She almost laughed aloud. Sarah Gillespie a spy! How Ma and Maura would have laughed and teased. And poor Da! He would have hated it so very much. So much, in fact, it gave her a little thrill. His shenanigans had been rooted in ideals few believed in any more, the cause of much pain and even death; at least what she would be doing would be fighting evil. If only she could tell Paul. She had no doubt he would be proud of her.

However, submitting to Northcott's demand without question didn't sit well with her. Surely spies were older, wiser and had access to major secrets; not lowly tracers who barely understood the plans they worked on?

But what were her choices?

He had placed her in a tricky position. Either she did as he asked to prove her loyalty to Britain, or she had to face the possibility of going home. That wasn't the end of the world – it was the threat to deport the Lambe family that was the death blow. And Northcott knew that. If that happened, the Lambes would never forgive her and she wouldn't blame them.

But what if Northcott or his source were mistaken? If Rob were wrongly accused, she would be a party to a travesty of justice. Was there even a modicum of due process during wartime? And didn't they execute traitors? Sarah shivered. She didn't want that on her conscience, even if he was guilty.

Shouldn't she do a little digging for information of her own? The notion appealed to her, but how was she to do it without drawing attention and giving herself away? So far, she only knew a handful of Supermarine staff. Would any of them be able to give her information? Ruth was an obvious choice, but there was something strange about her brief relationship with Rob. If Rob had tried to involve her in his scheme, as logic would suggest he must have, she hadn't agreed to it. And, if she knew Rob was a spy, why hadn't she informed on him? Unless, of course, she was Northcott's source – or a Nazi sympathiser herself. No, she would have to stay clear of Ruth.

Then she remembered. Didn't Vera who worked with her on the sets for the play work in Wages? If she could get Vera alone for a few minutes tomorrow night, she could ask a few general questions about the lads she worked with to see if anything popped up. The pretext for asking the questions might be fiddly; she'd have to be careful. Sarah couldn't risk Vera spooking Rob by letting something drop. However, overall, it seemed the most sensible course of action. Sarah would feel more comfortable if she could confirm some basis for Northcott's assertions.

Next, she had a pressing difficulty: figuring out how she was to secure the drawings without being caught. She wasn't even sure where they were kept. And how could she find out without giving herself away? Then there was the question of what a German spy would actually want. Even if she could get Rob the drawings he desired, wouldn't they be missed? And if they were, there would be an investigation.

With a shudder, Sarah's thoughts turned to Da. Was she never to be free of him and his vile past? Although she had played down Da's activities to Northcott, she knew well Da had been up to mischief over the years. He'd often boasted of his role in the War of Independence, but whether he had been active after that she hadn't been sure. There had been talk in the neighbourhood when they were children; insidious whispers about Da's violence and outspoken views, and scornful glances in the local shops as Sarah and Maura clung to their mother's hand. Sarah had grown up accepting it as normal, not comprehending how devastating and isolating it must have been for her mother.

Now, Sarah realised she had been naïve. Da must have been up to something for people to act like that. Did the British secret service know what he had been doing? If they did, it suggested the Irish authorities were feeding them information. That was a surprise, knowing how poor relations were between the two countries. And would Northcott's organisation really use Da's past against her if she didn't co-operate? They probably didn't even need an excuse to deport people. In a time of war, no one would question it. The irony didn't escape her. A fine legacy her Da had left her!

Sarah vented her frustration with a curse that caused the crows in the trees above to screech and take to the sky. Sarah watched them circle above her before they flew away. How she envied their freedom. Perhaps she should just take off; pack her bags and quietly disappear. But that would hurt her family, and she hadn't a friend in the world, except maybe Paul, and she didn't know where he was and had no way to find out. No, that was a daft idea. And what was there to stop Northcott carrying out his threat and deporting the Lambes in retaliation, anyway? Sarah gnawed at her lower lip.

Dare she enter Northcott's shadowy world? What the man

proposed was tantamount to using her as an *agent provocateur*. Wasn't that illegal? What protection would Northcott give her if it all went belly-up? Although new to these shady undertakings, she knew there would be nothing to link her to Northcott, and she had a sneaking suspicion he would deny all knowledge. She would be Northcott's scapegoat. There seemed to be only one solution to protect herself. She'd write it all down in a journal *as Gaeilge*; that way most people on finding it wouldn't be able to read it. But Uncle Tom would. That way, even if the plan resulted in her demise, the truth would come out.

There was one other rather thorny matter. She had declined Rob's requests that she go out with him, not only once, but twice. And the thought of being intimate with him made her stomach turn, particularly if he was a Nazi. She shuddered at the thought. How on earth could she do it without revealing her true feelings? There appeared to be only one way she could manage it, and that was to think of it as performing a role in a play. Yes, that might work.

However, to suddenly turn around and encourage Rob's advances now would look suspicious, wouldn't it? Especially if he were a fifth columnist in daily dread of being exposed, second-guessing everyone and everything? *Oh bother*, she huffed. This was going to be difficult. She would have to engineer a casual meeting and hope he might ask again. How to handle things after that, she had no clue.

Sarah took in the scene before her and knew she didn't want to leave; she loved her job and could see a life for herself here in England. She breathed out slowly. It was going to be dangerous, but now she had decided on a course of action, the near panic she had felt all afternoon lifted at last. She would act for Northcott and face the possible consequences.

17

14th October 1941, Otterbourne

With her decision made, Sarah didn't see much point in wasting time. She would contact Northcott that evening. However, she had to be careful. He had been adamant that any communication between them had to be kept secret. The phone box in Hursley was slap-bang in the middle of the village and in full view of almost everyone. She had never used it – for who would she be ringing? – so if one of the family spotted her making a call, it would be difficult to explain. Using a telephone box in another village would be a safer option.

Although all was quiet and few people were about, Sarah pedalled through Hursley with her head down. At the cross-roads she took the turn she hoped was for Otterbourne. All the road signs had been removed at the start of the war, but she recalled Martin talking about the other village only days before as they had passed the turn on their way to work. After fifteen minutes she was on the verge of turning back, thinking she must have taken a wrong turn, when she reached the outskirts of Otterbourne. She was taking a risk, but hopefully no one would recognise her; although it was possible some residents worked at Supermarine.

Sarah passed an elderly couple out for a stroll and heard the chatter from the open door of the pub as she cycled past. Finally, she spotted the red telephone box by the side of the road. To her relief, it wasn't in use. Leaning her bicycle up against it, she scanned the surroundings before ducking inside.

'Southampton 379,' Sarah asked the operator, looking down at Northcott's card.

'Insert your coins, caller,' she was instructed. Sarah did so, pushed button A, and waited for the connection. After several clicks, a female voice answered. It must be Mrs Northcott or a maid. Flustered, Sarah asked to speak to the captain in a faltering voice.

There was a pause followed by an icy: 'Who shall I say is calling?'

'Miss Gillespie,' Sarah replied. She caught her breath with a start. Should she have used her real name? Too late. Sarah heard the receiver being put down. Her heart was pounding; a few minutes more and she would have committed to carrying out Northcott's plan.

'Hello?' It was Northcott. She'd know that clipped accent anywhere.

'Good evening, Captain. It's Sarah Gillespie.'

'How delightful, Miss Gillespie. I do hope you have good news for me,' he drawled.

Sarah squeezed her eyes shut. 'Yes, I've come to a decision. I'm willing to help you.'

'Of course,' he answered, as if any other outcome hadn't even crossed his mind.

'There is one condition, sir, however.'

'Oh? Before you continue, might I remind you to be circumspect. This is a public line.'

'I am aware of that, Captain.'

'Jolly good. Do continue.'

'I would like your guarantee my family will not be affected by any of this. That they will not be . . . that you will not, you know, no matter what the outcome. I will do my best for you, but I cannot guarantee I will be successful. I've undertaken nothing like this before.'

'Don't fret, Miss Gillespie, I understand your concern, but I have every confidence in your abilities. I would only act in extreme circumstances.'

Not very much mollified by his answer, she swallowed a retort and replied. 'Thank you. What do I need to do now?'

'As I outlined to you earlier, you must reconnect with the gentleman. The sooner this is set in motion the better. Can't proceed until that happens.'

'That's all well and good, sir, but as I explained, that might be problematic,' she said.

'I hardly need to tell you what to do, Miss Gillespie; you're no schoolgirl. As he will be more than keen, I don't foresee any problem. Might I also remind you that this is your best chance to strike a blow and, in the process, help your adopted country.'

Sarah smarted and her grip on the receiver tightened. 'I'll try my best.'

'Excellent! I look forward to hearing your report. I will meet you on Friday evening at Farley Mount, at six o'clock. It's a famous local landmark. Do you know where it is? We can discuss the finer details there . . . in private.'

'I'll find it.' Farley Mount. Sarah hadn't heard of it, but hopefully it wasn't too far away.

'Jolly good. I wish you a pleasant evening, Miss Gillespie. Thank you for calling.' He hung up on her.

Sarah replaced the receiver. She'd hoped to get more information from him, but he must have feared someone was listening in on the line. With a sigh, she left the telephone box and wheeled her bicycle along the road. Despite Northcott's claim that reviving her 'relationship' with Rob would be easy, she couldn't see how it was to be achieved. If only she hadn't been so forthright with Rob at the dance that night. He would think she was barmy to change her mind. But first things first; she had to contrive an 'accidental' meeting. Work seemed the best place to do it.

'I don't think my painting skills are up to scratch,' Sarah remarked to her scene painting partner, Vera, the following evening at the Hut. They had spent the previous hour doing their best to create a garden scene backdrop. 'Though it could be more to do with only having three colours to work with.' Sarah stood back, but her efforts didn't look any better at a distance, even with her eyes scrunched up.

'We had to beg, borrow and steal to get even this much paint. And don't you dare ask for green! The army must have commandeered every tin in the country,' Vera said.

'If only we had some yellow to mix with that odd blue shade.'

'Well, we don't.' Vera joined her and surveyed their attempt, her expression as bleak as her tone.

'I guess it will have to be a winter scene if we have no paint for the leaves. This is beginning to look more Gothic horror than comedy,' Sarah said with a grin.

Vera's lips twitched. 'Don't let the cast hear you say that. They take it all very seriously.'

With a sigh, Sarah put down her brush. 'So would I if I had the chance to do more than backstage chores.' She looked past Vera to where the cast were rehearsing and had to suppress a pang of envy.

'Oh, it's not that bad, is it?' Vera replied. 'It's got to beat listening to the awful news about Russia on the radio every evening.'

'True!' Raised voices drifted through from the other room and Sarah gripped Vera's arm. 'Oh, no! They're at it again! I bet Anthony fluffed his lines once more.'

Vera followed her gaze to the outer room where the argument was in full flight. 'I don't think they have improved much, do you? The play will never be ready for Christmas.'

Sarah chuckled and clasped her hands together, putting on her poshest voice. '*The Times* review reads as follows: "Carnage near Southampton – The Hursley Players brought the long-awaited production of *Hay Fever* to the inhabitants of Hursley this Christmastide. However, we are sad to report that Mr Coward would not be amused to see the slaughter of one of his most celebrated plays. Luckily, the evening was saved by the exquisite scenery and clever stage management of Vera Taylor and Sarah Gillespie."' Vera bit her lip, trying not to laugh. Sarah reverted to her normal tone: 'Just you wait and see, Vera. We will be hunted down by Hollywood and whisked away to pursue our dreams of fame and fortune.'

Vera snorted and rolled her eyes. 'You do talk nonsense sometimes, Sarah.'

'It keeps me sane. Now, let's take a break. They'll want their tea soon, anyway.'

Vera, still shaking her head, led the way to the tiny kitchenette at the back of the hall. Sarah leaned against the cupboard as her companion filled the kettle. This was the perfect opportunity to do some digging.

'Vera, what's it like working with a mixture of lads and girls? Do the men talk a lot of boring old politics?'

Vera shot her a curious glance. 'Gosh, no. It's mostly sport. Some of them are obsessed with football, the rest with cricket. Tiresome for the most part.'

'But they must comment on the war sometimes?'

'Not often; only when something big happens. Half of them seem to feel guilty they aren't in the forces, fighting.'

'Of course, yes, though it's usually for a good reason, such as health or age,' Sarah replied.

Vera handed Sarah her tea. 'Why do you ask?'

'Oh, just curious. I've always worked in all-female offices. Was wondering what it was like, that's all.'

Vera rolled her eyes. 'To be honest, some of the lads are just big kids at heart. Us girls tend to avoid them outside the office.'

'Are office relationships discouraged?' Sarah asked.

'Not officially, but I've never indulged myself so I've no idea if it leads to a telling-off.' Vera gave her a knowing look. 'Has someone in Wages caught your eye?'

Sarah sipped her tea. 'Maybe.'

'Tell me more. I can be discreet.'

'Rob McArthur has asked me out a few times but I'm not sure about him. I went out with him once but came away puzzled. The fact is, I learned little about him.'

Vera shrugged. 'Rob's a nice enough lad and works hard. He's not long in the company and I don't know him that well. But I do suspect one thing.'

Sarah's heart leaped. 'Oh, what's that?'

'I reckon he's a lot younger than he makes out. He's always

messing around with the other lads or flirting with the girls, but sometimes it's as if he's putting on an act. Not that that should put you off. Could just be nerves.'

'And has he ever mentioned where he worked before or where he is from?'

'He has brought up Kent a few times in conversation, so I assume that's where he is from.'

Sarah nodded, but she was disappointed; she already knew that much. How far could she probe without drawing attention to either Rob or herself? She reckoned she only had a few more minutes before the others arrived for their tea. She'd risk it. 'He said some things which surprised me; political comments about the war.'

No reaction from Vera except another shrug. 'I can't recall hearing him say anything like that, but then I don't have lunch with the lads or go for tea break with them. Perhaps he is trying to impress you, Sarah. You know what lads are like.'

'Yes, that must be it,' Sarah said.

Before she could ask anything further, the cast piled in, led by Martin, clamouring for tea and biscuits.

It was Friday lunchtime. Sarah spotted Rob's tall form straight away. He was next in the queue in the canteen and she could not believe her luck. He had proven elusive the last few days, and she had despaired that the right opportunity might never arise.

As she approached, he turned around and greeted her with a friendly grin. 'Hello there, stranger.'

'Hi, Rob. How are you?' she replied with her most winning smile.

'All the better for seeing you, Sarah. I haven't seen you in ages. How are you?'

161

'Fine, thanks. Really busy; you know how it is.'

'I do. Here, let me get you a cuppa. Save you queuing with these reprobates.' Rob nodded towards his colleagues ahead of him and grinned again.

'Thanks, that would be super.'

'Would you like anything else?' he asked, indicating where the canteen staff were dishing up the food. With a shake of her head, Sarah held up her paper bag with her sandwiches. He glanced over her shoulder. 'The other girls not with you today?'

'They were down earlier.'

Rob smiled. 'Won't you join me, then? I'm sick of the sight of these lads. I wouldn't mind some civilised conversation for once.'

'Sure, thanks; I hate eating alone. I'll grab a table,' Sarah replied.

Heart thumping as if it would explode from her chest, she quickly scanned the room. This was going far better than she could have imagined. She spotted a small table at the back, away from most of the other staff. Sitting down, she opened her bag of sandwiches but her appetite had suddenly vanished. She kept her eyes on Rob as he progressed through the queue. If only she could like him. But the knowledge he was a Nazi sympathiser coloured everything else. Rob was always friendly, but it had a forced feel to it, and the expression in his eyes, as if he were constantly analysing her, was rather disconcerting. Even before she knew about his ulterior motive in getting to know her, there had been no fizz of excitement when she saw him, and that evening in the pub she had been uncomfortable and, worse still, bored. Now she had to resign herself to the fact that she would have to lap up his political ramblings and pretend to agree with them. Even worse, she would have to feign attraction to him, just as he was pretending to like her. It was almost comical. Above all, this was going to be so difficult; it went against everything she believed in when it came to matters of the heart. If he was who Northcott claimed, he deserved to be exposed and she would be doing the world a favour. Of course, there was the added incentive that the alternative to helping Northcott was too awful to contemplate.

As Rob made his way towards her, Sarah pasted a smile on her face, her heart beginning to pound. Well, she'd always dreamed of being a consummate actress; here was her chance to give the performance of a lifetime.

'Thank you, Rob, that's very kind of you,' she said as he placed the cup of tea in front of her, before taking the seat opposite.

'Do you always take your lunch this late?' he asked, stirring sugar into his tea.

'No. There was an urgent job and I wanted to complete it. The Dragon is a stickler when it comes to finishing jobs. A batch of drawings had to go to the printers by three o'clock and I didn't want to be the one to hold things up.'

Rob sat back in his chair with a smile. 'I've heard she's a hard taskmaster, all right.' He took a sip of tea. 'Is it always that pressurised, or are you particularly busy at the moment?'

Sarah stiffened. She didn't want to appear too eager to give information. 'No more than usual. New designs coming through all the time. The RAF is insatiable.' She picked up a sandwich and forced herself to eat.

'Yeah, so I've heard. I can't imagine why they keep wanting to change things. Surely the Spitfire can't be improved?'

Sarah shrugged. 'I'm sure whatever changes they make must be necessary.'

Rob narrowed his eyes and leaned forward. 'But what kind

of changes? I mean, the Spitfires that won the Battle of Britain were top class.'

'I don't know. I'm not an engineer, just a tracer. It's keeping us all in a job, so we really shouldn't complain.'

Rob nodded. 'Yes, indeed. But you are enjoying the work? Glad you came here?'

'No regrets so far.'

'All the same, it must be different to living in Ireland. I know we speak the same language, but we have quite different histories . . . and points of view.'

Sarah wasn't sure what he was driving at. Steady, girl, be careful! 'But a shared history, too.' She looked at her watch before draining her cup. 'I'm sorry to rush off, but I ought to get back,' she said, standing up. 'Thanks for the tea.'

'Do you have to go so soon?' he asked, disappointment in his eyes as he looked up at her.

'Sorry. I can't afford to linger; I'm still on probation.' She hoped he would discern regret behind the words, but she didn't want to seem too keen to stay. He might become suspicious after her previous coolness.

Rob rubbed his chin, his expression sympathetic. 'I understand; I've only just passed mine. But, before you rush off, I was wondering if you are interested in art by any chance?'

'I know little about it, Rob, to be honest. Why?' she replied.

'A friend of mine has paintings in an exhibition for young artists. Nothing grand, but he's awfully good and would appreciate the support. I have two tickets if you'd like to go along. It's on Sunday afternoon in Winchester.'

Sarah gave him a bright smile, her fingers crossed behind her back. 'That sounds great! Something different to do. Thanks, I'd love to go.'

18

17th October 1941, Farley Mount

The sky was almost black as Sarah reached Farley Mount on Friday evening. It hadn't been the easiest place to find with road signs removed. At first, all she could discover was that it was located west of Winchester. Luckily, she had come across a local map at Uncle Tom's and had made a quick sketch of the route when no one was around. For the entire journey she had worried that she hadn't made sufficient progress for Northcott. If displeased, how would the man react? Here she was, miles from home, about to meet a man she knew next to nothing about. She felt extremely vulnerable. To add to her woes, the rain had started during the twenty-minute cycle from Hursley. It was a drizzle at first, but by the time Sarah spotted Northcott's car pulled up at the base of the monument, her coat was soaked through and her mood was close to foul.

Sarah left her bicycle against a tree and obeyed the come-hither summons from Northcott, sitting in his nice dry car.

No rain-drenched bicycle ride for him. Pulling open the passenger door with a jerk, she greeted him, her tone short. 'Evening.' Sarah pulled the door shut and sat staring ahead.

'Good evening, Miss Gillespie.' Northcott glanced at her, his eyes straying to her damp and drooping beret. Sarah glared back at him, ready to scold if he made a nasty comment. Whatever he was about to say died on his lips, though they twitched in amusement. Northcott turned his gaze out towards the shadow of the mount and Sarah simmered.

While she regained her composure, she followed his gaze. Sarah could make out the silhouette of what looked like a church spire at the top of the hill. 'What is this place, Captain?' she asked at last.

'A ridiculous folly built by a man with more money than sense. In honour of his horse, would you believe.' Northcott snorted.

It was on the tip of Sarah's tongue to say something scathing about the English gentry and their quirks, but she thought the better of it. Northcott was obviously from such a background. No one rose from the gutter with an accent like that. Instead, she shifted in her seat, uncomfortably aware of the dampness seeping through her coat and into her dress. 'I would be grateful to know what it is you wish me to do, Captain. I need some guidance as I've never acted as a spy before.'

'I understand your concern but I have every faith in you. At the first opportunity, you must reignite your friendship with McArthur and gain his trust, whatever it takes. Most of all, you must encourage him to discuss politics as much as possible. If you hint that you have republican leanings, I think he will fall for it. If we are right about his intentions, he will be easily lured into revealing what he wants from you.'

'You make me sound like Mata Hari!' she said in dismay.

Northcott half-twisted in his seat, his lips a tight line of displeasure. 'Are you taking this seriously, or not?'

Despite being annoyed with *him*, Sarah felt the heat of embarrassment rise in her cheeks. 'I wouldn't be here if I weren't!' She flicked her hand out and skimmed the skirts of her coat. 'Nor would I have ventured out on this filthy evening on a bicycle unless I had resolved to do as you ask.'

Northcott harrumphed. 'I have no control over the weather. However, if you are squeamish about a little rain—'

Sarah wrung her hands and took a shuddering breath. 'I'm sorry; it's been a long week and I'm tired. But I'm a lot tougher than I look and you think. I *can* do this.'

'Excellent, excellent! I have no doubt you will unmask this scoundrel for us.' Northcott's fingers drummed the steering wheel. After a moment, he continued: 'The easy part will be reconnecting with McArthur. He has been systematically trying to find a co-conspirator amongst the tracing girls. You see, there is no one suitable for his needs in the Drawing Office. There's only one female employed there, and she's in her fifties.'

'Would that deter him?' Sarah asked.

'It would appear seducing older women is something he wishes to avoid,' he replied with a quirk of his lips.

'That would make sense. It would look odd and give rise to gossip. I can't imagine he would want that,' Sarah said. 'But how *do* you know what he has been up to? Is someone feeding you information from within Supermarine?'

'I have my sources,' he replied.

Fine – keep your secrets, she thought. Sarah ran through possible Northcott collaborators. Ruth was still top of her list. No one else jumped out, but it was something she would give plenty of thought to when she had the chance. If he had help within Supermarine, she would be watched, and reports sent back to him. She would have to be careful. Tempting as it might be to confide in someone, even Gladys, she could not risk it. Best not to trust anyone.

'How long has Rob been trying to find someone to help him?' she asked. 'Am I to understand no one was interested in him? Difficult to believe, for he's a good-looking fellow,' she said.

'According to the information I have, he was only a week at Hursley before he focused in on the tracing girls. Whether or not they were interested is irrelevant. That none suited his needs suggests romance was not his aim. His behaviour set off alarm bells and he has been watched ever since. It would appear once he found that the girls in question were useless to him, they were dropped,' Northcott said. 'He is clever, Miss Gillespie; don't underestimate him. I assume he is testing the water with each potential target to find—'

'A dupe?'

Northcott rolled his shoulders. 'To find a willing *accomplice*. Someone with your background will have his antennae twitching, and with your access to drawings you are ideally placed to help him.'

'Hence the many efforts to persuade me to go out with him, despite my reluctance.'

'Precisely. You are perfectly positioned to help him and I'm sure the possibilities have him salivating. Romance is the easiest way for him to find his helper, though these fellows aren't above paying for secrets, so don't be surprised if he should offer. Anyway, I'm sure I don't need to point out, this should make your job easy.'

Sarah almost laughed out loud. *Easy!*

'Well, as it happens, I have made some progress. I am accompanying him to an art exhibition on Sunday in Winchester.'

Northcott swung right round, eyebrows raised. 'I'm impressed, Sarah. Good work. You see; you're a natural.'

Sarah puffed. 'That's hardly a compliment. I hate deceit.'

'But it is for the right reasons and therefore justified. Think on that and how good it will feel when he is revealed to be a traitor. This is perfect. I know how much you want revenge for what happened to your family. Tell me, how did you manage it so quickly?'

Sarah explained about meeting Rob in the canteen.

'Excellent. I look forward to your report next week, Sarah. Time is of the essence; I cannot stress that enough. Be encouraging; do whatever you have to do.'

'But I cannot offer him plans just like that. Wouldn't it be suspicious?'

Northcott gave her a stern look. 'Of course it would. You wait until he suggests it. You must let him think he has persuaded you to act. I imagine he will encourage you to regard England as your natural enemy. McArthur will play on your republican sympathies – very well, you don't need to glare at me like that! – your *fictional* republican sympathies. Just ensure you create the right opportunity. Convince him you are sympathetic to his views.'

'But I was adamant I held the opposite view when we had that one disastrous night out.'

'Yes, but who would freely admit to being a Nazi sympathiser or a republican so soon in a relationship? If he questions it, tell him you couldn't admit to it when you didn't know him or his political stance. One has to trust someone before

169

you reveal something as dangerous as that. As I said before, talk about your father and his involvement with the IRA. If you come across as leaning that way yourself, he'll pounce on it.'

'I'm not sure I can convince him,' she said.

'You underestimate your abilities, Sarah. Few who have gone through what you have experienced bounce back so capably and rebuild their lives.' Was he being serious? Sarah studied his profile with interest. She hadn't expected so much empathy from him. 'Above all, act quickly. Time is not on our side, Sarah. I want him flushed out,' Northcott said. 'He is not the only fifth columnist the government needs terminated. The sooner he is dealt with, the sooner I can move on to the next rat in Berlin's pocket. These people pose a significant threat to this country. If McArthur were to obtain Spitfire plans unbeknownst to us, the damage to the war effort could be catastrophic. The Spitfire has proven to be a menace to their bombers – the Third Reich desperately want to know where the weaknesses in design might be so they can target them. But with you working for us, we can ensure McArthur is caught red-handed, mitigating any risk so the drawings don't end up in Germany. Just think of the consequences if he found a real ally and got the plans out of the country.'

'I understand all of that; however, what happens once an agreement is reached about the plans and I'm ready to hand them over?'

'If you can facilitate an exchange, my colleagues and I can be on standby, and will catch him in the act. And most importantly, the Jerries won't get their hands on the plans.' Northcott thumped the steering wheel, making Sarah jump. His pent-up frustration was seeping out. Precluded from active service, she

170

could understand his hatred of the Germans and his wish to scupper their plans and their agents.

'I'll do my best, Captain,' she muttered at last. 'Am I to write up reports for you? I assume most agents do?'

'Eh, no. Not in this instance, Sarah. I will write up any documentation required . . . based on what you tell me.'

'Are you afraid I'd leave something like that lying around?' she couldn't help but ask.

'Well, as it's your first time—'

'—and last!'

'Best leave it to me. Now, was there anything else?' he asked.

'Yes, actually. Do we have to meet here again? It's not very convenient . . . for me, it being so far from Hursley.'

Northcott sighed. 'It is imperative we are not seen together, Sarah. No one can know or suspect a connection. That is as much for your safety as mine.'

Sarah frowned at him. 'Then why did you approach me at Hursley Park?'

'I could hardly knock on your uncle's door. That was out of necessity and will not be repeated.'

'I don't have use of a car and would rather not have to travel so far,' Sarah said. 'Like you, I have an injured leg.'

Northcott stiffened and a swift glare made it clear he didn't wish to discuss such personal matters. 'Very well, where do you suggest?' he asked at last. 'It must be somewhere quiet and out of the way.'

'Do you know the ruins of Merdon Castle? It's at the northern end of Hursley Park. The laneway that runs behind it is quiet. No one ever goes there, especially in the evenings.'

He grunted. 'That sounds close to the village, but all right: I'll find it. Six thirty next Friday, then.'

It was a dismissal. 'Good evening, Captain,' Sarah said, pulling the door handle.

Northcott grunted again as he wiped the condensation from the inside of his windscreen. Just as she pushed the car door closed, to her surprise she heard: 'Do be careful, Miss Gillespie.'

No sooner was the door shut than he pulled away. *What a strange man*, she thought as she watched his car disappear down the laneway to be swallowed up by the dusk. With a weary sigh, she traipsed back to her bicycle.

At least the rain had stopped.

Upon her return home, Sarah stowed the bike in the shed. If her luck held, Martin and Uncle Tom would be sitting over their pints in the pub by now, and her aunt would be snoozing by the fire, allowing her to slip upstairs unseen and get out of her wet clothes. She crept into the house by the back door. To her consternation, Martin was leaning against the scullery door, cup of tea in hand, a reproving frown on his face.

'Well, well, where have you been?' he asked, his gaze sweeping up and down. 'Who's the lucky chap?'

Sarah pinked up but pulled a face. 'I wasn't meeting any fella. As it happens, I was meeting up with Gladys for a drink in Winchester. I'm sure I mentioned something about it at dinner.'

'I can't say I recall. A long way to go just for a drink,' he remarked with a frown.

'We didn't fancy the cinema and knew none of you were going this evening either. We just wanted a chat. It's been such a busy week.'

'Was Ruth there?' he asked.

'No, she wasn't able to come. She was preparing for her big date tomorrow . . . with you.'

'I see.' By his tone, she knew Martin wasn't convinced and wasn't to be thrown off by her mention of his love life. He went on: 'You look as if you got caught in the rain.'

'I did, but didn't you know bedraggled is the latest fashion? All the girls are going for it.' She spun around and made a mock curtsey, hoping her banter would put him off asking any more questions, but to no avail; Martin frowned at her again.

'If it was raining, why didn't you stay over with Gladys in Winchester? Seems silly to cycle home in a downpour; dangerous, too, in the dark on your own.'

'Oh, you know me, as silly as they come. It wasn't raining much in Winchester when I left. Besides, Gladys's landlady doesn't allow overnight guests and I always prefer to sleep in my own bed. Now, I best get out of these wet things straight away,' she said, moving past him towards the stairs.

'Sarah?'

She turned at the bottom step. 'Yes?'

'Is everything all right?'

He sounded concerned and she hated having to lie. 'Absolutely!'

'I have to admit I'm mystified,' he said, putting his cup down into the sink.

'Really? Why is that?'

'Mother told me you are going out with Rob McArthur on Sunday. I thought you didn't like him. You were very definite the other week after the dance. I seem to remember you saying something along the lines of "when hell freezes over".'

'Oh! That was the punch talking that night. I've given the matter a lot of thought since then and I decided to give him another chance. I can't become a hermit because of what happened with Paul. Weren't you the one who told me I must move on with my life? Rob asked me out again the other day when I bumped into him in the canteen, and I realised I might have been hasty before.' It felt as though she was betraying Paul's memory and a little piece of her died inside, but she had to be strong. She hated lying to Martin, but she had to make him believe it was genuine. If Martin were constantly questioning her motives, she knew she would fail. 'Since the bombing and all of that . . . well, I don't trust my own judgement. My head is all over the place.'

Martin sniffed. 'Will he be picking you up here?'

'No. Rob is taking me to an art exhibition in Winchester. I'm meeting him after Mass. I thought it would be an excellent opportunity to get to know him better as it wouldn't be a formal outing.'

Martin stared at her. 'Why would that be a problem if you like him? It doesn't sound terribly honest on your part.'

Flustered, and not a little ashamed, Sarah squeaked: 'Why all the questions?'

Martin's puzzled expression cleared, and he took a step towards her. 'Because I know damn well you're still hankering after that RAF chap. And yes, I did tell you to move on, but walking out with Rob on the rebound doesn't seem sensible to me.'

'Well, no one else has asked me out.' Sarah found there was a lump in her throat. 'What's the harm? I'd like to see if Rob and I can get along.' Even to her own ears, this sounded weak.

Martin's expression softened and he sighed. 'Sorry if I'm being intrusive, Sarah, but I feel like your big brother, I suppose. And Judith isn't here for me to boss around. If I don't practise on you, I might lose my touch; and that, my dear cousin, would be a tragedy.'

'Just my luck, eh? Thanks, you are a pet, and I do appreciate you looking out for me. You must miss her a lot. But isn't Judith coming home next weekend?'

'Unless she cancels again. I'll wring her neck if she does.'

'The lure of the big city. You cannot blame her, Martin. I wouldn't worry about Judith; she's just spreading her wings.'

'Oh, I don't worry that much. I know she's having a grand old time, but Mother and Father miss her, and I don't think she realises.'

'Don't be too hard on her, Martin. Maybe drop her a hint in a letter. And as for me, I'm no schoolgirl and I am used to looking after myself. Dublin was a tough enough place to grow up in, you know. I may be small, but I pack a punch. Now, I must get changed or I'll catch my death.'

'I'm off to join Dad in the King's Head. Fancy joining us? I can wait for you.' A strong undertone of apology was discernible in his words and she felt a surge of affection for him.

Sarah smiled back at him. 'Thanks, but not tonight. Work in the morning.'

'Aye, I know that, and that's why *I* need a pint,' he replied with a grin.

19

18th October 1941, Hursley Park

Sarah hadn't slept well and was panicking. Having lied to Martin on her return from meeting Northcott, she was anxious to cover her tracks. Martin was already far too inquisitive about everything she did; if he asked Gladys or Ruth about the previous evening, it could spell disaster. He would hound her for the truth. Worse than that, he would know she had lied to him and it would damage their relationship, something she prized highly. So now she would have to tell even more lies, this time to Gladys. In one fell swoop, Northcott was turning her into a vile human being. Only the thought her actions should result in the exposure of a dangerous man kept her from backing out.

As they finished their work at lunchtime on Saturday, Sarah caught Gladys's eye, leaned across to her and whispered: 'Fancy a walk before you head back to Winchester? Even a quick turn around the park?' She nodded to the window. 'The rain has stopped.'

'Sure. I'm not rushing back for anything. Ruth can go ahead without me, and I can catch the next bus.'

Once their work was handed up to Miss Sugden, Gladys strolled over to Ruth's desk. They chatted for a few moments before Ruth threw Sarah an offended glance. Then she waved goodbye and headed out of the door at speed. Gladys returned to Sarah, smiling. 'She wasn't happy at being left out, but I pointed out to her it was an ideal opportunity to waylay Martin on his way out of the gate.'

Sarah chuckled as they made for the cloakroom. 'How clever of you to use Martin. She did appear put out. That look she threw me could have curdled milk. I don't think we will ever be close friends. I can't help but find her annoying.'

'Don't mind her, she's as contrary as bedamned. Though I am fond of her, she always wants to know your business, yet she is the most secretive person I've ever met. I've lived with her for months and know next to nothing about her, other than she's from the southeast and has a couple of brothers.'

'Oh, really? I didn't even know that much. But now you say it, she rarely talks about her family. She doesn't make it easy for a person to get close to her. None of that would matter but I find the constant judging of my behaviour and my choices a little difficult to take.'

'I know what you mean. Luckily, she has given up on me,' Gladys replied with a smirk.

'How lucky you are! I wish she'd lose interest in my love life. The fact she's walking out with Martin makes things more difficult for me. She has a loose tongue, and there are certain things I'd rather didn't get back to him.'

'Ah! I'm intrigued. Tell me more.'

Sarah pulled on her coat and grinned. 'Not in here.'

They took the path away from the main house, heading towards the wooded area. 'Now, you best confess it all. What is it you don't want to get back to Martin?' Gladys asked once they were out of earshot of anyone else.

'It's complicated,' Sarah admitted.

'You'll feel better once you get it off your chest.' Gladys gave her a searching look. 'You seem distracted this morning.'

'A sleepless night is the reason, and it's entirely my own fault. Have you ever found yourself in a situation where you tell a small lie, but then you have to tell many more to cover it up?'

'Good Lord! That's most days for me.'

'Seriously, Gladys, I've messed up.'

Gladys tilted her head and gave her a kindly smile. 'I doubt it, not on the Gladys scale of messing up. You'd best spit it all out.'

Sarah took a deep breath. 'Well, there are two things. The first is I need to ask a massive favour of you.'

'Certainly; ask away.'

'If anyone should enquire, I met you in Winchester for a drink early yesterday evening. Just the two of us,' Sarah said, with a pleading smile.

'All right . . . am I allowed to ask why I need to say that?'

'It was stupid of me, but I had to meet someone. Well, to be honest, it was Rob. He has been at me for days to meet him for a chat. When I returned home, Martin started questioning me about where I had been. I didn't want to admit I'd met Rob. I panicked and told him—'

Gladys held up her hand. 'You were with me. I get it. No need to worry. That's what pals are for. Though I have to admit I'm surprised you were meeting Rob of all people. Not that I'm judging you. Listen, I'm happy to cover for you, and you should be ok; Ruth was out with a friend most of the evening, so if Martin should ask her, she won't know one way or the other.'

'God, yes, that's good to know,' Sarah replied with a sigh.

Gladys peered at her anxiously. 'But, well . . . you aren't in any kind of trouble, are you?'

'Oh no, not at all.' Sarah did her best to smile.

'Good. I don't mind covering for you as long as you don't make a habit of it. I'm so scatty I'd be bound to muddle it up on you.'

'You're the best. Don't worry, I won't ask again,' Sarah said.

'And the second thing?' Gladys asked.

'Well, that's more in the line of advice. I'm in a quandary, to be honest,' Sarah said. 'You see, last night I agreed to go out with Rob again.'

Gladys's eyes popped. 'He wore you down, then. My, but he's persistent. But . . . I was sure you didn't like him. I distinctly remember you saying he was boring.'

'Did I? It was more that he only wanted to talk about politics.'

'Exactly – dull as dishwater!'

'But you can't ignore what's happening in the world with a war on. Anyway, I think he was nervous.'

'Still, not my idea of the perfect night out,' Gladys replied. 'Although he's a nice-looking lad . . .'

. 'Yes, that is true, and that's why I'm so confused.' Sarah paused and stood staring off into the distance. 'I think I was too hasty in refusing him. You see, I still had . . . well, *have* feelings for someone else. What am I to do, Gladys? I do *like* Rob. But I still think about Paul.'

'Oh dear.'

'Yes, I know, but I've burned my bridges with Paul, and it is unlikely he will give me another chance. Anyway, I don't even know where he is.'

'I thought you said he had joined the RAF,' Gladys said, as they set forth again.

'Yes, but I don't know where he has been posted. There has been no communication from him, even though he promised to write. He has probably forgotten about me or met someone else. It's no use; there is no future in that.'

'That's not enough reason to date Rob. In fact, it's unfair on the lad.'

Sarah groaned. 'That's exactly what Martin said when I admitted I was going to go out with him, but I think what put me off Rob was you saying he had been sniffing around all the tracing girls at some point. That concerned me.'

Gladys laughed softly. 'It's true, though. When he first started in the company, he was always chatting up the ladies; but not only the tracers.'

'Did he approach you?'

'No. Why all the questions?' Gladys asked.

'I'm just trying to get a better picture of him before I take things any further.'

'Fair enough, but no, he never came near me. I know little about him other than that he lives in Winchester and works in Wages. I see him on the bus most days. Sorry, that's not much help. Ruth walked out with him as you know; maybe you should ask her,' Gladys said, looking amused.

'Oh no, I couldn't talk to her about him. That would be too personal. But you wouldn't know who broke it off?' she asked.

'No idea, Sarah. It didn't go on for long. Look, if you want my advice, why not give Rob a chance? He seems a nice enough lad. You have nothing to lose and if it doesn't work out, no harm done. Have you made arrangements to meet up?'

'Yes, tomorrow afternoon.'

'Excellent! You can give me all the grisly details on Monday.' Gladys wiggled her brows and tucked her arm through Sarah's. 'Now, did I tell you about Kenneth from the workshop?'

20

19th October 1941, Winchester

The tiny gallery-cum-shop was wedged between a post office and a fruit and veg shop. As Rob pushed open the door, a wave of heat and tobacco smoke washed over Sarah and she was instantly nauseous. The gallery was crammed with people, but Rob pushed forward. She hesitated at the door, breathing hard. A moment later, he turned and said something, but she couldn't hear him above the din. Sarah shook her head, hunching her shoulders, but he laughed, tugged her hand and drew her into the melee. Sarah's heart rate rocketed. Before she knew it, a glass of white wine was pushed into her hand by a young girl with a tray balanced precariously at shoulder height. Sarah took a sip: warm and it was nasty-tasting. Unfortunately, there was nowhere to put it, so she had to forge on, doing her best not to spill it over her dress.

Rob came to a stop and pulled her forward. 'This is Alfie, my artist friend,' he roared into her ear. He stood back as a lanky lad with scruffy clothes and unbrushed hair swung towards her. Alfie was barely out of his teens, Sarah reckoned. A pair of startling blue eyes scrutinised her.

Sarah held out her hand, but Alfie ignored it, continuing to look her up and down. After a moment, he turned to Rob and said something to him before moving away into the crowd.

'What did he say to you?' Sarah demanded, taken aback by the young man's rudeness.

Rob leaned down, gulping down his laughter, and shouted into her ear. 'Alfie approves.'

'Oh, well, that's all right, then,' she replied, with a quirk of her lips. 'Sociable chap?'

Rob chuckled. 'Not especially. Lives only for his art and pretty much oblivious to everyone and everything else.'

'How do you know him? Are you an artist too?'

'Good Lord, no. His father owns this building and happens to be my landlord. My flat is on the first floor and Alfie's studio is in the attic above me. Don't be put off by Alfie's manner; he's a fine painter. He's only seventeen, would you believe? Alfie's work is over on the far wall. Come on, I'll show you. I think it will impress you.'

They squeezed through to the other side of the room, and Rob indicated a section of the wall. Sarah gasped. There were about twenty miniature landscapes and they were exquisite.

'Wow! Alfie's really good,' Sarah said, peering closely. Rob smiled in response and identified some locations for her. She took her time examining the various pieces, enthralled by how Alfie had captured the scenes with seemingly so little paint or canvas. Sarah recognised one painting as a stretch of the quaint cottages of Hursley, and another as the Merdon Castle ruins. In fact, all the landscapes were typical Hampshire landmarks or countryside views, from what she could see. Looking at the prices beside each one, Sarah regretted she could not afford to buy one. Maybe someday.

'Afternoon, Rob,' a male voice piped up close by. Sarah turned to see an elderly man with dark-rimmed glasses shaking Rob's hand. 'Thanks for coming along. I appreciate your support.'

'My pleasure,' Rob said, before introducing him to Sarah as Alfie's father, Mr Atkins. They shook hands.

'Are you an art lover, Miss Gillespie?' Mr Atkins enquired.

'Not especially, sir, I'm afraid my knowledge of the art world is scant, but I know what I like. Have you heard of Edward Hopper? He's an American artist with a unique style. I read about him in a magazine last year. His work has an almost melancholy quality to it which, I have to say, I found appealing.'

Mr Atkins' face clouded. 'I don't hold much store by Yankee artists when we have so much talent here at home. In fact, I don't like them Yanks at all.' He turned to Rob. 'Why won't they help us out this time round? They should be fighting alongside us, not dragging their heels.'

Sarah winced at his words; she had unwittingly hit a nerve. Desperate to change the subject, she gushed: 'Yes, I couldn't agree more, Mr Atkins. We could really do with their help.' Sarah waved towards Alfie's paintings. 'And, sir, even I can tell your son is incredibly talented. You must be proud of him. He captures scenes so effortlessly. I'm only a short time here, but I recognise some of these places.'

Mr Atkins smiled. 'Thank you, yes, I am proud of him. Once this blasted war is over, he will go to art college: the finest I can afford.' He nodded towards the paintings. 'In the meantime,

I'm happy to facilitate little exhibitions for him and his friends. The proceeds go towards his university fund.'

'I'm sure he will be very successful, Mr Atkins,' she replied.

Alfie's father grunted, nodded to Rob, and moved away.

'I'm not proving popular with the Atkins family, am I?' she said to Rob with a self-effacing smile.

He chuckled in response. 'Never mind; I still like you. You do look pale, though; are you all right?'

'Sorry, I'm finding the heat and the crowd overwhelming. My head is throbbing.'

Rob tugged her sleeve. 'Come on, we've done our bit. Let's go for a stroll down by the river. That will help, I'm sure. It's a shame to waste a sunny afternoon cooped up in here. Besides, I can't afford for you to alienate any more of my friends.' Sarah glowered at him, but he just smiled and took her glass, placing it on the floor next to his own.

'Won't Alfie mind if we go?' she asked as they made for the door.

'Not a bit. There's a good turnout; he'll be happy enough I showed my face. That's if he even remembers I turned up!'

It was a relief to be out in the open air again. Rob appeared at ease as they walked along, but Sarah's heart was still pounding. The crowded gallery had made her fretful; the horrible sensation of being trapped was only a breath away. She kept a firm grip on Rob's arm as they walked on, and gradually the dread eased. If Rob noticed, he was kind enough not to draw attention to it, which was something in his favour.

Winchester's streets were busy with Sunday afternoon strollers taking advantage of the unseasonably good weather. It was so pleasant it would have been easy to forget, however briefly, that there was a war on, except for the number of uniformed personnel walking around. Just ahead of them, two small boys were ambushing anyone in uniform, looking for autographs. Sarah was impressed to see most of the personnel approached obliged the two small lads, sometimes bestowing a piece of chocolate or a sweet, which resulted in huge grins and much hilarity.

Eventually, Rob steered her down behind the cathedral enclosure before turning under an archway which brought them to a near-deserted street. Rob came to a halt, smiled down and swooped in for a kiss. Taken by surprise, she didn't quite stiffen, but at the back of her mind she was filled with distaste. Instinct made her jerk her head to the side and his kiss landed on her cheek. It took a deal of strength not to recoil completely.

He straightened up and frowned down at her.

'Gosh, I'm sorry. You took me by surprise,' she said, desperately trying to appear apologetic and not nauseous. Sarah knew well his pretence of romance was only a means to an end. She smiled up at him whilst digging her fingers into her palms. She should have been more prepared for something like this.

His frown melted away. 'No, I'm sorry. It's just . . . I couldn't help myself.'

She glanced away, feigning embarrassment with a hint of a smile. How much more of this would she have to tolerate? The physical side of this job was going to be the most difficult. Just how far would Northcott expect her to go? *I must remember why I'm doing this. This is for Maura. I'm doing this for revenge.*

Rob put his arm around her shoulder, and they ambled on down the street. 'I'm so glad I changed your mind, Sarah. I thought I had ruined my chances after our night out in Hursley,' he said. 'Sorry. I didn't behave very well. I guess I was trying to impress. I couldn't believe such a pretty girl as you had agreed to come out with me.'

What could she say in response? She rustled up another smile instead and cursed a certain naval captain and his machinations.

Away from the crowds, the street was a tiny haven of tranquillity, with only birdsong and the breeze in the treetops to be heard. It was as if they had stepped back in time. The ancient walls of Winchester College framed one side of the road, whilst on the other, the trees were sporting autumnal colours and throwing shifting shadows on the grass verge below. If only she weren't here under false pretences; she could have enjoyed the walk and Rob's company. Sarah hadn't missed the admiring glances he received from other girls as they walked along. They probably envied her. *If only they knew*. It was surprising he was unattached; but then, if he were what Northcott claimed, a girlfriend would be an impediment and a risk. With a sinking feeling, she concluded that it further validated Northcott's assertion that Rob McArthur was up to no good.

But how to reconcile all of it? On the whole, Rob appeared to be a decent bloke. It was hard to believe he could be a Nazi sympathiser; and worse, a spy willing to betray the country of his birth. At that moment, she hated Northcott and the world he represented. Asking her to use her sexuality to trap a man was repugnant; it made her feel cheap, even if it were all a ruse, and Sarah hated the deceit. The thought of this charade dragging on for months was almost intolerable. In fact, the more she thought about it, the more worried she became. If she didn't manage to convince Rob she was genuine and ready to help him, might he turn on her? Could he be a dangerous man to cross? Nazis weren't known for their forgiving nature.

'Have you been in this part of Winchester before?' Rob asked as they sauntered along.

'No. It's lovely here. This must be the oldest area of the city,' she said.

'Yes, as far as I know the college dates back to the thirteen hundreds, but I don't know exactly how old the buildings are. Of course, the cathedral is much older again. Have you been inside it yet?'

Sarah laughed. 'No. I'd be in serious trouble. Catholics don't enter Protestant churches. Well, at least back home they don't.'

'But that's just silly.'

'You underestimate the control of the Church back home. Protestant is equated to "English" and therefore "oppressor".'

'What did you say that night in the pub? Eight hundred years of British rule?'

'Exactly. Not something that can be wiped from the collective memory too quickly.'

'I think it's a shame. You would love the cathedral. It's a beautiful building, inside and out.'

'Would you take me to see it someday?' she asked. 'I'll risk being struck down by a bolt of lightning.'

Rob guffawed. 'Of course!'

Up ahead, Sarah saw the path narrowed and turned to the left. 'Is it far to the river?' She could just make out the sound of running water.

'Just a little further along. This is my favourite area of the city – I come down here often. It's a pleasant place to clear your head after a day's work. Though with the evenings starting to draw in, I don't get to enjoy it as much as I'd like. I find the flat claustrophobic. I'm not used to living in the city and I miss the open fields. But I'm slowly getting used to it.'

Rob motioned for Sarah to go ahead. Somewhere close by, Sarah could smell lavender in the air. Stretching, she could just see over a hedge into someone's garden. One small section of the garden was a riot of late autumn colour with salvia, aster and dahlias bursting from its borders. The rest was given over to vegetables. Sarah smiled; Uncle Tom's gardening tuition was paying off. A few months ago, she wouldn't have recognised any of the plants.

Rob poked her in the back. 'Come on, nosey parker! Don't dawdle. At this rate, it will be dark before we get to the water.'

The path swung round, and at last the river came into view. The Itchen was fast flowing after the recent rain. On the far bank, a weeping willow skimmed the water, and a raft of ducks swam downstream. The romance of the scene made Sarah sigh. It was inconveniently idyllic.

Rob moved up beside her on the path. He clutched at her hand awkwardly before capturing her fingers. Sarah was surprised to catch him blush before he looked away from her, out over the water. His other hand brushed along the top of the wooden railing between the path and the river. If she didn't know better, she would swear he was uncomfortable. She would have to try harder if he was unsure of her.

'This is lovely, Rob. To think you have this right in the middle of the city. It must be busy in the summer. Does the city get many visitors?'

'Yes, the place was full of cyclists and hikers during the summer. Many of them stay in the old mill up at the bridge. It's a hostel these days.' He frowned. 'I don't see the attraction of cycling around as a holiday, at least not in England with our unpredictable weather. Now, if it were somewhere foreign with lots of sunshine, I'd be far more likely to consider it.'

'Oh, I don't know, Rob. It could be fun to explore this area on a bike. Just taking your time, meandering about. I'd love to do something like that. Maybe next year.'

'You plan to stay around, then?' he asked.

'Why yes. I love my job and living with the Lambes. I don't miss Dublin as much as I thought I would.'

They stepped aside to let a couple stroll past, hand in hand. Sarah hoped he wouldn't feel obliged to be more lover-like again. That kiss earlier had felt like an afterthought rather than a romantic impulse. She almost laughed. Did he have a check-list of romantic gestures to draw her in? He wasn't terribly good at this game. If she didn't know he was a fraud, she would be confused by the mixed signals he was giving her. Most of the time, he chatted away as if she were his sister, not a poten-tial lover. Though her reaction to his attempts at intimacy on their first date might be holding him back. Perhaps he was afraid of scaring her off. It was almost funny: they were both acting their socks off.

'This path is famous hereabouts. It's known as the Weirs.' Rob broke into her thoughts.

'It's lovely. How far does it run?'

'Up to the bridge, but you can continue to walk the banks of the river for miles in both directions. Even as far south as Southampton if you have the stamina. This section of path only takes us up to Bridge Street.'

Sarah pulled a seedhead of grass from the verge and plucked the seeds out one by one. 'I can see why you like it here,' she commented at last. 'It's very peaceful.'

'There's an old bench a little further up,' he replied. 'It's a lovely place to sit when it's in the sun.'

'And watch the world go by?'

Rob chuckled. 'Yes, something like that. When I need to

mull over a problem, it seems to help. The solitude, I suppose, because the flat is always noisy.'

Sarah smiled half-heartedly, wondering what the nature of Rob's 'problems' might be. Perhaps persuading young ladies to help him betray his country?

'Noisy?' she asked. 'It didn't appear to be a busy street to me.'

Rob sighed. 'Traffic isn't the issue. The girls in the flat next door always have the radio on.' A flash of annoyance crossed his face. 'Ninnies the pair of them. And if that wasn't bad enough, Alfie likes to blare his music as he works. I've hinted to him several times it's a bit much, but he laughs it off, saying it "helps the creative flow", whatever that means. I can't complain to the landlord, now can I?'

'I suppose not. Mr Atkins would be unlikely to take your side. You could always hide Alfie's collection of records,' Sarah suggested with a grin.

Rob hooted with laughter. 'What an evil mind you have! Ah, I couldn't do it to him. I must put up with it for the sake of his art.'

'Or move,' she said.

'I wouldn't get anywhere else so cheap,' he replied with a self-effacing smile. 'Ah, we are in luck; there's no one else here.' Rob pointed to a lopsided wooden bench half-concealed by the pathside flora. 'Would you like to sit here for a while?'

'Sure!' Sarah sat down and sighed contentedly. As Rob joined her, he put his arm around her shoulders, but she had been expecting it this time, and she relaxed into him. This was going to be an audience-worthy performance. Only a shame Martin wasn't here to witness it. *Oh dear; probably not the cleverest idea to pop into my head right now,* she thought.

They sat unspeaking for several minutes and Sarah was happy

to take in the scenery. It was a beautiful spot, and anything was better than talk of treason.

'You know, Rob, this place reminds me of a spot back in Dublin near our old house. It was down by the canal. Not half as pretty as here, as it was a dumping ground for the locals, but it was a magnet for most of the kids in the area. Most days we played down there. My sister and I once found a couple of old crates and dragged them under the railway arch to use as seats and a table. We had some grand tea parties with the other kids down by the water until some of the boys thought it would be fun to throw our furniture into the canal.'

'Typical boys,' Rob said.

'I suppose so,' she said as she watched the ducks swim past again. 'Sometimes the swans would come. If we had stale bread in the house, we would sneak it out and feed them. Maura, my little sister, was half terrified of the birds, but I loved them. Such beautiful creatures, almost mythical. Have you ever heard of the Children of Lir, Rob?'

'No, tell me.'

Rob listened, head bent, as Sarah recounted the story. 'In ancient Ireland, there was a King named Lir. When Eve, his wife, died, he was left alone with his four children. Soon, however, he married again. At first his new wife loved his children, but eventually she grew jealous of their father's affection for them. One day, she took the children to a nearby lake. Using her magical powers, she put them under a spell, turning them into four white swans. She told them they would remain swans for nine hundred years, until such time as they heard the sound of a Christian bell. The poor swans endured endless misery, until one day they arrived at Erris in County Mayo. There they encountered St Mochaomhóg, who turned them back into humans. Taking pity on them as they were now withered with age, he baptised them and they were able to die peacefully.'

'That's powerful stuff! Can't say I know much about Irish mythology,' Rob said.

'I adored those stories. Probably the only thing the nuns at school taught me that I enjoyed. Those swans on the canal?' she looked at Rob, who nodded, 'I imagined they *were* the Children of Lir.'

'Of course you did! You have a fertile imagination, Sarah Gillespie.'

'Yep, and the nuns hated me for that. You had to conform, accept whatever they told you, or pay the penalty. But I couldn't help myself. I asked too many questions.'

'But it's healthy to question things. You must have posed a threat to their closed community.'

'And their closed minds.' Sarah winced as some bad memories came rushing back.

'I guess that comes from being cooped up with a load of women all the time,' Rob said with a shudder. 'Can't be a healthy environment.'

'They weren't all bad. Some of them were kind – the younger ones in particular – but there was one, Sister Brigid, who disliked me. I could never figure it out because I wasn't cheeky or bold, and I was reasonably bright, but she used to mispronounce my name deliberately. The first time she did it, I corrected her, thinking it was a genuine error. And that was my fatal mistake. From then on, she tormented me. One day the local priest visited and posed a Bible question to the class. Not one other child put up their hand, but I did and gave the right answer.' Sarah shrugged at the memory. 'That really annoyed her. When he left, she found an excuse to use the cane on me. Not that she was ever slow to use it. She was always going to my Da with tales of my so-called misdemeanours.'

'Of which there were many?' Rob asked, looking highly amused.

'In her eyes. I always suspected the old biddy got a sadistic pleasure from stirring up trouble.' Sarah cleared her throat. 'That woman is the reason I cannot, to this day, stand a bully.'

Rob smiled and took her hand, squeezing it. 'Good for you. Did you always live in the city?'

'Yes. A pure Dub, as we would say. Our house was close to the centre, but North Strand was almost like a village. A very close-knit community. Of course, it has been destroyed now. We've been scattered far and wide.'

'Do you miss it?' he asked.

'Yes, but it has changed forever now. It has lost its heart.' Sarah took a deep breath. 'Sorry for being mawkish. I have been avoiding thinking about home. It makes me angry to dwell on what the Germans did that night. I have to move forward and make a new life.'

Rob drew her closer. 'You have every right to be sad and upset. It must have been devastating. And to lose your family as well. I think you're coping very well, in the circumstances.'

Sarah shrugged, but there was a lump in her throat. 'Lots of people are in the same position. This bloody war! Did we learn nothing from the last one?'

'There were too many loose ends, particularly for Germany. It was bound to blow up again. Unfortunately, it doesn't look like it will end soon, either.'

Sarah frowned down into her lap, trying to think of something to say that would prompt him to reveal his true motives. If she kept talking about the war, would he jump at the opportunity? But instead, he lifted her chin and pressed his lips to hers. The kiss was gentle and not unpleasant, as she had dreaded when imagining how things would play out. But it still made her skin crawl. Obviously he would want to keep up the charade of romance for now. But it was depressing, not least because it could not have been more different to how Paul had made her feel. His kisses had been so welcome; they'd set off fireworks in her head and disturbing sensations throughout her body. Rob's kisses left her cold.

As he pulled away, she forced herself to smile up at him as dreamily as she could. She had to wonder if he was attracted to her on any level, but whether he was or not, he was using intimacy to trap her.

Suddenly, Rob's expression turned grim as he looked out over the water. 'I think there is something you should know. I don't want to upset you any further – you've been through enough – but there are many people who put forward the theory that it was us British who bombed Dublin, not the Germans.'

'Never!' she exclaimed, her heart thumping. 'I saw the planes; they were German all right.'

'Ah, but we have many downed Nazi planes from the Battle of Britain. It would be easy to repair some of them and use them to our advantage. In essence, to pretend to be a German squadron flying over Dublin. I know, I know; it's shocking. But don't you see? Churchill desperately wants the Irish to throw in their lot with the Allies. He is terrified the Germans will make a pact with Ireland. Just think, it would be the end of the war for Britain if the Nazis had airfields in Ireland. They'd be able to bomb us to smithereens. So Jerry might not have been responsible for that raid after all. Churchill is a cunning old fox and capable of anything. Look what happened at Mers-el-Kébir when he sent in the Navy to destroy the French ships.'

'But he couldn't risk the Germans using the French fleet,' she replied. 'It had to be destroyed.'

'There was no warning given. Many Frenchmen died, and they were our allies, Sarah. He'd hardly care more for Irish lives, now, would he, if it got him what he wanted?'

Her blood boiling, Sarah tried to calm down. So this was how he was going to try to turn her. Her reaction now would be crucial.

'But what you are implying is dreadful, Rob. I lost my family in that raid. I could have died.'

'I know,' he said, frowning down at her. 'But you may be blaming the wrong people. Hopefully, the truth will come out soon, though I have my doubts. The British government would never admit it.'

Sarah let out a slow breath and feigned outrage. 'If what you say is true—'

'Oh, it is! I have it on good authority.'

'Then I'm helping those murderers win the war!'

'Exactly!' he said, a triumphant gleam in his eyes.

197

21

20th October 1941, Hursley

At her aunt's behest, Sarah invited Gladys and Ruth to dinner with the family the following evening. Once the dinner things were washed and put away, Ruth and Martin went out for a walk and Gladys went upstairs to Sarah's room with her for a natter.

'Why, this is lovely. Lucky you to have your own room. I've never had that luxury,' Gladys said, plonking down on Sarah's bed and surveying the room.

'Yes, I know, me neither. I love it.' Sarah sat on the window seat. 'It was my cousin Judith's room for the brief time she was here.'

'Is that the girl who went off to London?' Sarah nodded. 'Tall, blonde girl? I only knew her to see; she worked in a different building. She was always very glamorous.' Gladys blew out her lips. 'I wonder what London's like. I'd love to go there someday. Do you fancy it? Could be fun. We'd have a ball! I hear there's plenty of work.'

Sarah tensed up. 'I'm not sure I do while Jerry is bombing the place to pieces. I think I'll stick with Hursley for now.'

'Must be exciting though. I've heard the nightlife is a deal better than sleepy Winchester.'

'That wouldn't be difficult,' Sarah replied. 'Even Dublin was livelier.'

'There you go. Think on it. It would be fun to share a flat and sample the delights.' Gladys sighed contentedly. 'That was a grand dinner. Your aunt puts on quite a spread. You should see the muck we get served up of an evening. No fear of me getting fat on my landlady's offerings.'

'My aunt never stints. I think she wanted to impress you.'

Gladys spluttered. 'Why on earth?'

'Aunty Alice is the most kind-hearted woman. She wants to welcome my friends to help me settle in, I suppose. She was very keen I invite someone here.' Sarah bit her lip. 'The best I could do was you and Ruth, of course.'

'Well, aren't *we* hilarious this evening? Just you be careful now. Don't forget I know secrets about you.' Gladys wagged her finger at her.

Sarah froze for a moment before she realised Gladys was referring to Paul and her doubts about walking out with Rob. Sarah made a face back at her.

'Charming! Well, spill the beans, girl. I'm dying to know how you got on with Rob yesterday.' Gladys smirked, settling back against the pillow she had propped against the wall.

'It was fine.'

Gladys wrinkled her nose. 'Fine! What kind of insipid word is that? Sounds awful.'

'No, no, it wasn't.' Sarah laughed. 'He was more relaxed and turned out to be good company. The exhibition was interesting, and Rob's friend is really talented.'

'Was it a posh do? Champers and caviar?'

'Not at all: cheap white wine.'

Gladys smirked. 'Oh well, there is a war on! So, was that it?'

'No. We didn't stay long in the end as it was crowded and uncomfortable. We went for a walk down by the Itchen before he walked me back to my bus.'

'Very romantic,' Gladys commented. 'I guess you enjoyed the *attention*. Was he all lovey dovey?'

Sarah pasted a smile on her face. 'Very. I think this is going to work out.' *God forgive me for lying to my friend.* Hopefully, someday she'd be able to tell Gladys the truth.

Sarah hesitated outside the Dragon's office door. She'd only just sat down at her desk when the summons had come. A little anxious, she knocked and waited, wondering what misdemeanour had brought her to Miss Whitaker's unwelcome attention.

'Come in!' the lady responded. Miss Whitaker was standing at the window as Sarah entered the room, and she greeted Sarah with a curt nod. Sarah always felt inadequate in her presence. It was difficult not to admire the lady's dedication to her job and her ruthless crusade for perfection, even if it meant misery for Sarah and her fellow tracers. Sarah guessed it wasn't easy to hold sway in a male-dominated arena with such aplomb. It was just a pity the woman was so utterly terrifying.

As ever, Miss Whitaker was perfectly groomed, leaving Sarah conscious of her own carelessness. Most mornings, she simply tied back her hair in a ponytail to keep it away from her face as she worked. When it came to clothes, her manager had a great fondness for tweed suits: today's ensemble was a russet-toned example, cream blouse, and her ubiquitous string of pearls.

'Miss Gillespie, do sit down.' The Dragon trained one of her withering stares on Sarah as she took her seat.

'Is something amiss, Miss Whitaker?' Sarah asked, bracing herself for the worst while racking her brains as to what she could have done wrong.

The Dragon clasped her hands where they lay on the desk and glanced at her over her spectacles. 'The very question I was about to ask you, Miss Gillespie.'

'Oh! I'm fine, thank you, Miss,' Sarah replied, taken aback.

'Are you sure there is nothing worrying you? Anything you would like to confide?'

'No, thank you, Miss Whitaker.' Sarah clenched her fists where they lay in her lap.

Her manager sat back in her chair. 'Forgive me, but you have been quiet of late. Your supervisor, Miss Sugden, has commented on it. I hope you realise that if anything were worrying you, of any nature, that you could come and talk to me. You are one of my gals now and, I like to think, under my wing. I won't beat about the bush, Miss Gillespie. Since you received that visit here in my office a couple of weeks ago, you appear preoccupied. I'm not trying to pry into your personal affairs, but I was concerned that the gentleman had imposed on you in some way.'

Sarah stiffened. If only things were different. Wouldn't it be lovely to have Miss Whitaker fighting in your corner: if it came to a showdown with anyone, Sarah would put her money on her for sure. Alas, that was not possible.

'Not at all, Miss. Captain Northcott's visit concerned my late father, that is all. He wished to check some details about his past.' Which was pretty close to the truth. She should have realised eagle-eyed Miss Whitaker would take note of the visit and the visitor and eventually ask questions. Was the Dragon curious or suspicious? The notion that Miss Whitaker worked for Northcott and was testing her suddenly popped into her head. Would she accept her answer? How best to fudge it if she didn't? She was reluctant to lie to the woman, not least because she suspected Miss Whitaker would see straight through any fabrication.

'I'm relieved to hear it, Sarah; however, I am still worried about you,' the Dragon replied.

'To be honest, Miss Whitaker, I haven't been myself of late. Some nights I have difficulty sleeping. I am missing my family, in particular my younger sister, Maura. We were close. My mother died some years ago, and I had to take care of Maura after that. I feel guilty, I suppose, that I survived, and she did not.' Well, it was true to a great extent, Sarah consoled herself. She missed Maura like crazy, but her lack of sleep these nights was more down to Northcott and his intrigues. How happy she would be when the day came that she no longer had to prevaricate or lie to anyone.

'That is understandable, of course. This war has already brought about so much suffering and pain, and few of us have escaped its reach. But I'm sure your family here can be a great support to you at this time. You should confide in your aunt, Miss Gillespie, or indeed your uncle. Tom Lambe is one of the kindest men I know. Wise, too.'

'Yes, he is. And they have been nothing but supportive; but I'd rather not worry them. I'm sure this will pass in time.'

'If I know your uncle, he is taking a fatherly interest in your welfare. Young girls stand in great need of an older man's guidance, I always say,' Miss Whitaker said, again with a stern glance.

'Of course,' Sarah replied. Miss Whitaker didn't need to know that it was a novelty for her to have any kind of father figure in her life who cared. 'The Lambes have been wonderful and I appreciate all they have done for me.' The Dragon nodded. 'I hope my state of mind hasn't affected my work, Miss Whitaker. I take pride in what I do,' Sarah continued.

'No, I have no issue with your performance. In fact, you are one of our best tracers, and that is why I am concerned. I feared you were unhappy or being imposed upon and might decide to leave. We do not wish to lose you to another company. Good tracers are in short supply.'

'Thank you, Miss Whitaker, but let me assure you there is no need for concern. I'm happy here at Supermarine.'

'Very good, you have eased my mind. However, there is one other matter before you return to work,' the Dragon said with a stiff smile. 'You are being courted by a co-worker, I understand.'

Sarah was impressed. Did Miss Whitaker have a network of spies or had she heard it from Northcott? There wasn't any point in denying it. 'I am seeing Rob McArthur from Wages. Is that an issue? I didn't think it was prohibited.'

'No, it isn't a problem as such. I merely wish to emphasise the need to be circumspect. You should not discuss your work outside the walls of the Tracing Room. I mentioned this the day you started here, if you recall.'

'I do, yes, Miss Whitaker. We don't discuss work.'

'Good, because you hold a responsible position with access to many secrets. This is something I highlight to all my gals, not just you, Miss Gillespie. Do I make myself clear?'

'Absolutely, Miss Whitaker. You have no need to worry. I am grateful to have this job and I would do nothing to betray the trust that has been placed in me.'

Lying was becoming far too easy. Skimming the depths of deceit, although currently necessary, shook her moral compass. Northcott had turned her into a horrible, deceitful person. Would the end result justify what she was doing? Eventually, when the truth was revealed, she would have to attempt to repair all the damage. That was, of course, if she survived.

'Excellent. We need say no more on the subject. Good day, Miss Gillespie.'

Sarah could have sworn she glimpsed disappointment on the Dragon's face as she turned and left the room. Whatever the test had been, Sarah had an uncomfortable feeling she had failed.

22

24th October 1941, Hursley

Sarah was sitting beside the fire after dinner, trying to concentrate on her book, but her mind kept wandering to her imminent meeting with Northcott. All day, her stomach had done somersaults at the mere thought of it, and all week her dreams had been haunted by him or Rob, to the point she dreaded the climb up the stairs to bed.

Hearing a step out in the hallway, she looked up to see Martin enter the room. He grabbed his hat and overcoat from the coatstand just inside the door.

'Won't you change your mind and come to see the film?' he asked. 'We could take the bus if you aren't up to the cycle. Is your leg acting up?'

'No, it's fine. Sorry, Martin, I'm going to give it a miss. As I said at dinner, it doesn't sound like my kind of picture.'

'I thought all films were your kind of film,' he replied, coming across the room to stand before her. 'Are you meeting

Rob instead? Is that it? I thought he loved going to the pictures.'

'No, I'm not meeting up with him tonight. We plan to meet in Winchester on Sunday, after church.' Sarah lifted her book up. 'I fancied a lazy evening. I want to finish this so I can return it to the library. It's nearly overdue and I can't afford the fines. Go on. Say hi to the girls from me. I'll see them in the morning.'

'Will do.' Martin treated her to a doubtful look before disappearing out the door.

Sarah sighed and closed her book. She hated deceiving Martin, but she couldn't risk telling him about the difficulties she faced. Glancing at her watch, she realised she only had twenty minutes before she had to meet Northcott on the road near Merdon Castle. Thankfully, Uncle Tom was out pottering in the back garden and Aunt Alice was at a neighbour's house, so there shouldn't be any awkward questions about where she was going. Hopefully, no one would pay too much attention to her evening stroll. And more importantly, she hoped Northcott would be happy with her limited progress.

Sarah spotted Northcott's car easily enough, as the setting sun reflected off the bonnet. He had reversed the Austin up to the gate of a field opposite the boundary of the Hursley Estate, close to where the fallen tree had damaged the wall. Northcott wore a grim expression as she approached the car, and her heart sank; he usually opened his conversations with bonhomie and smiles. His hat was half pulled down over his eyes and his coat collar was up. For a moment Sarah almost laughed. Every spy in every film she had ever seen acted like that when trying to be inconspicuous. Did he not realise how suspicious he looked? By his expression, she doubted he would see the funny side of the observation. Best to keep it to herself.

She climbed in beside him. 'Evening, Captain.'

Northcott turned and gave her a look which did little for her equilibrium. 'Miss Gillespie,' he said, unusually curt. He tapped his watch. 'You're late. Furthermore, this location is totally unsuitable as it is far too close to Hursley village. We will have to find a better meeting place than this. It is imperative we are not seen together.'

How paranoid he is, she thought, and mischief prompted her to flick a glance up at his hat. 'No one comes down here in the evening: you are unlikely to be spotted.' A grunt of disbelief was his response. She continued: 'It is difficult for me to travel great distances and not give rise to questions from my family. My cousin already suspects something is wrong and keeps asking if I'm all right. I had to lie to him last week when he caught me sneaking in the back door like a drowned rat, after our meeting at Farley Mount. Then I had to ask a friend to say I was with her because it was the only explanation that came to mind when he put me on the spot.'

'Did you convince him?'

'Yes,' she lied. All week, she had been catching Martin giving her funny looks. 'But the worst part is trying to defend my sudden interest in Rob McArthur. It has raised some awkward questions at home and my friends are mystified by my change of heart.'

Northcott frowned. 'You need to be more circumspect, Sarah. This isn't a game, you know.'

'That's jolly easy to say, but I might point out I was adamant I would not see him again after our first disastrous night out. And that all occurred before I met you and became involved in your delightful scheme.'

Northcott responded with a harrumph. 'Don't you realise? The merest whisper of something suspicious and McArthur might disappear without trace, and all my work will be undone. And that, my dear Miss Gillespie, will leave you in a difficult position.'

'On a boat back to Ireland, I suppose,' she said in disgust.

'Most likely, but never fear, you would have the company of your dear family to make the journey more pleasant.'

Sarah stared straight ahead. 'There is no need to reiterate that threat . . . sir.'

Northcott's laugh in response was humourless. 'I'm glad to hear it. Now, have you told your cousin anything?'

'No!'

'Will he try to interfere?'

'No. Martin's just concerned for me. It's not a problem. I am being careful.'

Northcott grunted again and drummed the steering wheel. 'Well then, have you anything to tell me? Anything *useful*?'

For a split second, Sarah considered lying again; but what was the point? Besides, the quicker this was over, the better for everyone. 'I met Rob in Winchester last Sunday.'

'I am aware of that,' he ground out. 'You told me you were going to meet him. Something about an exhibition?'

Sarah stiffened with annoyance. Northcott was showing a less pleasant side this evening. 'Yes. We attended the event, but it was uncomfortably crowded. Rob suggested a walk down by the river.'

'How delightful. Do go on. Did McArthur make his move?'

Sarah had to bite her tongue. 'He didn't waste much time at all. The conversation turned to the bombing in Dublin . . . the one—'

'Yes, Miss Gillespie; I do know to what you are referring.'

'And he tried to convince me it was a British plot to force the Irish to join the Allies.'

'Good Lord! That was a clever move. And did you fall for this ruse?'

Sarah sighed. 'Yes, I led him to believe I did.'

'And?'

'That was it. We talked of other things after that.'

'Hmm, so he has laid the groundwork. Very good. We shall have to hope he will broach the subject of plans sooner rather than later. You have hooked him. I knew you could do it. But you must appear co-operative. When he eventually asks for them, you must provide him with the most up-to-date drawings you can get your hands on. Working at Supermarine, he will know well what the latest mark will be. It is my understanding that a new high-altitude version is being worked on. Keep a lookout for those plans specifically. He won't be fobbed off with something out of date. It is imperative you convince him you are genuine and want to help him.'

'I'll do my best, sir.'

'When do you meet him again?'

'Sunday.'

'Do your best to encourage him along, Sarah.'

'Certainly; that is what I have been doing. I feel he is close to revealing his plans. However, there is something troubling me. Can I ask you something?'

Northcott grunted. 'Fire away, if it's relevant.'

'Rob seems to be close to one of the other tracing girls. A girl called Ruth Howard. They walked out together briefly, but they still seem to be on very good terms. Obviously, she has not provided him with plans or you would have no need of

211

me, but do you think she could be helping him? Or even just sympathetic to his cause? She was very annoyed with me initially when I didn't want to see him again. It didn't make much sense to me.'

Northcott continued to stare out the windscreen. 'I haven't heard of this girl. Trust me, if she were working with him, I would know about it. You are far too easily distracted. You must concentrate on the job in hand, Sarah.'

'I am doing my best in very difficult circumstances. Any advice you can offer would be appreciated. What do you suggest I do next . . . sir?' Sarcasm was the only weapon in her arsenal. Northcott threw her a nasty glance, but it was worth it to know she was needling him.

'McArthur is a fascist. Tell him about your father and his less-than-angelic past. McArthur may know of this already through his contacts, but either way he should be impressed. That should open up the conversation to all manner of—' He broke off as a head popped above the wall opposite. 'Good God!' Northcott froze, his hands gripping the steering wheel.

With dismay, Sarah watched the figure climb over the wall, then pull a large bag and an easel up after him, before walking down the boundary for a couple of yards. From there, the young man pulled a bicycle out from behind the hedgerow and strapped the bag and easel to the back carrier.

The man wheeled his bicycle along the road towards them. When he reached the car, he stopped and stared, first at Northcott, then at Sarah as if struggling to place her.

It was Alfie Atkins.

'Good heavens!' she exclaimed. 'Alfie must have been painting at Merdon Castle.'

Northcott swung round, his eyes wide. 'You know him!'

'Yes. What a coincidence! He was the artist whose exhibition I was at on Sunday. He's very talented.' Northcott gave her a look which bordered on murderous.

Afraid to react, Sarah sat still, cursing her bad luck, avoiding eye contact with Alfie. Of all the people to turn up! She knew Northcott would be mad with her, since she had claimed no one used this road. And worse still, someone who knew her had spotted them.

Alfie frowned at her, then continued on his way, wheeling his bicycle for several yards. Sarah sighed with relief; but to her horror, he stopped and looked back over his shoulder at the car once more before mounting the bicycle and heading towards the main road.

'What's his name and where does he live?' Northcott hissed the question.

'Why? I don't think he recognised me. He's just a harmless kid who paints landscapes,' she said. But Northcott's eyes blazed into hers. She crumbled. 'His name is Alfie Atkins, and he has a studio above Rob McArthur's flat in Winchester. I don't know his home address. He lives in his own little bubble, Captain. I doubt he even remembers who I am or where we met.' Sarah gave him Rob's address.

Northcott ignored her protestations and wrote it all down on a scrap of paper before tucking it into his pocket. 'Clearly, we cannot meet here again.' His voice shook with rage. 'I will contact you next week to make new arrangements.'

It was a dismissal. Sarah released the door lever, but just as she swivelled her legs around to exit the car, her arm was gripped tightly, forestalling her. She had to twist back to face him.

'Don't fail me, Miss Gillespie. Ensure you make progress with McArthur on Sunday or I will be extremely dissatisfied.

I have invested a huge amount of time and effort in this operation. I will not have it flounder because of you—' he glanced down the road at Alfie's retreating figure '—or a boy artist.'

Sarah glared back at him and ground out: 'Yes, sir.'

Northcott released her arm and started the engine. Sarah jumped out, then stood back and watched him pull off and speed away. *Hateful man!*

The light was fading as she trekked homeward, rubbing her upper arm. There would be a lovely bruise there in the morning, she had no doubt whatsoever.

23

Steel-grey clouds hung low on the horizon and the air held
the promise of rain as Sarah bade farewell to the Lambes outside
St Peter's Church after Sunday Mass. As she stood and watched,
they headed off to catch the bus back to Hursley. She waited
until they disappeared from view, half wishing she could go
with them. Aunt Alice was in poor spirits. Judith had cancelled
yet again, and at the last minute. Her excuse of being inundated
with work rang false to Sarah. Alice had spent all day Friday
baking in her honour, having saved up her rations for the
expected visit. If Sarah ever met this cousin, she'd have something to say to her about her treatment of her parents.

Sarah headed south towards the riverbank. A sharp breeze
met her as she turned the corner and she had to tuck her scarf
more securely round her neck. With a tug, she pulled her
knitted hat, which Aunt Alice had produced for her that very
morning, down around her ears. October was showing its teeth

215

today, Sarah thought, and increased her stride. Down by the river, the fast-flowing water reflected the bleakness of the sky. It wasn't half as inviting for a stroll on such a day; not one other person was walking the Weirs. Even the ducks were missing. Continuing at a brisk pace, she was relieved to see Rob sitting on the bench waiting. He was staring out over the water, preoccupied, and she wondered what mischief was brewing in his head.

'Hello, there,' she greeted him, stopping in front of him. 'Penny for those thoughts!'

Rob looked up and a flash of surprise crossed his features. 'Sarah!'

'Had you forgotten we were meeting today?'

'No, no. Sorry, I was miles away.' Rob patted the bench. 'Come and sit, please; you're a welcome sight.'

Sarah shivered as she sat down. 'Not too warm here today, is it?'

'Definitely a change for the worst.' He leaned over and kissed her, his lips a cold surprise and in sharp contrast to the warmth of his gaze. Luckily, she had expected it and didn't recoil.

'We might go for a coffee in a bit to warm up. How are you? I haven't seen you all week, not even at lunchtime. Are you busy?' he asked.

Sarah rolled her eyes. 'Need you ask? The work seems to increase exponentially every week. There's talk of them hiring more draughtsmen and tracers, though where they are going to put them, I do not know.'

Rob nodded, but it didn't look like he was listening. She studied his face; if she wasn't mistaken, he had been weeping; his eyes were red-rimmed. 'What's wrong, Rob? Are you unwell?'

'Ah, Sarah, you won't believe it. The most awful thing has happened. I heard about it yesterday afternoon.'

Sarah gripped his arm. 'Oh no! Is it one of your family? Your brother in Cairo?'

Rob shook his head and swallowed hard. 'No, my family is fine. It's young Alfie.'

'Alfie? What about him?'

'He's dead, Sarah.'

Sarah's breath caught in her throat. 'What? How?'

'He was found yesterday morning in a ditch just outside town. Looks like a hit and run some time on Friday night.' Rob sighed. 'He isn't the first, either. With practically no lights on bicycles these days, cars can't see you until they are right on top of you, and then it's too late.'

With horror, Sarah grappled with the news, her instincts screaming at her that this was no accident. 'Yes, it can be scary on the roads at night; but Alfie would have heard a car coming up behind him. Which road was it?'

'The road from Hursley. He must have been out painting somewhere Friday evening, poor sod. It happened on that dangerous bend.'

'My God! What a terrible waste. Alfie's family must be devastated, Rob.' Sarah's heart sank as she recalled Northcott's anger at Alfie's sudden appearance; his insistence on knowing his address. Her mind was churning with questions. When Alfie left Merdon Castle, he would have turned left and journeyed home via the Winchester Road. She tried to remember which way Northcott had turned when he got to the main road. But she had been too preoccupied, mulling over their conversation and nursing her grievances. Northcott lived in Southampton; he must have gone in the opposite direction to Alfie: he would have taken a right turn. Still, he had been livid. Was he that concerned about being seen with her that he would have—? Could Northcott have followed Alfie onto the Winchester Road and *killed him*? It would be easy to make it look like a hit and run. Everyone would assume it was a terrible accident.

'They are in an awful state, as you can imagine,' Rob said, breaking into her jumbled thoughts. 'Mr Atkins came by the studio first thing yesterday morning. Alfie hadn't come home on Friday evening and he was worried about him. He thought Alfie might have worked through the night in the studio. He had done so a couple of times before. Time was something Alfie didn't pay much attention to. But I would usually hear him knocking about or playing his music, and I told Mr Atkins I hadn't heard Alfie at all the previous evening. Of course he had to check, so I went upstairs with him. The attic was empty. The best advice I could give him was to go to the police and report Alfie missing. But just as Mr Atkins arrived at the station, a local farmer came in and reported finding a body out on the Winchester Road.'

'Poor Mr Atkins!'

'Yes, and then he had to identify the body once they brought Alfie to the morgue. Later, he came back to the studio and I found him sitting on the stairs, sobbing his eyes out, wondering how he was going to break the news to his wife. Alfie was their only child.'

Sarah closed her eyes as adrenaline pumped through her. If only she hadn't admitted she knew Alfie. This was all her fault. Unless it was a genuine accident . . . No! That would be too much of a coincidence. But what threat could Alfie have really posed to Northcott? It didn't make sense; but at least she knew what kind of ruthless man she was dealing with now. Could the secret service get away with such behaviour? Unfortunately, there was no one she could ask – certainly not Northcott.

An icy gust blew along the riverbank and Sarah shivered. She tucked her hand through Rob's arm. 'Come on, it's freezing here. I think we could both do with a stiff drink.'

Rob glanced at his watch. 'An excellent idea. If we hurry, we can catch the Fox and Goose before it shuts for the afternoon. It isn't too far from here.'

The Fox and Goose was half empty; most of the clientele were flat-capped old men, sitting over their pints, or nursing a glass of spirits in the gloom. A fire smouldered and smoked in the grate, and every so often released puffs of smoke out into the room. Sarah's eyes watered. Decades of that smoke had stained the ceiling and walls to a rich mahogany. Sarah headed for a table near the window, as far away from the fireplace as she could get, while Rob went to the bar. She was still shivering, but it wasn't from the cold. How was she to remain composed? The news about Alfie had shocked her deeply. But she had to act normally. To let down her guard now might prove fatal. How naïve she had been; this was no game.

The door pushed open and a middle-aged couple entered, arm in arm. The man's gaze swept the pub and rested on her for a few moments. Sarah froze. Did the man's gaze linger just a little too long? Under her lashes she watched the new arrivals, heart thumping, as they searched for a free table. Eventually, the couple sat at a table on the far side of the bar and Sarah's breathing slowed. She *was* becoming paranoid.

Rob returned and placed a welcome gin and tonic down in front of her. She had to resist the urge to down it in one go.

'To Alfie,' Rob said, clinking her glass with his malt whisky.

'To Alfie,' she echoed.

'I still can't believe it, Sarah. I'll miss the poor little blighter.' Rob scratched his head, as if bewildered. 'He was a queer fish; totally absorbed in his work. He was one of those characters you only come across once in a lifetime, I suspect. Sometimes, I'd sit and watch him paint up in the studio. He didn't even notice me, most of the time. It was a fascinating process, to watch a scene evolve before your eyes. The tiniest mark with his knife or a brush, and suddenly it would come to life. But I don't need to tell you. You saw the results for yourself.'

His words twisted her gut, but what could she say? 'Yes, he was exceptionally talented. Such a shame that so few will get to see his work now.' The platitudes rolled off her tongue far too easily. In that moment, she hated what she had become. It probably had something to do with the company she was keeping of late.

'Or the art he was yet to create,' Rob said with a sigh. 'He could have gone on to great things.'

'I'm glad I met him, even if it was only briefly,' she said.

'Poor old Alfie. Of course, you do realise he could have met you the following day and he wouldn't have had a clue who you were.'

His words stabbed her conscience, and she took another gulp of her gin. If only she hadn't said his name when he had stopped in front of Northcott's car. 'Did he often paint outdoors?' she asked.

'He did most days, weather permitting, but every evening he'd be up in the studio by the time I'd get home. I'd hear the music halfway down the street.' Rob's tone was bleak. Sarah reached over and held his hand. Rob couldn't be all bad to be so affected by the young man's death.

They sat in companionable silence for several minutes.

'Drew, is that you, old man?' A young man approached their table, a wide grin on his face. He slapped Rob's shoulder. 'I haven't seen you in ages. Not since we left school. What are you doing in Winchester?'

Rob's grip on her hand tightened. He turned to face the man and blinked. 'I'm sorry, I think you must have mistaken me for someone else.'

The man stalled, frowning down at Rob. 'Oh! Sorry, mate, my mistake.' His tone and puzzled expression suggested otherwise, and Sarah studied Rob's reaction closely. He was blushing.

Rob cast the man a peculiar glance before looking down into his glass, his body rigid. The stranger nodded to Sarah, his face flushing bright red before he walked away, shaking his head.

'He seemed sure he knew you,' Sarah said. *Rob isn't his real name.*

Rob shrugged. 'Happens all the time. I have one of those faces, I suppose.' Then he seemed to shake off his ghosts. 'Pity you didn't come to the cinema; I missed you on Friday night. It was a brilliant film.'

Sarah played along with the change of subject. 'I had an Agatha Christie to finish and I was dog tired. Martin told me all about *The Maltese Falcon* yesterday morning over breakfast. In fact, he has been raving about it ever since. He is a big Humphrey Bogart fan.'

'As am I! It was marvellous.'

'If it's still on next Friday, I'll go and see it,' she said.

'Let me know if you do want to go. I'd be only too glad to see it again.'

'Sure, why not?' she replied, doing her best to smile.

'Thank God the cinemas are open. Films are a great escape from reality just now.'

'Very true. It's nothing but bad news. The war, now Alfie . . .'

Rob frowned across at her. 'I know; poor Alfie's death must have come as a shock to you, too.'

A shock! It was utterly terrifying. *If only you knew!* Sarah sighed. 'I'm finding it difficult to comprehend. He was far too young to die.'

'I know. I'm struggling to make sense of it, too,' Rob said. 'If it wasn't for this bloody war and blackout, the poor little sod would still be alive.'

'I wish to God it would end soon,' she said.

'Well, it won't while people insist on casting the Germans as the only baddies, now will it?' Rob said with a frown. He swallowed the rest of his whisky. 'When will this country see sense?'

'You know, after what you said about what happened in Dublin . . .' she lowered her voice, '. . . that it might not have been Jerry? I have been thinking about little else. And do you know what? It makes so much sense. Now, I have to question what I am doing here helping the British war effort.'

He nodded vigorously. 'I can understand that completely. If it all became common knowledge, I think it would push the Irish towards the German cause.'

'You could be right. My father was a staunch republican. He believed that an alliance with Germany was the best option for the country, both economically and politically.'

'And what do *you* believe?' Rob asked, almost in a whisper.

'I think he may have had the right of it.' *God forgive me!* Sarah cast her eyes down before taking a large swallow of gin. If ever there was a time for Dutch courage, this was it.

'Well, I've read a lot, Sarah, and not just the British press, which you might not realise is heavily censored. The truth about the Nazis is different to what we are being fed here. My God, that country is a marvel. They have rebuilt their economy from the ruins of the Great War. Look what they have achieved in such a short time.'

'Yes, but what about the rumours about what they are doing to the Jews?' She couldn't help herself. The nonsense he was prepared to spout sickened her.

'All lies, Sarah. The Allies are carrying out a propaganda war because it is the only way they can justify keeping this ridiculous war going. And the Jews are funding it all.'

'I see.'

'Do you? You have been a direct victim. You lost your sister, your father, and your home in an instant. Don't you want revenge?'

A shiver ran through Sarah's body as she thought of her little sister. That much was true; she did want revenge, but the nature of it was not what Rob McArthur envisaged. 'Yes, but what can I do?' she asked at last, casting him her best doleful gaze.

Rob reached across and caressed her hand where it lay on the table. 'There's plenty you and I can do, Sarah. Finish up your drink and we can go back to my flat.' He looked around the pub. 'It's not safe to talk here.'

24

Sarah followed Rob up the dingy stairway to his first-floor flat and waited as he rooted in his overcoat pocket for his keys. A squeal of girlish laughter came from the flat down the hallway. Rob turned to Sarah and threw his eyes to heaven. Two other doorways led off the landing and another flight of stairs led upwards into the gloom: presumably to poor Alfie's attic.

'I can show you the studio, if you like,' Rob said, following her gaze. 'There's a lot of Alfie's stuff still up there. It might be your last chance to see his work. I imagine Mr Atkins will be along any day now to remove it.'

'Yes, I'd like that,' she said, happy to put off the conversation she was now dreading.

Rob put his keys back in his pocket and led the way up the narrow staircase. There was only one door off the tiny landing at the top, and it stood ajar. Rob waved her through. It was a much brighter space than Sarah had expected. Ancient roof beams formed an apex above her head, and two large roof lights let the daylight flood in to the area. Alfie's easel, with a half-completed canvas, stood in the centre. Beside it, a large table was covered in brushes, paint, and pieces of rag. A glass jar held a further array of clean brushes and scattered all about were paintings in various stages of completion. Some leaned against the walls, others were heaped up in piles.

'Gosh, he was prolific,' Sarah remarked, picking up a painting from the floor.

Rob walked further down the room to where an ancient gramophone and a stack of records teetered on a three-legged table. 'I might ask Atkins if I can have this blasted thing, for old times' sake,' Rob said.

'I thought you hated the racket it made.'

'I did, but I guess I'm a sentimental fool when it comes down to it. Anyway, it was more what Alfie played on it that I objected to.' Rob picked up the top record and cleaned off the dust with his sleeve. 'It's all classical stuff; not really my thing.'

Sarah doubted Rob was ever sentimental, but she smiled back at him. As a shiver-inducing draught swept through the attic, Sarah could see the old roof felt lifting in the wind. 'How did he work up here in the wintertime? It's absolutely freezing.'

'There are a few slates missing, but I don't think he noticed,' Rob grimaced. 'A strange kid at the best of times.'

'And what's through there?' Sarah asked, pointing to a door at the end of the room.

Rob swung around. 'A sheer drop if you're not careful. It's locked these days. They used to use this as a storeroom for the shop below. That door leads to a metal staircase which takes you down to the yard at the rear. The ladder is lethal, though; it's half rusted through.'

Sarah stooped down and picked up another canvas, showing a riverside scene. 'This must be along the Itchen somewhere,' she said, showing it to Rob.

He nodded. 'Could be.' Rob looked about the room. 'I'm going to miss him.'

'Let's go, Rob. It's too sad up here,' she said, looking down at another half-finished landscape. It was the church in Hursley.

Rob gave the key another twist and the door to his flat opened. He stood back and gestured for her to precede him. 'It's not much,' he said with a quirk of his eyebrow, 'but it's home sweet home.'

Sarah gazed around the tiny flat. It was basic but clean, though the threadbare condition of the rug on the floor hinted at better days, and the wallpaper bore the marks of a multitude of tenants over many years. An open door led off to another room, which she imagined was Rob's bedroom. Against the back wall was a rickety-looking sink, a gas ring and a couple of cupboards. The rest of the furniture comprised two arm-chairs, a small table and some shelves stacked with books and newspapers. As she took it all in, she realised that there was something peculiar about the place. There were no photographs or personal things lying about. In fact, it was the kind of place you could quit at speed and leave no trace of who you were. With a start, she realised she was thinking like a spy already.

Nerves jangling, Sarah went to the window and peered down into the street, while Rob bent down to light the paraffin heater. With relief, she noted that there was no sign of the couple from the bar. The man had looked up as they had left and had passed some remark to his companion. During the short walk to Rob's flat, Sarah had had to restrain the urge to keep looking back to check if they were being followed.

'I'd keep your coat on for now,' Rob said. 'The room will take a minute or two to warm up.' He reached over and pulled her towards him. 'Of course, there are other ways to keep warm,' he said, gazing down at her.

Doing her best to ignore the lurch of her stomach, she smiled. 'Now, now; I'm not that kind of girl, Rob.'

To her amazement, Rob released her, and coloured from the neck up. 'How about a cuppa?' he asked, his voice wobbling.

'Sure,' she said. 'Milk, no sugar.'

Rob crossed over to the small kitchen area and pottered about making the tea, his back to her. A convenient activity, she thought, to hide his obvious embarrassment.

Sarah went over to the shelves, pretending to scan them. What was that all about? Sometimes he came across as gauche; not the near-lothario Gladys made him out to be. But then she spotted something that struck her as incongruous. There were several books in foreign languages, stacked one on top of the other. One stood out. The title on the spine was in that strange font the Germans used. You saw it all the time in the newsreels. Sarah racked her brain: it was called 'Fraktur', wasn't it? She pulled the book out and flicked through the pages. She was sure it was German. Still, he had admitted he was something of a language expert. Was it suspicious that he had several books in German, or was it perfectly innocent?

'Do you read German?' Rob asked, almost making her jump.

'No, I'm afraid not. The nuns at school didn't think it a necessity,' she said, pushing the book back into its place.

Sarah sat down beside the heater and watched him. Soon the paraffin fumes were more noticeable in the room. They reminded her of home, and her grumblings about being sent by her mother to fetch fuel to keep their heater filled. They were horrible, smelly things, those old stoves, but you couldn't deny it was good to warm your hands and feet before one on a cold evening. Unfortunately, if Da was home, he always monopolised it. Thankfully, his love of drink and his mates kept him down the pub most evenings. A blessing in more ways than one. With a sigh, she dismissed the image of her father; he was the last person she wanted to think about.

'Darn it!' Rob exclaimed, turning towards her. 'I've no milk. I'll just run next door and borrow some from the girls.'

'Sure.'

As soon as he was out the door, Sarah jumped up and searched through the shelves again. Nothing else stood out. Dare she check out the bedroom? Quickly, she went to the door of the flat and listened. There was a distant rumble of voices but no footsteps. Sarah dashed to Rob's bedroom and looked around the door. A quick sweep of the room revealed a single bed, a nightstand and a chest of drawers on top of which lay more books. Sarah scooted over and scanned them. Several were about Irish history. Great hefty tomes they were, too. He probably knew more about the subject than she did if he had read all of these. No doubt it had been research to help him gain her trust. She took one last look around the room. Again, there was a strange absence of personal effects. She didn't dare stay any longer. Heart pounding, she leaped across the outer room, sitting back down just as Rob came in the door. He held a small jug aloft. 'Success.'

'That was lucky,' she replied.

'Yes, and I've no qualms borrowing from them. They are always at the door looking for something from me.' He pulled out some cups from the cupboard.

Sarah dreaded the conversation to come and hurriedly sought a safe topic. 'Do you think Mr Atkins will let out the attic?'

Rob gave a shrug. 'It would need a great deal of work to rent it out as a flat. He might just let it out as a studio to another artist. Hopefully one not so fond of loud music as Alfie. It will boil down to money and I don't think Atkins is flush with it. The gallery doesn't make much. He's a music teacher – piano, I believe.'

'Well, he hasn't spent much on this place, by the look of it. Gosh, sorry, Rob, that's a bit rude of me!'

Rob chuckled. 'No offence taken. I agree wholeheartedly. But that's why it's so cheap.' Rob turned back to the now boiling kettle. He sighed. 'Poor Alfie; still can't believe he's gone. And such a horrible way to die. I only hope it was instant.'

'I know. It would be awful to think he had been lying injured and could have been saved if he'd been found sooner.'

Rob paused with the kettle in his hand. 'Lord! What an awful thought.' He returned to his task.

'But doesn't it seem odd to you?' she asked.

'What?'

'Well, the driver of the car must have known they had hit something. Wouldn't they stop and check?'

'I don't know. Maybe they only clipped Alfie's bike, or they passed him at speed and he just lost his balance. He probably had art stuff on the back carrier – that would have made him unstable. Could have hit his head when he fell.'

'Yes, of course, it must have been something like that.'

If only she could be sure Northcott hadn't done it. But how was she to find out? Another part of her didn't want it confirmed.

Sarah watched as Rob stirred the milk into the tea. 'How domesticated you are!' she said, hoping to lighten the mood.

'Needs must. I'm almost a year living away from home. My mother would be proud,' he quipped. 'So, what do you make of *chez Rob*?' he asked.

'It's perfect for you, isn't it?'

'Without doubt; otherwise I would have had to share some place with a group of lads, and I didn't fancy that. I prefer my own company after years of having to share with my brother. My only gripe is sharing the bathroom with the two other flats.' He sighed heavily. 'There are girls in both, God help me, and they hog the bathroom. The things I find in there sometimes!'

Sarah laughed. 'Things to make you blush?'

Rob nodded. 'They just laugh when I complain. Still, I hope to find somewhere better in the near future.'

I bet you do, with your ill-gotten gains! Sarah forced herself to smile up at him, taking the cup. 'It must be nice to have your own place. Someday, I'd like to have my own flat, but I couldn't afford it at the moment. I am doing my best to put a little by every week, but it's hard.'

'Good for you. I'm doing the same. But would you not be lonely on your own?' he asked, sitting down on the chair opposite. 'You're used to living with family.'

'True, but it's academic until the war is over. I can't see my circumstances changing much. If my cousin Judith should return from London, it would be a tight squeeze at the house in Hursley. That would be my cue to move on. Though I'd be sad to leave the Lambes and the job.'

'Where does your cousin work?'

'The Home Office, I believe, but it's all very hush-hush. I haven't met her yet, but I think she is due to visit soon.'

Rob frowned over his cup. 'What does she do there?'

'I'm not sure; a secretary, as far as I understand.'

For a moment or two, he stared down into his tea, as if trying to come to a decision. Sarah's heart thumped, and a shiver ran down her spine. Her instincts were screaming at her to run out the door before they both committed to something terrifyingly dangerous.

When Rob looked up, his expression was serious. 'About what we were talking of earlier in the pub, Sarah: I'm not sure you realise how lucky you are.'

'How so?'

'Your job puts you in a unique position to do a lot of good.'

'What do you mean? A unique position for what exactly?' she asked. He cleared his throat and she realised he was nervous. *He knows what he is about to propose to me is treason.* But grasping that fact didn't comfort her.

'You have access to information – Spitfire plans – that the Germans would find especially useful. If they saw the plans, they could take advantage of any design weaknesses or strengths. Wouldn't it be easy enough for you to take some drawings out of Hursley?'

'Well, no, I doubt it would. The originals are kept in a safe. Once we do our tracings, the original drawings go straight back to the Drawing Office at the end of each day. They'd know if one was missing.'

'Couldn't you copy one then? Do a second tracing perhaps?' Rob asked, his voice low.

Sarah took her time in answering. She still didn't want to appear too keen, or suggest that it was something she had given thought to – even though, most nights, she thought about little else. 'No, that would not be possible without the drawings, and we have to hand those back as soon as we are finished.'

'There must be some way, Sarah.'

She made a show of mulling over it. Eventually she said: 'I suppose it might be done. I'll have to think about it. But don't get your hopes too high. It may not be possible, and it certainly won't be easy. I can hardly tell the Dragon I'm working late on some plans for the Germans.'

Rob smarted. 'No, of course not; but you're a clever girl, I'm sure you could come up with a way. And just think – not only would you be helping the Germans, but you would earn enough money to start afresh. I know people who are willing to pay well for those kinds of secrets. Very well indeed.'

Sarah's hands were shaking, so she gripped the cup tightly. 'Really?'

'And, if it helped Jerry, it would be fitting revenge on Churchill and his ilk for what they have done to your family, wouldn't it?'

'Yes . . . but are you positive about that British plot? If you're wrong—'

'I have it on the best authority, Sarah. It was a deliberate ploy to force the hand of the Irish government. The Germans deny any involvement in that incident and I believe them. It makes perfect sense. The last thing the Germans want is the Irish to side with the Allies, which rather gives credence to it being a British plot.'

'When you put it like that . . . But, Rob, I have no idea how to go about this kind of thing. What if I were caught? I'd be in serious trouble. I could go to jail – or worse.'

'Don't worry, you won't be caught, because we will plan it all very carefully. And once I have the drawings, I know who to pass them on to. My friend will ensure they go to the right people in Berlin.'

Sarah put the cup down. 'Who are these people, Rob?'

'Don't worry about who they are. Let's just say they are Brits like me who believe this war is misguided. I have one friend in particular who has German ancestry, and over the last few months he has been telling me so much about the Nazis. You can't believe all the propaganda from the British government.'

'What's his name?' she asked.

'I'd rather not say. He wouldn't like it. To be honest, he's a ruthless man: doesn't trust anyone; but then I suppose he has a lot to lose. Even for a German, he's rather zealous. But he assures me it's only a matter of time before the Germans are here. Hitler will soon turn his attention back to the Western Front once the Russians are defeated. When that time comes, some of us will be eager to help them. Of course, as fascists, we must remain secret. But trust me, we have cells all over the country, ready to rise up and help make Britain great again.'

'I'm not sure, Rob. I need to think about this,' she replied. 'It's very risky.'

'That's all right; I know it's a big decision. But let me assure you, I'm willing to help in any way I can. I would do it myself if I could, but I could never access those plans without raising suspicion, whereas you handle them every day. So, you see, it has to be you.' Sarah nodded slowly. 'However, I must warn you to be careful. Don't trust anyone – and do not discuss this with anyone else, in particular those girls you are friendly with. They are shocking gossips.'

'I won't say a word, I promise,' she said.

Rob looked so relieved. He believed he had reeled her in so easily. It made her blood boil. In the last few weeks she had often questioned her motivation, but any doubts she had about what she was doing were gone now. Bringing him and his Nazi friends to justice would be so satisfying.

'All right,' he answered, reaching across and squeezing her hand. 'Fancy some whisky in that tea to warm you up? You look like you've seen a ghost!'

25

29th October 1941, Hursley

Sarah arrived home from work a few days later and was met by her aunt at the door. Alice was beaming as she handed Sarah a letter.

'Must be that young man from Dublin you told us about?' Aunt Alice's eyes were alight with curiosity. 'Now, what was his name again?'

Sarah recognised Paul's hand and a rush of excitement swept through her. The letter bore a Yorkshire postmark. So that's where he was! But more importantly, he had remembered her.

'Yes – Paul.' Sarah stared at the letter for several moments before pushing it into her coat pocket.

'You're going to wait to read it?' her aunt asked, her brows raised. 'Go on with you, girl. Catch up on the news and you can tell me all after dinner.'

Torn between her evening-time duty to her aunt, and the

fact that the letter was already burning a hole in her pocket, Sarah crumbled. 'Would you mind terribly . . . ?'

'Of course not. I don't need help this evening. Dinner will be in half an hour – that should give you plenty of time to read it.' Aunt Alice actually winked at her before waving her off and returning to the kitchen.

There were no secrets in the Lambe house; everything was openly discussed by the family, which was lovely, and a novelty to her, but in this instance, she longed for privacy. If Uncle Tom or Martin found her downstairs with the letter, they would plague her to know what was in it, but Paul was her last link to Dublin, and she could not bear the thought of sharing him with the others just yet. With a light heart, Sarah tore up the stairs to her room. She was greedy for news. For weeks now she had pushed all thoughts of him to the back of her mind; it was the only way she could cope with the forced intimacy with Rob. Despite Northcott's insistence that what she was doing was for the greater good, it still felt like betrayal. If Paul ever learned of her actions, would he understand or approve? She had difficulty justifying them to herself as it was.

Sitting on the bed, she ran her fingers over the envelope. The accusations she had thrown at Paul on the night of the bombing were echoing in her head. Was she to spend the rest of her life regretting them? She paused. Could this letter be the longed-for reconciliation, or might it be the final curtain falling on what remained of their relationship?

With mixed emotions, she slit open the envelope. To her surprise, her hands trembled, and tears weren't far off either. The stress of the last few weeks had grown to a point where she even wondered if she could carry on with Northcott's plan. The worst thing was not having anyone to confide in or to seek advice from. If ever she had needed contact from a true friend, it was now. Paul's continued silence had been difficult to understand, and she had feared it meant he had totally rejected her. Well, the letter was proof she had been mistaken. For better or worse, she had to read it. She slipped the letter out of the envelope and was delighted to see it covered three pages; that had to be a good omen. Taking a deep breath, she dived in.

24th October 1941
Prince of Wales Hotel,
Scarborough.

Dear Sarah,
  I hope this letter finds you well. You must forgive the delay in writing to you, but we have been moving from Billy to Jack for ages. Life has been quite mad, and I have hardly had time to think, but you have never been far from my thoughts and when I do have a quiet moment, I wonder how you are getting on. Hopefully, you continue to recover from your awful ordeal and have settled in with your family. I'm dying to hear all about them. It seems a lifetime ago that we last met at the cemetery that day, and so much has happened to me since then.

And to me, Sarah thought gloomily, before continuing to read.

A week later, I travelled up to Belfast and presented myself at the recruitment centre, suddenly very unsure of myself. I needn't have worried: I was welcomed with open arms. However, I had no idea it would take so long for my paperwork to be processed. I suppose because I'm Irish they insisted on several references and there were strict criteria to be followed. Someone in the pub told me they are terrified some IRA good-for-nothings might try to enlist and get up to mischief. Anyway, luckily for me, my old boss back in Dublin and Sergeant Mulligan from Store Street Station were more than willing to provide what the RAF required. However, until those documents came through, I had to kick my heels in Belfast. Fortunately, the owner of the hostel where I was staying heard of work at a local factory, so for six weeks I worked there, making tank parts. Much as I enjoyed doing something for the war effort, it was a great relief when the call finally came. I left for Doncaster with several other fellows. We arrived on a wet and dismal day at the aircrew selection board and I must admit I was awfully nervous. There were two days of intelligence tests (yes, I can hear you laughing about that!) and a medical which included colour-blindness and eye tests. Gosh, I was anxious about those, as bad eyesight runs in the family. We even had a night vision test where you sit in a dark room and you have to name the objects or shapes which flash up on a small screen.

Next thing we knew, we were on a train to London, of all places. You can imagine our astonishment to discover we would be starting our service life at Lord's Cricket Ground. On arrival we were issued with our kit and uniform (nice and smart, I think you will agree when you see me) and then another shock ensued. Our digs were luxury flats in St John's Wood. In case you don't know, that's quite a posh area. Do not get too envious, however, as the flats had been stripped of all extravagances before we arrived. Still, it was wonderful to have access to decent bathrooms; no outdoor privies for us, like at home. The following day we had the compulsory razor haircut. All I can say is that it is practical!

I won't bore you with my daily routine, but you can be sure there was plenty of drilling and the like. They continuously tested us to see if we were fit to fly. The first time I went up, I was absolutely terrified, shaking like a leaf, and wondered what the hell I had been thinking. But oh, it was glorious and once my nerves settled, I began to enjoy it. Now I am totally addicted to it. And, by the grace of God, I am proud to say that I am now officially an RAF Cadet!

After a couple of days, we were allowed out into the city and I visited all the London tourist attractions. I've never walked so much in my life. The people were amazing, and we received nothing but kindness as we explored the sights. I suppose the uniform helped! Despite the bombing, the city is incredible, and I don't just mean the buildings. It's hard to explain. There's a kind of excitement in the air there. I've certainly experienced nothing like it. There were a few air-raid warnings, but all were false alarms.

After two weeks we were posted here to the Initial Training camp where things became serious. We are billeted in a hotel which has been requisitioned for our use. It would be a wonderful place for a holiday – it is beautifully situated on a clifftop overlooking the sea, and the food isn't half bad, but, unfortunately, that is the best I can say for it. The physical training is relentless and the lectures tough. I had always considered myself a fit man, but I had no real concept of what is meant by physical exhaustion. I think the worst was the cross-country march in the most appalling weather, with heavy kit, and dare I admit, a heavier heart. There have been a few moments when my commitment has wobbled, but it always comes back to the planes. I desperately want to fly and now I am determined to stick it out, no matter what.

This week sees the end of my initial training and we have been given permission to take some downtime. My next posting will be to Elementary Flying School at Brough, so I was hoping we could meet up this weekend. I am planning to get the train to Southampton with one of the lads this Friday. Ralph has invited me to stay at his folks' place. Of course, I jumped at the chance, knowing it wouldn't be too far from where you are living, and it might be possible for us to meet. Perhaps we could get together on Saturday afternoon? My friend says there's a nice little café called Mrs Delaney's Tea Rooms on Commercial Road, close to the station. I'll be there for 3.30 pm and will wait outside for you. I really hope you can make it but don't worry if it doesn't suit you, I'll understand.

Yours affectionately,

Paul.

Sarah skimmed through the letter a second time, her heart thumping. He was giving her an out in that last sentence. Paul was unsure of her, which made her sad. She still wondered whether she should have told him her true feelings that day at the cemetery. But regrets were pointless. If she had learned anything in the last few months, it was to grab life and its opportunities without hesitation, for you did not know what life had in store.

Wild horses wouldn't keep her away from that rendezvous. It would be wonderful to see him again. A tiny flicker of optimism ignited in her heart. There was an undercurrent of warmth to his words, and she dared to hope he still had feelings for her. His letter could not have come at a better time. Since Sunday, she had nearly fallen into despair. What Rob and Northcott were asking of her was tearing her apart. She glanced at the letter again. After the way she had treated Paul, she didn't deserve his friendship. If only she could pour her heart out to him! But she couldn't tell Paul anything about what was happening with Rob and Northcott. Not after what had happened to Alfie. The risk was too great, and Paul was . . . still special. There! She had admitted it fully now. So often she had buried her feelings, as it was the only way she could pretend to like Rob. What a mess! Still, perhaps there was a glimmer of hope. That was, of course, if she wasn't hanged for treason in the near future.

With a groan, her thoughts turned reluctantly to Northcott. A telegram from him had landed on her desk that morning, proposing a new rendezvous point down in Southampton, and as it happened, he was suggesting early Saturday evening, the same day she would meet Paul. He expressed a hope that the bus journey would not be too *fatiguing*. My, but he was a sarcastic so-and-so. Southampton was no easier a location for her to get to, but nice and convenient for him. Sarah sucked in a breath: she dreaded meeting him again, not least because of the strange circumstances of Alfie's death. On top of that, he would expect her to have a plan in place now that Rob had openly encouraged her to steal drawings. Both men were becoming more demanding, and stalling wasn't an option with either of them. Greatly agitated, she sprang up from the bed and went to the window.

Down below in the garden, Martin was leaning against the wall chatting to his father as Uncle Tom turned over the soil in one of the empty vegetable beds. Their laughter floated up, catching her heart. Life was so normal here in this house. How she longed to embrace it! But until the job with Northcott was concluded, she could only be a bystander.

26

1st November 1941, Southampton

It was Saturday afternoon. With an hour to spare before meeting Paul, Sarah walked over to High Street, where she was to meet Northcott at five o'clock in the Victoria Hotel. The street was long, stretching from the Bargate down to the port. It was bitterly cold, and a sharp breeze was blowing up from the harbour as she headed southward. Every so often, the wind picked up eddies of dust which pirouetted upwards, stinging her nostrils and eyes. Sarah had to hold her scarf up over her mouth and squint to avoid it.

The Blitz the previous November had left the thoroughfare a pitiful sight, with large tracts of it still in ruins. Tomb-like mounds of debris and scorched timbers bordered the pavement, stark reminders of the Jerry attacks. One or two shops in between had survived, their windows valiantly declaring that Jerry wasn't going to put them out of business. One had to admire the shopkeeper's resolute spirit. Sarah knew there had been hundreds of lives lost in the Blitz, but people were picking up the pieces and carrying on. It was defiance in the face of near-annihilation, and she found it incredibly moving.

So much destruction was hard to take in, and for one brief moment she was back in North Strand. She wondered if it was still in a similar state of bleak emptiness, haunted by uneasy ghosts. Poor Mrs Twohig, alone with her memories in that tiny cottage. That final visit to North Strand had been a defining moment for Sarah. Staring at No. 18, self-pity had been pushed aside and a burning desire to avenge Maura's death had taken hold. If she could pull off Northcott's plan, that desire for revenge would be satisfied.

But why did she feel so uneasy about it all?

As she continued down the street, she wondered why Northcott had chosen such a public place to meet, particularly after his reaction to being seen by Alfie. Did he not run the risk of being seen with her by friends or colleagues, or was there safety in a crowd? Would he claim she was a colleague?

She was almost at the harbour when she spotted the hotel across the street. It was a beautiful double-fronted building, with rounded bays protruding from the second and third floors. Judging by its architecture, she reckoned it must have stood on the spot for centuries, serving the passengers for the port. It was incredible it had escaped the destruction that had demolished half the buildings in the surrounding area.

Just as she was about to retrace her steps, an all-too-familiar cane-wielding figure limped out of the hotel door. Sarah turned and gazed in blind panic into the butcher's shop window, pulling her scarf further up around the bottom half of her face, while her heart beat a drum tattoo against her chest. Gradually, she calmed enough to focus, and through the reflection in the shop window she watched Northcott. Still outside the hotel, he consulted his watch then stood for a moment, his hand tapping his leg as he looked up and down the street. Was he worried he was being watched? Sarah stepped closer to the shop window, hoping the awning and the passers-by would shield her from view. A few moments more, and to her great relief he turned left towards the harbour. Thank goodness he hadn't spotted her. If he had seen her, what would he have thought? That she was spying on him? That she really *was* an IRA plant at Supermarine planning to double-cross him?

Turning her head ever so slightly, Sarah followed his progress. Even with his limp, he set a brisk pace and was soon lost from view around a corner. Maybe the hotel was a favourite haunt of his for lunch or a drink. As she contemplated what to do next, she observed that many of the clientele entering and exiting the premises were servicemen and women. Calmer, she laughed at herself. Southampton was a naval port and the hotel was close to the harbour. It made sense that naval officers would frequent it.

And then, a minute later, the most extraordinary thing happened. A grey-haired woman in a russet tweed suit with a matching coat and hat emerged from the hotel. The lady stood surveying the street before walking away in the opposite direction to Northcott. Sarah froze, dumbfounded. This was so bizarre, so unexpected, that for a moment Sarah wondered if she was imagining things. What on earth was Miss Whitaker doing coming out of the same hotel as Northcott? It could not be a coincidence. *Good grief*, she thought, *she must have been meeting Northcott*. The Dragon must be Northcott's eyes and ears at Supermarine! That strange interview with Miss Whitaker two weeks before made much more sense now. The woman *had* been testing her. All that concern for her welfare had been a trick to see if Sarah would betray Northcott. What a tangled web of deceit!

Still perplexed, Sarah slowly made her way back up High Street, not sure whether to laugh or cry, but keeping well back from Miss Whitaker, who was striding away in a most purposeful manner.

By the time Sarah neared the tea rooms, she was calm again. Although puzzled, at least now she knew how careful she would have to be in formulating her plans and copying the drawings. But she did question why Northcott hadn't told her about Miss Whitaker being on their side. Surely the woman could only be an asset to their plan? Sarah could see how it would be impossible for someone in Miss Whitaker's position to risk providing the plans – and besides, it was unlikely that Rob would target or trust such a senior member of staff – but at the very least, she could assist Sarah by suggesting a way to copy a drawing without being caught. Still, it was hard to know how Northcott's mind worked; and if she were honest, she didn't want to dwell on that. No doubt Miss Whitaker's role in all of this would become apparent in due course.

At last Sarah caught sight of Paul, and suddenly her heart was pounding with anticipation; but she was scared too. He was so much more to her than just a face from the past or a link to her previous life. Did he still view her as just a friend? What she would give to be able to confide in him; not just about Rob and Northcott, but about how she felt about him. Dare she tell him how much she loved him? That she craved the warmth of his embrace? It would be wonderful to salvage some of their former intimacy, but that would be impossible, sitting in a café surrounded by strangers. And what if she took the plunge and he rejected her? There was no guarantee that he wished to rekindle their romance. There had been no hint of it in his letter.

Her breath caught in her throat as all the old feelings stirred within her. *What an idiot you are, Sarah Gillespie*, she berated herself. *Look what you threw away!* How handsome he looked as he stood waiting outside the tea rooms, looking about anxiously, and blowing into his cupped hands. In fact, he was such a welcome sight she had to resist the urge to rush up and hug him. The RAF uniform, with its smart overcoat, made him look older somehow, but when he saw her and smiled, he was her old Paul again.

'You're a sight for sore eyes,' he said as she approached.

'As are you!' she answered, almost on the verge of tears.

He bent down to kiss her cheek. At the same time, she lunged forward to hug him. They both ended up laughing and blushing furiously. 'I'm so glad you could make it,' he said, clearing his throat.

'Did you doubt me?' she asked.

'Well . . . I wasn't sure if you'd want to see me again. Sorry it took so long to get in touch. Come on; let's go inside, it's perishing out here,' he said before she could answer.

A young waitress showed them to a table.

'I was thrilled to receive your letter,' Sarah said as they settled down. 'I thought I'd never see you again. It seems so long since I saw you last.'

'I know, it's hard to believe it was only three months ago. It's all been a bit mad, hasn't it? Well, it has for me. I only hope once my training is complete, we have some kind of permanent base. Though, it may not be in England. Still, time enough to worry about that.' Paul grinned across at her, making her heart skip a beat. He reached across and took her hand. 'You look well, Sarah. Have you recovered from your injuries?'

'Yes. A little stiffness in my leg sometimes, but otherwise I'm fine. It was lucky I broke my left arm, not my right, otherwise I might not have been able to take up my new job. You need a steady hand to trace.' She held out her left hand and wrinkled her nose. 'See? It shakes a bit.'

'That's marvellous,' he said. 'I mean that you are ok and that you got the job. But seriously, Sarah, it was a bloomin' miracle you survived at all. That day I went to the house and saw the state of it, I really feared you could not have survived.'

'There isn't a day I'm not thankful they found me and dug me out. It was a miracle they found me so quickly. I only realised that when I visited and saw the ruins for myself. I only wish . . .'

'Yes, poor Maura. She didn't deserve to meet such an untimely end. God rest her soul. You must miss her dreadfully.'

'I do.'

If only he knew. Missing Maura and loving him were the two constants in her life. Missing Maura was what made it possible to continue Northcott's mission. Whenever she questioned the appropriateness of revenge as a motive for what she was undertaking, she would recall her sister's last moments and how she had died, and the anger would flare up once more. It was always there in the background, bubbling away, driving her forward when the doubts threatened to overwhelm her.

Sarah glanced out of the window and took a deep breath. 'Let's not talk about it, Paul, please. I'm just so glad to see you here. I was afraid you were so busy having adventures that you had forgotten all about me, and I had no way of contacting *you*.'

'Yes, I'm sorry about that. We can stay in touch now . . . but only if you want, of course.'

'I'd like that very much, Paul,' she said, suddenly shy. *What is wrong with me? This is foolish; he would not be here if he didn't care.*

The waitress appeared at the table and took their order.

'I hadn't realised how much I missed hearing a Dublin accent,' Sarah said once the waitress had left.

Paul hooted with laughter. 'Lord, I'm constantly ribbed about it by the fellows at the camp. Sometimes they pretend they can't understand me.'

'Oh no, is it awful there? Do you hate it?'

'No, no; it's all part of the camaraderie. Don't be concerned. I give as good as I get,' he said with a smirk. 'They are a good bunch of lads.'

'You're enjoying it all, then?' she said, relieved.

His face lit up. 'I've never been happier, Sarah. I'm doing what I always wanted to do. The only fly in the ointment is my parents.'

'I'm sorry to hear that – but you knew how it would be, especially with your father and his leanings.'

Paul pulled a face. 'Oh yes, I was prepared for a backlash, but not the extent of it. All my letters have been returned unopened. My Da, of course.'

'How cruel of him. You are risking so much to fight for a cause you believe in. It might not be a cause he agrees with, but he must remember why he took up arms during the War of Independence. It's simply a matter of good versus evil. That generation have short memories when it comes to some things.'

'That's it exactly. He can't see beyond his hatred for the Brits. Can't admit Hitler and his chums are a worse threat to our freedom.'

'Your mother must be frantic,' Sarah said. 'Does he not consider her feelings?'

'Of course not. Ma's wishes have always been at the bottom of his list of priorities. She was upset at first, of course, but I've been able to write to her via my sister Deirdre, and vice versa. I send my letters to Deirdre's workplace and she smuggles them home to Ma.'

'That's clever, but a pity you have to go to such lengths,' Sarah remarked.

'Yes, but hopefully Da won't find out I have found a way around the problem.'

'Families, huh?' The waitress appeared with their order. Sarah waited for her to leave before saying: 'Perhaps he will come round, eventually. He must see what you are doing is honourable.'

Paul shrugged. 'I doubt it. Too damn proud. I'll never go back, Sarah. If I survive this war, I'm staying in England and making a life here.'

Sarah sighed. 'I'm thinking along those lines myself.'

His eyes lit up. 'Really?'

'Yes, why not? With Maura and Da gone, there's no reason to go back to Dublin.'

'I'm glad for you, Sarah. You've had a hard time of it,' he said.

'No more than others.'

'Don't you . . .'

'What?' she asked.

'Well, don't you think it's much freer here? I think that's what appeals to me most. I hadn't realised how restrictive life was back home. The Church dictates everything.'

'Yes, I suppose you're right. I hadn't given it much thought.

Maybe it's the war; people here are determined to enjoy themselves whenever they can. They have realised how precious life and time really are. They've been to hell and back.'

'And more importantly, they don't feel guilty for enjoying themselves,' Paul said. 'Anyway, what have you been up to?'

On receiving his letter, she had considered confiding in him, but had concluded it was safer for them all if he knew nothing about Northcott. She didn't want Paul to worry about her. Besides, as much as she longed to talk to someone about it, there was very little Paul could do to help her. In a few hours, he would be back in Yorkshire, blissfully ignorant of the situation she found herself in.

Pasting a smile on her face, she said: 'Settling in, mostly. You know how challenging life could be with Da back in Dublin?' He nodded. 'Well, it's the complete opposite here. The Lambes have welcomed me with a generosity that overwhelms me at times. I feel as though I belong. My only regret is that Maura isn't here to share it.'

'Of course.' His eyes were full of sympathy. 'And the work?'

'I love it. I'm with a nice group; the girls are friendly. We usually go to the cinema once a week and there's a fabulous library in Winchester. And you won't believe it, but my cousin Martin persuaded me to join the local dramatic society.'

'That's lucky. I wouldn't have thought such a small place would have anything like that.'

'I know, but although the village is small, there are many displaced people working and living there at the moment. The local clubs and societies are thriving as a result.'

'I have to admit I do miss the North Strand Players,' Paul said with a wistful sigh. 'Will you ever forget that dingy old hall and the hole in the stage floor?'

'Gosh, no. That night Mary Wilson got her foot stuck and went flying!'

'Poor girl! At least the audience thought it was part of the play.' Paul chuckled. 'We had some good laughs, didn't we?'

'Yes . . . and that's where we met, so it will always hold a special place in my heart,' Sarah said.

Sarah could have sworn Paul flinched at her words, and he didn't meet her eye. 'How life has changed for all of us since then,' he said. 'Innocent days, really.' When he finally looked up, his expression was neutral once more. 'I hope you were given a good part. You never got a chance to shine with the plays we did back home.'

'I'm afraid I was too late to audition, so I'm working backstage; but I'm enjoying it and meeting lots of new people.'

'Sounds like you have landed on your feet. I am pleased for you; you deserve some happiness.' He paused. 'I suppose there are plenty of young lads where you are working, too?'

'Yes. It's a big place with many departments. Oh! I see. Are you asking if I am walking out with someone?' she asked, with a tilt of her head. How on earth could she explain Rob? It felt disloyal, which was bizarre in the circumstances. But she had to be honest without giving away Northcott's mission.

Inwardly cringing, she said: 'I am seeing someone, but it's nothing serious.' Paul's eyes widened, but he didn't comment. What was he thinking? She continued in a rush: 'It doesn't feel like the right time to get too involved with anyone. In fact, I can't see it lasting long. We've little in common.' *Except treason, of course*, she thought. At that moment she would have gladly run Northcott through. It was his fault she was having to lie, yet again.

'And you?' she asked, doing her best to sound nonchalant.

Paul chuckled. 'I don't have the time. Training is intense and we are moving on again next week.'

'Oh, come on! You must socialise a bit.' Sarah knew from the gossip at work that the armed services' social lives were always lively. Some of Gladys's stories had been shocking.

'We sometimes go out for a quiet pint in the town,' he said.

'You'll be struck down for telling me such a whopper of a lie. I'd say you're last to leave every night. In fact, they probably have to throw you out!'

'You know me too well, Sarah Gillespie,' he said, laughing. 'However, we are under strict orders and have to be back at camp by a certain time. If you're late, there is hell to pay.'

'And are the Yorkshire ladies to your liking?'

'I refuse to answer that,' he replied. 'Here; you're neglecting your duties. Pour us a cuppa.'

As Sarah poured, she said, 'This new place you are going to; what will you be doing there?'

'It's final selection, so it will be crunch time. We will train in Tiger Moths and based on how well we do, we will be selected for further pilot training.'

'What happens if you're not selected to be a pilot?'

'Don't even say that!' he said, his mouth turning down. 'I would be devastated. I'd probably cry.'

'Don't be daft!' she laughed.

Paul took a sip of his tea, his eyes alight. 'Some will train as navigators or bomb aimers. But not me; I *will* be a pilot, come hell or high water. Even if I have to steal a plane to do it!'

Sarah grinned back at him. 'I don't doubt it for a moment. Does the RAF realise what an obstinate man you can be?'

'Don't be cheeky, Sarah Gillespie. Eat your cake.'

27

1st November 1941, The Victoria Hotel, Southampton

Sarah made her way across the marble-floored entrance hall to the reception desk of the hotel, the echo of her footsteps adding to her discomfort. The foyer was all gilt and glass and screamed luxury. The guests she passed were well-to-do and fashionably dressed; most of the men were in uniform and the women in exquisite evening wear. Sarah glanced down at her sensible woollen coat and low-heeled shoes and shrugged. This was an alien world she had dropped into, one of glamour and money. But it didn't matter what she looked like; she would not be here for long. The niggling notion that Northcott had deliberately chosen such a place to intimidate her crossed her mind, and she smiled.

Behind the reception desk, a young man made no attempt to disguise his scrutiny as she approached. Sarah guessed it was a practised look to intimidate any riffraff and send them scurrying back out the door.

'Good evening . . . madam,' the receptionist greeted her. 'May I be of assistance?'

Sarah almost smiled in response. What he really wanted to ask her was what she was thinking coming into his high-class hotel dressed like a refugee. 'Good evening. I do hope so. I'm here to meet Captain Northcott. He's expecting me,' she answered, chin up, channelling Joan Fontaine to the best of her ability.

The receptionist flicked a glance off to the right. 'If madam would care to take a seat in the lounge, I'll inform the captain you are here when he arrives,' he replied in a slightly warmer tone than absolute zero. With a pained smile and a flick of his wrist, he indicated a doorway off the foyer.

'Much obliged,' Sarah replied, her nose in the air.

The guest lounge was a handsome room, with red wing-backed chairs grouped around tables, potted palms aplenty, and white panelled walls. A pianist was tinkling the ivories in the far corner, ignored by the various groups sitting around. *What a thankless job,* she thought, and nodded to him in acknowledgement. His answering quirk of a smile spoke volumes. Noticing a table in a quiet corner, Sarah walked over to it. No sooner had she sat down than a waiter materialised at her side.

'A gin and tonic, please,' she told him. 'Actually, make that a double.' If Northcott insisted on dragging her to Southampton, the least he could do was stand her a decent drink.

The waiter drifted away and Sarah glanced at her watch: five to five. He should be here soon. As she sat people watching, she noticed a few curious glances aimed in her direction. Aware she stuck out like a sore thumb amongst the glamorous clientele, she returned their impudent stares with a raised brow and what she hoped was an icy gaze. She'd just have to brazen it out until Captain Northcott appeared. Hopefully, he would not be late.

A stylish couple at the next table caught her eye. The lady's dress was beautiful. It consisted of swathes of pink chiffon that swept elegantly to the floor. How on earth had the woman sourced a dress like that on clothes rations? But then, if one had money, anything was possible. A tendril of envy caught Sarah by surprise, and she had to look away.

What a day it had been! Parting from Paul had been awful. The afternoon had flown by, every minute of it precious to her. It had been like old times and they had fallen into easy conversation, full of banter. It felt right. It had only emphasised how dishonest she felt to be entangled with Rob, no matter how much duty demanded it. When Paul had finally looked at his watch and said he had to leave, she had almost panicked. She didn't know when she might see him again . . . or if.

With his friend Ralph present at the station, not hiding his curiosity as to their relationship, their farewell had been frustratingly restrained. At one point on the platform, she thought Paul was going to say something affectionate, perhaps even intimate, but the words never materialised. Instead, he had hugged her awkwardly and promised to write. She had waved the men off, doing her best not to show how much the parting affected her.

The idea the war might rob her of Paul dominated her thoughts as she walked away from the station. With growing panic, she tried to put things into perspective. Was her desire to be with Paul real, or was she just being contrary? Maura had always accused her of being just that. Did she only want him because she had pushed him away? Paul was her only link to home and her past; perhaps she was afraid of losing that.

Lost in her thoughts on her way to the hotel, she had come to an abrupt stop on the sidewalk and a man had cursed her as he dodged around her, but she was barely aware of his presence. Self-realisation had crashed through the jumble of her thoughts, leaving her appalled. The truth was that it was pointless to continue to pine for him – she had no hold on him now, and no right to expect him to remain loyal. She would have to be content in the knowledge that he was happy pursuing his dream, no matter where that might lead . . . even if it were into the arms of someone else. All she could do was hope and pray that they would both survive whatever lay ahead for them in this war. Maybe, if fate were kind enough, they might get a second chance in the future.

The sight of Northcott in the doorway of the lounge brought her back to the present and their eyes met just as the waiter turned up with her drink.

'Good evening, Sarah,' Northcott said as he approached the table, his glance flicking down to her glass. To her amazement, a grin lit up his face. He turned to the waiter. 'I'll have my usual.'

'Yes, sir, of course,' the waiter replied, and floated off.

'Is this setting more to your liking?' Northcott asked as he sat down opposite.

Sarah looked about the room, then gave him her blandest smile. 'Perfection. It beats rain-soaked national monuments any day.'

The captain laughed softly. 'That tongue of yours is far too sharp, Sarah. Be careful you don't cut yourself.'

Sarah took a sip of her gin, too irked to respond. How did he manage to get under her skin so often?

With casual ease, he scanned the room before his gaze settled back on her. 'Well, this is jolly pleasant, but shall we get down to business? Have you made any progress with our friend?'

'I have agreed in principle to secure what he wants.'

'Excellent, Sarah,' he said. 'You see, your fears were groundless. I told you he would be keen. And when do you propose to acquire it?'

She paused while the waiter placed Northcott's whisky on the table. 'I hope to make a start next week.'

'Only a start? Have you figured out how to do it?'

'Yes.'

'How?' he asked, his brows snapping together.

She needed to prevaricate, as she hadn't a clue. 'This isn't the place to go into it,' she answered *sotto voce*, looking around the room.

'You intrigue me, Sarah. You have quite the talent for this kind of thing. Must be hereditary.' Sarah threw him a dirty look. Northcott smiled back at her. 'But perhaps you are correct; best to be careful. Very well, I will trust you have it all under control. However, I must stress how important it is that what you acquire for our *friend* is of value.' He leaned towards her. 'Our foreign friends would love to get their hands on something like that.'

'But Rob hasn't asked for anything in particular,' she replied.

'I'd imagine it's only a matter of time. I would stress there is a need for something special to hold his interest. The new variation preferably – do you understand?'

'He's not going to know one end of a . . . from another.'

'Perhaps not, but I would prefer he is discovered with something that would be of great value to the other side. It will make his downfall more worthwhile; wouldn't you agree?'

Sarah was puzzled. Why would it matter what Rob was found with as long as they outed him as a German spy? Surely the act of receiving the stolen drawing would be sufficient evidence against him. 'I don't have much choice about what I work on, Captain: I have to take the next available . . . thing, you know what I mean?' He nodded. 'But I will do my best,' she said at last.

'Good. Does McArthur know when you propose to do it?'

'I had lunch with him yesterday. We have a plan outlined,' Sarah said. 'But until I have the job completed, we can't set a date for a handover.'

'Hmm, all right.' He sighed. 'When you are ready, phone and leave a message for me here giving me location, date and time. Not my flat, please.' He flicked a glance around the room and smiled. 'I pop in here most days. They are used to taking messages for me.'

'Fine; I will do that. There is one thing that worries me, however.'

'And what is that?' he asked, taking a sip of his drink.

'What will happen at the handover? Will you be there to ensure nothing goes awry? He has mentioned another party being involved,' she said.

'Has he now!' Northcott's cheek twitched and his jaw clenched. 'That is an interesting development. His handler, I assume. Did he give you a name?'

'No, but I didn't like the sound of this other man. From what Rob has told me, he's a nasty piece of work. What am I to do if this other person is there? I have no way to defend myself. I would be outnumbered.'

'Don't worry about that end of it, Sarah. I will have it all in hand. Let me assure you, it will be the last time our friend and his colleagues get up to mischief in this country.' Sarah froze as poor Alfie's fate loomed large in her mind. For a moment she was tempted to bring up Alfie's accident. Her gut feeling was that Northcott had been responsible. He was ruthless, she was certain of it, and his methods for dealing with problems didn't sit easy with her. But of course, she had no evidence. Just a hunch. Perhaps when this was all over she could plant a seed of doubt with the Winchester police, anonymously.

'I hope so. What will happen to Rob afterwards?' Sarah asked.

'Don't worry your pretty little head about it. Justice will be served, I assure you,' he said. 'There are special court sittings to deal with the likes of him.'

'If it goes to court, will I have to testify?'

'All these questions, Sarah. I hope you aren't getting cold feet?'

'Of course not, but I want to be prepared.'

'It is unlikely you will have to testify, mainly because it is best to keep agents out of the limelight. This will be dealt with swiftly and out of the public eye.'

Sarah stiffened. '"Out of the limelight"? That suggests our business won't be complete. You implied this was a one-off.'

Northcott frowned. 'Did I?' He leaned across as if to impart something further. Sarah moved forward in her chair. His mouth twitched. 'Now, drink up, there's a good girl; I have a dinner engagement with my wife.'

What a lucky lady! Livid, Sarah snatched up her glass and downed her gin. 'And I have a bus to catch.'

As she passed his chair, he stood and took her hand. 'Good

luck, Sarah.' His grip was firm. 'I have every faith in you. You are doing a great job.'

'Thank you,' she replied, holding his gaze. 'I wish you a pleasant evening, Captain.'

28

3rd November 1941, Hursley Park

'Morning, Sarah,' Gladys called out as she walked down towards her through the coat racks. Sarah had only arrived in the cloakroom a few minutes earlier and was sitting on a bench, deep in thought. 'Well, did you meet the lovely Paul?' probed Gladys. 'I'm dying to hear all about your dilemma.'

'How do you know I have one?' Sarah asked, half laughing.

'Stands to reason. Being courted by one fellow and then meeting a former boyfriend. Bound to produce all sorts of problems. Does Rob know about this clandestine meeting?'

Sarah glanced behind Gladys to see if anyone else was about and lowered her voice. 'It wasn't clandestine. You make it sound awful! And no; he does not need to know. It's none of his business if I meet an old friend.'

Gladys snorted. 'Old lover, you mean!'

Sarah threw her a stern look. 'I'm sorry I told you about it now. And I hope you didn't tell Ruth.'

Gladys took off her coat, shaking her head. 'What do you take me for? Course I didn't tell Ruth. But I think you are courting trouble, in every sense of the word.' Gladys plopped down beside Sarah and gave her a nudge. 'Come on, spill the beans. Was it all hearts and flowers? Or awkward silences?'

Sarah briefly outlined her encounter with Paul. 'And so I'm more confused than ever. I can't get him out of my mind, but I may never see him again.'

Gladys puckered her lips. 'It doesn't sound promising, Sarah. Sounds like he wants to remain friends.' She blew out her lips. 'That dreaded phrase. You might be best to forget about him and give Rob a decent chance.'

Sarah's stomach churned at the thought and she blurted out: 'I can't see us lasting much longer.'

'Well, you won't with that attitude.' The door opened and a group of girls came in. 'Come on, best we get to work. We can talk more at lunchtime if you wish,' Gladys said as she stood.

Despite her assurances to Northcott that she knew what she was doing, Sarah still didn't know how she was going to pull it off. Racked with doubt, she formulated and rejected plan after plan. There were so many factors to consider; the most important ones being how to take the most recent plans, as Northcott was being so precise about what she should give to Rob, and how to get them out of Hursley Park without being caught. As far as she knew, the originals were logged in and out of the Drawing Office, checked by the Tracing Room supervisor before and after the girls had done their work, and then returned to the Drawing Office safe. Even if she used the excuse of visiting her uncle or cousin, she had no business being in that part of Hursley or going near that safe. The crazy idea of sneaking into the Drawing Office and snatching a drawing from a drawing board when no one was looking brought her out in goose bumps. She wasn't that desperate yet.

The only viable option was to copy an original schematic. But the tracings she made were immediately taken away once completed. There was one possible technique she wanted to try, but that entailed copying the drawing at her desk in full view of her colleagues. However, she wasn't sure her idea would work, and she ran the risk that someone in the Tracing Room might work out what she was attempting to do.

She was still mulling it all over on Monday evening after dinner. Her aunt and uncle sat either side of the fire and Martin sat across the table from her, and though her mind focused in on the family chatter now and then, she always came back to the knotty problem of getting that damned drawing. What she was planning was very risky. If she were caught, she'd lose her job and most likely be hauled off by the police to face God-knows-what. What was worse was that the two *gentlemen* involved were running none of that risk. Both would deny any involvement, she was sure of that. She would be totally abandoned if exposed.

The mention of a new Spitfire mark by Martin pulled her attention back into the room and she realised Uncle Tom and Martin were discussing aspects of the new design.

'I only hope this newer high-altitude Spit will make a difference and give those blasted German Junkers a run for their money,' Uncle Tom said. 'If we get it right, the new mark will not only prey on Jerry bombers, but will also protect our own lads on raids over Germany. Which part has Manning got you working on?'

'The new wing tips. We're opting for the C type universal wings,' Martin said.

'Ah, good choice. They can handle up to eight machine guns. But don't you have to extend the wing tips like on the Mark VI?'

'Yep, and we have to integrate thirteen-gallon fuel tanks to the wing leading edges between the wing-root and the inboard cannon bay.'

'From what Manning said, the main difference from the Mark VI is the cockpit door. My understanding is the pilots didn't like the fact the fixed version had to be locked in place,' said Uncle Tom.

'I'd say not!' Martin exclaimed. 'Imagine if you were stuck and couldn't open it and the plane was spinning down out of control.' He gave a shudder. 'It has happened. Poor blighters!'

'Why do they have to lock them in place?' Sarah asked.

'To facilitate high-altitude flying, the cockpits have to be pressurised and sealed. If you lose pressure, the pilot can pass out.' Uncle Tom looked across at Martin. 'In the new model, they're putting in a newly designed sliding mechanism on the cockpit door. Should be easier to use and safer for the pilots. They are also upgrading the air pump, which will be a significant improvement.'

'Why?' Sarah asked. This sounded like just the thing a Nazi would be very interested in.

'Air is pumped into the sealed cockpit to keep the pilot conscious at high altitudes,' her uncle explained.

'So without the sealing of the cockpit and the air pump, it would not be possible for the Spitfire to go to the higher altitudes?' she asked.

'That's it exactly,' said Tom.

Martin glanced at Sarah and smiled. 'Sorry. We shouldn't be talking shop, but you should be getting the drawings in the Tracing Room later this week.'

'Great,' Sarah answered, putting down her book. 'I'll look out for them. Actually, I find it fascinating to know that minor changes can make such a difference to performance.'

'Aye, they do,' said Tom. 'We have to stay one step ahead of Jerry because whenever they get their dirty hands on a downed Spit, they copy our technology if it suits their needs. Of course, the same is true for us. The Germans are fine engineers, it has to be said.'

Martin gave a snort. 'That's about the only good thing one can say about the blighters.'

'Very true, son. But isn't it grand?' Uncle Tom said with a beaming smile. 'The possibility of both your names being on the same plan for posterity. I couldn't be prouder.'

'Ah, Dad, stop that,' Martin laughed.

Aunt Alice put down her knitting and glowered at Martin. 'And why shouldn't we be proud of ye? Sure aren't you both contributing hugely to the defeat of the enemy? I don't know why you always underestimate what you do, Martin.'

Sarah's gut twisted in uncertainty about what her contribution would be, ultimately; she only hoped her aunt was right.

29

The next morning, Sarah arrived at Hursley Park slightly earlier than usual in the hope she would be first into the Tracing Room. Once she had left her coat and bag in the cloakroom, she made her way to the office, but to her dismay, Miss Sugden was already at her desk. Sometimes, Sarah wondered if the woman ever went home. She was married to her job, just like the Dragon.

'Good morning, Sarah. How are you?' the supervisor greeted her as she approached her desk. Miss Sugden handed her a schematic. 'Isn't it nice to start the day with a new one?'

'Yes, indeed,' Sarah answered with a smile, marvelling at the woman's enthusiasm. As far as she knew, Miss Sugden had worked at Supermarine for over ten years. Would you not get bored doing the same work day in, day out? Sarah wondered. She moved across to the table which held the tracing cloths. As she reached out to pick one up, the door opened and Gladys and Ruth burst into the room, chattering away. This was Sarah's chance. While Miss Sugden welcomed them, and while all three were distracted, Sarah slid a second tracing cloth from the top of the pile, and made for her desk. She sat down, breaking out in a cold sweat.

Gladys soon joined her and sat down at the adjacent desk with a sigh. 'How are you, Sarah? Fancy going for a drink after work? I can't bear the thought of another evening in that dreary flat. Ruth is driving me barmy with her constant whining about Martin.'

'Sorry, Gladys, I've promised to help my aunt tonight. How about some other evening?'

'All right. There's no new film on this week, so let's make it Friday.'

'What about Friday?' Ruth enquired as she sat down on the other side of Gladys.

'Drinkies, after work in the King's Head. Want to come?' Gladys asked.

'Sure,' Ruth replied, looking past Gladys to Sarah. 'Will Martin be there?'

Gladys rolled her eyes at Sarah. 'Are we not good enough company for you?'

Ruth pouted. 'You're a pig, sometimes, Gladys, you really are.'

'Ladies, shall we get started? Plenty of time to chat at lunch,' Miss Sugden interrupted from the top of the room.

Sarah had managed to place both tracing cloths on top of the drawing before the girls had joined her. It was a gamble, but she hoped if she leaned hard enough on her pen, the drawing outline would imprint on the second cloth. She took her time setting up, securing the tracing cloths over the original with drawing pins, then cleaning the top surface. All set. Although the tracing cloths were generally robust, she didn't know if the added pressure would damage the top copy and raise suspicion. With some trepidation and a prayer, she took up her pen, dipped it in the ink and began.

The drawing she was working on was complex, and it was well into the afternoon before Sarah was happy enough to slow her pace. She hoped to co-ordinate the end of the job with going-home time. At one point, Miss Sugden walked past, then stepped in between Sarah and Gladys's desks.

'That line isn't consistent in width, Gladys. I suggest you go over it once more,' she said, peering down at Gladys's work and pointing at one particular section.

'Very good, Miss Sugden,' Gladys replied meekly.

Sarah broke out in a sweat again, every nerve end dancing. *Please, God, don't let her look at my board. Make her move on!*

After a few heart-stopping moments, Miss Sugden moved away, and Sarah realised she had been holding her breath. Keeping her head down, she released it slowly and unclenched her pen. *I've aged ten years today. I'm not cut out for this malarkey.*

With a few more strokes of the pen, she completed the tracing. Now for the tricky bit. Sarah loosened the pins securing her work but remained hunched over the drawing as if still working on it, waiting for an opportunity to slide the second sheet out. She didn't have long to wait. Five minutes later, Gladys rose from her seat with a finished tracing and original in her hand. Keeping her eyes on the other girls, Sarah gently tugged the underlying tracing cloth down into her lap and quickly folded it over several times, before guiding it up the sleeve of her jumper. As Gladys walked back down the room towards her, Sarah picked up her drawing and tracing and headed for Miss Sugden.

As usual, the supervisor examined the tracing but, to Sarah's relief, didn't appear to notice anything amiss. She smiled up at Sarah. 'Very good, Sarah.' Then she consulted her watch. 'Twenty past five; hardly worth your while starting a new one. Since you were early this morning, why don't you head off now?'

'Thanks very much, Miss Sugden. See you tomorrow.' Sarah escaped out the door before the supervisor could change her mind.

Sarah could not believe her bad timing. As she scurried down the path towards the gates, she heard Martin calling out to her. She had to stop and wait, all too conscious of the tracing up her left sleeve. Every time she moved, the blasted thing crackled.

'Hello there,' he said as he caught up with her. 'Early release for good behaviour?'

'Funny! But yes, actually. I'm a star tracer, or didn't you know? One day there will be a plaque on the wall in my honour.'

'I wouldn't be getting too big a head about it, kiddo. The Dragon is bound to take you down a peg or two at some point.' Martin tucked his arm through hers and Sarah cringed. It was her left arm. 'What's wrong with your arm?' he asked, glancing down at the sleeve of her coat.

'That's the arm I broke,' she said. 'On days like this, when it's cold and wet, it aches something terrible. If I keep it straight, it doesn't hurt quite as much.'

'Sorry, am I hurting you?' he asked. 'I didn't realise.'

'It's not too bad, but take my other arm. It will be more comfortable.'

Martin obliged, and she breathed a sigh of relief.

As soon as Sarah gained the privacy of her bedroom, she pulled the tracing from her sleeve. So far, so good. But had it worked? Holding the unfolded sheet under her bedside light, she twisted it around, hoping to see an outline of the drawing. The surface was frustratingly smooth. She tried a different angle, then groaned. It hadn't worked. There was barely any impression left on the sheet. Totally despondent, Sarah slumped down onto the bed. Now what was she to do? She couldn't risk using more pressure on the top cloth; she'd go through it for sure, and might even damage the drawing underneath. That would be an absolute disaster, and she would be caught red-handed.

Jumping up, she paced the room. She'd have to think of another way of getting a copy. If only she were clever enough to draw something, just make it up; but she was useless at that sort of thing, and besides, if it wasn't on tracing cloth as she had told Rob, he and his *friend* might be suspicious. She glanced down at the cloth in despair. Now she had the added problem of having to dispose of it. She couldn't risk it being found in the house.

Sarah slept fitfully during the night, and dawn brought little consolation to her troubled mind. If she couldn't find a solution, would Northcott carry out his threat to deport her? There was no one who could advise her on a method that might work, or indeed on her legal position. She could not risk putting anyone in danger by implicating them in the plot. Northcott didn't strike her as a patient man, and lately he had shown little in the way of empathy for her situation. She suspected he was enjoying playing with all their lives, a puppet master in every sense.

The only bit of good fortune was an empty parlour when she came down to breakfast. There was a roaring fire in the grate. It was the perfect chance to dispose of the tracing cloth, hidden in the sleeve of her coat upstairs. She dashed back up the stairs, retrieved it and hurried back down. But as she stood over the fire, ready to chuck the cloth in, Aunt Alice came in from the kitchen.

'Morning, Sarah,' her aunt said as she placed her tray down on the table. 'Sleep well?'

'Morning! Yes, thanks,' Sarah answered, keeping the cloth behind her back. Alice looked surprised to see her standing at the fireplace, so Sarah grabbed the poker and prodded the fire before moving away and sitting down on the sheet to hide it. As soon as Aunt Alice went back into the kitchen, Sarah ran back upstairs with it. She couldn't risk Martin or Uncle Tom appearing at any moment either, as they were bound to be more observant than her aunt. Muttering under her breath, she folded the sheet over several times, and pushed it into her pillowcase, hoping an opportunity to destroy it would materialise later. It was too creased now anyway to bring it back to Hursley Park. In frustration, she almost thumped the pillow. She was being thwarted at every turn. Was it a sign from on high to abandon the entire endeavour? She could be back in Ireland by tomorrow if she left now. Staring at her battered case jutting out over the top of the wardrobe, she was sorely tempted.

★ ★ ★

The taste of failure lay bitter in her mouth as she sat over her breakfast a little while later. Absentmindedly, she twisted her toast into pieces, then looked down at the mess on her plate, bemused by her own actions.

When Martin arrived downstairs, he glanced at her in surprise. 'If you didn't want that toast, you could have saved it for me. Waste not, want not.'

Sarah forced herself to smile back. The last thing she needed was her cousin making a fuss. 'I happen to like it this way,' she said, popping some in her mouth.

Martin looked at her askance, took a fresh piece from the plate his mother had just brought in, and started to spread margarine on it. 'Fair enough.'

'Will you be joining us in the pub Friday night?' she asked.

'Ruth mentioned something about it. Yes, I probably will. Straight after work?'

'Yes. Gladys is on a mission. There is to be fun, and lots of it, and she's not to hear any excuses. Don't dare show up unless you are prepared to be chipper. I am, of course, quoting her.'

'Lord, that girl is so empty-headed,' he said with a quirk of his mouth. 'Is she ever serious about anything?'

'That's harsh, Martin. Is it a crime to enjoy yourself? You'd understand if you knew some of her history. From what she has told me, she had a miserable childhood. Her family was extremely poor. Her dad was injured in the Great War – gassed, I think. Anyway, he couldn't work and when she was old enough, she was pretty much told to leave and fend for herself.'

'That's as may be, and I'm sorry to hear it, but she's a bad influence on Ruth. I wish they didn't share a flat.' A frown settled on his brow as he munched his toast. 'Gladys is far too flighty for my liking.'

'Oh, come on; Ruth is a bit ditzy too,' she said. 'Anyway, I am rather fond of Gladys. We have a lot in common.'

Martin snorted. 'I doubt it. You're well-read and interested in the world around you. I can't imagine Gladys ever reads a book or a newspaper or listens to the radio.'

'You're such a snob!' she exclaimed. 'And she does listen . . . if they play swing.'

Martin rolled his eyes, drained his tea, and stood. 'I rest my case. Are you ready to go? Work's a-calling.'

30

It was with a heavy heart that Sarah entered the Tracing Room half an hour later. She still hadn't figured out an alternative to using a second tracing cloth. It was frustrating because she had hoped that method would work. Neither man would be happy with her lack of progress, and she could almost envisage Northcott's reaction when she told him, which left her with a churning stomach. Would he give her any credit for at least trying? Her thoughts turned to Alfie and his fate. Her answer probably lay there. What she needed now was divine intervention. That, or an escape plan.

Sarah greeted Miss Sugden and took the next drawing from the top of the stack on the supervisor's desk. At once, she spotted Martin's name in the title block. It looked like Uncle Tom's wish was about to come true.

Gladys was at the other table picking up a new tracing cloth. 'What's up with you? You do look glum,' Gladys commented,

279

nudging her with her elbow as she drew alongside. 'Please cheer up before Friday evening's outing. I need distraction; I want to have some fun. The foul weather and this place are getting to me.'

'You got a rollicking, then?'

Gladys had been hauled up before the Dragon the previous afternoon, as one of her tracings had not been accurate enough. Unfortunately, it was a regular occurrence for Gladys: concentration often eluded her.

'I'll say! Lord, being skinned alive would be more pleasant.' Gladys gave an exaggerated shudder. 'She's put me on a warning.'

'Oh no, Gladys! You must be more careful.'

Gladys made a face. 'Maybe I should look for a different job. London's looking more and more inviting.'

'Don't you dare quit!' Sarah hissed at her. 'The place would not be the same without you.'

Gladys grinned at her. 'You old softie.' She lowered her voice after flicking a glance at Miss Sugden. 'Do you think it's true what the lads say about the Dragon?'

'What's that?'

'That it's vinegar, not blood, that runs in her veins,' Gladys said.

Sarah chuckled. 'Some kind of acid for certain. But she's not that bad; I've met worse.' Gladys looked at her askance. Sarah continued: 'You've just been unlucky. By the way, do you happen to know where she lives?'

Gladys's brow puckered. 'Southampton, I think. As far as I know, she didn't move closer when we relocated here. I think she is from there originally and still lives with her mother. I'd say that's a fun household. Can't you imagine the larks they'd get up to?'

Sarah spluttered. 'You're too cruel.'

Gladys sniffed. 'It's what keeps me sane. Anyway, why do you want to know where she lives?'

'Oh, no reason. I thought I spotted her there on Saturday when I was meeting Paul.'

'Hmm, it was probably her. Mind you, it's hard to envisage her anywhere but here behind that desk of hers, giving someone short shrift.'

Sarah was sure there was far more to the lady. Particularly if she was Northcott's accomplice. 'Oh, you never know. She may lead a secret life we know nothing about.'

Gladys snorted with laughter. 'I doubt it!'

Sarah stifled a yawn.

Gladys tilted her head. 'Are you still having those awful nightmares of yours, or are you dreaming of lover boy?'

Sarah snorted. 'As if!'

Gladys tapped her chin with a finger. 'Of course, the real question is which lad you dream about. Poor Rob. How can he compete with a dashing bloke in an RAF uniform?'

'Shush, Gladys, I told you about Paul in confidence, and that's all over, more's the pity,' Sarah said with a stern look. 'Rob is a nice lad, but you know well I haven't made up my mind about him. I am not ready to get too involved with anyone. I'm still finding my feet.'

'You're dead right. Time enough to get tied to one man and the kitchen sink. I've certainly no intention of doing it yet. Far too much fun to be had these days. Think how much freer our lives are compared to our mothers.'

'That's true.'

'Anyway, does Rob know he is only temporary? The poor bloke is keen on you. Always looking out for you in the canteen and asking if you are coming to lunch. Can't remember the last time you had lunch with us girls.'

Sarah pulled a face at her. 'You're just jealous.'

'Course I am!' Gladys spluttered as the door opened and more of the girls entered.

'And I had lunch with you yesterday,' Sarah hissed back.

Gladys bowed. 'So you did. Awfully honoured, I felt, too. Uh-oh, here's the Dragon. Heads down, pens at the ready.'

The morning dragged. Sarah tried her best to work steadily on her drawing, but Martha in the row ahead was ill, constantly coughing and snuffling. Sarah didn't normally find such things distracting, but today it was getting on her nerves. All of a sudden, there was an explosion of sneezing and Sarah looked up to see Martha rummaging frantically up her sleeve. Pulling a handkerchief out, Martha's hand glanced off her inkwell and she jumped off her seat with a cry. Sarah soon saw why. A creeping stain of ink was devouring the girl's tracing as gravity did its worst. Martha stood frozen by the side of the drawing board, watching in horror. Everyone in the room stopped working. Some shook their heads, while others looked more sympathetic. But for each of them, it was their worst nightmare.

Miss Sugden rushed down the room, muttering under her breath, a cloth and sheets of blotting paper clutched in her hand. She righted the now-empty inkwell and stared at the mess on Martha's desk. 'Not again, Martha. How clumsy you are!' The supervisor pulled off the drawing pins and picked up the tracing cloth, being careful to avoid spilling the ink onto the original drawing underneath. 'Oh dear; it's ruined. You will have to start again.'

Martha stood by in misery, her lower lip trembling as she

nodded. 'So sorry, Miss Sugden. It was an accident, honest.' Martha blew her nose, her eyes bright with tears.

Miss Sugden's expression softened. 'Yes, I know. Here, leave this in the tray with the other spoilt tracings. It can be washed off at the end of the day. Take a fresh tracing cloth and start again.' Shaking her head, she handed the blemished sheet to Martha. Her gaze swept around the room. 'Ladies, return to your work, please.'

Sarah's heart began to race. She sucked in her breath as her heart lifted. That was it: that was how she would do it!

Rob was waiting for her in the canteen. Since the Sunday in his flat, they had had lunch together nearly every day. In public, he seemed determined to keep up the deception that their relationship was a romantic one. Though she had no choice but to play along, she dreaded the meetings as Rob spouted more of his fascist nonsense in an attempt to bolster her confidence and urge her to action. It had the opposite effect, leaving her drained and fractious. Thankfully, in private, all pretence of romance had vanished now that his real purpose in pursuing her was out in the open. If anything, Sarah was relieved. Handsome as he was, his political beliefs and traitorous nature were abhorrent.

From Rob's expression as she approached the table, she knew he was eager for news of yesterday's trial run. Sarah was composed as she sat down to join him. 'Can you stay or are you heading back to the office now?' she asked.

'I don't have long, but I was hanging on in the hopes of seeing you.' He lowered his voice. 'How did it go yesterday? Did you manage to get something interesting? Was it successful? Do you have it?'

Sarah unwrapped her sandwich slowly. 'Sorry, Rob. I'm afraid it didn't go well. In fact, it didn't work at all.'

'What! Why?'

'Keep your voice down, for God's sake!' she hissed at him. A couple of the lads at the next table looked over and smirked. One of them piped up: 'Uh-oh, lover's tiff! Poor old Rob!'

Rob threw him a dirty look before sitting back with a frown. 'Don't mind those idiots. Tell me what went wrong? Why didn't it work?' He barely kept the exasperation from his voice.

Sarah whispered: 'The cloth was too thick, and the second sheet didn't take an imprint. I couldn't risk going harder with the pen, even if I'd known at the time it wasn't working. If I had damaged the top sheet, there would have been questions asked. As it was, getting that sheet out without anyone noticing was almost impossible.'

'How did you do it?' he asked.

'Shoved it up my sleeve. Not ideal, I can tell you, as I had to fold it over. Every time I bent my arm you could hear it move. I nearly got caught out by my cousin, of all people. I'll have to find a safer and better way of removing one from the premises.'

'For the next time? Ah! You have another idea. There's something else you can try?' he asked, all eagerness.

Sarah glared at him. 'Yes, but I would appreciate if you didn't put so much pressure on me, Rob. Need I remind you I'm the one running the risk here, not you?'

With a sigh, he leaned forward and reached for her hand. 'Sorry. Yes, I know that. It's just, well, I have promised someone that I can get . . . you know. I don't want to let them down. He came to my flat the other night, demanding we get a move on. Doesn't like being refused anything, you see. I'm almost sorry I gave my word. Sometimes the people you have to deal with are not those you'd choose.'

Sarah almost spluttered: she couldn't agree more. 'Why should I care about this friend of yours? You shouldn't have promised him anything. It's no simple thing, what I'm trying to do.'

'But the cause is the most important thing, Sarah.'

'Perhaps, but there's a strong possibility I may not be able to pull it off. Have you considered that?'

Rob let go of her hand. 'Yes, I know. Sorry. Where does that leave us, then?'

'There is another option. It's a bit mad, and highly risky, but just might work if I'm lucky.'

'Great – what is it?' Rob's eyes were alight.

'I'd rather not say now, Rob, but I'm going to attempt it tomorrow or Friday.'

'How will I know if you are successful?'

'You must be patient until lunch on Friday. I'll see you then,' she replied, finishing her tea and checking the time. 'My thirty minutes are up. I have to get back. Won't you wish me luck? God knows, I need it.'

'Of course I will.'

Sarah stood and looked down at him. 'If it doesn't work, you may see me being carted off and the Dragon breathing real fire for once.'

'Don't be silly. If anyone can do it, it's you.'

Was there a shade of uncertainty behind his words? She couldn't blame him for doubting her. As Sarah walked away, she had never felt so weary.

31

Sarah's head was throbbing. The reality of what she was about to attempt brought her out in a cold sweat. There could be only one shot at this. Sarah took another look around the room before she picked up her pen and resumed her tracing. As if the universe were mocking her, her original drawing for the day was another one of Martin's Mark VII schematics. It looked like the cockpit door mechanism Martin had mentioned to Uncle Tom. Her heart raced. If her cousin was to be believed, this design would enable the Spit to go even higher than before and give the RAF a huge advantage over Jerry. This was perfect: just what Northcott had described.

For a brief moment, she sat back and admired Martin's skill. The drawing was so intricate and yet had a lightness of touch, as if his pen had danced across the page. There was beauty and a kind of magic to it. For the first time she wondered how it felt to be the one creating something new. Was there a thrill when you saw the prototype, or finished plane, and knew you had contributed to its creation?

It felt so wrong to blithely hand the drawing over to a traitor such as Rob and his vile conspirators. In fact, it made her blood boil. What if Northcott failed to stop the transfer and the drawing ended up in Berlin as Rob hoped? If that happened, she might be complicit in the possible defeat of the Allies. However, now was not the time to contemplate such things. She was committed, even if it was giving her restless nights and many a nightmare. Her hand shook as she gripped the pen tighter. She wasn't sure which emotion was driving her most: fear or hatred. Not for the first time, she cursed her luck in coming to the attention of Captain Northcott of His Majesty's Royal Navy.

She checked her watch. It was now ten past five. Timing was crucial if her plan was to work. The tracing was almost finished; one more flourish of her pen and the final sign-off were all that was required. Her hands were clammy as she completed the line, drawing her pen smoothly along the ruler. Under her brows, she surveyed the room. Everyone was working away in silence and Miss Sugden, glasses on the end of her nose, was inspecting someone's tracing. Sarah filled in her name and the date below Martin's. She had to implement her plan now or miss her chance for another day.

But just then, Gladys's head popped up and looked across at her, a wide grin on her face as her eyes flicked towards the clock on the wall and back again. Sarah smiled back in acknowledgement. Gladys – an inveterate clock-watcher – wiggled her brows at her before returning to her work. If only Gladys knew how much Sarah wished the day was over too. She could feel her blouse clinging to her back, damp beneath her cardigan, and it wasn't the warmth of the room that was the cause.

Sarah couldn't stall any longer. With as little movement as possible, she eased out the drawing pins so they were barely holding the tracing cloth and drawing in place. Speed would be vital when the moment came. She reached towards the inkwell. It took some effort to control the shake in her hand. Her aim was to tip enough of the ink to make the tracing unusable, but not unreadable. When setting up earlier, she had positioned the drawing so that the title block was in the top right corner, close to the inkwell. With a jerk of her hand, as if she were reaching out for a pen, her fingers brushed against the inkpot. It tipped slightly, and an ugly, black pool of ink landed on the title block. Perfect. The stain was small but sufficient for her purposes. Sarah grabbed the inkwell and righted it, cursing under her breath.

Gladys looked over and mouthed: 'Oh, no!'

Sarah bit her bottom lip, breathing rapidly, doing her best to look flustered. Gladys, wide-eyed, glanced up the room to the supervisor's desk. Sarah scowled and nodded in response. Thank goodness for those acting opportunities last year. She took a few deep breaths before slipping the tracing cloth free. Slowly, she made her way up the room to the supervisor. Sarah felt her face burn, but the blush in her cheeks suited the situation perfectly. Miss Sugden would not know it was anxiety induced, rather than embarrassment.

'I'm terribly sorry, Miss Sugden, I'm afraid I knocked over my inkwell,' Sarah said, showing the damage to the supervisor. 'It's just the title block, though.'

Miss Sugden's eyebrows shot up. 'Oh dear, that's not like you, Sarah. You are usually so careful.'

'It was very clumsy of me. Is the damage too great? What should I do with it?'

Miss Sugden gestured towards a tray at the end of her desk. 'You can add it to those to be soaked and cleaned off. Such a shame, my dear, I'm afraid even that small amount of damage is too much. You will have to start over in the morning. Tut-tut. What a pity: your work is always perfect.'

'That's kind of you to say, Miss.' Sarah looked down at the floor for a moment, before moving to the tray. She made a show of placing the tracing down in the tray, then turned back to the supervisor. Her heart was in her mouth: this was the key part of her plan. 'I feel really bad about this, Miss. May I be of help? I can take these out to the cloakroom and clean them off for you, if you like?'

Miss Sugden glanced at the spoilt tracings in the tray and then at the clock. 'That's kind of you, Sarah. It will save my old legs. Do you know what to do?'

'I do, Miss. I soak them in the sink and then rinse them off.'

'Yes, Sarah. Once they are clean, bring them back in here and put them on the radiators to dry off. Hopefully, they will be usable tomorrow. Waste not, want not!'

'Indeed, Miss. Don't worry, I'll sort them out for you. I really am very sorry.'

Miss Sugden melted. 'Don't fret, my dear, these things happen to the best of us. Now, before you go out, fetch the original drawing and I will keep it safe for you to use tomorrow.'

Sarah hurried back to her desk and retrieved Martin's drawing. Gladys gave her a sympathetic look, which she returned with a self-effacing smile, before heading back to Miss Sugden.

'Here it is, Miss.' Sarah handed the drawing over.

Miss Sugden examined it closely. 'That's a relief: no damage to the original.' Then she turned and placed it in the cupboard behind her desk and turned the key.

Sarah took up the damaged sheets and hurried out of the door. Out in the corridor, she was almost light-headed with relief and paused to catch her breath. But she couldn't hang around for long. The girls would leave the room as soon as the clock struck five thirty. Sarah strode to the cloakroom and quickly closed the door behind her.

She had deliberately left her coat on a hook at the back of the room to give herself some cover in case anyone should come in. When she found it, half-hidden beneath someone else's coat, she turned to the inside and found the opening she had made in the front lining the night before. But perhaps her gas mask box would be better? She stood uncertain, eyeing the box. No. The tracing would become very creased, as she would have to fold it over many times. Decision made, she went with her original plan. Sarah carefully fed her tracing into the gap in her coat lining and turned the coat interior to face the wall.

Sarah filled the sink with water and plunged the other tracings in. Tapping her foot, she waited for the water to take effect. She pulled the top one out. The ink began to blur and run. Sarah took up the cloth, which was always there for that very job, and scrubbed off the ink. It took her several minutes to clean off the remaining cloths. Using a dry towel, she soaked up the excess water. Her watch read five twenty. She'd have to hurry.

With a prayer of thanks foremost in her mind, she exited the cloakroom and hurried back to the Tracing Room. The other girls were finishing up their work, the silence of the afternoon now broken by their chatter. Sarah nodded to Miss Sugden and made for the radiators. She spread the cloths along the top, checked they would not slip off, and returned to her drawing board. As the others left the room, she tidied up her equipment. She needed time to recover, and wanted to avoid being caught by Ruth or Gladys on her way out. The quicker she got home, the sooner she could breathe easy again.

On her return to the cloakroom ten minutes later, Sarah was surprised to find a few of the girls still there chatting, including Gladys.

'I thought you'd already left,' Gladys said to her, as she pulled on her coat.

Sarah threw her eyes to heaven. 'Silly me, I was so flustered over that stupid tracing, I forgot to put on my coat before I brought the cloths back inside.'

'You were lucky, my friend. I thought Miss Sugden would have had a fit when she saw that tracing. She really hates when that happens. If that had been me . . .'

'I know. She was awfully good about it. I guess we are all allowed one mistake.'

Gladys giggled. 'I'm well past that quota! Come on; let's get out of here. I'll walk out with you.'

To Sarah's horror, as they walked down towards the gate, she spotted a queue at the hut. That could only mean one thing: they were doing checks of the staff as they exited. Of all the days for them to do it! Would this nightmare never end? To get this far and now *this*. Gladys was chatting away, but she barely heard her. What if they found the tracing? Should she make an excuse and go back in and wait? Perhaps she should try leaving from the Southend House gate instead? But there was no guarantee they weren't carrying out checks there too. Running around like a headless chicken would only draw attention. Too late now. With her heart pounding, they joined the queue: she'd have to brave it.

Gladys groaned. 'Oh no, I'll miss the bus at this rate. Do they not realise the likes of us don't need to be checked? I wish they'd hurry up.' Sarah nodded. It was all she could do in response, for she feared if she tried to speak, it would come out as a squeak.

When they reached the two soldiers on duty, Gladys sidled up to the nearest one and piped up: 'Hello, Frank, pet. Any chance you could let me through?' She pointed to the bus stop. 'Look, my bus has just pulled in and I don't want to miss it. Be a dear.'

Frank checked to see if his superior officer inside the hut was occupied, then winked at Gladys. 'Gladys, you should know better.' Gladys beamed at him and he visibly melted. 'Oh, all right, you know I can't resist that cheeky smile of yours. Quick – just show me the insides of your handbags, ladies.' He peeked inside each of their bags and nodded. 'That's fine. Go on. Just this once, mind! You'll get me in trouble, Gladys, you will.'

Gladys blew him a kiss and took off at speed for the bus stop. Heart thumping, Sarah stood outside the gate and watched while her friend jumped onto the bus. Gladys turned and waved back to her.

Thank God for flirts! That had been far too close for comfort.

32

Much to Sarah's disgust, Rob was waiting at the army hut at the entrance to Hursley Park on Friday morning. Rob hassling her was all she needed. She was already tense; she didn't know what awaited her inside. Could her theft have been discovered? As the time for the handover approached, she was getting extremely nervous. Rob's constant badgering was only making things worse. It was bad enough having lunch with him every day without being ambushed at the gate. Keeping up the pretence of romance was really getting to her. The sooner this was all over, the better.

She showed her ID to the soldier on duty and didn't make eye contact with Rob. She kept walking, her irritation bubbling up inside.

'Sarah?' He gasped as he came level with her. 'Hey, hold up,' Rob demanded, catching her arm and forcing her to stop.

'What?' Sarah turned on him, wrenching her arm from his grasp. Over his shoulder and not far behind, she saw Martin and Uncle Tom coming up the path, as were a few of the tracing girls. 'For goodness' sake, why are you waylaying me here?' she hissed. 'I told you I'll meet you for lunch. We can talk then.'

Rob frowned at her. 'I only wanted to know if you had any success. No need to bite my head off!'

Sarah greeted the group of girls as they passed, then turned back to Rob. 'Have you no patience?'

'Frankly, no!' Rob spluttered. 'There is so much at stake, Sarah. You can't leave me in the dark. I need to know.'

Martin and Uncle Tom walked past, her uncle winking at her. But Martin threw her a questioning glance. She indicated it was all right with a shake of her head and he continued on, turning back to his conversation with his father.

Rob glanced at Martin's retreating back. 'What's up with him?' Rob asked.

'Nothing. Like me, I'm sure he is wondering why you are accosting me on the way into work,' Sarah ground out, looking at her watch.

Rob's eyebrows shot up. 'For God's sake, do you think I got any sleep last night, wondering what happened yesterday?'

'It might surprise you to know that sleep was fairly elusive for me as well.'

'You succeeded then?'

'Yes!' She sighed. 'Now, if you don't mind, I need to get to my desk. I'm already in trouble for messing up my tracing yesterday. I don't want to draw any further attention to myself.' The look of relief which spread over Rob's face was almost comical, but it just added to her irritation. He moved as if to link her arm. 'Please, Rob, don't,' she said, and strode away.

★   ★   ★

By lunchtime, there had been no mention of any missing tracing sheets and Sarah's mood had mellowed. To her surprise when she arrived at the canteen, there was no sign of Rob. She found an empty table and waited. As she finished her sandwiches, he finally appeared in the doorway. Ruth was by his side and they were in deep conversation. As Sarah looked on, Ruth touched his arm and leaned in even closer to say something. Rob became agitated, shaking his head. *Now, what's that all about?* Sarah wondered. They seemed very chummy for supposed ex-lovers. It gave further credence to her suspicion that they were in league. But could she be mistaken? Perhaps Ruth was still interested in Rob romantically? That raised the question of whether she should warn Martin. Sarah didn't want to see him get hurt.

Just then, Rob caught sight of her, muttered something to Ruth, and made for Sarah's table. Ruth joined the queue, but Sarah noticed her gaze followed Rob across the room.

'Are you still speaking to me? May I join you?' he asked, his expression a trifle sheepish as he stood looking down at her.

'Of course,' she replied. Once he sat down, she couldn't resist: 'Is Ruth all right? She looks upset.'

'What?' he replied, looking flustered. 'Ruth Howard? I don't know, she seemed ok to me. Met her just outside on my way in.'

Not at all convinced he was telling the truth, Sarah flicked a glance over to the queue, but Ruth now had her back to them. Sarah turned to Rob. 'Look, I'm sorry about earlier, but I didn't know what I'd be facing this morning. I was all on edge.' She lowered her voice. 'If Miss Sugden or the Dragon cottoned on to what I'd done . . .'

'Don't worry, I understand. I'm pretty stressed myself.' She noted that the enthusiasm with which he launched into his sandwiches belied his claim. 'When I saw the check at the gates yesterday evening, I was concerned you might be caught.'

'I nearly did. It was only thanks to Gladys using her charms that we weren't thoroughly searched.'

'Excellent, but you still haven't told me how you got the copy.'

Sarah briefly outlined the previous afternoon's venture.

'I'm impressed,' he said. 'That was inspired. It's not too damaged, is it? I'll get a telling-off if it's not of use.'

'The only unreadable bit is the title block; I made sure of that,' she answered. 'The drawing itself is perfect.'

'Well done. My friend will be so grateful.'

Sarah sniffed. 'I hope so, because I won't be doing that again in a hurry. I was scared to death I'd be caught.'

'But you weren't. I must admit, I'm not sure I'd have had the gumption to do it. You must have nerves of steel, Sarah. Now the sooner we pass it on, the better. Can you meet me this evening?' he asked.

A wave of panic swept over Sarah. She needed more time. There was no guarantee Northcott would be available at such short notice. She licked her lips and swallowed hard. 'No, I'm afraid not. It will have to be Sunday.'

'Why?'

'What's wrong with Sunday? That's the day we normally meet up. It might raise questions otherwise.'

'I think we could make an exception in the circumstances. Besides, who would question it? We're walking out, aren't we?'

'But I already have plans,' she said, desperately trying to think of an excuse.

'Change them.' Rob glared at her, and for the first time she was afraid of him.

'I can't. I'm meeting up with the girls tonight, and tomorrow is a family night out at the local. My cousin Judith is coming down from London for the weekend. I have to be there. My aunt and uncle would be very hurt if I didn't go.'

'I see,' he said, frowning over his tea.

'What's the rush, Rob? It's not going anywhere.'

'But is it safe? I hope you have hidden it well. The last thing we need is for your nosy cousin to find it and start asking questions.'

'Trust me, no one will find it. It's in a safe place where no one would think to look.' Rob didn't look satisfied, but she brazened it out by giving him a long hard stare with her chin up.

He looked away first. 'All right; Sunday it is. Can you come to the flat?'

'Sure. Straight after Mass – about one o'clock?'

Rob nodded. 'You will be careful, won't you?'

'Of course. Will your friend be there too? I'm not sure I want to meet him from the way you described him.'

'He may insist on it, but I'll try to put him off.'

'Is he German secret service?' she asked in a whisper.

'He has hinted at it, but he's not the kind of man you question. All I know is he can pass information on to where it is greatly appreciated and will do the most good. Best of all, he is willing to pay handsomely for it. If he's happy on Sunday, he'll pay us then.'

'Hmm, I don't really care about that. This was never about money, Rob.' Rob shrugged. 'Do you think he will be armed?' she asked.

'Possibly, but he won't harm you, not after what you have achieved for the cause.' Rob frowned. 'He's bound to be pleased.'

Sarah smiled: *Well, your friend won't be so pleased when he comes face to face with Captain Northcott!*

The phone box in Otterbourne was again an unwelcome sight, but it was still the safest option. As she waited to be put through to the Victoria Hotel, she once again marvelled at how quickly the lies came to her. Rob had really pressured her, but she supposed he was anxious to get the whole thing over with as soon as possible. A lot appeared to hinge on the success of the operation for him. His German friend didn't sound like a man you would want to disappoint.

Using Cousin Judith as an excuse for putting Rob off had been inspired, her only regret being that it wasn't true. A letter had arrived earlier in the week, full of excuses for Judith's absence, yet again. Poor Aunt Alice had done her best not to show how disappointed she was, and how much she missed her daughter, but Sarah had seen her uncle become enraged for the first time. He had immediately written a response, and Sarah had no doubt he wouldn't have minced his words.

The phone clicked and a male voice answered. 'Good evening, the Victoria Hotel; how may I help you?'

Sarah could have sworn it was Mr Snooty from her visit the previous Saturday. 'I'd like to leave an urgent message for Captain Northcott, please.'

'Certainly, madam. I shall just fetch a pen,' he answered, and she heard the receiver being placed on the desk, then picked up again. 'Sorry, madam. Please go ahead.'

'One o'clock, Sunday afternoon, 35 Albert Place, Winchester,' Sarah said.

'And would madam care to leave a name?'

'No, madam would not. Just that message, please.'

'Very good, madam,' he replied frostily.

Sarah had to admit he sounded unsurprised at the cryptic nature of her communication, and she wondered if Northcott was often the recipient of strange messages. The receiver went dead.

Sarah leaned against the side panel of the telephone box, breathing hard. Had she given enough information? Should she have warned Northcott about Rob's friend? But it wasn't something she could have said over the phone to the receptionist at the hotel, and when she had mentioned the man's existence to Northcott, and the likelihood of his being present, he hadn't appeared fazed by it.

With a muttered curse, she picked up the receiver once more. 'Southampton 379, please, operator.'

'One moment please,' the disembodied voice replied. Sarah fed in her coins.

A click and a voice came on the line. 'Hello?' Sarah reckoned it was the same lady from last time.

'Hello. May I speak to the captain, please?'

'I'm afraid he is out. May I take a message?'

'Could you just say Miss Gillespie is expecting company on Sunday afternoon? He'll know what it means.'

There was a sigh, followed by silence on the other end for a few moments. Was she writing it down? 'Very well, I will pass it on.' The phone line went dead.

Sarah looked at the receiver and wondered if she had done the right thing. However, it was too late for regrets. For any of it.

33

Sitting between her aunt and cousin in church on Sunday, Sarah could not focus. When her fidgeting prompted a reproving glance from Martin, she mouthed 'sorry' and tried to relax. Breakfast that morning had probably been a mistake. It was now a cold slab of undigested food sitting in her gut. To distract herself, she followed the shafts of light coming through the stained-glass windows as they flickered across the congregation: ripples of colour as transient as her composure. It didn't help. Sarah concentrated on the priest instead. There was some comfort in the musicality of his voice and the rhythm of the familiar Latin phrases. But his words washed over her, compounding the hollow ache in her stomach. When she managed to pray, it was a plea to God to keep her safe: to bless her mission if it was, as Northcott claimed, the right thing to do. The possible consequences of her involvement in Northcott's scheme made her shudder. Would her actions mean that Rob would face a traitor's rope? The doubts kept bubbling up, undermining her composure, and it took a deal of courage to suppress them and act normally in front of the family.

'Don't be late for dinner, you two,' Aunt Alice said to Sarah and Martin as they parted outside the church.

Uncle Tom grinned at them and wiggled his brows from behind her back. 'Stop fussing, woman. We'll miss our bus.'

Aunt Alice darted a look at him from the corner of her eye. 'I won't be a minute, Tom; have some patience.'

'We won't be late, Mother. Enjoy your afternoon and don't be anxious about us. Our plan is to meet up again and get the six o'clock bus home,' Martin said, giving her a peck on the cheek.

'Say hello to Ruth from me,' she said, smiling up at him.

'I will. Go on with ye; it's too cold to be standing about.'

But Alice didn't move. 'I meant to say, Martin. Perhaps it's time Ruth came around for dinner again some evening after work. I'd like to get to know her better.'

Sarah and Martin exchanged an amused glance. 'I'll see, Mum,' he replied.

Alice frowned at him before turning to Sarah. 'Have fun, my dear. Make sure you don't miss that bus, now. I don't like the thought of you travelling home on your own when it's dark.'

'Thank you, but you don't need to fret, Aunty Alice. I'll see you later,' Sarah answered. It took a great deal of restraint not to hug her aunt. The possibility that she might never see any of them again brought a lump to her throat.

Sarah and Martin stood together and watched Alice and Tom walk away.

'Will we be hearing wedding bells any time soon?' Sarah teased.

'Don't you start. Mum is bad enough,' he said with a smirk. 'I'll see you later, Sarah; you mind yourself.'

Ten minutes later, Sarah stood at the corner of Albert Place, surveying the almost deserted street. She felt in her pocket, her fingers curling around Mrs Twohig's Iron Cross. If ever there was a test for how lucky the trophy was, it was today. Mind you, it would take some explaining if she was found with it on her person; or worse, on her corpse. *My, how dark my thoughts have become*, she thought with a slight shake of her head. But the gloomy thoughts were starting to numb her senses just when she could not afford to be emotional and mess things up. She had to think of this as a job, a duty to her adopted country and, above all, an opportunity to settle a score with Jerry.

She scanned the street again. Where might Northcott be hiding? There was no sign of his car. He must have left it close by; on the next street, perhaps. Would he have accessed the house before her, or was he watching and waiting for her to go in first? A million other questions ran through her head, and she realised just how unprepared she was for this. Did she possess the ability to react quickly enough to whatever might await her at Rob's flat? She should have insisted Northcott tell her exactly what was going to happen. With a start, she remembered she hadn't specified which flat belonged to Rob. How would Northcott figure it out? Worse still, she had no way to defend herself if things took a nasty turn with Rob's friend. Was it too late to turn and run?

On the gable wall of the end house were numerous pasted posters. One in particular caught her eye. It was of a Tommy pointing to his helmet, and the caption read: 'Beware Spies: Keep it under your hat'. *Oh, the irony; that's the last place a tracing would fit!*

With an unsteady hand, she gently pushed against the front panel of her coat and met resistance. The tracing was still there. The night before, she had dreamt she had arrived at Rob's flat only to find the tracing had slipped out from her coat and was lying in the street for anyone to pick up. And that was only one nightmare she had endured.

With her senses humming, she walked towards the gallery building. As she put her hand to the side door which led to the upstairs flats, she spied Mr Atkins through the gallery window. She waved hello, but he was sitting at the desk, staring into space, oblivious to her presence. Sarah suspected he was oblivious to everything. Her heart went out to him, but his grief, no more than her own, had to be pushed aside for now.

This was for Maura.

Taking a deep breath, she pushed the door open and entered the gloom of the hallway. The only light came from the grimy windowpane above the door. For a moment, she stood and listened, peering up into the shadows. The muted sound of the radio or a gramophone was coming from one of the flats above, but she could distinguish no other sound. With her heart hammering in her chest, she climbed the flight of stairs. Much to her relief, there was no one waiting for her on the landing. She almost laughed. What had she expected? A Nazi uniformed officer hailing Hitler, welcoming her to the Third Reich with all its glories? *Too much imagination, my girl.*

At the top step, she hesitated. The music was louder now, coming from a flat further down the corridor. It wasn't too late to change her mind. She gripped the banister as a tremor of pure terror ran through her; she wanted to retch, but no: she had to keep control. This had to end today for the sake of her sanity, if nothing else.

She knocked on Rob's door.

'Come in, come in, Sarah,' Rob said, with a bob of his head and a bright smile, as he opened the door wide. *He's cheerful*, she thought, with a further twist to her beleaguered stomach. Of course, this was the culmination of his scheming: he had every reason to be delighted with himself. She stepped over the threshold and was relieved to see there was no one else in the room. Sarah turned to him with a questioning glance. 'Are we alone?'

'Yes, of course,' he replied. 'Is everything ok with you?' he asked. 'You do look tense.'

'I am. It's not surprising, given the circumstances.'

'I suppose so, but there's no reason to be. What you have done is positively heroic. I'm quite envious. I'm only a facilitator: you have done all the hard work. Here, give me your coat,' Rob waved towards a chair, 'and take a pew.' She watched him hang up her coat on the back of the door. He was paler than usual, and his movements were jerky: she realised he was just as uneasy and trying to hide it. Rob turned around. 'Well, have you got it?' he asked, his voice hinting at hoarseness. 'Is it in your handbag?'

'No. It's in the lining of my coat. If you look, there is a slit in the front seam on the right-hand side.'

'Oh, how clever of you,' he said, pulling the coat away from the door and feeling the inside of the lining. A slow smile spread over his face. 'Is that how you got it out of Hursley?' She nodded.

Taking his time, he pulled the tracing cloth free of the lining.

Once at the table by the window, he smoothed it out, almost reverently. Sarah recoiled. He could hardly contain his excitement. *Bloody traitor!* If only he could be caught at this moment when his treachery was so plain to see. Taking a deep breath, she joined him at the table, hoping Northcott would make his appearance sooner rather than later, because she didn't know how much longer she could maintain the pretence.

'This looks great, Sarah,' Rob said, peering at it closely. 'What is the drawing?'

'The release mechanism for the newly designed cockpit for the Mark VII,' she told him.

He pointed to the ink stain. 'Is there anything crucial under there?'

'No. That's the title block. It only has names and dates, and version number – that kind of thing. As I planned, the ink only affected that part of the tracing. That was one of the tricky bits of the whole operation because if I had misjudged it, and the spill had spread over the drawing, it would be useless to anyone. Luckily, the stain was enough to make the tracing unusable from Supermarine's point of view, but the actual tracing is an exact replica of the original. You need not worry.' He nodded vigorously whilst staring at the sheet. 'So, will this do, do you think?' she prompted. 'Will it satisfy your friend?'

'Looks marvellous to me,' he said, smiling up at her. 'Well done. I think he will be more than happy.' Rob tapped the drawing. 'Don't worry, he will make sure the Luftwaffe get this. Then it's up to them to make the best use of the information.'

'Well, that's a relief,' she sighed. 'I don't want to go through that again, I can tell you.'

Rob patted her arm. 'Don't worry, Sarah. This should be enough.'

Her insides twisted again. 'But what if it isn't, Rob? I took an enormous risk getting this. It was sheer luck I got away with it. I want you to tell him I won't be repeating the exercise.'

'All right! Take it easy. Look, you can tell him yourself. We will meet him shortly.'

'Is that necessary?' she asked.

Where the hell was Northcott? Things were moving too fast. How was she to stall them?

'Yep. He wants to meet you and pay you in person.' Rob grinned at her. 'I think you will find he will be more than generous. Of course, he also wishes to convey his thanks for your service to the Fatherland.' Rob placed his hand down on the tracing. 'This kind of information could actually save lives.'

He said it with so much sincerity, she was nauseous. 'Do you think so? That's gratifying, I'm sure. Where are we meeting him?' Sarah asked, worried he was going to say they had to go elsewhere. She had no way of letting Northcott know if there was a change of location. She only hoped the captain had the building under surveillance and could follow them. But where *was* he? Time was running out.

Rob smiled and tapped the side of his nose. 'He's here already.'

Sarah glanced around. 'Where?' Was he in the bedroom? Had he been listening the whole time? Suddenly, her hands were clammy.

'He's waiting for us upstairs, in fact. By a stroke of luck, Mr Atkins cleared out most of Alfie's stuff from the attic last week. It's the perfect spot to meet as we won't be disturbed up there.' Rob waved his hand around the room. 'The walls are pretty thin down here. Do you hear that racket from the girls in the flat next door? When their radio isn't blaring, I can hear every word they say. It's too dangerous to chance being overheard here.'

Sarah thought it was an odd arrangement, despite his explanation. Something wasn't right. Her instincts were screaming at her to run.

'But I saw Mr Atkins down in the gallery as I came in. This is risky, is it not? He might go up to the attic for some reason. How would we explain our presence?'

Rob frowned. 'I doubt he will. The poor man is still in a state. Sits down there mulling over what might have been most days.' Rob rolled the tracing up and tucked it under his arm. 'Come on, let's get this over with. Then we can go for a celebratory drink.' Rob held the door open for her.

'Oh, good,' she replied half-heartedly. 'I have more than earned one.'

34

9th November 1941, Winchester

Sarah hung back and let Rob precede her up the narrow flight of stairs to the attic. Despite the chill of the house, her blouse was stuck to her back with perspiration and her hands were damp. Taking deep breaths helped her keep control, even though she had every reason to panic. Rob already had the tracing and Northcott hadn't been present to see or stop the hand-over. What was she to do? Should she grab it back from Rob and run? In a few moments, it would end up in German hands. She couldn't let that happen, not after all she had been through.

This would be an excellent moment to appear, Captain Northcott.

Rob turned at the top and gave her an encouraging smile, his eyes bright with excitement, evidently pleased with himself and his achievements. Then he pushed open the attic door and disappeared from view. She followed him inside.

The room was as cold as she remembered, but most of Alfie's clutter was gone. Instead, an armchair now stood where the easel used to be. A silver-topped cane leaned against the arm of the chair, and sitting in it was . . .

Rob stepped forward. 'Here she is, Northcott, and I think you will be very pleased with what she has brought along for us today.' Rob grabbed her arm and pulled her forward, before throwing her a triumphant glance. 'You were right about her in every respect, Captain. She's a republican, and a traitor to this country.' Rob held up the tracing. 'She didn't need much encouragement to steal this when she thought it would find its way to Germany. You have your spy.'

'Well done, McArthur. Do come and join us, Miss Gillespie.' Northcott smiled at her.

'You!' Sarah found her voice at last.

What was going on? This didn't make any sense.

Rob swung around, frowning. 'You two know each other?'

'Very well, indeed,' drawled Northcott. 'Isn't that so, Sarah?'

'Yes!' She almost choked on the word as her mind raced. What the hell was he playing at? Northcott was Rob's contact? Rob thought *she* was a republican and a traitor.

'But . . . I don't understand, Northcott,' Rob said, his gaze flicking between Sarah and the captain. 'How does she know you already? What's going on?'

'A good question, Rob. What *is* going on, Captain?' Sarah asked, stepping closer. 'You asked me to root out your fascist fifth columnist.' Furious, she waved her hand at Rob. 'That's you, Rob, in case you haven't worked it out yet.'

'What?' Rob shouted, his bewildered gaze swinging wildly back and forth.

The captain chuckled softly. 'What a pair of gullible fools. This has been almost too easy.'

Sarah grabbed Rob's arm and hissed, dismayed that he did

not comprehend what was happening: 'For God's sake, Rob. He isn't who he claims.'

Rob shook her off and shot her an angry glare. 'I don't *understand.*' Then he stepped towards Northcott. 'Explain!' he demanded, his voice cracking.

'Oh, I'm sure you can figure it out, old chap. Now, give me the tracing,' Northcott said, easing up out of the chair. 'We can't let all of Sarah's excellent work go to waste.'

With her heart hammering in her chest, Sarah stared at Northcott. His face was twisted, and his eyes filled with mania. A zealous Nazi; isn't that what Rob had described to her? Well, even if Rob had given her the impression that his Nazi contact might be German, it was an unerringly accurate description of the captain at this moment. As the pieces fell into place, she was filled with rage. They had both been duped. She had to make Rob understand that they were in real danger from this lunatic.

'He has tricked both of us, Rob. I don't know who you really are, but I bet he convinced you I was dying to sell secrets. All the while he set me up to out you as the spy at Hursley. Don't you see? We did his dirty work for him. We stole the plans *he* wanted.'

Northcott smiled and nodded. 'Indeed, you did, my dear girl, and I'm ever so grateful.'

Rob looked at her aghast. 'He said you were IRA and had been planted at Hursley to get Spitfire drawings for the Germans. All you needed was a way of getting them out of England and I was to provide that.'

'No, no, you have it all wrong.' She had to convince Rob they had both been manipulated. 'He lied to both of us. He told me you had similar aims.'

'What?' Rob went deadly pale. 'That's utter nonsense. I'm a journalist. He promised me a scoop if I helped him reveal the spy at Supermarine. I only pretended about all that fascist nonsense so we could flush you out. He was desperate to expose *you.*' Slowly, he turned back to Northcott. He was trembling. 'You bastard! What are you playing at?'

'Now, now, McArthur; language, please: there is a lady present,' the captain said. 'I suggest you both calm down.' He held out his hand. 'The tracing, please.'

'Rob, I'm telling you: *he* is the fifth columnist,' Sarah cried. 'We have been double-crossed.'

'No, I don't believe you. He can't be. He's Royal Navy, for goodness' sake.'

'Which makes him all the more dangerous. I don't know his motivation, but his sympathies clearly lie with Germany. What's more, if you hand over that tracing, he will kill us.'

'Why would he do that?' Rob asked, his voice rising, his expression wild.

Sarah glanced at Northcott. A smug smile played about his mouth. He was thoroughly enjoying the situation. Enraged, she swung back around to Rob. 'Good God, you idiot, don't you realise? He has too much to lose to let us go free. We know who he is. We are witnesses. If he is arrested for treason, he will hang.'

'Might I also point out that you are both accomplices?' Northcott chipped in. 'Well, this is all lovely – a real tête-à-tête – however, I am in a hurry.' Northcott eased a revolver out of his pocket and pointed it at Rob. 'You should listen to her, McArthur. She's far cleverer than I had anticipated. If I had known, I would have ensured she secured more than one drawing for me. Alas, this one will have to suffice. I do

314

hope you heeded my words, Sarah, and brought me something of worth.'

Suddenly, Northcott lunged forward and grabbed the tracing from Rob, pushing him backwards to the floor. Sarah leapt forward and tried to hit the revolver out of Northcott's grip. In the tussle, the captain dropped the tracing. With a curse, he pulled her by the arm and twisted her around, just as Rob gained his feet. Northcott's arm was like a band of steel around her stomach, pinning her arms. She was stuck fast and no match for the captain's strength.

'Pick the tracing up and hand it to me or I will put a bullet in her,' Northcott told Rob.

Sarah was all too aware of the cold metal barrel of the gun pressed to her temple. She could see no way out of this situation. Once that tracing was in Northcott's hand she was a dead woman. In despair, she realised Rob was frozen in indecision: he had a rigid stance and a wild stare. After a moment, his gaze fixed upon the tracing. 'Don't!' she warned him. 'He is going to kill us both if you hand it over. Take it and run, Rob. Get out of here!'

'Shut up!' the captain hissed in her ear. 'Now, McArthur, I'm running out of patience with you. Pick up the damned tracing.'

Rob's lower lip trembled. He reached down and lifted the tracing from the floor.

'No!' Sarah cried out and tried to twist out of Northcott's grip, but he just tightened his hold.

'I'm sorry, Sarah, I don't know what is happening, but I can't let him shoot you. I won't have that on my conscience,' Rob said, swallowing hard and holding out the tracing to Northcott.

All of a sudden, Northcott released Sarah and pushed her to the floor. The force of impact winded her. When she rolled over, it was in time to see Northcott raise the gun and fire. Rob staggered, then crumpled to the floor as Northcott grabbed the tracing from him. In horror, Sarah saw the blood pumping from Rob's stomach as he lay moaning on the floor. On her hands and knees, she crawled over to him.

'Oh, no, Rob!' she cried out, her voice shaking. In desperation, she pressed down on his blood-soaked shirt above the wound, but the blood oozed, warm and sticky, through her fingers, the metallic smell of it in her nostrils. Rob had put himself in danger to save her. Panic gripped her. It looked hopeless: there was too much blood. It would take a miracle to save him.

'I wouldn't bother, Sarah. He won't last long.' Northcott sighed. 'I do so hate goodbyes.' The captain took a step closer.

'You won't get away with this,' Sarah hissed as she looked up at him, consumed with a burning rage. 'I've left a written account of it all. The truth will come out.'

'No matter, my dear. I hate to disillusion you, but no matter what evidence you have left, I have no intention of being caught. I pride myself on always having a perfect plan in place.' He pointed towards the door at the back of the attic. 'My car awaits at the rear entrance. I shall be long gone by the time they find your bodies here. The only thing that stands between me and my duty to the Fatherland is . . . well, my dear young lady, you.' Northcott nodded down at the groaning Rob. 'It would be a shame for him to go on his own to the next world, now wouldn't it?'

Slowly, with a smile on his face, Northcott raised his gun again.

Sarah grabbed Rob's hand and squeezed her eyes shut, her body tensing up in dread. In that split second, she knew she'd never see Paul again, or her family and friends. Then Maura's face flashed into her mind and a strange calmness settled over her. She began to pray.

A gunshot reverberated around the attic, followed by a thump. Time stopped.

Something wasn't right. There was no pain! Sarah's eyes flew open. To her astonishment, Northcott lay on the floor right in front of her, and he wasn't moving.

'I hope you are unhurt,' a brisk female voice said from the doorway. Sarah recognised that voice. No, it couldn't be! Sarah scrambled to her feet and faced the speaker in disbelief.

Miss Whitaker advanced into the room, putting her pistol away in her coat pocket. Behind her, several men stood out on the landing. Miss Whitaker followed Sarah's gaze. 'Oh, these are Special Branch officers, Miss Gillespie.' Miss Whitaker turned towards them. 'This man needs help, urgently,' she said, waving towards Rob. 'Call for an ambulance, please.'

One man ran back down the stairs, and another came forward and knelt beside Rob. 'He doesn't look good, ma'am.'

Miss Whitaker grimaced.

'He's lost a good deal of blood,' Sarah heard herself say as if from a distance. 'I couldn't stop it. I tried my best.' She stretched out her blood-soaked hands and turned them over. They shook violently.

Miss Whitaker grunted before stripping off her scarf. She gave it to the officer. 'Bind this tightly around the wound.'

'Yes, ma'am.'

Sarah watched as the man pulled the scarf taut around Rob's stomach. Rob was whimpering in pain and she was consumed by guilt. He had tried to save her. She watched as Miss Whitaker walked around the captain's body, tut-tutting under her breath. Sarah turned away: she could not bear to look at him.

'Such a shame he won't face a trial,' Miss Whitaker said. 'I would have enjoyed seeing him squirm in the witness box.'

'He's definitely dead?' Sarah asked.

Miss Whitaker nudged his arm with her shoe. 'As a Dodo.'

Sarah forced herself to look at Northcott. There was no doubt the captain was dead: there was a bullet hole right in the middle of his forehead.

The perfect execution.

35

The afternoon light was fading. Sarah lay in bed staring up at the ceiling, reluctant to close her eyes because every time she did so, Northcott shooting Rob replayed in graphic detail. She pulled her hands out from under the covers, fully expecting to see blood on them. There was none, of course, but they still trembled. The slickness of the blood on her fingers the previous afternoon, that feeling of repulsion, would stay with her forever. Sarah gulped down her tears. She hoped she would never witness someone being shot in cold blood ever again.

How could Northcott have shot him so casually? He'd shown no remorse as he had looked down on his handiwork, and he would have done the same to her if Miss Whitaker had not intervened. His cold-bloodedness only confirmed that he must have been responsible for Alfie's 'accident' too, though she had no proof. Was it enough that Northcott was dead and could no longer harm anyone else, or should she try to convince the police of his involvement in Alfie's death? She had a feeling Miss Whitaker would not be pleased if she did so, for she had been adamant the entire episode should remain secret. Sarah's conscience, however, was nagging at her. She couldn't get Mr Atkins' sorrowful expression out of her head. Did she not owe it to him and his wife to speak up? To at least try?

What a disaster. So much for gaining her revenge. It felt such a hollow victory now, and it could all be traced back to that one fateful Whitsuntide Eve. That cruel decision by a Luftwaffe pilot, flying over Dublin all those months ago, had led to this unholy mess. Every choice Sarah had made since that dreadful night had led her to this moment. Two men dead, another almost, and for what? The only consolation was that her desire to strike a blow against Germany had succeeded, just not in the way she had expected. Her face burned. How could she have been so mistaken? Rob had been a victim, just like her, trying to do his duty as he perceived it. She hoped Northcott would burn in hell.

She still couldn't believe what had happened the previous afternoon. Talk about walking blindly into a trap! How had she been so stupid? And all that time, Rob had been innocent. Had there been clues? What had she missed in his behaviour? The shock of seeing Northcott and not Rob's chum, and realising they were one and the same, had left her scrambling to make sense of what was happening. If only she had not taken Northcott at his word. If only she had investigated Rob a little more, she might have . . . She sighed. Too late now. It was a valuable but unfortunate lesson. She had completely underestimated the danger she faced and the men she had been dealing with.

How clever Northcott had been, using them both to get what he wanted. He had orchestrated it all so well that she had never suspected him. That was embarrassing. Now it was all over, there was nothing left but unanswered questions, chief of which were two: who exactly was Rob McArthur, and where had he come from?

She remembered that man in the bar calling him 'Drew'. That must be his real name. And if he was a journalist looking for a story, as he claimed, he must have given false references to be recruited to Supermarine. No doubt Northcott had taken care of all of that for him. Northcott had been very clever, using loyalty and duty as bait for both of them. She had never suspected the game the captain was playing. He had been so believable. She hadn't liked him, but she had never doubted he was genuine secret service. It rankled that Northcott had deceived her so thoroughly, but at least she had survived relatively unscathed. Poor Rob. When she closed her eyes, she saw him again, twisting in agony on the floor and then drifting in and out of consciousness as the loss of blood took its toll. She wondered if there was any news of his condition. Could he have survived such a serious wound?

Sarah heard the creaking of the floorboard outside her bedroom just before Aunt Alice popped her head around the door and smiled down at her.

'Ah, you are awake, Sarah. May I come in?' she asked.

'Of course.'

'Tom has just arrived home from work, and he has a visitor with him who'd like to see you.'

Sarah sat up. 'Miss Whitaker?'

Alice sat down on the edge of the bed. 'Yes. Are you up to it? I can always say you're still asleep.'

'No, it's fine, really. Best I talk to her sooner rather than later. Is Martin home too?'

Alice patted her hand. 'Yes, he is.' Her aunt squeezed her hand where it lay on the eiderdown. 'Though he has to leave for Winchester shortly. Ruth's brother has had an accident and is in hospital. I understand it's very serious and he may not make it. Martin wants to be there to support her.'

'Oh, no. I'm sorry to hear that. Poor girl. I must write her a note. Perhaps Martin would take it to her?'

'I'm sure he would.'

Sarah gave her aunt a sheepish glance. 'Are you cross with me?'

'Cross? Heavens, no. But, my dear, I only wish you had come to one of us. I'm sure we could have helped, whatever the problem was. Miss Whitaker says we are not to ask you anything about it. But just remember, we're your family.'

'Thank you; but you see, I couldn't risk putting you in danger,' Sarah replied.

'What's the country coming to when vulnerable girls like yourself are put in danger?' Alice clenched her hands. 'This stupid war! Making us all question our loyalties and forcing us to tell lies. How will we ever recover and get back to normal?'

'Aunty, please don't distress yourself. I'm sorry I can't tell you what happened, but it's probably for the best. Most of all, don't worry about me. I'm fine now.'

Alice didn't look convinced as she rose from the bed. 'Hmm. I'll put the kettle on. Olivia does like her tea.' She paused at the door. 'She has always been a good friend to us, so I trust she has your best interests at heart. You have nothing to fear from her. And even if there is trouble, your uncle and I will stand by you. Martin, too.'

Sarah nodded but couldn't speak, her emotions bubbling up. She'd have to pull herself together. As soon as her aunt left the room, she stretched her arms above her head. Whatever the

322

doctor had given her the previous evening had done the trick, for she had slept for most of the day. However, there was tension in her muscles as if she had undergone strenuous exercise, and her old injuries were aching. But that was nothing. Now she had to face Miss Whitaker and explain her actions. The thought made her gulp.

Hope that Miss Whitaker would have news of Rob's condition spurred her on, and Sarah got out of bed and dressed quickly. As she tied up her hair in front of the mirror, an unbidden image flashed into her mind: Northcott lying dead. Her last glimpse of him would be ingrained in her memory forever – his vacant eyes staring up, wide in surprise, and the bullet hole livid against his pale forehead.

As she turned from the mirror, her eyes fell on the box containing the Iron Cross on her bedside locker. Pulling it out, she outlined its shape with a finger. Had it been lucky? It was daft to think that something like that might have influenced her fate. And yet it was Rob who had been shot and was fighting for his life, and Northcott who had met the stickiest of ends. Unsettled by the thought, Sarah shoved the cross into a drawer. She would decide its fate at a later date.

Sitting on the edge of the bed, her thoughts returned to the previous afternoon. Once Northcott had been shot, everything had taken on a dreamlike quality. The Special Branch officers with Miss Whitaker had taken over the scene immediately. One peeled Northcott's fingers from around his revolver, emptied the bullets, and pocketed the gun. The other man remained at Rob's side, talking softly to him, trying to keep him conscious.

'Best cover the captain until the police surgeon gets here,' Miss Whitaker had said, gesturing towards the body.

'Right-oh, ma'am,' the officer said. He took off his jacket and placed it over Northcott's head.

'We are in the way,' Miss Whitaker said to Sarah, suddenly brisk. 'We will wait downstairs in McArthur's flat.' The officer had nodded in agreement.

Miss Whitaker had shooed Sarah down the stairs to wait for the arrival of the ambulance. As they descended to the lower landing, they were met by the inquisitive occupants of the other flats, who had come out to see what all the commotion was. One girl was adamant she had heard gunshots and demanded to know what was going on. Miss Whitaker had dealt with her with a few sharp words, as only she could. The girls returned to their flats to wait for the police, duly chastened, and locked their doors as instructed.

Sarah had followed Miss Whitaker into Rob's flat. Conscious of the state of her hands, she had hurried to the sink. In disbelief, she had stood and watched the red-stained water drain away. Was any of this real? Could Rob survive that wound?

Miss Whitaker paced the floor, glancing at her watch every so often. 'What is keeping that damn ambulance?' she muttered.

Sarah had sat down, suddenly feeling weak. As the minutes ticked by, her composure slipped. She began to shake again. Instantly, Miss Whitaker was by her side. Sarah could not remember what she said, but Miss Whitaker's words had been soothing, and eventually Sarah calmed down. Soon after, through the open door of the flat, she had seen the ambulance crew rush up the stairs and had made to get up.

The Dragon pushed her back into the chair. 'We need to let them do their job, Sarah. We'd only be in the way.'

'Will he make it?'

'I've no idea. It's in God's hands now.' Miss Whitaker's face creased in pain. 'If only we had arrived sooner. I'll never forgive myself.' She glanced down at Sarah. 'I think we could both do with a drink. Do you know if he keeps any here?'

Sarah nodded. 'Try that press above the sink.'

Miss Whitaker retrieved and poured the whisky, handing her a glass. 'You've been through an extremely traumatic experience. You're in shock, Sarah. But I'm very proud of you, you know. Not many girls would be so brave.'

'More foolish, than brave, Miss Whitaker. I was an idiot to trust that man.'

'Don't dwell on it now. I've no doubt he was very convincing. Drink up; you look like you've seen a ghost.'

Sarah flinched. Was it only two weeks before that Rob had said exactly the same thing in this very room?

Shortly after, the ambulance men had stretchered Rob out of the building.

'My Special Branch friends will go to the local police and give an explanation for what has happened. A sanitised version, you understand, that will involve neither of us due to the sensitivity of the situation. I will ask one of the Special Branch officers to bring you home. It would be best you say nothing when you get there. Is that clear, Sarah? I need to come up with an account that will satisfy your family whilst protecting the service. I will drop by and talk to them later this evening.'

'Thank you. But are you sure I shouldn't talk to the police? Those girls in the other flats have seen me. I'm sure they know I was involved in what happened upstairs,' Sarah said, not quite liking the cover-up.

'The official version is that *nothing* occurred. Trust me, it's for the best,' answered Miss Whitaker with a stern look. 'If the public were to learn that an officer of the Royal Navy was a fifth columnist, it would shatter their confidence. The preservation of morale is paramount. Do you understand?'

Eventually, Sarah nodded, and Miss Whitaker grunted. 'Very good. I will go to the hospital now; someone should be with the poor lad.'

Out in the hallway, Miss Whitaker had hesitated before running back up the stairs to the attic. A minute later she had reappeared, the tracing rolled up under her arm. 'Almost forgot it. Now, that would be shockingly remiss of me!' she had exclaimed to Sarah, before disappearing down the stairs.

'Bloody hell!' Sarah had sat staring out of the door after her manager. Who *was* Miss Olivia Whitaker?

36

10th November 1941, Hursley

Halfway down the cottage stairs, Sarah wavered as her nerves kicked in. How much trouble was she in? There was no one to verify her version of events, in particular her meetings with Northcott and Rob. The question was: could she retrieve the situation and avoid the boat back to Dublin? Would anyone believe her innocence?

Much to her surprise, Sarah entered the parlour to find only Miss Whitaker present, sitting by the fire, sipping her tea and looking relaxed.

'Good evening, Miss Whitaker,' Sarah said. Suddenly conscious of how quiet the house was, she craned her neck to see into the kitchen. 'Where are the others?'

'Good evening. Don't be concerned, Sarah. Your aunt and uncle have adjourned to the King's Head for a wee while. I understand Martin has gone to Winchester. I thought it best we have a little chat, just the two of us. We have matters to discuss that are best kept between us.' Then she jumped up and walked across to Sarah. She held out her hand and bestowed one of her rare smiles. Her grip was firm. 'How are you feeling?' she asked.

'A little confused, if I'm honest,' Sarah replied. 'Everything happened so quickly yesterday. I'm still trying to sort it out in my head.'

'That's understandable. Did you get any sleep?'

'Yes, I did. I'm afraid I didn't handle things very well after I got home. Don't worry; I didn't tell the family anything. I said there had been an accident and that you would explain it all later. But I couldn't stop thinking about poor Rob. I cried so much that Uncle Tom became alarmed and fetched the doctor. He gave me something to help me sleep.'

'That's understandable after what you witnessed. I was able to ease their minds somewhat when I spoke to them last night. At that stage, you were sound asleep.'

'What did you tell them?'

Miss Whitaker took a deep breath before she spoke. 'I told them that you were involved in a secret undertaking for the government which had gone slightly awry, and that you had witnessed a shooting. Of course, I had to emphasise that under no circumstances were they to tell anyone about it.'

Sarah sagged. 'No doubt Uncle Tom will send me back to Ireland. I wouldn't blame him.'

'Nonsense! If anything, they are proud of you.'

'And what about work? The girls will wonder why I wasn't in today.'

'Relax, Sarah, they are none the wiser and will remain so. Miss Sugden informed them you have a heavy cold and won't be in for a few days. Will that do? Now, come and sit down at the table with me.' She picked up the teapot. 'Shall I pour?'

Sarah nodded. 'Thank you.' She watched Miss Whitaker for a moment, her heart thumping. Best to get it over with straight away. 'I'm sorry. I've put you to a lot of trouble.'

Miss Whitaker laughed. 'My dear girl, you have single-handedly neutralised a most dangerous man.'

'Oh no, I think you did that, Miss Whitaker.'

A smile twitched at the corner of the lady's mouth. 'Perhaps. But you set him up nicely for me.'

'Not knowingly.'

'We won't fight over it,' Miss Whitaker said, her eyes glinting. 'Drink your tea.'

Sarah obeyed but there was a question she was burning to ask. 'Tell me, please, is there any news of Rob?'

Miss Whitaker's expression became serious. 'He underwent surgery last night at the Royal Hampshire. The last I heard, which was about an hour ago, he was still in a critical condition. They have him heavily sedated and his parents arrived this afternoon. The next few days will be crucial. We must hope for the best.' Miss Whitaker frowned. 'It was most unfortunate he was shot. I wish I could have prevented it.'

'The situation evolved rapidly; there was little you could have done in the circumstances.'

Miss Whitaker flashed her a sad smile. 'It is good of you to say, my dear. Biscuit?' she asked, holding out the plate.

Sarah stared at her. What an extraordinary woman; and always so composed. 'If anything, it's my fault. I told Rob not to hand over the tracing. I knew once Northcott had it in his possession, he would kill us. Poor Rob didn't realise what was going on and thought he could save me if he complied. When he hesitated, Northcott lost patience and shot him.'

'Sarah, Northcott planned to shoot both of you anyway. He

never intended to let you simply walk free, knowing what you did. His escape route was planned. Out through Wales and Ireland and then on to Germany. We found false papers and his travel documents in his car.'

What she said made sense, and there was nothing Sarah could do about it now except pray for Rob's recovery.

'The captain was very clever,' Sarah muttered, as a wave of anger swept through her.

'But not clever enough,' Miss Whitaker said with a sniff. 'Now, before we go any further, there is something you need to know about Rob.' Miss Whitaker opened her handbag and pulled out a small picture frame. 'One of the Special Branch officers found this hidden in his flat, under the mattress.'

Sarah looked at the photograph. It had been taken in a garden or a park. The group stood close together and were smiling into the camera. 'But . . .' Sarah looked up, confused. 'That's Ruth Howard beside Rob. They look . . .'

'Miss Howard and Rob are brother and sister. His real name is Andrew Howard.'

Sarah sat back in her chair, staring at the picture. 'Now that you say it, I can see a resemblance. Why didn't I see it before? Oh my!'

'What is it?' Miss Whitaker asked.

'There was an incident some weeks ago. A man came up to Rob in the pub and called him Drew. Rob told him he was mistaken and made some silly excuse to me. Gosh, so it *was* someone he knew. Even at the time, I had suspected the man claiming recognition was genuine, but I had assumed Rob's false name was to cover up his identity as an impostor, in keeping with Northcott's claim.'

'That must have given him a fright. He must have feared his identity would be revealed.'

'Yes, and we left that pub rather quickly afterwards.' Sarah looked at the photograph again. 'The story at Hursley was that Rob and Ruth had been walking out together. Even Gladys spoke of it. I never saw their relationship in any other light.'

'Don't worry. No one else grasped it, either. They were a support to each other and so they were happy for everyone to think their relationship was a romantic one. It meant they could meet and talk and no one would bat an eyelid. At some stage, Rob decided it was too risky and they pretended to break up. Ruth, in her way, was trying to help him root out the spy. Northcott had recruited them both.'

'And that was why she was so anxious that I walk out with him. She must have believed I was the spy.'

'Northcott had convinced them of it.'

'The whole situation can't have been easy for her. No wonder she didn't appear to like me much,' Sarah groaned. 'I put it down to jealousy over Rob.'

'More likely it was concern; she feared you would do him harm.'

'Yes, I suppose you could be right. This is dreadful. Is she all right, Miss Whitaker?'

'Obviously, she is distraught. As soon as I saw the photo yesterday evening, I went to her lodging and confronted her about it. She was already in a state, as she knew the handover was to take place yesterday afternoon, and she hadn't heard from Rob. I took her straight to the hospital. She is there now with their parents,' she replied.

'This will make things very difficult for her and Martin; she will blame me for her brother's misfortune.'

'You must give her more credit, and you underestimate my ability to smooth over matters. Now, my dear, if you are up to it, you had best tell me everything, from the beginning.'

Sarah gathered her courage. 'Before I do, I'd like to know who you are. Who you *really* are. I'm sorry if that comes across as rude, but having trusted so many people lately, only for them to betray me—'

'A friend: that is all you need to know for now.' Miss Whitaker reached across the table and patted her hand. 'You *can* trust me.'

'I thought I could trust Northcott, but look where that got me!'

'A fair point, my dear.' Miss Whitaker hesitated. Her brow creased and she rested her chin on her steepled fingers. 'Very well, I think you have earned the right to know. However, what I am about to tell you must not be repeated, is that clear? Not even to the rest of your family. I know your Uncle Tom suspects, but he is enough of a gentleman not to press me.'

'Yes, I understand.'

'My father worked in army intelligence during the last war. Many of his fellow officers frequented our home, and one in particular—' Miss Whitaker paused, and sadness flashed momentarily in her eyes, '—there was a . . . a romance; however, it didn't lead to anything and we went our separate ways. Then in '39, when war seemed inevitable, this man contacted me again, quite out of the blue. He had joined MI5.'

'I've never heard of it. What is MI5?'

'Military intelligence, Sarah, and part of the secret service. The Colonel wished to recruit agents in strategic industries. My position in Supermarine had come to his attention. There was a fear that such places, handling the country's secrets, could be vulnerable to Nazi sympathisers and their schemes.'

'Men such as Northcott.'

'Exactly, though you would be surprised how many spies are women. In fact, they are often the nastiest to deal with. However, about a year ago, Captain Northcott came to MI5's attention.'

'Was he really a naval officer?' Sarah asked.

'Oh yes, indeed, with quite a record too; but he was badly injured at Dunkirk.'

'Hence the cane.'

Miss Whitaker nodded. 'He requested a transfer to Naval Intelligence, and on the face of it, that wasn't suspicious. His injuries precluded him from active service. However, an eagle-eyed officer at MI5 spotted something interesting: his grandmother was German and over the last ten years he had travelled to Germany almost every year on the pretext of visiting her. Further enquiries led to the discovery of her death in 1932. That set off alarm bells and he was put on a watch list for this county, something I am privy to. As you can imagine, the day he turned up and looked for you, my antennae began to twitch.'

Sarah let out a slow breath. 'I wish you could have warned me.'

Miss Whitaker smiled. 'Without being sure of your allegiances . . .'

'Because of my father?'

'Yes. It made the situation difficult. I could not risk exposure, especially to Northcott. I have no doubt he used your father's history as leverage?'

'That and my wish to avenge my sister's death. I always

333

suspected my father's past was shameful. Did you know the extent of it?'

'Of course. It came up in your background check and your Uncle Tom had already hinted at it but had vouched for you, so we decided to take the risk. After all, you had the right experience and we are, as you are aware, extremely short-staffed. To be honest, in normal circumstances, you would not have been employed. Our decision appeared to be the correct one, until Northcott showed up that day demanding to see you. There didn't appear to be any logical explanation for it. How could he have known about you unless he had been keeping an eye on the security clearance reports for Supermarine and had spotted your name? I knew he had to be up to something, but all I could do was watch and wait.'

'I have a confession, Miss Whitaker,' Sarah said a little sheepishly. 'I saw you in Southampton one Saturday. You came out of the Victoria Hotel, minutes after Northcott. I assumed you had been meeting him and that you were working with, or for, him.'

Miss Whitaker scowled. 'Oh dear, how clumsy of me to be spotted. I must be losing my touch. That would have been at the beginning of the month?' Sarah nodded. 'I had alerted London that Northcott was acting suspiciously and I was instructed to keep a watch on him, if possible. That particular day, he met with one of his fellow fascists in the bar of the hotel. We were on high alert after that, I can tell you. But I wasn't sure what role he had for you until I found the discrepancy.'

'What discrepancy?' Sarah asked, intrigued.

'The spoilt tracings. Did you not realise Miss Sugden keeps a tally? She came to me, rather upset as she considers you one of her best tracers, to tell me that you had taken four spoilt tracings to wash out but returned with only three. We also monitor how many clean tracing cloths are laid out each morning and check them off against the number of cloths returned at the end of each day. Therefore, I knew it was a possibility you had two tracing cloths in your possession. It seemed too much of a coincidence that a cloth would go missing two days in a row.'

Sarah groaned. 'Really? I had no idea she kept a record of those things. How unobservant I am.' Miss Whitaker smiled and nodded. Sarah was disgusted with herself. 'And there I was thinking I was ever so clever.'

Miss Whitaker chuckled. 'But you were, my dear. You were just missing that vital piece of information. As soon as I realised you had at least one tracing, I was deeply concerned as to what you might do with it. I suspected you were not working alone, and we stepped up our surveillance on Northcott. I began to wonder about your relationship with Rob, too.'

'Poor Rob! Northcott convinced him I was an IRA spy.'

'Unless he comes round, we may never know the full details; but yes, it appears likely. Rob is young and, it would appear, quite gullible. Now, tell me about that tracing you handed over. There was something wrong with it, wasn't there?'

Sarah was puzzled. How had she figured that out? But there was little point in not being honest. She drained her tea and refilled her own and Miss Whitaker's cup. 'Yes, it was fake. On Thursday, when I brought the tracing home, I realised I couldn't go through with it. I couldn't just hand over a vital Spitfire plan, mostly because I feared Northcott might leave me high and dry. His plan was so vague, and even when I pressed him, he just told me not to worry about it. That bothered me. I thought, what if he didn't turn up to the handover and the tracing ended up with Rob's Nazi? Of course, I didn't know that Northcott *was* that Nazi. Anyway,

I mulled it over for hours. What could I do to mitigate any damage if the tracing fell into the wrong hands? In the end, the best solution I could come up with was a fake tracing; that way if things went wrong, Rob's contact would pass on something useless to Berlin.'

'Excellent!' Miss Whitaker beamed across at her. 'So, what did you do?'

Sarah gave a dry laugh. 'Oh, it took me hours. Luckily, Uncle Tom has some drawing equipment at home, and I was able to bring it up to my room without anyone noticing. Then I had to carefully rub out parts of the tracing with a damp cloth. That gave me some heart-stopping moments, I can tell you. But it worked. I adjusted the drawing to make it useless by taking out vital details and adding others which were false, including some of the dimensions. I told Rob it was top secret and brand-new technology for the new cockpit door on the Mark VII. I prayed I had changed it enough to make it useless but look authentic at the same time.'

'Ah, I did wonder. First thing this morning, I checked that tracing against the most recent original drawings held in the Drawing Office, including the drawing you had been working on when you had your ink spill. I couldn't find a match.'

'There was no way I was handing over the real thing, even though I knew it would increase the risk. I didn't know how knowledgeable Rob's contact was about these types of drawings. Worst case, I was hoping the man would not examine it too closely.'

'You have good instincts, Sarah, and I am glad you went with them. If the real tracing had found its way to Berlin, the consequences would have been dire. We need to keep our design edge over the Luftwaffe.'

'But Miss Whitaker, Rob nearly ruined everything on me. He was insistent that I hand over the tracing on Friday evening after work, but of course I couldn't, as I needed time to work on the fake drawing. In fact, it took me all that evening and a good deal of Saturday as well to complete it. I was supposed to be going on a girls' night out on Friday, so I claimed I could not go due to a bad headache. Anyway, I had to use all kinds of excuses to put Rob off until Sunday.'

'Well done, Sarah. I wish we had more like you in the secret service.'

Sarah shuddered. 'I had luck on my side and I only did what I had to do to survive, nothing more. If you hadn't turned up Northcott would have killed me in cold blood, just like Rob. My only consolation in those last moments was that the tracing Northcott had tricked us into providing was useless.'

'No matter what the outcome might have been, Sarah, I can assure you he would never have made it out of Winchester. Luckily, we were in time to save you.'

'But how on earth did you find us?'

'As I said, once I knew you had a tracing, we increased our surveillance on Northcott. As it happens, there had been a few suspect transactions on his bank account over the last few months, which a bank employee had brought to our attention. Money had been transferred into it from an account in Denmark.'

'Why would that be suspicious?'

'Denmark is occupied territory and teeming with Abwehr agents. The money was traced back to the account of a man we suspected to be a handler. Northcott was probably acting as a go-between, paying other agents based here. We asked the bank to keep us informed, and lo and behold, on Friday, Special Branch were tipped off that Northcott had cleared out his account. We knew something was afoot. Then on Saturday morning, his wife was seen leaving their flat with a suitcase.'

'So you knew he was up to something.'

'Yes, and that he was most likely planning to leave the country. My colleagues followed him to Winchester to Rob's flat on Sunday morning. They contacted me, and the rest you know. His wife was picked up in Cardiff on Sunday evening and is currently undergoing interrogation.'

Sarah nodded and sipped her tea, but her curiosity about the lady across from her was raging: she had to ask. 'Miss Whitaker, how on earth did you manage that shot?'

The Dragon's eyes lit up. 'I learned to handle a gun at a young age. My father insisted I was taught before he headed off to France in 1914. It was only my mother and me left at home, you see, and he was anxious that we could defend ourselves if the worst happened. As it transpired, it was my old flame who took on the task of teaching me. I'll never forget that summer.' Her eyes misted up in memory. 'Happy times.' Then her expression cleared. 'A long time ago, of course, but a skill that has been of use on more than one occasion.'

Good Lord, Sarah thought, *I really don't know this woman at all.* 'Well, I'm very grateful he taught you so well or I would not be here today.'

Miss Whitaker dismissed this with a wave of her hand. 'It's over now. We must move on. Obviously, it's best not to discuss it any further. The fewer people who know about the Northcott affair, the better.'

'I see. I'd best destroy the journal then,' Sarah said.

Miss Whitaker's brows snapped together. 'What journal?'

'When I decided to help Northcott — when I felt I had no choice — I was afraid I would not survive to give my version of events. I kept a journal, written in Irish, outlining it all so that if the worst happened, my family would find it. It was to give them comfort – to know I did it to keep them safe, and that I wasn't of my father's persuasion.'

The Dragon stared at her for a moment. 'Extraordinary!'

Not quite sure how to take that, Sarah continued. 'And what will the consequences be for me? I suppose you will want me to leave the country quietly.'

Miss Whitaker's eyebrows shot up. 'Leave? Good Lord, girl, whatever are you talking about? On the contrary, I insist you *stay* in England.'

Sarah was astonished; she had fully expected a boat ticket to be produced at any moment. And she couldn't help but be suspicious about such leniency. 'There's a "but", isn't there?'

'Well, actually, there is.' Miss Whitaker shifted in her seat and shot a wary glance at Sarah. 'Of course, you can refuse to help us, and I have no wish to put you under pressure, particularly after what you have been through.' She splayed her fingers out on the table, then looked across at Sarah with an eager expression. 'However, you see, we have a tricky situation . . .'

Sarah held up her hand. 'Oh, no. Please, no more.'

'But you are wasted here as a tracer, Sarah. London is extremely interested in you. In fact,' Miss Whitaker broke into a grin and held out her hand, 'I have been instructed to welcome you into the ranks of MI5.'

All Sarah could do was stare. Miss Whitaker was obviously quite mad.

37

It was a couple of days later, and Sarah had just recounted a sanitised version of the Northcott affair to Martin. It was all very well Miss Whitaker insisting on secrecy, but Sarah was prepared to take the risk. She knew for the sake of her sanity she had to have someone to confide in.

'You have got to be joking, Sarah!' Martin stared back at her, open-mouthed. 'That's incredible! Actually, I'm not sure I believe a word of it.'

Sarah groaned. 'You have to believe me. It's all true. Every word of it.'

Martin blew out his cheeks. 'I never suspected a thing, though I suppose if I think about it, your relationship with Rob did seem a bit strange at times. You're a secretive one, aren't you?'

Sarah grabbed his hand, anxious to make amends. 'Not normally, and I hated every minute of it. Forgive me, but I had to lie to protect the family. The situation was impossible

341

with the threat hanging over us. I do value your friendship. Please say you can forgive me?'

Martin stared at her for a moment, then narrowed his eyes. 'Well, I suppose I could, just this once. You'll be a celebrity now, won't you, when all of this becomes common knowledge. I will be able to bask in the second-hand glory and all that.'

'Martin!'

He roared with laughter. 'I'm teasing, silly. I know it must stay a secret. But I'm only sorry you didn't confide in me at the beginning. What a team we would have made. I think I'd make a very good spy.'

'Trust me, it was terrifying. You were well out of it. And Martin, you can't breathe a word of this to anyone. Is that clear? If you do, you will have the Dragon to deal with.' Sarah made a shooting motion with her hand.

'Thanks very much!' he exclaimed. 'Nothing like vile threats between cousins. Oh, very well, spoilsport.' Martin sat back in his chair. 'Well, well . . . and the Dragon is a secret agent. I'm actually impressed. It makes her even more terrifying, somehow.'

'You should have seen her in action,' Sarah said. 'Cool as you please.'

'I wish I could thank her,' he said.

Sarah's heart jumped. 'You can't! She mustn't know you know.'

'Relax, relax; I know that. Good gracious, what a web of deceit!'

'Dear Martin, you have no idea.'

'Well, I'm just glad you weren't harmed. Pity about poor Rob – well, I suppose we should call him by his real name now.'

'Have you heard from Ruth?' Sarah asked.

'Yes. His condition deteriorated last night.'

'Oh no! This is awful.' Sarah's stomach lurched. It was the news she had been dreading.

'But it isn't unexpected, Sarah. The doctors were never really hopeful. Too much blood loss, and the bullet did an enormous amount of internal damage.'

'I feel so guilty, Martin.' Sarah gnawed her bottom lip. 'Do you know, I think I'll go to the hospital. Maybe they'll let me see him. I'd like a chance to say goodbye.'

'Do you want me to come with you?' Martin asked.

'No, I'm sure you need a break. You've been with Ruth every evening this week. It's fine. I'll ask Gladys to accompany me.'

Sarah was relieved when Gladys agreed to go with her to visit Rob, and they met up in Winchester later that evening. Gladys, of course, questioned her relentlessly all the way to the hospital. Ruth had already told Gladys that Rob was her brother and that he had been at Supermarine trying to get a story. But by agreement with Miss Whitaker and Ruth, Gladys was to stay ignorant of Rob's part in Northcott's plans. Much to Sarah's relief, Gladys believed the story that Rob had been shot during an attempted armed robbery.

The hospital was eerily quiet as visiting time was nearly over. Once again, Gladys saved the day by charming the porter with a sob story to get them past the door. As they walked down the brightly lit corridor, Sarah suddenly felt uneasy. The harsh lighting and the all-pervading smell of disinfectant reminded her of the hospital back in Dublin all those months ago. She tucked her arm through Gladys's and squeezed it. Her friend gave her an encouraging smile. However, Sarah's heart pounded as they followed the signs to where Rob's ward was located. Sarah hoped they could give Ruth some comfort, but she feared Ruth would blame her for her brother's situation and shun her.

They turned a corner and spotted a small group of people huddled together outside a room at the far end. Sarah instantly recognised Ruth and hesitated.

'Come on, it will be ok,' Gladys said, tugging her arm. 'We've come this far.'

When they were about halfway down, Ruth looked in their direction. A lady who Sarah assumed was Ruth's mother was leaning against a gentleman's shoulder, her face desolate. The man was unmoving and deadly pale, staring across the corridor, also looking distraught.

Sarah was filled with dread; the family's distress suggested they were too late.

Ruth stood and walked towards them slowly, trying her best to smile; but her chin wobbled, and her cheeks were wet with tears.

Sarah heard Gladys sniff and murmur: 'Oh, no.'

As Ruth approached, Gladys broke free from Sarah's arm and rushed towards their friend. She enveloped her in a hug. Sarah kept back, unsure what to do, anxious not to give offence, but to her astonishment Ruth eventually withdrew from Gladys's embrace, closed the gap between them and hugged her.

'He's gone,' Ruth said, her words muffled into Sarah's shoulder. 'Andrew died half an hour ago.'

Sarah was devastated. 'I'm so sorry, Ruth. For all of it.'

Ruth pulled back and gazed at her. 'It wasn't your fault, Sarah.' She touched Sarah's shoulder gently. 'Come and meet my parents.' She turned to Gladys. 'You, too.'

★ ★ ★

Andrew's parents listened to Sarah and Gladys's condolences and thanked them for coming to the hospital. They were in shock, and after one last visit to Andrew's room, they said they wanted to go back to their hotel.

'I'd like to stay a little longer, Mother. I'll go back to the flat with Gladys,' Ruth said. 'I'll see you in the morning.'

Once everyone else had gone, the three girls sat outside Andrew's room in silence for some time. Now and then, Ruth would cry, and they comforted her as best they could.

'I'm just going to the ladies. Back in a jiff,' Gladys said.

With Gladys out of earshot, Sarah finally had the chance to apologise to Ruth; but the words would not come. Sarah's mind was churning. How much did Ruth know of what had transpired at the flat?

'It's so unfair,' Ruth said at last. 'He didn't deserve to die like that. He was only trying to do the decent thing.'

Her words cut Sarah to the quick. She felt so guilty. She reached over and squeezed Ruth's hand. 'No, he didn't deserve to be shot. You must know he was a hero, Ruth. He risked his own life trying to save mine. Unfortunately, he didn't realise how ruthless Northcott could be. Well, neither of us did. Do your parents know the real circumstances?'

'No, they have been spared that. Miss Whitaker swore me to secrecy. They were told it was a robbery in the gallery and that Andrew tried to intervene. I know,' she sighed, 'it's tenuous, but they couldn't handle the truth. Of course, I knew what was going on . . . well, Andrew's part in it. You must have thought I was daft the way I was acting, but we fell for every word Northcott said. He had us both convinced you were the enemy.' Ruth bit her lip. 'I'm sorry for my part too. Andrew and I . . . we thought we were doing the right thing by helping him. We were convinced you were as bad as he claimed.'

'Northcott was a clever so-and-so. He fooled us all.'

'He certainly did.' Ruth dried her eyes. 'Was Andrew really a hero?'

'Yes. Andrew was incredibly brave and tried to trade the drawing for my life, but Northcott . . . he never intended to let either of us go.'

'What a wicked man! At least he didn't kill you too,' Ruth said.

'That is generous of you to say, Ruth, in the circumstances, and I know Miss Whitaker is deeply sorry that she could not save your brother.'

'I know. Tell me, did you love him?' Ruth asked.

'I'm sorry, but no. There is no point in me lying about that now. I was following Northcott's orders. He had a hold over me, and he knew how much I wanted revenge for my sister's death. But I liked Andrew, and now that I have learned the truth, I know I caught glimpses of the real man. He was so distressed about young Alfie's death: I should have realised at that point he was someone of deep feeling, and not the traitor Northcott had portrayed to me. The irony is we both played our roles too well.'

'Thank you for being honest. Strangely enough, Andrew said something similar about you. Said he couldn't understand how you could be one of those nasty IRA supporters.'

That sent a chill down Sarah's spine as her Da's ghost flitted into her mind. Well perhaps now she could lay him to rest, once and for all.

'Would it be all right for me to say goodbye to Andrew?' Sarah asked when she regained her composure.

346

Ruth sighed. 'Of course.'

'Will you be all right out here on your own?' Sarah asked as she stood.

'Go on. Gladys will be back in a minute.'

Sarah closed the door and gazed at the figure on the bed from across the room. He looked so young and so vulnerable. It was hard to believe that only a few days ago, Andrew had been full of life; triumphant when he believed he had caught a spy and served his country. She would never forget how his eyes had shone as he had presented her to Northcott like a trophy. It was clear he had never doubted Northcott; he had always believed he was on a heroic mission to out a traitor. Northcott had used Andrew's loyalty to his country against him for his own vile ends.

Sarah moved over to the bed and looked down at Andrew's sunken face, now serene in death. As far as she knew, he had never regained consciousness. Perhaps that was just as well. She leaned down and kissed his forehead. With a heavy heart, Sarah pulled a chair closer to the bed and sat down. She thanked God and asked him to take care of Andrew and comfort his family, then she reached out and touched Andrew's hand where it lay above the sheet. If only it were possible to turn back time.

Racked with guilt that she had survived and he had not, she recalled their times together. If circumstances had been different, if they had met innocently, would they have got along? But then she recalled that disastrous first date in Hursley. Perhaps not; and it was probably her fault. It dawned on her in that instant that she had resented Andrew the entire time, and not because she thought he was a Nazi. She had seen him only as a poor substitute for Paul, the man she really wanted in her life. That realisation didn't sit easy. Recent events had revealed aspects of her character she wasn't sure she liked, and above all, the last few days had revealed just how explosive a mixture loyalty and lies could be.

With a start, she realised she was crying; not only for Andrew, but for her own lost innocence.

38

11th December 1941, Paddington, London

To put an end to Miss Whitaker's constant badgering, Sarah agreed to go to London to hear what MI5 had to say. However, by the time she arrived at the guesthouse near Paddington Station on a cold but dry December afternoon, she was exhausted and dispirited. Thankfully, the journey had been uneventful, except for the letter burning a hole in her handbag. It had arrived at the house in Hursley just as she was heading out of the door to catch the train to London. Sarah knew it was from Paul, but she was half terrified to read it. She had shoved it into her bag and promised herself she would open it later when she would have some privacy. For the entire journey in the crowded train carriage, she could think of little else.

The excitement of finally being in London faded somewhat when she saw where she was to stay. The unprepossessing exterior of Horgan's Guesthouse gave her pause, and her fears were confirmed once inside. The house was in need of attention, with peeling paint, threadbare carpets, and an overpowering smell of cooked cabbage. A narrow hallway brought her to a reception desk, home to a large woman of indeterminate years, puffing on a cigarette and flicking through a copy of *Woman's Own*. Sarah had to cough to get her attention. A scrutiny followed which bordered on impertinent.

'Looking for a room, lovey?' the woman drawled, putting down the magazine.

'There should be a booking already made . . . for tonight. My name is Sarah Gillespie.'

'Just the one night, then? Can't tempt you to stay longer?' the landlady asked, before exhaling the smoke from the cigarette wedged in the corner of her mouth. The smoke stung Sarah's eyes and she took a step back. The landlady's eyes narrowed. 'Could offer you a great rate for an extra night, and my long-term rates can't be beaten. You just ask any of the ladies who lodge 'ere.'

'No, thank you; I return home tomorrow.'

'I'll need payment in advance,' the woman said with a weary sigh. She tucked a stray strand of greasy hair back under the scarf which just about covered the rollers on her head.

'I believe that has already been taken care of,' Sarah said. Aunt Alice had assured her Judith would make all the arrangements, including finding her a room for the night and paying up front.

With a grunt, the landlady bent down and pulled out a large ledger from under the desk. She thumbed through the pages.

'Ah, yes,' she said, as if disappointed, 'Sarah . . . Gillespie, you said?'

'Yes.'

'All right and tight, so.' She craned her neck over the desk and glanced down at Sarah's feet. 'Just that small bag?'

'That's right.'

'Good, cos we ain't got no porter 'ere!' She burst into a cackle of laughter. A slob *and* a wit, Sarah thought, and waited for her to recover from the fit of coughing which had quickly followed the laughter. The lady's eyes narrowed again and with a harrumph, she plucked a key from the rack on the wall behind her. She slid it across the desk towards Sarah and nodded to the narrow stairway. 'Top floor, room nine. Bathroom is at the end of the corridor. Breakfast seven sharp or do without, and no male visitors. We ain't that kind of establishment. Only good Catholic girls stay 'ere.'

'I'm relieved to hear it,' Sarah replied. A suspicious frown flashed across the lady's brow. Sarah jumped in: 'And if there is an air raid?'

'Down the basement, dearie. Hasn't failed us yet,' the landlady said with a smirk, pointing to a door down the corridor.

'Thanks,' Sarah said, and escaped up the stairs.

Her expectations of the room weren't high and proved well-founded. It was rather dark, with a grand view of the bare wall of another building almost in touching distance. There was hardly a need to draw the curtains, but blackout was blackout, and avoiding the awful landlady was foremost in Sarah's mind. However, the room was clean, and the bed springs didn't bite back when she tested them. Other than the single bed, there was only a small wardrobe. She unpacked her things and made herself comfortable on the bed, Paul's letter in hand.

9th December 1941
No. 4 Elementary Flying Training School,
Brough,
Yorkshire

Dear Sarah,

Thank you for your letter. I'm so glad you wrote to me. Our last meeting didn't go as I had planned, you see, and I have been trying to summon the courage to write ever since. I meant what I said that day — that I think of you often. In fact, I had hoped to be brave enough to ask for a second chance. There! Why are these things so much easier to say in a letter? Please don't think me a coward, but you sounded so settled and happy that I didn't want to upset you, particularly after all you had been through back home. When you admitted you were seeing someone, I was gutted, but not surprised. I feared you would be snapped up. Ralph ribbed me the entire journey back to Yorkshire, as in a moment of weakness, I had told him all about us and how I felt. Let's hope I'm braver when I have to face Jerry!

The truth is, my feelings have never changed, and I still think you are the most marvellous girl I've ever met. It would be wonderful if you felt the same, but if you consider a reconciliation impossible, I understand, and wish good luck to that other chap. I just hope he realises how lucky he is and I hope we can remain friends.

I do have some cracking news. As I told you, this is make-or-break time for us lads at Brough, and I am proud to tell you that I managed a solo flight after eight hours' training. Unfortunately, it took me several attempts to land as I kept coming in too close to the riverbank. It was only afterwards one of the chaps told me my instructor had hidden himself in the flight hut, thinking I was going to crash his precious plane. The upshot of all of this, however, is the best news ever. I have been selected for further pilot training and you will never guess where I will be doing it: America! Alabama, in fact. Fancy that – an Irish lad flying US planes in an RAF uniform. I'll write again when I have more details. It would be wonderful if we could meet again before I depart.

In the meantime, try to stay out of trouble and, of course, let me know if there is any chance for us.

Yours in hope,

Paul.

If it were not for a lack of pen and paper, Sarah would have replied to the letter straight away. For the guts of twenty minutes, all she could do was sit there, turning the letter over and over in her hands. She could hardly believe it. Paul still loved her. My God, she had broken his heart and yet he had remained loyal all these months. Many times, she had wished she could have turned the clock back. All those nights she had tossed and turned, wishing she had been brave enough to ask his forgiveness. Loving Paul had made her liaison with Rob almost impossible. If Northcott had not kept the pressure up, she might have abandoned the scheme with Rob and faced the consequences. If she had known Paul loved her, it would have made it all so much more bearable. This letter changed everything. As soon as possible the next day, she would write that letter and reassure him she felt the same way.

The following morning would be busy. First thing, she was to meet Cousin Judith at a Lyons Corner House. It promised to be an interesting meeting. Not that she was nervous about it, having met with nothing but kindness from the rest of the family, but

Judith was an unknown quantity. Sarah's impression of her wasn't great, based on her constant neglect of her parents. However, Martin's fondness for his sister had to carry some weight. She would hold off judging her cousin until she met her.

Immediately after that, she was due to meet Colonel Everleigh of MI5, Miss Whitaker's old beau. Why on earth did he want to meet her? Miss Whitaker would not tell her anything about what was to be discussed, insisting that Sarah had to hear it from the colonel. In the end, she had given up asking Miss Whitaker, and allowed her to confirm the meeting. Of course, there was an element of curiosity in Sarah's decision. She was dying to see the man who had stolen the heart of the Dragon and been brave enough to walk away.

Her dreams that night were not of MI5 officers, but of a certain RAF pilot who looked rather dashing in that uniform.

39

12th December 1941, Piccadilly Circus, London

It was early on Friday morning when Sarah arrived in Piccadilly. As she stood taking in the multistorey buildings and the logjam of red buses, black taxis and delivery vans, she recalled Paul's comment about London's energy compared to sleepy Dublin. There were so many people milling about, it was extraordinary. She had to admit she liked the air of excitement. All of a sudden, a stream of people emerged from the depths of the Tube station close to where she was standing. Everyone blinked as they came out into the daylight. Some were holding bags, some had blankets rolled up under their arms, and all wore a relieved expression.

'I tell you wot, Flo, if I have to stay one more night down there, I'll lose my marbles, I will,' one woman remarked to her friend as they walked past.

'Too right, Elsie. Can't get a wink of sleep with those cryin' babies and noisy young 'uns. It's enough to make you chance stayin' at home.'

Sarah knew that people used the underground stations as air-raid shelters. God love them, for it didn't sound pleasant, and she was glad it was something she would not have to experience during her brief stay. All being well, she planned to be back on a train to Winchester by late afternoon. Martin had promised to meet her at the station.

'Watch out, love,' an elderly man said, as he brushed past her.

'Sorry!' she said, but he was already lost in the crowd.

Everyone was in a tearing hurry, and she wondered if they were going to work or going home, for some looked as though they had pulled an all-nighter. Perhaps they were ARP wardens or Home Guard, or maybe they worked the night shift in the factories.

Dawdling along, she examined the shop windows and marvelled at the array of items to purchase. Dublin shops, even before the war, hadn't anything to compare with what was on offer in London. Someday, when rationing was over, she'd come back to London and splurge.

Looking up from a shoe display, she suddenly realised she needed to get her bearings. She pulled out the rough sketch one of her fellow guests had provided on overhearing her ask the landlady for directions. Mrs Horgan had stared at her, grabbed the large metal teapot off the table and quit the room, leading one of the other guests at the table to pipe up with, 'I won't be sending my children to whatever finishing school she attended!' They'd all laughed.

'Here, you say you want to go to Coventry Street?' Sarah had nodded and the woman had drawn the map on a scrap of paper. 'There you are, and if you get lost, ask a policeman.'

Sarah strolled down Coventry Street until she reached the Lyons Corner House where she was to meet Judith. Even at this early hour, it was busy with a constant flow of people in and out. Sarah checked her watch. She had timed it well: a few more minutes and Judith should be here. Her cousin's message said to meet her on the tea shop floor. Aunt Alice had gone to great pains to explain that there were in fact five floors, each serving a unique menu and with a different theme. Her aunt remembered the Lyons on Coventry Street with great fondness, as it had been a haunt of hers and Uncle Tom's for the brief time they'd lived in London. 'Neither too posh nor working class, my dear,' she had said with a twinkle in her eye.

A young woman greeted Sarah as she entered the main door. 'Second floor, Miss, is where you want,' the girl informed her when Sarah enquired. 'Stairs is at the back over there.'

Sarah made her way past the delicatessen counter and the packed tables to the rear of the shop. An archway led to the stairwell.

As soon as Sarah went through the doorway on the second floor, she stalled, amazed at the sight before her. The tea room was hopping with people and their chatter lifted her spirits. It was so lively it was easy to forget there was a war playing out. But perhaps that explained their high spirits. One thing was certain: she could get used to this buzz of excitement. No wonder Cousin Judith didn't want to leave London. Then, just above the din, she thought she could hear music. To her amazement, she spotted a small orchestra playing at the far end of the room. And such a room! The décor was 1920s Art Deco and she loved the geometric shapes and the monochrome colour scheme. Then, realising she must look a bit odd, all agog standing in the doorway, she schooled her features. *Try not to look like a complete country bumpkin*, she told herself.

A waitress in black with a white apron and cap approached. 'Miss, may I help you?' she asked.

'A table for two, please. I'm waiting for a friend,' Sarah replied.

'No problem, Miss, this way.' Sarah was seated at a table with a menu in her hand before she knew what was happening. The waitress drifted away to another table.

Sarah opened her menu and smiled, for at the top in bold lettering was 'Food is a munition of war – don't waste it!' After her meagre breakfast at Horgan's that morning, there was little chance of that. Her stomach rumbled and she shifted in her seat, hiding a smile. She ran her finger down the listings. A cuppa was only thruppence and a fresh scone only a penny-halfpenny – more than affordable, even for her. Still, she was grateful Uncle Tom had slipped her some money the night before she left: 'in case of emergencies', he had said. He was such a dear man.

As she waited, her nerves grew. Should she order or wait? Again, she glanced at her watch. This was silly. Meeting Judith should not be making her nervous. She was bound to be as nice as the others. It had to be the meeting afterwards that was putting her on edge. What could MI5 want with her? Miss Whitaker had assured her it was simply a chat. She took a deep breath and smoothed her aunt's pale-blue scarf where it lay over the collar of her coat. She had agreed to wear it so Judith could find her without too much trouble; but what if another lady had a similar scarf?

As Sarah scanned the room a voice at her side enquired: 'Cousin Sarah?'

'Oh! Yes,' she answered, looking up at a willowy blond, smartly dressed in a stylish suit, with a natty hat perched on the side of her head. Sarah stood and held out her hand, but Judith ignored it and hugged her instead, just like Uncle Tom had done the day Sarah had arrived in Southampton.

Judith held her at arm's length. 'My, but you're tiny! And as pretty as a doll,' she said, her eyes alight. 'Gosh, you're just like your photograph.'

'So are you!' Sarah exclaimed.

Once settled at the table, Judith smiled across at her. 'Dad loves all those old photographs. He is so sentimental. Martin and I used to call it his Irish rogues' gallery. All those cousins we had never met. Dad was always reminiscing about Ireland and the family, but we used to make up alternative histories to amuse ourselves. And don't ask me what those tall tales were, because it was so long ago and very silly stuff indeed. So, in a way, we grew up with you in our lives.' Judith caught her breath, her hand flying up to her mouth. 'How awful of me! I'm deeply sorry for what happened to you all. Poor Cousin Maura and Uncle Jim. You were lucky not to have met the same fate. We were so shocked to hear about Dublin being bombed, and when Dad saw where the bombs had dropped . . . well, he was frantic. It was two weeks before we got any news. You would not believe his relief when he found out you were alive, but he was devastated about poor Cousin Maura.'

'I was lucky, both to survive and for Uncle Tom being so generous in bringing me here,' Sarah said.

Judith reached for her hand, her brow furrowed. 'It was only right and proper, what with you left without a soul to take care of you. Well, you are a Lambe now. We'll look after you.' Sarah felt a rush of affection for her cousin, but found she couldn't speak. 'Now, we should order,' Judith said, all business.

She consulted her watch as the waitress appeared at the table. 'We'll have tea and scones, please, and we're in a hurry.'

'Very good, Miss,' the waitress answered, not looking the least put out.

'I was beginning to think we'd never meet,' Judith continued. 'Mum and Dad must be mad with me for not going home . . . well, actually I know they are. But, you see, work is horrendously busy.'

'Well, now that you say it, I do think you should make the effort,' Sarah said, recalling her poor aunt's face on hearing of the last cancellation.

'Lord! You are forthright.' Cousin Judith sized her up for several seconds before breaking into a smile. 'And you are dead right. I am such a coward, and I don't want to upset them, so it's just easier to stay in London and not face the questions.'

'I'm not sure what you mean,' Sarah replied.

'Golly, this is awkward. Most weekends we have to work right through, but there is another reason,' she said with a meaningful look.

'Ah! A man.'

'How clever of you. Yes.'

'I don't think they would mind,' Sarah said, perplexed.

'It's complicated . . . he's my boss and . . . he's married.'

'Oh! I can see how that would be difficult. But, forgive me, will you not have to tell them at some stage? Putting it off will only make it worse.'

'You're a wise old thing, and you're right; but the fact is I'll not be able to get away this side of Christmas. Not after what happened yesterday when all hell broke loose at the office. Such a commotion.'

'What happened?' Sarah asked, wondering what she had missed.

'Don't you know? Did you not see the papers this morning?'

'No.'

'Germany and Italy declared war on the US. You can imagine what that means. Anyway, it was well after midnight when I got back to the flat, and then I slept it out this morning.' Judith removed her gloves and sighed. 'I expect it will be hell today. Still, far more exciting than any day at Supermarine, wouldn't you say?'

It was on the tip of Sarah's tongue to contradict her, but Miss Whitaker's stern features floated before her. 'Yes, it can be awfully dull.'

'It's such a pity you're stuck down in Hursley. This is the centre of things. It's much more fun here, I can assure you . . . well, when you're not trapped behind a desk at work, that is. How are you getting on in the job? I worked for them in Southampton for about a year as a secretary, but when they moved to Hursley, I decided it was time to move on. Miss Whitaker found me my present job you-know-where . . .' Judith said this *sotto voce* before glancing around. 'Can't be too careful. Loose talk and all that.'

Sarah was just about keeping up with her garrulous cousin. 'But you like it – where you work now?'

Judith leaned towards her. 'It's wonderful! You get to meet the most amazing people. Gerald, my boss, is such a dear, though he works me hard.' Judith sighed. 'The best bit is the nightlife in London. Just can't be beaten. I share a flat with two other girls, Maisie and Anne. Like me, they aren't Londoners and they're enjoying their newfound freedom, if you know what I mean.'

Sarah laughed. 'Martin suspected you were having a grand old time.'

361

'Dear Martin! How is he? I wish he'd come to London and see me. It's too bad of him neglecting me like this. Though I hear from Mother there is a lady in his life.'

'Oh dear, I'm afraid that is over. Ruth has left Supermarine and gone back home to Kent.'

'Really? Poor Martin. We were as thick as thieves growing up, you know. Mind you, he can be a real bossy boots.' Judith sat back and giggled. 'And eagle-eyed. Perhaps it's just as well he isn't in London.'

'Don't worry, he has found a new target. I keep him busy in that regard.'

'Oh good, I hope he will ease up on me then. His last letter was vile, full of recriminations.' Judith leaned forward, her blue eyes alive with mischief. 'My advice is not to take any guff from Martin. Some fellows need to know their place.' As she sat back, she laughed. 'Do you know, I have just had the most marvellous idea. Perhaps you could persuade him to visit me in London. In fact, both of you should come up for the weekend. Isn't that a wonderful idea? We'd have such fun: see the sights and have a night out.'

'That sounds brilliant. I'll persuade him, you can depend on it,' Sarah answered, suddenly thinking of Gladys. 'I might drag a friend of mine along as well.'

'Excellent. Oh, here's our food. Tuck in, and then we must get you safely to St James's Street.'

40

Judith insisted on walking Sarah all the way, chatting away ten to the dozen. With her stomach doing flip-flops, Sarah hadn't refused the offer, even though it was only a short walk from Coventry Street and she had memorised the route.

'Well, my dear, here we are,' Judith said, stopping outside an unremarkable building with a rundown appearance compared to its neighbours.

'Are you sure?' Sarah asked, looking at the 'To Let' sign hanging above the door.

Her cousin grinned back at her and leaned close. 'They like to be inconspicuous. Now, give your cousin a goodbye hug.'

They embraced, and for a split second Sarah was tempted to ask Judith to wait for her. Instead, she asked: 'Have you any messages for home?'

'Best to be honest. As I said, it doesn't look like I will be home until Christmas, especially after what happened yesterday.

Tell Mother I'll write to her this week. And ask her if there is anything special she would like me to bring home for the holidays. It's much easier to find things here if you know the right people,' Judith said with a wink. 'Now, will you be ok?' she asked, glancing up at the building.

Sarah lifted her chin. 'Yes, it's just a chat.'

Judith's expression was full of sympathy. 'If you say so. And now I really must fly, or my boss *will* skin me alive. Don't forget our plan for a weekend here. Take care, and safe journey home.' And with that Judith was gone.

Sarah took a deep breath, climbed the steps, and rang the bell.

Sarah followed the porter through a labyrinth of corridors and up several flights of stairs before he stopped at an unmarked door.

'Please, Miss,' the man said, opening the door and waving her through.

'Miss Gillespie.' The man behind the desk jumped up and came forward to greet her. 'Do come in.' He held out his hand. 'Colonel Everleigh, at your service.' Black slicked-back hair, piercing blue eyes and a hook nose gave the colonel a striking appearance. Sarah could imagine the effect it must have had on a young Miss Whitaker all those years ago.

They shook hands and he pulled out a chair for her. When he was settled back behind the desk, he folded his arms. Sarah knew he was sizing her up. 'It is good of you to come to London. My travelling to Hampshire was out of the question. As you can imagine, we are extremely busy at present.'

'I'm sure you are. It was no trouble. In fact, it was an opportunity to meet one of my cousins and see a bit of London, too.'

He smiled. 'Ah yes, Miss Lambe.'

'You know my cousin?'

His gaze strayed to a file on the desk. 'I know of her.'

'I see.' She should have expected he'd know all about her and her family. Was she always going to be on the back foot with these people?

'And what do you make of London?' the colonel asked.

'From the little I have seen, I like it very much,' she replied.

'Few fail to fall for its charms. I still recall the first time I came here. I was barely nineteen, green as they come, and had seen nothing of the world outside Harrogate. I was fascinated by the city and never wanted to leave. London was a different place then, of course, in the days before the last war. I had only begun to explore its delights, and a Civil Service career, when the Kaiser intervened. Unfortunately, life's pleasures had to be abandoned to fight the Hun, and my life took a very different turn.'

'You enlisted straight away?'

'Yes. The fellows I worked with thought it would be a grand idea if we all signed up together. Poor blighters; more than half never made it back.'

'Miss Whitaker told me you served under her late father, sir.'

'Yes, indeed. General Whitaker was my commanding officer during the Great War,' he said. 'It was an honour to serve under him. He was one of the best. Old school, of course.'

'He was a general? She never said.'

'With Miss Whitaker it is always on a need-to-know basis,' he replied with a quirk of a brow. He placed his hand on the closed folder on the desk. 'Now, I have no wish to waste your time, Miss Gillespie. The reason I was anxious to make your acquaintance was to express our gratitude for your help in bringing down Captain Northcott. We were impressed by your courage and quick thinking. These are not common traits in someone so young, let me tell you.'

'Thank you, but I was merely thinking on my feet on finding myself in a difficult situation.'

'Many in your position would have hightailed it back to Ireland.'

'It crossed my mind,' she admitted. 'Several times, in fact, when things got sticky.'

'What stopped you?'

'Loyalty to my family. I believed Northcott's threat to deport them.'

He nodded. 'Loyalty is a precious commodity these days.'

Sarah was uncomfortable. She had an inkling where he was going with this. 'And I have proven where mine lies.'

'Indeed you have, Miss Gillespie. There can be no doubt about it.'

'Then why am I here, sir? Why was Miss Whitaker so insistent I speak to you?' There was no point in prevaricating. As far as Sarah was concerned, she was here merely to repay a debt of gratitude to the Dragon.

'She is not a lady to be thwarted, is she?' he said, his eyes alight.

'She is certainly not what she seems on first acquaintance,' Sarah replied.

Colonel Everleigh burst out laughing. 'No indeed, and many have made the mistake of underestimating her. She is one of my best agents.'

'Northcott certainly underestimated her.'

Everleigh nodded. 'And paid a heavy price for it. But his greatest error was trying to recruit you into his scheme.'

'No doubt you are trying to compliment me, Colonel, but

the reality is I made a mess of it. There is no other way to describe what happened that day in Winchester. I regret the outcome – and by that, I mean *both* deaths – though I am grateful to Miss Whitaker for saving my life. I just wish it could have had a different conclusion.'

'Northcott would have hanged either way. I would not waste any sympathy on him.' Sarah shrugged. The colonel went on: 'Regrettably, there are many more like him.'

Sarah sighed. 'Is that the reason you asked me here? Miss Whitaker has been pestering me for weeks, wanting me to join your . . . organisation, but as I made it plain to her – or at least I thought I had – that is not going to happen. Whatever debt I owed, real or imagined, is paid. I have no wish to end up like poor Andrew Howard.'

The colonel pursed his lips. 'Yes, it was a shame he didn't pull through; I understand the bullet did too much damage to his liver.'

'And there will be no justice for his family with Northcott dead. Do you have any idea how he became involved with Northcott and his plans?' Sarah asked.

'We do. His sister told Miss Whitaker everything, in the end.'

'Miss Whitaker never told me.'

'Olivia Whitaker is always circumspect, Miss Gillespie. For the sake of Howard's family, and in particular his sister, we need to keep the entire episode secret, especially Miss Whitaker's role. We wish to keep the fact that she works for us out of the public domain. Not even Supermarine is aware of her MI5 status. However, as you were involved, I'm happy to give you some detail regarding Howard, with the stipulation it goes no further.'

'It won't, sir. Thank you.'

'Andrew met Northcott through his father. Mr Howard

played golf with Northcott. No doubt Mr Howard spoke of his family and where his daughter worked. Northcott must have been delighted with his good fortune. No doubt, he had been looking for a suitable person to help him carry out his plan. Learning that Ruth Howard worked at Supermarine must have ignited his interest. However, he didn't approach Ruth, seeing a better target in her brother. It would appear he approached Andrew first at a family event. At the time, Andrew was working as an office junior for a Kent newspaper. It wasn't an exciting job for a lad who wanted to fight but was precluded on health grounds. Andrew had been desperate to join the Navy, and we believe the captain played on that and persuaded Andrew that he knew of an opportunity for him to make a name for himself. If he would pose as a fascist, Northcott would supply him with a spy to uncover. It would be a great story for his newspaper, gain him a promotion, and he would be doing his country a service.'

'And Andrew jumped at the chance to be a hero.'

'He did. Northcott tipped him off about you as a promising opportunity for mischief and encouraged him to out you as a republican spy. The rest you know.'

Sarah nodded in acknowledgement. 'Northcott was a nasty piece of work. But did he have to kill Andrew?'

'As you are fond of plain speaking – and you will find I'm rather fond of it myself – Howard's death, like many others, is collateral damage to people like Northcott.'

'Sir, I believe he may have killed someone else.' Sarah outlined her suspicions surrounding Alfie's hit and run.

'It would be difficult to prove, Miss Gillespie, but I don't doubt the man was capable of it. When this is over, we will mourn all the innocents; but for now this is total war, Miss

Gillespie. We are not playing parlour games. Northcott and his many friends are a threat to our very way of life. Despite official denial, we know there are networks of fascists throughout the country, doing their best to undermine us. They are like weeds: you pluck one and a dozen pop up in its place. You would be amazed if I were to tell you some of those involved. Public figures, some of them, and proving untouchable.'

'Perhaps I'm happy to remain ignorant, Colonel. I am well aware of the price this war is exacting, and I am happy to do my bit, but that is working for Miss Whitaker in my *current* role.'

'But that would be such a waste of your talents.' Sarah protested and he held up his hand. 'Hear me out, please. Have you any idea how difficult it is to find suitable agents? You have more than proven yourself capable of thinking clearly in a crisis. Faking that drawing was, I have to say, inspired. Do you believe that a fluke?'

'No, it was the sensible solution in the circumstances. I didn't want to risk using a real drawing.'

'Exactly! Look; I'm a busy man, Miss Gillespie. The plain fact is that we want you to work for us.'

Sarah leaned forward, more than angry now. 'And are you going to threaten me like Northcott did? Because, I assure you, it will not work on me again.'

'I don't use threats, Miss Gillespie, nor do I believe I need to.'

Sarah stared at him, half suspicious, half curious. 'And why is that?'

Everleigh sighed. 'We have a very special kind of problem and we believe you can solve it for us. I believe when you learn some of the details you will change your mind.'

'I doubt it!' Sarah exclaimed. The temptation to get up and

walk out was strong, but her curiosity was stronger. Everleigh sat back in his chair and remained silent, putting her in mind of a spider. Finally, she succumbed, digging her fingers into her palms. 'What details?' she asked. The colonel's shoulders relaxed. *Damn*, she thought. *He has drawn me in far too easily.*

'I will be frank with you, Miss Gillespie. Your recent adventure and your nationality give you a particular insight that would be useful to us.'

'Oh, no, not this again.' With a shake of her head, she stared down into her lap. All this familiar scene would need now would be for the man to bring up the republicans.

'You are uniquely placed to root out someone for us. He is a ghost. A dangerous man who is orchestrating the escape of fascists from this country back to Germany before we can lay our hands on them. Our fear is that he may also be facilitating German agents, enabling them to access this country without our knowledge. If so, he is providing these people with false identities so they can vanish into the ether or meld into English society.'

Sarah frowned across at the colonel. 'Why can't you find this man, this *ghost*?'

'He is deeply embedded in an organisation which has invested in his protection. He gets the job done for them and is paid well for it. In return, they keep him safe.' Everleigh sighed. 'He has more aliases than you can shake a stick at, and he flits from one town to another with ease. We are always one step behind.' He reached inside the file and pulled out a small photograph. He slid it across the table to her. 'You need to see this, Miss Gillespie.'

Sarah picked up the photo and shot him a furious glance. 'Is this some kind of joke? Because if it is, it's not terribly funny.' As she stared at the picture, a rush of pure anger surged through her.

'That was taken two weeks ago in Cardiff.'

'What? That is impossible.'

'The man who took the photograph managed to get the film into the post to us. Unfortunately, the following day he was found dead in the back garden of his home, which had been ransacked. I'm sure this is a shock for you, Miss Gillespie, but you of all people know what this man is capable of.'

Rigid with fury, Sarah crushed the photograph in her hand. 'I think you had better explain, Colonel, because I thought he was lying in the family plot in Glasnevin Cemetery.'

'I'm afraid not. Jim Gillespie is alive and well and causing us considerable inconvenience.'

In an effort to calm her breathing, Sarah stared out of the window behind Everleigh. This was madness: she should walk away right now. The day she left Ireland she had jettisoned the bad memories. Now they were regurgitated, flashing before her eyes like a sick magic-lantern show: the bruises on her mother and sister; on her own skin in the mirror. All that pain, the constant fear and rumours, and worst of all, a lifetime of flinching at the sound of a key in the door . . .

'As you can probably guess, the bombing of North Strand was the perfect opportunity for your father to disappear. His sources had informed him that Irish Special Branch were on to him. We know this because the authorities in Dublin had sent us their surveillance reports when we had raised concerns about him. They were just as alarmed by his antics. They didn't want fascists or Germans using Ireland as a springboard to Germany as it would cause considerable embarrassment to the Irish government, having declared neutrality. When the bombs dropped, he made straight for the train station. I imagine he couldn't believe his luck. The pandemonium was the perfect cover. We believe he slipped out of Ireland through Northern Ireland on the first of June, then managed to find passage to England on a boat out of Belfast. After that, the trail goes cold; he was welcomed with open arms by his friends here and quickly disappeared.'

Sarah shook with anger. 'He abandoned us without a second thought, even though he must have known where the bombs fell,' she choked out. 'He never sought us out to see if we were alive or dead, or considered we might be mourning him needlessly. My God, his ring. He must have planted it on someone else before he left. How cruel!'

The colonel shrugged. 'Efficient and effective. That's why he is so dangerous.'

'And I identified it – I played right into his hands and helped him to disappear.' A cold shiver went down her back. 'Maura and I were just baggage to be discarded,' she said at last, appalled.

Breathing hard, Sarah regained control of her temper. She knew this man sitting opposite was manipulating her to take advantage of her burning hatred of her father, but if she was honest, hadn't her anger at all of the injustice of this war still been bubbling away beneath the surface, even after Northcott's death? She still wanted revenge for Maura, and now for Andrew, but if she took this step, it would change her irrevocably. She might even die trying to track her father down.

Sarah exhaled slowly and met Colonel Everleigh's steady gaze. 'When do I start?'

THE END

Acknowledgements

One of my earliest memories is accompanying my father to our local library. Both my parents encouraged me to read, and as an only child, books provided a safe and beguiling way to explore the world. However, it was my father's love of history which resonated with me the most, and although I devoured crime novels as a teenager, historical fiction has always been my first choice. It is hardly any surprise that it is my chosen genre both for reading and writing to this day.

No writing journey is possible without support from family and friends. This, I have in abundance. My long-suffering hubby Conor and my three wonderful children, Stephen, Hazel and Adam, have endured many a hastily thrown together dinner for my craft! To friends and work colleagues: thanks for the words of encouragement over the years. It kept me going when hope and belief sometimes faltered.

I would like to take the opportunity to thank one incredibly special lady, Thérèse Coen, my agent. It was her suggestion of a WW2 novel with an Irish slant that resulted in *Her Secret*

War. For your continued support, guidance and hard work, I am extremely grateful. A big thank you to all the team at Hardman & Swainson. You guys are the best.

My local and family history inspired *Her Secret War,* and I am immensely proud of this novel. However, it would not have been possible to bring this book into the world without the keen eye and enthusiasm of Katie Loughnane, my editor at Avon Books UK. Katie and all the team at Avon and HarperCollins have polished my story and made it shine. Thank you.

I owe so much to my incredible and loyal readers of all my first drafts, namely Lorna, Terry, Joan, Kevin and Keith. Thank you from the bottom of my heart.

The cornerstone of historical fiction is research. In this regard, I was extremely lucky to come across the fabulous Supermariners website, hosted by David Key. The in-depth research David had already carried out enabled me to recreate those war years at Vickers Supermarine at Hursley Park in Hampshire with confidence. I am deeply indebted to you, David, and thanks so much. To Cheryl Morris at Diagio who so promptly answered my queries regarding the distinctive smell which used to emanate from the Guinness brewery at St. James's Gate in Dublin; thank you for resolving the argument! And finally, thanks to Kevin C. Kearns, author of *The Bombing of Dublin's North Strand 1941: The Untold Story.* This book was a wonderful resource of eyewitness accounts, which brought the events of that fateful night to life. Thank you for your painstaking research.

I am extremely grateful to have such loyal readers, who are so kind and generous. For those of you who take the time to leave reviews, please know that I appreciate them beyond words.

To the amazing book bloggers, book tour hosts and reviewers who have hosted me and my books over the years – thank you.

Last, but not least, I am incredibly lucky to have a network of writer friends who keep me sane, especially Sharon Thompson, Valerie Keogh and Fiona Cooke. Special thanks to the members of the Historical Novel Society and RNA Irish Chapters, and all the gang at the Coffee Pot Book Club.

Go raibh míle maith agat!

Pam Lecky, October 2021